GREAT LOVE STORIES

GREAT LOVE STORIES

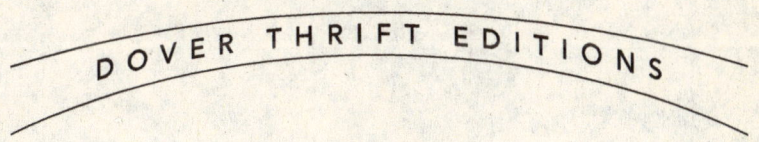

DOVER THRIFT EDITIONS

Edited by
Bob Blaisdell

DOVER PUBLICATIONS, INC.
MINEOLA, NEW YORK

DOVER THRIFT EDITIONS

GENERAL EDITOR: MARY CAROLYN WALDREP
EDITOR OF THIS VOLUME: SUSAN L. RATTINER

ACKNOWLEDGMENTS: SEE PAGE XIII.

Bibliographical Note

Great Love Stories, first published by Dover Publications, Inc., in 2016, is a new anthology, reprinted from standard sources. A new introductory Note has been specially prepared for this edition.

Library of Congress Cataloging-in-Publication Data

Great love stories / edited by Bob Blaisdell.
     pages cm. — (Dover thrift editions)
   ISBN-13: 978-0-486-79382-5 (paperback) — ISBN-10: 0-486-79382-6
1. Love stories.   I. Blaisdell, Robert, editor.
PN6120.95.L7G68 2016
808.83'85—dc23
                                                  2015005961

Manufactured in the United States by LSC Communications
79382602   2017
www.doverpublications.com

Contents

Note

WHAT A MISFORTUNE it is to lose one's will, to abandon one's family and career, to be crippled by a force stronger than one's self, to be invaded by visions! And yet most of us can't help envying the lovesick hero of Anton Chekhov's "A Misfortune," who complains to his beloved: "What am I to do if your image has grown into my soul, and day and night stands persistently before my eyes, like that pine there at this moment? Come, tell me, what hard and difficult thing can I do to get free from this abominable, miserable condition, in which all my thoughts, desires, and dreams are no longer my own, but belong to some demon who has taken possession of me? I love you, love you so much that I am completely thrown out of gear; I've given up my work and all who are dear to me; I've forgotten my God! I've never been in love like this in my life."

Meanwhile, in another century, in another country, the besotted Ethel, in William Carlos Williams's "The Knife of the Times," must suffer for years before she begins to understand the unthinkable, that she is in love with her correspondent Maura, her childhood friend:

> . . . as these letters continued to flow, there came a change in them. First the personal note grew more confidential. Ethel told about her children, how she had had one after the other—to divert her mind, to distract her thoughts from their constant brooding. Each child would raise her hopes of relief, each anticipated delivery brought only renewed disappointment. She confided more and more in Maura.

Before lovers understand they're in love, they wonder: What's wrong with me? Am I sick? Am I *dying*? Realizing that the answer to the mystery is "love" has the impact of religious revelation:

> She loved her husband; it was not that. In fact, she didn't know what it was save that she, Ethel, could never get her old friend Maura out of her mind.
>
> Until at last the secret was out. It is you, Maura, that I want. Nothing but you. Nobody but you can appease my grief. Forgive me if I distress you with this confession.

But if love is an illness, why do we all want to catch it or at least, having recovered from it and now seemingly immune, fondly recall our lovesick days and nights?

Fortunately, inevitably there is more comedy than tragedy in love stories. People in love make us laugh! How revealing is a lover's joy and misery! Anthony Trollope's narrator observes of one of Miss Ophelia Gledd's suitors: ". . . in the society of Boston generally he was regarded as a stout fellow, well able to hold his own,— as a man by no means soft, or green, or feminine. And yet now, in the presence of me, a stranger to him, he was almost crying about his lady love." However sympathetic we are to the suitor, we smile because we know the brilliant intensity of those feelings won't last!

We know that the suffering in love is just as unimaginably debilitating as the joys are blissful. In "White Night," Colette describes the quiet ecstasy of physical love:

> How my heart beats! I also hear yours under my ear. You're not sleeping? I lift my head a bit, I imagine the paleness of your upside-down face, the tawny shadow of your short hair. Your knees are fresh as two oranges . . . Turn to my side, so that mine can steal this smooth freshness.

When we condescendingly refer to lovers as living in their own little world, we're wrong; these stories will remind us that we've only *forgotten* the grace of that experience! The world, for lovers, isn't small, it's only so focused, so essential; it's we undizzy ones who are distracted by the inessentials; we're the ones content with our carved-out routines and busy practicalities in a tiny circumscribed neighborhood. It's Heinrich von Kleist's heroes, Jeronimo and Josefa (with their divine baby Felipe) who have their heads and hearts in the right place. The most dramatic of writers, Kleist imagines his lovers, after being persecuted by the church for their love affair, witnessing and surviving a devastating earthquake in Santiago that miraculously reunites them:

> . . . they had an infinite number of things to talk about, the convent garden, and the prisons, and what they had gone through for each other; and they were very moved when they thought of how much misery had to come upon the world for them to be happy.

Yes, the happiness (or despair) of lovers is the only human state that detaches itself from the gravitational pull of the Earth's woes. But love has so much power that no lover, except in his joys, feels himself content and sure of himself. Love is an imbalance because nothing can avert it; no amount of leaning away from it will restore our equilibrium. Who's stronger than the Goddess of Love? Not the old Greek gods, who were continually dazzled by Aphrodite's charms, and for whose "weakness" there are some—too wise for *this* world—who have rebuked them for their immorality rather than sympathized with them for their vulnerability. We've all heard enough stories to know that any being who declares himself physically or spiritually invulnerable to love, as does the hero of Yukio Mishima's "The Priest of Shiga Temple and His Love," is due for a fall:

> Unwittingly the Great Priest glanced in her direction and at once he was overwhelmed by her beauty. His eyes met hers and, as he did nothing to avert his gaze, she did not take it upon herself to turn away. . . .
>
> In the twinkling of an eye the present world had wreaked its revenge on the priest with terrible force. What he had imagined to be completely safe had collapsed in ruins. . . .

After all, someone invulnerable to love is nobody at all. We would despise Mishima's priest if he could deny the *reality* of his feelings:

> A woman's beauty, he told himself, was but a fleeting apparition, a temporary phenomenon composed of flesh—of flesh

that was soon to be destroyed. Yet, try as he might to ward it off, the ineffable beauty which had overpowered him at that instant by the lake now pressed on his heart with the force of something that has come from an infinite distance. The Great Priest was not young enough, either spiritually or physically, to believe that this new feeling was simply a trick that his flesh had played on him. A man's flesh, he knew full well, could not alter so rapidly. Rather, he seemed to have been immersed in some swift, subtle poison which had abruptly transmuted his spirit.

So these two dozen stories could be called tales about *vulnerability*; it's not that lovers are especially susceptible (most of us could plausibly deny *susceptibility*, because we know we can always apply resistance to an inclination), but vulnerability, on the other hand, is humankind's common lot. The God of Reason can't fend it off, as the Cajun store-clerk 'Polyte discovers (in Kate Chopin's "Azélie") when he falls in love with a thief:

> The very action which should have revolted him had seemed, on the contrary, to inflame him with love. He felt that love to be a degradation—something that he was almost ashamed to acknowledge to himself, and he knew that he was hopelessly unable to stifle it.

Our spiritual or psychological balance, so otherwise essential, teeters every which way under love's influence and even shows us that such balance is a sad meager goal. The distraught and frustrated narrator of James Joyce's "Araby" recalls his youthful encounter with love:

> I could not call my wandering thoughts together. I had hardly any patience with the serious work of life which, now that it stood between me and my desire, seemed to me child's play, ugly monotonous child's play.

Love is amusing and ridiculous, mockable, as long as it's not, *mis*fortunately, happening to us.

★ ★ ★

Preceding each story, I have offered short biographical notes, with a detail or two about the author's love life. Such details, it seems to me, are too often ignored or discounted by us editors or professors when we present thumbnail sketches of artists' lives; in a collection of brilliant love stories, however, by some of the greatest authors of the past and present, these details will seem, perhaps, justified and relevant.

I would like to acknowledge my appreciation to a friend, the poet John Wilson, for his suggestion of a couple of these stories, and to Ekaterina Rogalskaya, for her help in translating Chekhov's "A Misfortune" (though we finally decided Constance Garnett's superb version was the best). I dedicate this collection to Suzanne Carbotte, my wife, the heroine of my own ongoing love story.

—*B.B.*
New York City
January 1, 2015

Acknowledgments

Chinua Achebe: "Marriage Is a Private Affair," copyright © 1972, 1973 by Chinua Achebe; from *Girls at War: And Other Stories* by Chinua Achebe. Used by permission of Doubleday, an imprint of the Knopf Doubleday Publishing Group, a division of Penguin Random House LLC. All right reserved.

Jorge Luis Borges: "Ulrikke," from *Collected Fictions* by Jorge Luis Borges, translated by Andrew Hurley, copyright © 1998 by Maria Kodama; translation copyright © 1998 by Penguin Random House LLC. Used by permission of Viking Books, an imprint of Penguin Publishing Group, a division of Penguin Random House LLC.

Géza Csáth: "Erna" from *The Magician's Garden and Other Stories* by Géza Csáth. Copyright © 1980 Columbia University Press. Reprinted with permission of the publisher.

Junot Díaz: "The Sun, the Moon, the Stars," from *This Is How You Lose Her* by Junot Díaz, copyright © 2012 by Junot Díaz. Used by permission of Riverhead, an imprint of Penguin Publishing Group, a division of Penguin Random House LLC.

Gabriel García Márquez: All pages from "The Handsomest Drowned Man in the World" from *Leaf Storm and Other Stories* by Gabriel García Márquez. Copyright © 1971 by Gabriel García Márquez. Reprinted by permission of HarperCollins Publishers.

Yukio Mishima: "The Priest of Shiga Temple and His Love" by Yukio Mishima, translated by Ivan Morris, from *Death in Midsummer,* copyright

GREAT LOVE STORIES

CHINUA ACHEBE

[Nigeria]

CHINUA ACHEBE's greatest work, the novel *Things Fall Apart* (1958), describes the culture of a remote Nigerian village dividing against itself after Christianity arrives. "Marriage Is a Private Affair" is another tale of culture-clash, as the hero, a young teacher in metropolitan Lagos, breaks his home village's seemingly eternal tradition of parents arranging their children's marriages. Achebe was born in 1930 in an Ibo village in southern Nigeria. His father became a Christian, and Achebe was educated in schools modeled after those of the British. He graduated from the university in Ibadan, and then worked for the BBC in London and in Lagos. He was married in 1961 to Christiana Okoli, and they had four children. Achebe spent parts of the last few decades of his life teaching literature in American universities, and died in 2013.

Marriage Is a Private Affair (1952)

"HAVE YOU WRITTEN to your dad yet?" asked Nene one afternoon as she sat with Nnaemeka in her room at 16 Kasanga Street, Lagos.

"No. I've been thinking about it. I think it's better to tell him when I get home on leave!"

"But why? Your leave is such a long way off yet—six whole weeks. He should be let into our happiness now."

Nnaemeka was silent for a while, and then began very slowly as if he groped for his words: "I wish I were sure it would be happiness to him."

"Of course it must," replied Nene, a little surprised. "Why shouldn't it?"

"You have lived in Lagos all your life, and you know very little about people in remote parts of the country."

"That's what you always say. But I don't believe anybody will be so unlike other people that they will be unhappy when their sons are engaged to marry."

"Yes. They are most unhappy if the engagement is not arranged by them. In our case it's worse—you are not even an Ibo."

This was said so seriously and so bluntly that Nene could not find speech immediately. In the cosmopolitan atmosphere of the city it had always seemed to her something of a joke that a person's tribe could determine whom he married.

At last she said, "You don't really mean that he will object to your marrying me simply on that account? I had always thought you Ibos were kindly disposed to other people."

"So we are. But when it comes to marriage, well, it's not quite so simple. And this," he added, "is not peculiar to the Ibos. If your father were alive and lived in the heart of Ibibio-land he would be exactly like my father."

"I don't know. But anyway, as your father is so fond of you, I'm sure he will forgive you soon enough. Come on then, be a good boy and send him a nice lovely letter . . ."

"It would not be wise to break the news to him by writing. A letter will bring it upon him with a shock. I'm quite sure about that."

"All right, honey, suit yourself. You know your father."

As Nnaemeka walked home that evening he turned over in his mind the different ways of overcoming his father's opposition, especially now that he had gone and found a girl for him. He had thought of showing his letter to Nene but decided on second thoughts not to, at least for the moment. He read it again when he got home and couldn't help smiling to himself. He remembered Ugoye quite well, an Amazon of a girl who used to beat up all the boys, himself included, on the way to the stream, a complete dunce at school.

I have found a girl who will suit you admirably—Ugoye Nweke, the eldest daughter of our neighbour, Jacob Nweke. She has a proper Christian upbringing. When she stopped schooling some years ago her father (a man of sound judgment) sent her to live in the house of a pastor where she has received all the training a wife could need. Her Sunday School teacher has told me that she reads her Bible very fluently. I hope we shall begin negotiations when you come home in December.

On the second evening of his return from Lagos Nnaemeka sat with his father under a cassia tree. This was the old man's retreat where he went to read his Bible when the parching December sun had set and a fresh, reviving wind blew on the leaves.

"Father," began Nnaemeka suddenly, "I have come to ask forgiveness."

"Forgiveness? For what, my son?" he asked in amazement.

"It's about this marriage question?"

"Which marriage question."

"I can't—we must—I mean it is impossible for me to marry Nweke's daughter."

"Impossible? Why?" asked his father.

"I don't love her."

"Nobody said you did. Why should you?" he asked.

"Marriage today is different . . ."

"Look here, my son," interrupted his father, "nothing is different. What one looks for in a wife are a good character and a Christian background."

Nnaemeka saw there was no hope along the present line of argument.

"Moreover," he said, "I am engaged to marry another girl who has all of Ugoye's good qualities, and who . . ."

His father did not believe his ears. "What did you say?" he asked slowly and disconcertingly.

"She is a good Christian," his son went on, "and a teacher in a Girls' School in Lagos."

"Teacher, did you say? If you consider that a qualification for a good wife I should like to point out to you, Emeka, that no Christian woman should teach. St. Paul in his letter to the Corinthians says that women should keep silence." He rose slowly from his seat and paced forwards and backwards. This was his pet subject, and he condemned vehemently those church leaders who encouraged women to teach in their schools. After he had spent his emotion on a long homily he at last came back to his son's engagement, in a seemingly milder tone.

"Whose daughter is she, anyway?"

"She is Nene Atang."

"What!" All the mildness was gone again. "Did you say Neneataga, what does that mean?"

"Nene Atang from Calabar. She is the only girl I can marry." This was a very rash reply and Nnaemeka expected the storm to burst. But it did not. His father merely walked away into his room. This was most unexpected and perplexed Nnaemeka. His father's silence was infinitely more menacing than a flood of threatening speech. That night the old man did not eat.

When he sent for Nnaemeka a day later he applied all possible ways of dissuasion. But the young man's heart was hardened, and his father eventually gave him up as lost.

"I owe it to you, my son, as a duty to show you what is right and what is wrong. Whoever put this idea into your head might as well have cut your throat. It is Satan's work." He waved his son away.

"You will change your mind, Father, when you know Nene."

"I shall never see her," was the reply. From that night the father scarcely spoke to his son. He did not, however cease hoping that he would realize how serious was the danger he was heading for. Day and night he put him in his prayers.

Nnaemeka, for his own part, was very deeply affected by his father's grief. But he kept hoping that it would pass away. If it had occurred to him that never in the history of his people had a man married a woman who spoke a different tongue, he might have been less optimistic. "It has never been heard," was the verdict of an old man speaking a few weeks later. In that short sentence he spoke for all of his people. This man had come with others to commiserate with Okeke when news went round about his son's behaviour. By that time the son had gone back to Lagos.

"It has never been heard," said the old man again with a sad shake of his head.

"What did Our Lord say?" asked another gentleman. "Sons shall rise against their Fathers; it is there in the Holy Book."

"It is the beginning of the end," said another.

The discussion thus tending to become theological, Madubogwu, a highly practical man, brought it down once more to the ordinary level.

"Have you thought of consulting a native doctor about your son?" he asked Nnaemeka's father.

"He isn't sick," was the reply.

"What is he then? The boy's mind is diseased and only a good herbalist can bring him back to his right senses. The medicine he requires is *Amalile*, the same that women apply with success to recapture their husbands' straying affection."

"Madubogwu is right," said another gentleman. "This thing calls for medicine."

"I shall not call in a native doctor." Nnaemeka's father was known to be obstinately ahead of his more superstitious neighbours in these matters. "I will not be another Mrs. Ochuba. If my son wants to kill himself let him do it with his own hands. It is not for me to help him."

"But it was her fault," said Madubogwu. "She ought to have gone to an honest herbalist. She was a clever woman, nevertheless."

"She was a wicked murderess," said Jonathan who rarely argued with his neighbours because, he often said, they were incapable of reasoning. "The medicine was prepared for her husband, it was his name they called in its preparation and I am sure it would have been perfectly beneficial to him. It was wicked to put it into the herbalist's food, and say you were only trying it out."

Six months later, Nnaemeka was showing his young wife a short letter from his father:

> *It amazes me that you could be so unfeeling as to send me your wedding picture. I would have sent it back. But on further thought I decided just to cut off your wife and send it back to you because I have nothing to do with her. How I wish that I had nothing to do with you either.*

When Nene read through this letter and looked at the mutilated picture her eyes filled with tears, and she began to sob.

"Don't cry, my darling," said her husband. "He is essentially good-natured and will one day look more kindly on our marriage." But years passed and that one day did not come.

For eight years, Okeke would have nothing to do with his son, Nnaemeka. Only three times (when Nnaemeka asked to come home and spend his leave) did he write to him.

"I can't have you in my house," he replied on one occasion. "It can be of no interest to me where or how you spend your leave— or your life, for that matter."

The prejudice against Nnaemeka's marriage was not confined to his little village. In Lagos, especially among his people who worked there, it showed itself in a different way. Their women, when they met at their village meeting were not hostile to Nene. Rather, they paid her such excessive deference as to make her feel she was not one of them. But as time went on, Nene gradually broke through some of this prejudice and even began to make friends among them. Slowly and grudgingly they began to admit that she kept her home much better than most of them.

The story eventually got to the little village in the heart of the Ibo country that Nnaemeka and his young wife were a most happy couple. But his father was one of the few people who knew nothing about this. He always displayed so much temper whenever his son's name was mentioned that everyone avoided it in his presence. By a tremendous effort of will he had succeeded in pushing his son to the back of his mind. The strain had nearly killed him but he had persevered, and won.

Then one day he received a letter from Nene, and in spite of himself he began to glance through it perfunctorily until all of a sudden the expression on his face changed and he began to read more carefully.

> . . . *Our two sons, from the day they learnt that they have a grand-father, have insisted on being taken to him. I find it impossible to tell them that you will not see them. I implore you to allow Nnaemeka to bring them home for a short time during his leave next month. I shall remain here in Lagos . . .*

The old man at once felt the resolution he had built up over so many years falling in. He was telling himself that he must not give in. He tried to steel his heart against all emotional appeals. It was a re-enactment of that other struggle. He leaned against a window and looked out. The sky was overcast with heavy black clouds and a high wind began to blow filling the air with dust and dry leaves. It was one of those rare occasions when even Nature takes a hand in a human fight. Very soon it began to rain, the first rain in the year. It came down in large sharp drops and was accompanied by the lightning and thunder which mark a change of season. Okeke was trying hard not to think of his two grandsons. But he knew he was now fighting a losing battle. He tried to hum a favourite hymn but the pattering of large rain drops on the roof broke up the tune. His mind immediately returned to the children. How could he shut his door against them? By a curious mental process he imagined them standing, sad and forsaken, under the harsh angry weather—shut out from his house.

That night he hardly slept, from remorse—and a vague fear that he might die without making it up to them.

SHERWOOD ANDERSON

[U.S.A.]

SHERWOOD ANDERSON (1876–1941) was, before becoming one of America's short-story masters, an ad-writer in Chicago. With his first wife (Cornelia Lane, the daughter of a wealthy businessman), he had three children. After a nervous breakdown, and despite success running his own business, Anderson Manufacturing Company, Anderson took to writing full-time in 1912. "The Other Woman" was published after Anderson's second marriage and before his third and fourth marriages, the last of which was happy.

The Other Woman (1921)

"I AM IN love with my wife," he said—a superflous remark, as I had not questioned his attachment to the woman he had married. We walked for ten minutes and then he said it again. I turned to look at him. He began to talk and told me the tale I am now about to set down.

The thing he had on his mind happened during what must have been the most eventful week of his life. He was to be married on Friday afternoon. On Friday of the week before he got a telegram announcing his appointment to a government position. Something else happened that made him very proud and glad. In secret he was in the habit of writing verses and during the year before several of them had been printed in poetry magazines. One of the societies that give prizes for what they think the best poems published during the year put his name at the head of its list. The story of his triumph was printed in the newspapers of his home city and one of them also printed his picture.

As might have been expected he was excited and in a rather highly strung nervous state all during that week. Almost every evening he went to call on his fiancée, the daughter of a judge. When he got there the house was filled with people and many letters, telegrams and packages were being received. He stood a little to one side and men and women kept coming up to speak to him. They congratulated him upon his success in getting the government position and on his achievement as a poet. Everyone seemed to be praising him and when he went home and to bed he could not sleep. On Wednesday evening he went to the theatre and it seemed to him that people all over the house recognized him. Everyone nodded and smiled. After the first act five or six men and two women left their seats to gather about him. A little group was formed. Strangers sitting along the same row of seats stretched their necks and looked. He had never received so much attention before, and now a fever of expectancy took possession of him.

As he explained when he told me of his experience, it was for him an altogether abnormal time. He felt like one floating in air. When he got into bed after seeing so many people and hearing so many words of praise his head whirled round and round. When he closed his eyes a crowd of people invaded his room. It seemed as though the minds of all the people of his city were centred on himself. The most absurd fancies took possession of him. He imagined himself riding in a carriage through the streets of a city. Windows were thrown open and people ran out at the doors of houses. "There he is. That's him," they shouted, and at the words a glad cry arose. The carriage drove into a street blocked with people. A hundred thousand pairs of eyes looked up at him. "There you are! What a fellow you have managed to make of yourself!" the eyes seemed to be saying.

My friend could not explain whether the excitement of the people was due to the fact that he had written a new poem or whether, in his new government position, he had performed some notable act. The apartment where he lived at that time was on a street perched along the top of a cliff far out at the edge of his city, and from his bedroom window he could look down over trees and factory roofs to a river. As he could not sleep and as the fancies that kept crowding in upon him only made him more excited, he got out of bed and tried to think.

As would be natural under such circumstances, he tried to control his thoughts, but when he sat by the window and was wide awake a most unexpected and humiliating thing happened. The night was clear and fine. There was a moon. He wanted to dream of the woman who was to be his wife, to think out lines for noble poems or make plans that would affect his career. Much to his surprise his mind refused to do anything of the sort.

At a corner of the street where he lived there was a small cigar store and newspaper stand run by a fat man of forty and his wife, a small active woman with bright grey eyes. In the morning he stopped there to buy a paper before going down to the city. Sometimes he saw only the fat man, but often the man had disappeared and the woman waited on him. She was, as he assured me at least twenty times in telling me his tale, a very ordinary person with nothing special or notable about her, but for some reason he could not explain, being in her presence stirred him profoundly. During that week in the midst of his distraction she was the only person he knew who stood out clear and distinct in his mind. When he wanted so much to think noble thoughts he could think only of her. Before he knew what was happening his imagination had taken hold of the notion of having a love affair with the woman.

"I could not understand myself," he declared, in telling me the story. "At night, when the city was quiet and when I should have been asleep, I thought about her all the time. After two or three days of that sort of thing the consciousness of her got into my daytime thoughts. I was terribly muddled. When I went to see the woman who is now my wife I found that my love for her was in no way affected by my vagrant thoughts. There was but one woman in the world I wanted to live with and to be my comrade in undertaking to improve my own character and my position in the world, but for the moment, you see, I wanted this other woman to be in my arms. She had worked her way into my being. On all sides people were saying I was a big man who would do big things, and there I was. That evening when I went to the theatre I walked home because I knew I would be unable to sleep, and to satisfy the annoying impulse in myself I went and stood on the sidewalk before the tobacco shop. It was a two story building, and I knew the woman lived upstairs with her husband. For a long time I stood in the darkness with my body pressed against the wall of the building, and then I thought of the two of them up there and no doubt in bed together. That made me furious.

"Then I grew more furious with myself. I went home and got into bed, shaken with anger. There are certain books of verse and some prose writings that have always moved me deeply, and so I put several books on a table by my bed.

"The voices in the books were like the voices of the dead. I did not hear them. The printed words would not penetrate into my consciousness. I tried to think of the woman I loved, but her figure had also become something far away, something with which I for the moment seemed to have nothing to do. I rolled and tumbled about in the bed. It was a miserable experience.

"On Thursday morning I went into the store. There stood the woman alone. I think she knew how I felt. Perhaps she had been thinking of me as I had been thinking of her. A doubtful hesitating smile played about the corners of her mouth. She had on a dress made of cheap cloth and there was a tear on the shoulder. She must have been ten years older than myself. When I tried to put my pennies on the glass counter, behind which she stood, my hand trembled so that the pennies made a sharp rattling noise. When I spoke the voice that came out of my throat did not sound like anything that had ever belonged to me. It barely arose above a thick whisper. 'I want you,' I said. 'I want you very much. Can't you run away from your husband? Come to me at my apartment at seven tonight.'

"The woman did come to my apartment at seven. That morning she didn't say anything at all. For a minute perhaps we stood looking at each other. I had forgotten everything in the world but just her. Then she nodded her head and I went away. Now that I think of it I cannot remember a word I ever heard her say. She came to my apartment at seven and it was dark. You must understand this was in the month of October. I had not lighted a light and I had sent my servant away.

"During that day I was no good at all. Several men came to see me at my office, but I got all muddled up in trying to talk with them. They attributed my rattle-headedness to my approaching marriage and went away laughing.

"It was on that morning, just the day before my marriage, that I got a long and very beautiful letter from my fiancée. During the night before she also had been unable to sleep and had got out of bed to write the letter. Everything she said in it was very sharp and real, but she herself, as a living thing, seemed to have receded into the distance. It seemed to me that she was like a bird, flying far away in distant skies, and that I was like a perplexed bare-footed boy standing in the dusty road before a farm house and looking at her receding figure. I wonder if you will understand what I mean?

"In regard to the letter. In it she, the awakening woman, poured out her heart. She of course knew nothing of life, but she was a woman. She lay, I suppose, in her bed feeling nervous and wrought up as I had been doing. She realized that a great change was about to take place in her life and was glad and afraid too. There she lay thinking of it all. Then she got out of bed and began talking to me on the bit of paper. She told me how afraid she was and how glad too. Like most young women she had heard things whispered. In the letter she was very sweet and fine. 'For a long time, after we are married, we will forget we are a man and woman,' she wrote. 'We will be human beings. You must remember that I am ignorant and often I will be very stupid. You must love me and be very patient and kind. When I know more, when after a long time you have taught me the way of life, I will try to repay you. I will love you tenderly and passionately. The possibility of that is in me or I would not want to marry at all. I am afraid but I am also happy. O, I am so glad our marriage time is near at hand!'

"Now you see clearly enough what a mess I was in. In my office, after I had read my fiancée's letter, I became at once very resolute and strong. I remember that I got out of my chair and walked about, proud of the fact that I was to be the husband of so noble a woman. Right away I felt concerning her as I had been feeling about myself before I found out what a weak thing I was. To be sure I took a strong resolution that I would not be weak. At nine that evening I had planned to run in to see my fiancée. 'I'm all right now', I said to myself. 'The beauty of her character has saved me from myself. I will go home now and send the other woman away.' In the morning I had telephoned to my servant and told him that I did not want him to be at the apartment that evening and I now picked up the telephone to tell him to stay at home.

"Then a thought came to me. 'I will not want him there in any event,' I told myself. 'What will he think when he sees a woman coming in my place on the evening before the day I am to be married?' I put the telephone down and prepared to go home. 'If I want my servant out of the apartment it is because I do not want him to hear me talk with the woman. I cannot be rude to her. I will have to make some kind of an explanation,' I said to myself.

"The woman came at seven o'clock, and, as you may have guessed, I let her in and forgot the resolution I had made. It is likely I never had any intention of doing anything else. There was a bell on my door, but she did not ring, but knocked very softly. It seems to me that everything she did that evening was soft and quiet, but very determined and quick. Do I make myself clear? When she came I was standing just within the door where I had been standing and waiting for a half hour. My hands were trembling as they had trembled in the morning when her eyes looked at me and when I tried to put the pennies on the counter in the store. When I opened the door she stepped quickly in and I took her into my arms. We stood together in the darkness. My hands no longer trembled. I felt very happy and strong.

"Although I have tried to make everything clear I have not told you what the woman I married is like. I have emphasized, you see, the other woman. I make the blind statement that I love my wife, and to a man of your shrewdness that means nothing at all. To tell the truth, had I not started to speak of this matter I would feel more comfortable. It is inevitable that I give you the impression that I am in love with the tobacconist's wife. That's not true. To be sure I was very conscious of her all during the week before my marriage, but after she had come to me at my apartment she went entirely out of my mind.

"Am I telling the truth? I am trying very hard to tell what happened to me. I am saying that I have not since that evening thought of the woman who came to my apartment. Now, to tell the facts of the case, that is not true. On that evening I went to my fiancée at nine, as she had asked me to do in her letter. In a kind of way I cannot explain the other woman went with me. This is what I mean—you see I had been thinking that if anything happened between me and the tobacconist's wife I would not be able to go through with my marriage. 'It is one thing or the other with me,' I had said to myself.

"As a matter of fact I went to see my beloved on that evening filled with a new faith in the outcome of our life together. I am afraid I muddle this matter in trying to tell it. A moment ago I said the other woman, the tobacconist's wife, went with me. I do not mean she went in fact. What I am trying to say is that something of her faith in her own desires and her courage in seeing things through went with me. Is that clear to you? When I got to my fiancée's house there was a crowd of people standing about. Some were relatives from distant places I had not seen before. She looked up quickly when I came into the room. My face must have been radiant. I never saw her so moved. She thought her letter had affected me deeply, and of course it had. Up she jumped and ran to meet me. She was like a glad child. Right before the people who turned and looked inquiringly at us, she said the thing that was in her mind. 'O, I am so happy,' she cried. 'You have understood. We will be two human beings. We will not have to be husband and wife.'

"As you may suppose everyone laughed, but I did not laugh. The tears came into my eyes. I was so happy I wanted to shout. Perhaps you understand what I mean. In the office that day when I read the letter my fiancée had written I had said to myself, 'I will take care of the dear little woman.' There was something smug, you see, about that. In her house when she cried out in that way, and when everyone laughed, what I said to myself was something like this: 'We will take care of ourselves.' I whispered something of the sort into her ears. To tell you the truth I had come down off my perch. The spirit of the other woman did that to me. Before all the people gathered about I held my fiancée close and we kissed. They thought it very sweet of us to be so affected at the sight of each other. What they would have thought had they known the truth about me God only knows!

"Twice now I have said that after that evening I never thought of the other woman at all. That is partially true but, sometimes in the evening when I am walking alone in the street or in the park as we are walking now, and when evening comes softly and quickly as it has come to-night, the feeling of her comes sharply into my body and mind. After that one meeting I never saw her again. On the next day I was married and I have never gone back into her street. Often however as I am walking along as I am doing now, a quick sharp earthy feeling takes possession of me. It is as though I were a seed in the ground and the warm rains of the spring had come. It is as though I were not a man but a tree.

"And now you see I am married and everything is all right. My marriage is to me a very beautiful fact. If you were to say that my marriage is not a happy one I could call you a liar and be speaking the absolute truth. I have tried to tell you about this other woman. There is a kind of relief in speaking of her. I have never done it before. I wonder why I was so silly as to be afraid that I would give you the impression I am not in love with my wife. If I did not instinctively trust your understanding I would not have spoken. As the matter stands I have a little stirred myself up. To-night I shall think of the other woman. That sometimes occurs. It will happen after I have gone to bed. My wife sleeps in the next room to mine and the door is always left open. There will be a moon to-night, and when there is a moon long streaks of light fall on her bed. I shall awake at midnight to-night. She will be lying asleep with one arm thrown over her head.

"What is it that I am now talking about? A man does not speak of his wife lying in bed. What I am trying to say is that, because of this talk, I shall think of the other woman to-night. My thoughts will not take the form they did during the week before I was married. I will wonder what has become of the woman. For a moment I will again feel myself holding her close. I will think that for an hour I was closer to her than I have ever been to anyone else. Then I will think of the time when I will be as close as that to my wife. She is still, you see, an awakening woman. For a moment I will close my eyes and the quick, shrewd, determined eyes of that other woman will look into mine. My head will swim and then I will quickly open my eyes and see again the dear woman with whom I have undertaken to live out my life. Then I will sleep and when I awake in the morning it will be as it was that evening when I walked out of my dark apartment after having the most notable experience of my life. What I mean to say, you understand is that, for me, when I awake, the other woman will be utterly gone."

ANONYMOUS

[West and South Asia]

THE ANONYMOUS authors of *The Thousand and One Nights* were Middle Eastern, African, and South Asian storytellers in the oral tradition. The stories, probably first collected from Persian and Indian sources, were translated into Arabic and gathered into books starting in the eighth century. Their most famous English-language translator from the Arabic, Richard F. Burton, whose versions we use here, scandalized and delighted his British readers in the 1880s with a privately published ten-volume collection entitled *The Book of the Thousand Nights and a Night* (he supplemented those volumes with six more). We present the dramatic opening story that establishes the pretext for the story-cycle as well as the cycle's happy conclusion.

The Thousand and One Nights ("Story of King Shahryar and His Brother" and "Conclusion")
(c. 900)

(Translated from the Arabic by Sir Richard F. Burton)

THERE HE SAT him upon his throne and sending for the Chief Minister, the father of the two damsels who (Inshallah!) will presently be mentioned, he said, "I command thee to take my wife and smite her to death; for she hath broken her plight and her faith." So he carried her to the place of execution and did her die. Then King Shahryar took brand in hand and repairing to the Serraglio slew all the concubines and their Mamelukes. He also sware himself by a binding oath that whatever wife he married he would abate her maidenhead at night and slay her next morning to make sure of his honour; "For," said he, " there never was nor is there one chaste woman upon the face of earth." Then Shah Zaman prayed for permission to fare homewards; and he went forth equipped and escorted and travelled till he reached his own country. Meanwhile Shahryar commanded his Wazir to bring him the bride of the night that he might go in to her; so he produced a most beautiful girl, the daughter of one of the Emirs and the King went in unto her at eventide and when morning dawned he bade his Minister strike off her head; and the Wazir did accordingly for fear of the Sultan. On this wise he continued for the space of three years; marrying a maiden every night and killing her the next morning, till folk raised an outcry against him and cursed him, praying Allah utterly to destroy him and his rule; and women made an uproar and mothers wept and parents fled with their daughters till there remained not in the city a young person fit for carnal copulation. Presently the King ordered his Chief Wazir, the same who was charged with the executions, to bring him a virgin as was his wont; and the Minister went forth and searched and found none; so he returned home in sorrow and anxiety fearing for his life from the King. Now he had two daughters, Shahrázád and Dunyázád hight, of whom the elder had perused the books, annals and legends of preceding Kings, and the stories, examples and instances of by-gone men and things; indeed it was said that she had collected a thousand books of histories relating to antique races and departed rulers. She had perused the works of the poets and knew them by heart; she had studied philosophy and the sciences, arts and accomplishments; and she was pleasant and polite, wise and witty, well read and well bred. Now on that day she said to her father, "Why do I see thee thus changed and laden with cark and care? Concerning this matter quoth one of the poets:—

Tell whoso hath sorrow   ★ Grief never shall last:
E'en as joy hath no morrow ★ So woe shall go past."

When the Wazir heard from his daughter these words he related to her, from first to last, all that had happened between him and the King. Thereupon said she, "By Allah, O my father, how long shall this slaughter of women endure? Shall I tell thee what is in my mind in order to save both sides from destruction?" "Say on, O my daughter," quoth he, and quoth she, "I wish thou wouldst give me in marriage to this King Shahryar; either I shall live or I shall be a ransom for the virgin daughters of Moslems and the cause of their deliverance from his hands and thine." "Allah upon thee!" cried he in wrath exceeding that lacked no feeding, "O scanty of wit, expose not thy life to such peril! How durst thou address me in words so wide from wisdom and un-far from foolishness? Know that one who lacketh experience in worldly matters readily falleth into misfortune; and whoso considereth not the end keepeth not the world to friend, and the vulgar say:—I was lying at mine ease: nought but my officiousness brought me unease." "Needs must thou," she broke in, "make me a doer of this good deed, and let him kill me an he will: I shall only die a ransom for others." "O my daughter," asked he, "and how shall that profit thee when thou shalt have thrown away thy life?" and she answered, "O my father it must be, come of it what will!" The Wazir was again moved to fury and blamed and reproached her, ending with, "In very deed I fear lest the same befal thee which befel the Bull and the Ass with the Husbandman." "And what," asked she, "befel them, O my father?" whereupon the Wazir began the

TALE OF THE BULL AND THE ASS

Know, O my daughter, that there was once a merchant who owned much money and many men, and who was rich in cattle and camels; he had also a wife and family and he dwelt in the country, being experienced in husbandry and devoted to agriculture. Now Allah Most High had endowed him with understanding the tongues of beasts and birds of every kind, but under pain of death if he divulged the gift to any. So he kept it secret for very fear. He had in his cow-house a Bull and an Ass each tethered in his own stall one hard by the other. As the merchant was sitting near hand one day with his servants and his children were playing about him, he heard the Bull say to the Ass, "Hail and health to thee O Father of Waking! for that thou enjoyest rest and good ministering; all under thee is clean-swept and fresh-sprinkled; men wait upon thee and feed thee, and thy provaunt is sifted barley and thy drink pure spring-water, while I (unhappy creature!) am led forth in the middle of the night, when they set on my neck the plough and a something called Yoke; and I tire at cleaving the earth from dawn of day till set of sun. I am forced to do more than I can and to bear all manner of ill-treatment from night to night; after which they take me back with my sides torn, my neck flayed, my legs aching and mine eyelids sored with tears. Then they shut me up in the byre and throw me beans and crushed-straw, mixed with dirt and chaff; and I lie in dung and filth and foul stinks through the livelong night. But thou art ever in a place swept and sprinkled and cleansed, and thou art always lying at ease, save when it happens (and seldom enough!) that the master hath some business, when he mounts thee and rides thee to town and returns with thee forthright. So it happens that I am toiling and distrest while thou takest thine ease and thy rest; thou sleepest while I am sleepless; I hunger still while thou eatest thy fill, and I win contempt while thou winnest good will." When the Bull ceased speaking, the Ass turned towards him and said, " O Broad-o'-Brow, O thou lost one! he lied not who dubbed thee Bull-head, for thou, O father of a Bull, hast neither fore-thought nor contrivance; thou art the simplest of simpletons, and thou knowest naught of good advisers. Hast thou not heard the saying of the wise:—

For others these hardships and labours I bear ⋆ And theirs is
    the pleasure and mine is the care;
As the bleacher who blacketh his brow in the sun ⋆ To whiten
    the raiment which other men wear.

But thou, O fool, art full of zeal and thou toilest and moilest before the master; and thou tearest and wearest and slayest thyself for the comfort of another. Hast thou never heard the saw that saith, None to guide and from the way go wide? Thou wendest forth at the call to dawn-prayer and thou returnest not till sundown; and through the livelong day thou endurest all manner hardships; to wit, beating and belabouring and bad language. Now hearken to me, Sir Bull! when they tie thee to thy stinking manger, thou pawest the ground with thy forehand and lashest out with thy hind hoofs and pushest with thy horns and bellowest aloud, so they deem thee contented.

And when they throw thee thy fodder thou fallest on it with greed, and hastenest to line thy fair fat paunch. But if thou accept my advice it will be better for thee and thou wilt lead an easier life even than mine. When thou goest a–field and they lay the thing called Yoke on thy neck, lie down and rise not again though haply they swinge thee; and, if thou rise, lie down a second time; and when they bring thee home and offer thee thy beans, fall backwards and only sniff at thy meat and withdraw thee and taste it not, and be satisfied with thy crushed straw and chaff; and on this wise feign thou art sick, and cease not doing thus for a day or two days or even three days, so shalt thou have rest from toil and moil." When the Bull heard these words he knew the Ass to be his friend and thanked him, saying, "Right is thy rede;" and prayed that all blessings might requite him, and cried, "O Father Wakener! thou hast made up for my failings." (Now the merchant, O my daughter, understood all that passed between them.) Next day the driver took the Bull, and settling the plough on his neck, made him work as wont; but the Bull began to shirk his ploughing, according to the advice of the Ass, and the ploughman drubbed him till he broke the yoke and made off; but the man caught him up and leathered him till he despaired of his life. Not the less, however, would he do nothing but stand still and drop down till the evening. Then the herd led him home and stabled him in his stall: but he drew back from his manger and neither stamped nor ramped nor butted nor bellowed as he was wont to do; whereat the man wondered. He brought him the beans and husks, but he sniffed at them and left them and lay down as far from them as he could and passed the whole night fasting. The peasant came next morning; and, seeing the manger full of beans, the crushed-straw untasted and the ox lying on his back in sorriest plight, with legs outstretched and swollen belly, he was concerned for him, and said to himself, "By Allah, he hath assuredly sickened and this is the cause why he would not plough yesterday." Then he went to the merchant and reported, "O my master, the Bull is ailing; he refused his fodder last night; nay more, he hath not tasted a scrap of it this morning." Now the merchant-farmer understood what all this meant, because he had overheard the talk between the Bull and the Ass, so quoth he, "Take that rascal donkey, and set the yoke on his neck, and bind him to the plough and make him do Bull's work." Thereupon the ploughman took the Ass, and worked him through the livelong day at the Bull's task; and, when he failed for weakness, he made him eat stick till his ribs were sore and his sides were sunken and his neck was flayed by the yoke; and when he came home in the evening he could hardly drag his limbs along, either forehand or hindlegs. But as for the Bull, he had passed the day lying at full length and had eaten his fodder with an excellent appetite, and he ceased not calling down blessings on the Ass for his good advice, unknowing what had come to him on his account. So when night set in and the Ass returned to the byre the Bull rose up before him in honour, and said, "May good tidings gladden thy heart, O Father Wakener! through thee I have rested all this day and I have eaten my meat in peace and quiet." But the Ass returned no reply, for wrath and heart-burning and fatigue and the beating he had gotten; and he repented with the most grievous of repentance; and quoth he to himself: "This cometh of my folly in giving good counsel; as the saw saith, I was in joy and gladness, nought save my officiousness brought me this sadness. But I will bear in mind my innate worth and the nobility of my nature; for what saith the poet?

Shall the beautiful hue of the Basil fail ★ Tho' the beetle's foot o'er the Basil crawl?
And though spider and fly be its denizens ★ Shall disgrace attach to the royal hall?
The cowrie, I ken, shall have currency ★ But the pearl's clear drop, shall its value fall?

And now I must take thought and put a trick upon him and return him to his place, else I die." Then he went aweary to his manger, while the Bull thanked him and blessed him. And even so, O my daughter, said the Wazir, thou wilt die for lack of wits; therefore sit thee still and say naught and expose not thy life to such stress; for, by Allah, I offer thee the best advice, which cometh of my affection and kindly solicitude for thee. "O my father," she answered, "needs must I go up to this King and be married to him." Quoth he, "Do not this deed;" and quoth she, "Of a truth I will:" whereat he rejoined, "If thou be not silent and bide still, I will do with thee even what the merchant did with his wife." "And what did he?" asked she. Know then, answered the Wazir, that after the return of the Ass the merchant came out on the terrace-roof with his wife and family, for it was a moonlit night and the moon at its full. Now the terrace overlooked the cowhouse and presently, as he sat there with his children playing about him, the trader heard the Ass say to the Bull, "Tell me, O father Broad o' Brow, what thou purposest to do to-morrow?" The Bull answered, "What but continue to follow thy counsel, O Aliboron? Indeed it was as good as good could be and it hath given me rest and repose; nor will I now depart from it one tittle: so, when they bring me my meat, I will refuse it and blow out my belly and counterfeit crank." The Ass shook his head and said, "Beware of so doing, O Father of a Bull!" The Bull asked, "Why," and the Ass answered, "Know that I am about to give thee the best of counsel, for verily I heard our owner say to the herd, If the Bull rise not from his place to do his work this morning and if he retire from his fodder this day, make him over to the butcher that he may slaughter him and give his flesh to the poor, and fashion a bit of leather from his hide. Now I fear for thee on account of this. So take my advice ere a calamity befal thee; and when they bring thee thy fodder eat it and rise up and bellow and paw the ground, or our master will assuredly slay thee: and peace be with thee!" Thereupon the Bull arose and lowed aloud and thanked the Ass, and said, "To-morrow I will readily go forth with them;" and he at once ate up all his meat and even licked the manger. (All this took place and the owner was listening to their talk.) Next morning the trader and his wife went to the Bull's crib and sat down, and the driver came and led forth the Bull who, seeing his owner, whisked his tail and brake wind, and frisked about so lustily that the merchant laughed a loud laugh and kept laughing till he fell on his back. His wife asked him, "Whereat laughest thou with such loud laughter as this?"; and he answered her, "I laughed at a secret something which I have heard and seen but cannot say lest I die my death." She returned, "Perforce thou must discover it to me, and disclose the cause of thy laughing even if thou come by thy death!" But he rejoined, "I cannot reveal what beasts and birds say in their lingo for fear I die." Then quoth she, "By Allah, thou liest! this is a mere pretext: thou laughest at none save me, and now thou wouldest hide somewhat from me. But by the Lord of the Heavens! an thou disclose not the cause I will no longer cohabit with thee: I will leave thee at once." And she sat down and cried. Whereupon quoth the merchant, "Woe betide thee! what means thy weeping? Fear Allah and leave these words and query me no more questions." "Needs must thou tell me the cause of that

laugh," said she, and he replied, "Thou wottest that when I prayed
Allah to vouchsafe me understanding of the tongues of beasts and
birds, I made a vow never to disclose the secret to any under pain
of dying on the spot." "No matter," cried she, "tell me what secret
passed between the Bull and the Ass and die this very hour an thou
be so minded;" and she ceased not to importune him till he was
worn out and clean distraught. So at last he said, "Summon thy
father and thy mother and our kith and kin and sundry of our
neighbours," which she did; and he sent for the Kazi and his asses-
sors, intending to make his will, and reveal to her his secret and die
the death; for he loved her with love exceeding because she was his
cousin, the daughter of his father's brother, and the mother of his
children, and he had lived with her a life of an hundred and twenty
years. Then, having assembled all the family and the folk of his
neighbourhood, he said to them, "By me there hangeth a strange
story, and 'tis such that if I discover the secret to any, I am a dead
man." Therefore quoth every one of those present to the woman,
"Allah upon thee, leave this sinful obstinacy and recognise the right
of this matter, lest haply thy husband and the father of thy children
die." But she rejoined, "I will not turn from it till he tell me, even
though he come by his death." So they ceased to urge her; and the
trader rose from amongst them and repaired to an outhouse to
perform the Wuzu-ablution, and he purposed thereafter to return
and to tell them his secret and to die. Now, daughter Shahrazad,
that merchant had in his out-houses some fifty hens under one
cock, and whilst making ready to farewell his folk he heard one of
his many farm-dogs thus address in his own tongue the Cock, who
was flapping his wings and crowing lustily and jumping from one
hen's back to another and treading all in turn, saying "O
Chanticleer! how mean is thy wit and how shameless is thy conduct! Be he disappointed who brought thee up? Art thou not
ashamed of thy doings on such a day as this?" "And what," asked
the Rooster, "hath occurred this day?," when the Dog answered,
"Dost thou not know that our master is this day making ready for
his death? His wife is resolved that he shall disclose the secret taught
to him by Allah, and the moment he so doeth he shall surely die.
We dogs are all a-mourning; but thou clappest thy wings and
clarionest thy loudest and treadest hen after hen. Is this an hour for
pastime and pleasuring? Art thou not ashamed of thyself?" "Then
by Allah," quoth the Cock, "is our master a lack-wit and a man

scanty of sense: if he cannot manage matters with a single wife, his life is not worth prolonging. Now I have some fifty Dame Partlets; and I please this and provoke that and starve one and stuff another; and through my good governance they are all well under my control. This our master pretendeth to wit and wisdom, and he hath but one wife, and yet knoweth not how to manage her." Asked the Dog, "What then, O Cock, should the master do to win clear of his strait?" "He should, arise forthright," answered the Cock, "and take some twigs from yon mulberry-tree and give her a regular back-basting and rib-roasting till she cry:—I repent, O my lord! I will never ask thee a question as long as I live! Then let him beat her once more and soundly, and when he shall have done this, he shall sleep free from care and enjoy life. But this master of ours owns neither sense nor judgment." "Now, daughter Shahrazad," continued the Wazir, "I will do to thee as did that husband to that wife." Said Shahrazad, "And what did he do?" He replied, "When the merchant heard the wise words spoken by his Cock to his Dog; he arose in haste and sought his wife's chamber, after cutting for her some mulberry-twigs and hiding them there; and then he called to her, "Come into the closet that I may tell thee the secret while no one seeth me and then die." She entered with him and he locked the door and came down upon her with so sound a beating of back and shoulders, ribs, arms and legs, saying the while, "Wilt thou ever be asking questions about what concerneth thee not?" that she was well nigh senseless. Presently she cried out, "I am of the repentant! By Allah, I will ask thee no more questions, and indeed I repent sincerely and wholesomely." Then she kissed his hand and feet and he led her out of the room submissive as a wife should be. Her parents and all the company rejoiced and sadness and mourning were changed into joy and gladness. Thus the merchant learnt family discipline from his Cock and he and his wife lived together the happiest of lives until death. And thou also, O my daughter! continued the Wazir, "Unless thou turn from this matter I will do by thee what that trader did to his wife." But she answered him with much decision, "I will never desist, O my father, nor shall this tale change my purpose. Leave such talk and tattle. I will not listen to thy words and, if thou deny me, I will marry myself to him despite the nose of thee. And first I will go up to the King myself and alone and I will say to him:—I prayed my father to wive me with thee, but he refused, being resolved to disappoint his lord, grudging the like of me to the like of thee." Her father asked, "Must this needs be?" and she answered, "Even so." Hereupon the Wazir being weary of lamenting and contending, persuading and dissuading her, all to no purpose, went up to King Shahryar and, after blessing him and kissing the ground before him, told him all about his dispute with his daughter from first to last and how he designed to bring her to him that night. The King wondered with exceeding wonder; for he had made an especial exception of the Wazir's daughter, and said to him, "O most faithful of Counsellors, how is this? Thou wottest that I have sworn by the Raiser of the Heavens that after I have gone into her this night I shall say to thee on the morrow's morning:—Take her and slay her! and, if thou slay her not, I will slay thee in her stead without fail." "Allah guide thee to glory and lengthen thy life, O King of the age," answered the Wazir, "it is she that hath so determined: all this have I told her and more; but she will not hearken to me and she persisteth in passing this coming night with the King's Majesty." So Shahryar rejoiced greatly and said, "'Tis well; go get her ready and this night bring her to me." The Wazir returned to his daughter and reported to her the command saying, "Allah make not thy father desolate by thy loss!" But Shahrazad rejoiced with exceeding joy and gat ready all she required and said to her younger sister, Dunyazad, "Note well what directions I entrust to thee! When I have gone into the King I will send for thee and when thou comest to me and seest that he hath had his carnal will of me, do thou say to me:—O my sister, an thou be not sleepy, relate to me some new story, delectable and delightsome, the better to speed our waking hours;" and I will tell thee a tale which shall be our deliverance, if so Allah please, and which shall turn the King from his blood-thirsty custom." Dunyazad answered "With love and gladness." So when it was night their father the Wazir carried Shahrazad to the King who was gladdened at the sight and asked, "Hast thou brought me my need?" and he answered, "I have." But when the King took her to his bed and fell to toying with her and wished to go in to her she wept; which made him ask, "What aileth thee?" She replied, "O King of the age, I have a younger sister and lief would I take leave of her this night before I see the dawn." So he sent at once for Dunyazad and she came and kissed the ground between his hands, when he permitted her to take her seat near the foot of the couch. Then the King arose and did away with his bride's maidenhead and the three

fell asleep. But when it was midnight Shahrazad awoke and sig-
nalled to her sister Dunyazad who sat up and said, "Allah upon
thee, O my sister, recite to us some new story, delightsome and
delectable, wherewith to while away the waking hours of our latter
night." "With joy and goodly gree," answered Shahrazad, "if this
pious and auspicious King permit me." "Tell on," quoth the King,
who chanced to be sleepless and restless and therefore was pleased
with the prospect of hearing her story. So Shahrazad rejoiced; and
thus, on the first night of the Thousand Nights and a Night, she
began with the "Tale of the Trader and the Jinni."

CONCLUSION

Now, during this time, Shahrazad had borne the King three boy-
children: so, when she had made an end of the story of Ma'aruf, she
rose to her feet and kissing ground before him, said, "O King of the
time and unique one of the age and the tide, I am thine handmaid
and these thousand nights and a night have I entertained thee with
stories of folk gone before and admonitory instances of the men of
yore. May I then make bold to crave a boon of Thy Highness?" He
replied, "Ask, O Shahrazad, and it shall be granted to thee."
Whereupon she cried out to the nurses and the eunuchs, saying,
"Bring me my children." So they brought them to her in haste, and
they were three boy children, one walking, one crawling and one
sucking. She took them and setting them before the King, again
kissed the ground and said, "O King of the age, these are thy children and I crave that thou release me from the doom of death, as a
dole to these infants; for, an thou kill me, they will become moth-
erless and will find none among women to rear them as they should
be reared." When the King heard this, he wept and straining the
boys to his bosom, said, "By Allah, O Shahrazad, I pardoned thee
before the coming of these children, for that I found thee chaste,
pure, ingenuous and pious! Allah bless thee and thy father and thy
mother and thy root and thy branch! I take the Almighty to witness
against me that I exempt thee from aught that can harm thee." So
she kissed his hands and feet and rejoiced with exceeding joy, saying, "The Lord make thy life long and increase thee in dignity and
majesty!"; presently adding, "Thou marvelledst at that which befel
thee on the part of women; yet there betided the Kings of the
Chosroës before thee greater mishaps and more grievous than that

which hath befallen thee, and indeed I have set forth unto thee that which happened to Caliphs and Kings and others with their women, but the relation is longsome and hearkening groweth tedious, and in this is all-sufficient warning for the man of wits and admonishment for the wise." Then she ceased to speak, and when King Shahryar heard her speech and profited by that which she said, he summoned up his reasoning powers and cleansed his heart and caused his understanding revert and turned to Allah Almighty and said to himself, "Since there befel the Kings of the Chosroës more than that which hath befallen me, never, whilst I live, shall I cease to blame myself for the past. As for this Shahrazad, her like is not found in the lands; so praise be to Him who appointed her a means for delivering His creatures from oppression and slaughter!" Then he arose from his séance and kissed her head, whereat she rejoiced, she and her sister Dunyazad, with exceeding joy. When the morning morrowed, the King went forth and sitting down on the throne of the Kingship, summoned the Lords of his land; whereupon the Chamberlains and Nabobs and Captains of the host went in to him and kissed ground before him. He distinguished the Wazir, Shahrazad's sire, with special favour and bestowed on him a costly and splendid robe of honour and entreated him with the utmost kindness, and said to him "Allah protect thee for that thou gavest me to wife thy noble daughter, who hath been the means of my repentance from slaying the daughters of folk. Indeed I have found her pure and pious, chaste and ingenuous, and Allah hath vouchsafed me by her three boy children; wherefore praised be He for his passing favour." Then he bestowed robes of honour upon his Wazirs, and Emirs and Chief Officers and he set forth to them briefly that which had betided him with Shahrazad and how he had turned from his former ways and repented him of what he had done and purposed to take the Wazir's daughter, Shahrazad, to wife and let draw up the marriage-contract with her. When those who were present heard this, they kissed the ground before him and blessed him and his betrothed Shahrazad, and the Wazir thanked her. Then Shahriyar made an end of his sitting in all weal, whereupon the folk dispersed to their dwelling-places and the news was bruited abroad that the King purposed to marry the Wazir's daughter, Shahrazad. Then he proceeded to make ready the wedding gear, and presently he sent after his brother, King Shah Zaman, who came, and King Shahriyar went forth to meet him with the troops. Furthermore, they decorated the city after the goodliest fashion and diffused scents from censers and burnt aloes-wood and other perfumes in all the markets and thoroughfares and rubbed themselves with saffron, what while the drums beat and the flutes and pipes sounded and mimes and mountebanks played and plied their arts and the King lavished on them gifts and largesse; and in very deed it was a notable day. When they came to the palace, King Shahriyar commanded to spread the tables with beasts roasted whole and sweetmeats and all manner of viands and bade the crier cry to the folk that they should come up to the Divan and eat and drink and that this should be a means of reconciliation between him and them. So, high and low, great and small came up unto him and they abode on that wise, eating and drinking, seven days with their nights. Then the King shut himself up with his brother and related to him that which had betided him with the Wazir's daughter, Shahrazad, during the past three years and told him what he had heard from her of proverbs and parables, chronicles and pleasantries, quips and jests, stories and anecdotes, dialogues and histories and elegies and other verses; whereat King Shah Zaman marvelled with the uttermost marvel and said, "Fain would I take her younger sister to wife, so we may be two brothers-german to two sisters-german, and they on like wise be sisters to us; for that the calamity which befel me was the cause of our discovering that which befel thee and all this time of three years past I have taken no delight in woman, save that I lie each night with a damsel of my kingdom, and every morning I do her to death; but now I desire to marry thy wife's sister Dunyazad." When King Shahriyar heard his brother's words, he rejoiced with joy exceeding and arising forthright, went in to his wife Shahrazad and acquainted her with that which his brother purposed, namely that he sought her sister Dunyazad in wedlock; whereupon she answered, "O King of the age, we seek of him one condition, to wit, that he take up his abode with us, for that I cannot brook to be parted from my sister an hour, because we were brought up together and may not endure separation each from other. If he accept this pact, she is his handmaid." King Shahriyar returned to his brother and acquainted him with that which Shahrazad had said; and he replied, "Indeed, this is what was in my mind, for that I desire nevermore to be parted from thee one hour. As for the kingdom, Allah the Most High shall send to it whomso He chooseth, for that I have no longer a desire for the kingship." When King

Shahriyar heard his brother's words, he rejoiced exceedingly and said, " Verily, this is what I wished, O my brother. So Alhamdolillah— Praised be Allah—who hath brought about union between us." Then he sent after the Kazis and Olema, Captains and Notables, and they married the two brothers to the two sisters. The contracts were written out and the two Kings bestowed robes of honour of silk and satin on those who were present, whilst the city was decorated and the rejoicings were renewed. The King commanded each Emìr and Wazir and Chamberlain and Nabob to decorate his palace and the folk of the city were gladdened by the presage of happiness and contentment. King Shahriyar also bade slaughter sheep and set up kitchens and made bride-feasts and fed all comers, high and low; and he gave alms to the poor and needy and extended his bounty to great and small. Then the eunuchs went forth, that they might perfume the Hammam for the brides; so they scented it with rose-water and willow-flower-water and pods of musk and fumigated it with Kákilí eagle-wood and ambergris. Then Shahrazad entered, she and her sister Dunyazad, and they cleansed their heads and clipped their hair. When they came forth of the Hammam-bath, they donned raiment and ornaments; such as men were wont pre-pare for the Kings of the Chosroës; and among Shahrazad's apparel was a dress purfled with red gold and wrought with counterfeit presentments of birds and beasts. And the two sisters encircled their necks with necklaces of jewels of price, in the like whereof Iskander rejoiced not, for therein were great jewels such as amazed the wit and dazzled the eye; and the imagination was bewildered at their charms, for indeed each of them was brighter than the sun and the moon. Before them they lighted brilliant flambeaux of wax in can-delabra of gold, but their faces outshone the flambeaux, for that they had eyes sharper than unsheathed swords and the lashes of their eyelids bewitched all hearts. Their cheeks were rosy red and their necks and shapes gracefully swayed and their eyes wantoned like the gazelle's; and the slave-girls came to meet them with instruments of music. Then the two Kings entered the Hammam-bath, and when they came forth, they sat down on a couch set with pearls and gems, whereupon the two sisters came up to them and stood between their hands, as they were moons, bending and leaning from side to side in their beauty and loveliness. Presently they brought forward Shahrazad and displayed her, for the first dress, in a red suit; where-upon King Shahriyar rose to look upon her and the wits of all present, men and women, were bewitched for that she was even as saith of her one of her describers:—

> A sun on wand in knoll of sand she showed, ★ Clad in her cramoisy-hued chemisette:
> Of her lips' honey-dew she gave me drink ★ And with her rosy cheeks quencht fire she set.

Then they attired Dunyazad in a dress of blue brocade and she became as she were the full moon when it shineth forth. So they displayed her in this, for the first dress, before King Shah Zaman, who rejoiced in her and well-nigh swooned away for love-longing and amorous desire; yea, he was distraught with passion for her, whenas he saw her, because she was as saith of her one of her describers in these couplets:—

> She comes apparelled in an azure vest ★ Ultramarine as skies are deckt and dight:
> I view'd th' unparallel'd sight, which showed my eyes ★ A Summer-moon upon a Winter-night.

Then they returned to Shahrazad and displayed her in the second dress, a suit of surpassing goodliness, and veiled her face with her hair like a chin-veil. Moreover, they let down her side-locks and she was even as saith of her one of her describers in these couplets:—

> O hail to him whose locks his cheeks o'ershade, ★ Who slew my life by cruel hard despight:
> Said I, "Hast veiled the Morn in Night?" He said, ★ "Nay I but veil Moon in hue of Night."

Then they displayed Dunyazad in a second and a third and a fourth dress and she paced forward like the rising sun, and swayed to and fro in the insolence of beauty; and she was even as saith the poet of her in these couplets:—

> The sun of beauty she to all appears ★ And, lovely coy she mocks all loveliness:
> And when he fronts her favour and her smile ★ A-morn, the sun of day in clouds must dress.

Then they displayed Shahrazad in the third dress and the fourth and
the fifth and she became as she were a Bán-branch snell or a thirst-
ing gazelle, lovely of face and perfect in attributes of grace, even as
saith of her one in these couplets:—

> She comes like fullest moon on happy night, ★ Taper of waist
>   with shape of magic might:
> She hath an eye whose glances quell mankind, ★ And ruby on
>   her cheeks reflects his light:
> Enveils her hips the blackness of her hair; ★ Beware of curls
>   that bite with viper-bite!
> Her sides are silken-soft, that while the heart ★ Mere rock
>   behind that surface 'scapes our sight:
> From the fringed curtains of her eyne she shoots ★ Shafts that
>   at furthest range on mark alight.

Then they returned to Dunyazad and displayed her in the fifth dress
and in the sixth, which was green, when she surpassed with her
loveliness the fair of the four quarters of the world and outvied,
with the brightness of her countenance, the full moon at rising tide;
for she was even as saith of her the poet in these couplets:—

> A damsel 'twas the tirer's art had decked with snare and
>   sleight, ★ And robed with rays as though the sun from her
>   had borrowed light:
> She came before us wondrous clad in chemisette of green, ★
>   As veilèd by his leafy screen Pomegranate hides from sight:
> And when he said, "How callest thou the fashion of thy
>   dress?" ★ She answered us in pleasant way with double
>   meaning dight,
> "We call this garment crève-coeur and rightly is it hight, ★ For
>   many a heart wi' this we brake and harried many a sprite."

Then they displayed Shahrazad in the sixth and seventh dresses and
clad her in youth's clothing, whereupon she came forward swaying
from side to side and coquettishly moving and indeed she ravished
wits and hearts and ensorcelled all eyes with her glances. She shook
her sides and swayed her haunches, then put her hair on sword-hilt
and went up to King Shahriyar, who embraced her as hospitable
host embraceth guest, and threatened her in her ear with the taking

of the sword ; and she was even as saith of her the poet in these words:—

> Were not the Murk of gender male, ★ Than feminines sur-
>   passing fair,
> Tirewomen they had grudged the bride, ★ Who made her
>   beard and whiskers wear!

Thus also they did with her sister Dunyazad, and when they had made an end of the display the King bestowed robes of honour on all who were present and sent the brides to their own apartments. Then Shahrazad went in to King Shahriyar and Dunyazad to King Shah Zaman and each of them solaced himself with the company of his beloved consort and the hearts of the folk were comforted. When morning morrowed, the Wazir came in to the two Kings and kissed ground before them; wherefore they thanked him and were large of bounty to him. Presently they went forth and sat down upon couches of Kingship, whilst all the Wazirs and Emirs and Grandees and Lords of the land presented themselves and kissed ground. King Shahriyar ordered them dresses of honour and largesse and they prayed for the permanence and prosperity of the King and his brother. Then the two Sovrans appointed their sire-in-law the Wazir to be Viceroy in Samarcand and assigned him five of the Chief Emirs to accompany him, charging them attend him and do him service. The Minister kissed the ground and prayed that they might be vouchsafed length of life: then he went in to his daughters, whilst the Eunuchs and Ushers walked before him, and saluted them and farewelled them. They kissed his hands and gave him joy of the Kingship and bestowed on him immense treasures; after which he took leave of them and setting out, fared days and nights, till he came near Samarcand, where the towns-people met him at a distance of three marches and rejoiced in him with exceeding joy. So he entered the city and they decorated the houses and it was a notable day. He sat down on the throne of his kingship and the Wazirs did him homage and the Grandees and Emirs of Samarcand and all prayed that he might be vouchsafed justice and victory and length of continuance. So he bestowed on them robes of honour and entreated them with distinction and they made him Sultan over them. As soon as his father-in-law had departed for Samarcand, King Shahriyah summoned the Grandees of his realm and made them a stupendous banquet of all manner of delicious meats and exquisite sweetmeats. He also bestowed on them robes of honour and guerdoned them and divided the kingdoms between himself and his brother in their presence, whereat the folk rejoiced. Then the two Kings abode, each ruling a day in turn, and they were ever in harmony each with other while on similar wise their wives continued in the love of Allah Almighty and in thanksgiving to Him; and the peoples and the provinces were at peace and the preachers prayed for them from the pulpits, and their report was bruited abroad and the travellers bore tidings of them to all lands. In due time King Shahriyah summoned chroniclers and copyists and bade them write all that had betided him with his wife, first and last; so they wrote this and named it "The Stories of the Thousand Nights and A Night." The book came to thirty volumes and these the King laid up in his treasury. And the two brothers abode with their wives in all pleasance and solace of life and its delights, for that indeed Allah the Most High had changed their annoy into joy; and on this wise they continued till there took them the Destroyer of delights and the Severer of societies, the Desolator of dwelling-places and Garnerer of grave-yards, and they were translated to the ruth of Almighty Allah; their houses fell waste and their palaces lay in ruins and the Kings inherited their riches. Then there reigned after them a wise ruler, who was just, keen-witted and accomplished and loved tales and legends, especially those which chronicle the doings of Sovrans and Sultans, and he found in the treasury these marvellous stories and wondrous histories, contained in the thirty volumes aforesaid. So he read in them a first book and a second and a third and so on to the last of them, and each book astounded and delighted him more than that which preceded it, till he came to the end of them. Then he admired whatso he had read therein of description and discourse and rare traits and anecdotes and moral instances and reminiscences and bade the folk copy them and dispread them over all lands and climes; wherefore their report was bruited abroad and the people named them "The marvels and wonders of the Thousand Nights and A Night." This is all that hath come down to us of the origin of this book, and Allah is All-knowing. So Glory be to Him whom the shifts of Time waste not away, nor doth aught of chance or change affect His sway: whom one case diverteth not from other case and Who is sole in the attributes of perfect grace. And prayer and peace be upon the Lord's Pontiff and Chosen One among His creatures, our lord MOHAMMED the Prince of mankind through whom we supplicate Him for a goodly and a godly.

GIOVANNI BOCCACCIO

[Italy]

ALONG WITH *The Canterbury Tales* by his English successor Geoffrey Chaucer and his anonymous predecessors who composed *The Thousand and One Nights*, *The Decameron* by Giovanni Boccaccio (1313–1375) is one of world literature's most famous story-cycles. Though he had probably composed some of the stories of his *Decameron* before the terrible plague of 1348 afflicted the city of Florence, it was the chaos brought by the Black Death that inspired the book's neat, symmetrical framework: ten days of stories by ten attractive young women and men who assemble in various idyllic locales outside the plague-ravaged city. Boccaccio seems never to have married.

Seventh Day: Ninth Story ("Lydia, wife of Nicostratus, loves Pyrrhus") (c. 1353)

(Translated from the Italian by J. M. Rigg)

Lydia, wife of Nicostratus, loves Pyrrhus, who to assure himself thereof, asks three things of her, all of which she does, and therewithal enjoys him in presence of Nicostratus, and makes Nicostratus believe that what he saw was not real.

IN ARGOS, THAT most ancient city of Achaia, the fame of whose kings of old time is out of all proportion to its size, there dwelt of yore Nicostratus, a nobleman, to whom, when he was already

35

verging on old age, Fortune gave to wife a great lady, Lydia by name, whose courage matched her charms. Nicostratus, as suited with his rank and wealth, kept not a few retainers and hounds and hawks, and was mightily addicted to the chase. Among his dependants was a young man named Pyrrhus, a gallant of no mean accomplishment, and goodly of person and beloved and trusted by Nicostratus above all other. Of whom Lydia grew mighty enamoured, insomuch that neither by day nor by night might her thoughts stray from him: but, whether it was that Pyrrhus wist not her love, or would have none of it, he gave no sign of recognition; whereby the lady's suffering waxing more than she could bear, she made up her mind to declare her love to him; and having a chambermaid, Lusca by name, in whom she placed great trust, she called her, and said:—

"Lusca, tokens thou hast had from me of my regard that should ensure thy obedience and loyalty; wherefore have a care that what I shall now tell thee reach the ears of none but him to whom I shall bid thee impart it. Thou seest, Lusca, that I am in the prime of my youth and lustihead, and have neither lack nor stint of all such things as folk desire, save only, to be brief, that I have one cause to repine, to wit, that my husband's years so far outnumber my own. Wherefore with that wherein young ladies take most pleasure I am but ill provided, and, as my desire is no less than theirs, 'tis now some while since I determined that, if Fortune has shewn herself so little friendly to me by giving me a husband so advanced in years, at least I will not be mine own enemy by sparing to devise the means whereby my happiness and health may be assured; and that herein, as in all other matters, my joy may be complete, I have chosen, thereto to minister by his embraces, our Pyrrhus, deeming him more worthy than any other man, and have so set my heart upon him that I am ever ill at ease save when he is present either to my sight or to my mind, insomuch that, unless I forgather with him without delay, I doubt not that 'twill be the death of me. And so, if thou holdest my life dear, thou wilt shew him my love on such wise as thou mayst deem best, and make my suit to him that he be pleased to come to me, when thou shalt go to fetch him."

"That gladly will I," replied the chambermaid; and as soon as she found convenient time and place, she drew Pyrrhus apart, and, as best she knew how, conveyed her lady's message to him.

Which Pyrrhus found passing strange to hear, for 'twas in truth a complete surprise to him, and he doubted the lady did but mean to try him. Wherefore he presently, and with some asperity, answered thus:—"Lusca, believe I cannot that this message comes from my lady: have a care, therefore, what thou sayst, and if, perchance, it does come from her, I doubt she does not mean it; and if, perchance, she does mean it, why, then I am honoured by my lord above what I deserve, and I would not for my life do him such a wrong: so have a care never to speak of such matters to me again."

Lusca, nowise disconcerted by his uncompliant tone, rejoined:— "I shall speak to thee, Pyrrhus, of these and all other matters, wherewith I may be commissioned by my lady, as often as she shall bid me, whether it pleases or irks thee; but thou art a blockhead."

So, somewhat chafed, Lusca bore Pyrrhus' answer back to her lady, who would fain have died, when she heard it, and some days afterwards resumed the topic, saying:—"Thou knowest, Lusca, that 'tis not the first stroke that fells the oak; wherefore, methinks, thou wert best go back to this strange man, who is minded to evince his loyalty at my expense, and choosing a convenient time, declare to him all my passion, and do thy best endeavour that the affair be carried through; for if it should thus lapse, 'twould be the death of me; besides which, he would think we had but trifled with him, and, whereas 'tis his love we would have, we should earn his hatred."

So, after comforting the lady, the maid hied her in quest of Pyrrhus, whom she found in a gladsome and propitious mood, and thus addressed:—

"'Tis not many days, Pyrrhus, since I declared to thee how ardent is the flame with which thy lady and mine is consumed for love of thee, and now again I do thee to wit thereof, and that, if thou shalt not relent of the harshness that thou didst manifest the other day, thou mayst rest assured that her life will be short: wherefore I pray thee to be pleased to give her solace of her desire, and shouldst thou persist in thy obduracy, I, that gave thee credit for not a little sense, shall deem thee a great fool. How flattered thou shouldst be to know thyself beloved above all else by a lady so beauteous and high-born! And how indebted shouldst thou feel thyself to Fortune, seeing that she has in store for thee a boon so great and so suited to the cravings of thy youth, ay, and so like to be of service to thee upon occasion of need! Bethink thee, if there be any of thine equals whose life is ordered more agreeably than thine will be if thou but be wise. Which of them wilt thou find so well furnished with arms and horses, clothes and money as thou shalt be, if thou but give my lady thy love? Receive, then, my words with open mind; be thyself again; bethink thee that 'tis Fortune's way to confront a man but once with smiling mien and open lap, and, if he then accept not her bounty, he has but himself to blame, if afterward he find himself in want, in beggary. Besides which, no such loyalty is demanded between servants and their masters as between friends and kinsfolk; rather 'tis for servants, so far as they may, to behave towards their masters as their masters behave towards them. Thinkest thou, that, if thou hadst a fair wife or mother or daughter or sister that found favour in Nicostratus' eyes, he would be so scrupulous on the point of loyalty as thou art disposed to be in regard of his lady? Thou art a fool, if so thou dost believe. Hold it for certain, that, if blandishments and supplications did not suffice, he would, whatever thou mightest think of it, have recourse to force. Observe we, then, towards them and theirs the same rule which they observe towards us and ours. Take the boon that Fortune offers thee; repulse her not; rather go thou to meet her, and hail her advance; for be sure that, if thou do not so, to say nought of thy lady's death, which will certainly ensue, thou thyself wilt repent thee thereof so often that thou wilt be fain of death."

Since he had last seen Lusca, Pyrrhus had repeatedly pondered what she had said to him, and had made his mind up that, should she come again, he would answer her in another sort, and comply in all respects with the lady's desires, provided he might be assured that she was not merely putting him to the proof; wherefore he now made answer:—

"Lo, now, Lusca, I acknowledge the truth of all that thou sayst; but, on the other hand, I know that my lord is not a little wise and wary, and, as he has committed all his affairs to my charge, I sorely misdoubt me that 'tis with his approbation, and by his advice, and but to prove me, that Lydia does this: wherefore let her do three things which I shall demand of her for my assurance, and then there is nought that she shall crave of me, but I will certainly render her prompt obedience. Which three things are these:—first, let her in Nicostratus' presence kill his fine sparrow-hawk: then she must send me a lock of Nicostratus' beard, and lastly one of his best teeth."

Hard seemed these terms to Lusca, and hard beyond measure to the lady, but Love, that great fautor of enterprise, and master of stratagem, gave her resolution to address herself to their performance: wherefore through the chambermaid she sent him word that what he required of her she would do, and that without either reservation or delay; and therewithal she told him, that, as he deemed Nicostratus so wise, she would contrive that they should enjoy one another in Nicostratus' presence, and that Nicostratus should believe that 'twas a mere show. Pyrrhus, therefore, anxiously expected what the lady would do. Some days thus passed, and then Nicostratus gave a great breakfast, as was his frequent wont, to certain gentlemen, and when the tables were removed, the lady, robed in green samite, and richly adorned, came forth of her chamber into the hall wherein they sate, and before the eyes of Pyrrhus and all the rest of the company hied her to the perch, on which stood the sparrow-hawk that Nicostratus so much prized, and loosed him, and, as if she were minded to carry him on her hand, took him by the jesses and dashed him against the wall so that he died.

Whereupon:—"Alas! my lady, what has thou done?" exclaimed Nicostratus: but she vouchsafed no answer, save that, turning to the gentlemen that had sate at meat with him, she said:—

"My lords, ill fitted were I to take vengeance on a king that had done me despite, if I lacked the courage to be avenged on a sparrow-hawk. You are to know that by this bird I have long been cheated of all the time that ought to be devoted by gentlemen to pleasuring their ladies; for with the first streaks of dawn Nicostratus has been up and got him to horse, and hawk on hand hied him to the champaign to see him fly, leaving me, such as you see me, alone and ill content abed. For which cause I have oftentimes been minded to do that which I have now done, and have only refrained therefrom, that, biding my time, I might do it in the presence of men that should judge my cause justly, as I trust you will do."

Which hearing, the gentlemen, who deemed her affections no less fixed on Nicostratus than her words imported, broke with one accord into a laugh, and turning to Nicostratus, who was sore displeased, fell a saying:—"Now well done of the lady to avenge her wrongs by the death of the sparrow-hawk!" and so, the lady being withdrawn to her chamber, they passed the affair off with divers pleasantries, turning the wrath of Nicostratus to laughter.

Pyrrhus, who had witnessed what had passed, said to himself:—Nobly indeed has my lady begun, and on such wise as promises well for the felicity of my love. God grant that she so continue. And even so Lydia did: for not many days after she had killed the sparrow-hawk, she, being with Nicostratus in her chamber, from caressing passed to toying and trifling with him, and he, sportively pulling her by the hair, gave her occasion to fulfil, the second of Pyrrhus' demands; which she did by nimbly laying hold of one of the lesser tufts of his beard, and, laughing the while, plucking it so hard that she tore it out of his chin.

Which Nicostratus somewhat resenting:—"Now what cause hast thou," quoth she, "to make such a wry face? 'Tis but that I have plucked some half-dozen hairs from thy beard. Thou didst not feel it as much as did I but now thy tugging of my hair."

And so they continued jesting and sporting with one another, the lady jealously guarding the tuft that she had torn from the beard, which the very same day she sent to her cherished lover. The third demand caused the lady more thought; but, being amply endowed with wit, and powerfully seconded by Love, she failed not to hit upon an apt expedient.

Nicostratus had in his service two lads, who, being of gentle birth, had been placed with him by their kinsfolk, that they might learn manners, one of whom, when Nicostratus sate at meat, carved before him, while the other gave him to drink. Both lads Lydia called to her, and gave them to understand that their breath smelt, and admonished them that, when they waited on Nicostratus, they should hold their heads as far back as possible, saying never a word of the matter to any. The lads believing her, did as she bade them. Whereupon she took occasion to say to Nicostratus:—"Hast thou marked what these lads do when they wait upon thee?"

"Troth, that have I," replied Nicostratus; "indeed I have often had it in mind to ask them why they do so."

"Nay," rejoined the lady, "spare thyself the pains; for I can tell thee the reason, which I have for some time kept close, lest it should vex thee; but as I now see that others begin to be ware of it, it need no longer be withheld from thee. 'Tis for that thy breath stinks shrewdly that they thus avert their heads from thee: 'twas not wont to be so, nor know I why it should be so; and 'tis most offensive when thou art in converse with gentlemen; and therefore 'twould be well to find some way of curing it."

"I wonder what it could be," returned Nicostratus; "is it perchance that I have a decayed tooth in my jaw?"

"That may well be," quoth Lydia: and taking him to a window, she caused him open his mouth, and after regarding it on this side and that:—"Oh! Nicostratus," quoth she, "how couldst thou have endured it so long? Thou hast a tooth here, which, by what I see, is not only decayed, but actually rotten throughout; and beyond all manner of doubt, if thou let it remain long in thy head, 'twill infect its neighbours; so 'tis my advice that thou out with it before the matter grows worse."

"My judgment jumps with thine," quoth Nicostratus; "wherefore send without delay for a chirurgeon to draw it."

"God forbid," returned the lady, "that chirurgeon come hither for such a purpose; methinks, the case is such that I can very well dispense with him, and draw the tooth myself. Besides which, these chirurgeons do these things in such a cruel way, that I could never endure to see thee or know thee under the hands of any of them: wherefore my mind is quite made up to do it myself, that, at least, if thou shalt suffer too much, I may give it over at once, as a chirurgeon would not do."

And so she caused the instruments that are used on such occasions to be brought her, and having dismissed all other attendants save Lusca from the chamber, and locked the door, made Nicostratus lie down on a table, set the pincers in his mouth, and clapped them on one of his teeth, which, while Lusca held him, so that, albeit he roared for pain, he might not move, she wrenched by main force from his jaw, and keeping it close, took from Lusca's hand another and horribly decayed tooth, which she shewed him, suffering and half dead as he was, saying:—"See what thou hadst in thy jaw; mark how far gone it is."

Believing what she said, and deeming that, now the tooth was out, his breath would no more be offensive, and being somewhat eased of the pain, which had been extreme, and still remained, so that he murmured not little, by divers comforting applications, he quitted the chamber: whereupon the lady forthwith sent the tooth to her lover, who, having now full assurance of her love, placed himself entirely at her service. But the lady being minded to make his assurance yet more sure, and deeming each hour a thousand till she might be with him, now saw fit, for the more ready performance of the promise she had given him, to feign sickness; and Nicostratus, coming to see her one day after breakfast, attended only by Pyrrhus, she besought him for her better solacement, to help her down to the garden.

Wherefore Nicostratus on one side, and Pyrrhus on the other, took her and bore her down to the garden, and set her on a lawn at the foot of a beautiful pear-tree: and after they had sate there a while, the lady, who had already given Pyrrhus to understand what he must do, said to him:—"Pyrrhus, I should greatly like to have some of those pears; get thee up the tree, and shake some of them down."

Pyrrhus climbed the tree in a trice, and began to shake down the pears, and while he did so:—"Fie! Sir," quoth he, "what is this you do? And you, Madam, have you no shame, that you suffer him to do so in my presence? Think you that I am blind? 'Twas but now that you were gravely indisposed. Your cure has been speedy indeed to permit of your so behaving: and as for such a purpose you have so many goodly chambers, why betake you not yourselves to one of them, if you must needs so disport yourselves? 'Twould be much more decent than to do so in my presence."

Whereupon the lady, turning to her husband:—"Now what can Pyrrhus mean?" said she. "Is he mad?"

"Nay, Madam," quoth Pyrrhus; "mad am not I. Think you I see you not?"

Whereat Nicostratus marvelled not a little; and:—"Pyrrhus," quoth he, "I verily believe thou dreamest."

"Nay, my lord," replied Pyrrhus, "not a whit do I dream; neither do you; rather you wag it with such vigour, that, if this pear-tree did the like, there would be never a pear left on it."

Then the lady:—"What can this mean?" quoth she: "can it be that it really seems to him to be as he says? Upon my hope of salvation, were I but in my former health, I would get me up there to judge for myself what these wonders are which he professes to see."

Whereupon, as Pyrrhus in the pear-tree continued talking in the same strange strain:—"Come down," quoth Nicostratus; and when he was down:—"Now, what," said Nicostratus, "is it thou sayst thou seest up there?"

"I suppose," replied Pyrrhus, "that you take me to be deluded or dreaming: but as I must needs tell you the truth, I saw you lying upon your wife, and then, when I came down, I saw you get up and sit you down here where you now are."

"Therein," said Nicostratus, "thou wast certainly deluded, for, since thou clombest the pear-tree, we have not budged a jot, save as thou seest."

Then said Pyrrhus:—"Why make more words about the matter? See you I certainly did; and, seeing you, I saw you lying upon your own."

Nicostratus' wonder now waxed momentarily, insomuch that he said:—"I am minded to see if this pear-tree be enchanted, so that whoso is in it sees marvels"; and so he got him up into it.

Whereupon the lady and Pyrrhus fell to disporting them, and Nicostratus, seeing what they were about, exclaimed:—"Ah! lewd woman, what is this thou doest? And thou, Pyrrhus, in whom I so much trusted!"

And so saying, he began to climb down. Meanwhile the lady and Pyrrhus had made answer:—"We are sitting here": and seeing him descending, they placed themselves as they had been when he had left them, whom Nicostratus, being come down, no sooner saw, than he fell a rating them.

Then quoth Pyrrhus:—"Verily, Nicostratus, I now acknowledge, that, as you said a while ago, what I saw when I was in the pear-tree was but a false show, albeit I had never understood that so it was but that I now see and know that thou hast also seen a false show. And that I speak truth, you may sufficiently assure yourself, if you but reflect whether 'tis likely that your wife, who for virtue and discretion has not her peer among women, would, if she were minded so to dishonour you, see fit to do so before your very eyes. Of myself I say nought, albeit I had liefer be hewn in pieces than that I should so much as think of such a thing, much less do it in your presence. Wherefore 'tis evident that 'tis some illusion of sight that is propagated from the pear-tree; for nought in the world would have made me believe that I saw not you lying there in carnal intercourse with your wife, had I not heard you say that you saw me doing that which most assuredly, so far from doing, I never so much as thought of."

The lady then started up with a most resentful mien, and burst out with:—"Foul fall thee, if thou knowest so little of me as to suppose that, if I were minded to do thee such foul dishonour as thou sayst thou didst see me do, I would come hither to do it before thine eyes! Rest assured that for such a purpose, were it ever mine, I should deem one of our chambers more meet, and it should go hard but I would so order the matter that thou shouldst never know aught of it."

Nicostratus, having heard both, and deeming that what they both averred must be true, to wit, that they would never have ventured upon such an act in his presence, passed from chiding to talk of the singularity of the thing, and how marvellous it was that the vision should reshape itself for every one that clomb the tree. The lady, however, made a show of being distressed that Nicostratus should so have thought of her, and:—"Verily," quoth she, "no woman, neither I nor another, shall again suffer loss of honour by his pear-tree: run, Pyrrhus, and bring hither an axe, and at one and the same time vindicate thy honour and mine by felling it, albeit 'twere better far Nicostratus' skull should feel the weight of the axe, seeing that in utter heedlessness he so readily suffered the eyes of his mind to be blinded; for, albeit this vision was seen by the bodily eye, yet ought the understanding by no means to have entertained and affirmed it as real."

So Pyrrhus presently hied him to fetch the axe, and returning therewith felled the pear; whereupon the lady, turning towards Nicostratus:—"Now that this foe of my honour is fallen," quoth she, "my wrath is gone from me." Nicostratus then craving her pardon, she graciously granted it him, bidding him never again to suffer himself to be betrayed into thinking such a thing of her, who loved him more dearly than herself. So the poor duped husband went back with her and her lover to the palace, where not seldom in time to come Pyrrhus and Lydia took their pastime together more at ease. God grant us the like.

JORGE LUIS BORGES

[Argentina]

JORGE LUIS BORGES (1899–1986) was and is Argentina's most popular literary export. Elegantly fluent in English, he read and spoke a variety of languages, translating many works by American and British writers into Spanish, and specialized in writing (in Spanish) short forms: essays, poetry and, most popularly, the peculiar hyper-literary "ficciones" that have coined their own adjective, Borgesian. He was a librarian, but began going blind in his forties; he lost his ability to read in his fifties and yet never stopped being a completely literary man, lecturing and teaching at the University of Buenos Aires and other universities around the world. He first married in 1967. In 1986, a few months before he died, he married again, this time to a former student who had assisted him in his work for many years, Maria Kodama.

Ulrikke (1975)

(Translated from the Spanish by Andrew Hurley)

Hann tekr sverthit Gram ok leggr i methal theira bert
Volsunga Saga, 27

MY STORY WILL be faithful to reality, or at least to my personal recollection of reality, which is the same thing. The events took place only a short while ago, but I know that the habit of literature is also the habit of interpolating circumstantial details and accentuating certain emphases. I wish to tell the story of my encounter with Ulrikke (I never learned her last name, and

45

perhaps never will) in the city of York. The tale will span one night and one morning.

It would be easy for me to say that I saw her for the first time beside the Five Sisters at York Minster, those stained glass panes devoid of figural representation that Cromwell's iconoclasts left untouched, but the fact is that we met in the dayroom of the Northern Inn, which lies outside the walls. There were but a few of us in the room, and she had her back to me. Someone offered her a glass of sherry and she refused it.

"I am a feminist," she said. "I have no desire to imitate men. I find their tobacco and their alcohol repulsive."

The pronouncement was an attempt at wit, and I sensed this wasn't the first time she'd voiced it. I later learned that it was not like her—but what we say is not always like us.

She said she'd arrived at the museum late, but that they'd let her in when they learned she was Norwegian.

"Not the first time the Norwegians storm York," someone remarked.

"Quite right," she said. "England was ours and we lost her—if, that is, anyone can possess anything or anything can really be lost."

It was at that point that I looked at her. A line somewhere in William Blake talks about girls of soft silver or furious gold, but in Ulrikke there was both gold and softness. She was light and tall, with sharp features and gray eyes. Less than by her face, I was impressed by her air of calm mystery. She smiled easily, and her smile seemed to take her somewhere far away. She was dressed in black—unusual in the lands of the north, which try to cheer the dullness of the surroundings with bright colors. She spoke a neat, precise English, slightly stressing the *r*'s. I am no great observer; I discovered these things gradually.

We were introduced. I told her I was a professor at the University of the Andes, in Bogota. I clarified that I myself was Colombian.

"What is 'being Colombian'?"

"I'm not sure," I replied. "It's an act of faith."

"Like being Norwegian," she said, nodding.

I can recall nothing further of what was said that night. The next day I came down to the dining room early. I saw through the windows that it had snowed; the moors ran on seamlessly into the morning. There was no one else in the dining room. Ulrikke invited me to share her table. She told me she liked to go out walking alone.

I remembered an old quip of Schopenhauer's.

"I do too. We can go out alone together," I said.

We walked off away from the house through the newly fallen snow. There was not a soul abroad in the fields. I suggested we go downriver a few miles, to Thorgate. I know I was in love with Ulrikke; there was no other person on earth I'd have wanted beside me.

Suddenly I heard the far-off howl of a wolf. I have never heard a wolf howl, but I know that it was a wolf. Ulrikke's expression did not change.

After a while she said, as though thinking out loud:

"The few shabby swords I saw yesterday in York Minster were more moving to me than the great ships in the museum at Oslo."

Our two paths were briefly crossing: that evening Ulrikke was to continue her journey toward London; I, toward Edinburgh.

"On Oxford Street," she said, "I will retrace the steps of de Quincey, who went seeking his lost Anna among the crowds of London."

"De Quincey," I replied, "stopped looking. My search for her, on the other hand, continues, through all time."

"Perhaps," Ulrikke said softly, "you have found her."

I realized that an unforeseen event was not to be forbidden me, and I kissed her lips and her eyes. She pushed me away with gentle firmness, but then said:

"I shall be yours in the inn at Thorgate. I ask you, meanwhile, not to touch me. It's best that way."

For a celibate, middle-aged man, proffered love is a gift that one no longer hopes for; a miracle has the right to impose conditions. I recalled my salad days in Popayán and a girl from Texas, as bright and slender as Ulrikke, who had denied me her love.

I did not make the mistake of asking her whether she loved me. I realized that I was not the first, and would not be the last. That adventure, perhaps the last for me, would be one of many for that glowing, determined disciple of Ibsen.

We walked on, hand in hand.

"All this is like a dream," I said, "and I never dream."

"Like that king," Ulrikke replied, "who never dreamed until a sorcerer put him to sleep in a pigsty."

Then she added:

"Ssh! A bird is about to sing."

In a moment we heard the birdsong.

"In these lands," I said, "people think that a person who's soon to die can see the future."

"And I'm about to die," she said.

I looked at her, stunned.

"Let's cut through the woods," I urged her. "We'll get to Thorgate sooner."

"The woods are dangerous," she replied.

We continued across the moors.

"I wish this moment would last forever," I murmured.

"*Forever* is a word mankind is forbidden to speak," Ulrikke declared emphatically, and then, to soften her words, she asked me to tell her my name again, which she hadn't heard very well.

"Javier Otárola," I said.

She tried to repeat it, but couldn't. I failed, likewise, with *Ulrikke*.

"I will call you Sigurd," she said with a smile.

"And if I'm to be Sigurd," I replied, "then you shall be Brunhild."

Her steps had slowed.

"Do you know the saga?" I asked.

"Of course," she said. "The tragic story that the Germans spoiled with their parvenu Nibelungen."

I didn't want to argue, so I answered:

"Brunhild, you are walking as though you wanted a sword to lie between us in our bed."

We were suddenly before the inn. I was not surprised to find that it, like the one we had departed from, was called the Northern Inn.

From the top of the staircase, Ulrikke called down to me:

"Did you hear the wolf? There are no wolves in England anymore. Hurry up."

As I climbed the stairs, I noticed that the walls were papered a deep crimson, in the style of William Morris, with intertwined birds and fruit. Ulrikke entered the room first. The dark chamber had a low, peaked ceiling. The expected bed was duplicated in a vague glass, and its burnished mahogany reminded me of the mirror of the Scriptures. Ulrikke had already undressed. She called me by my true name, Javier. I sensed that the snow was coming down harder. Now there was no more furniture, no more mirrors. There was no sword between us. Like sand, time sifted away. Ancient in the dimness flowed love, and for the first and last time, I possessed the image of Ulrikke.

ANTON CHEKHOV

[Russia]

ANTON CHEKHOV (1860–1904), Russia's and perhaps the world's greatest author of short fiction, wrote hundreds of short stories, none of them, according to him, about himself. When as a young man Chekhov was in medical school, he supported his parents and siblings by writing skits and tales for humor magazines. By the time he wrote "A Misfortune" (in Russian "Несчастье") at age twenty-six, he had begun to take his art "seriously," as one of his admirers had suggested he do. Among his new favorite subjects were star-crossed lovers. How is it that people destined for one another meet at the wrong time? When Chekhov was forty-one, he married the actress Olga Knipper, but because he suffered from tuberculosis, she and he were often separated, he on the sea-coast for his health, she in Moscow for her work in theater.

A Misfortune (1886)

(Translated from the Russian by Constance Garnett)

SOFYA PETROVNA, THE wife of Lubyantsev the notary, a handsome young woman of five-and-twenty, was walking slowly along a track that had been cleared in the wood, with Ilyin, a lawyer who was spending the summer in the neighbourhood. It was five o'clock in the evening. Feathery-white masses of cloud stood overhead; patches of bright blue sky peeped out between them. The clouds stood motionless, as though they had caught in the tops of the tall old pine-trees. It was still and sultry.

Farther on, the track was crossed by a low railway embankment on which a sentinel with a gun was for some reason pacing up and down. Just beyond the embankment there was a large white church with six domes and a rusty roof.

"I did not expect to meet you here," said Sofya Petrovna, looking at the ground and prodding at the last year's leaves with the tip of her parasol, "and now I am glad we have met. I want to speak to you seriously and once for all. I beg you, Ivan Mihalovitch, if you really love and respect me, please make an end of this pursuit of me! You follow me about like a shadow, you are continually looking at me not in a nice way, making love to me, writing me strange letters, and . . . and I don't know where it's all going to end! Why, what can come of it?"

Ilyin said nothing. Sofya Petrovna walked on a few steps and continued:

"And this complete transformation in you all came about in the course of two or three weeks, after five years' friendship. I don't know you, Ivan Mihalovitch!"

Sofya Petrovna stole a glance at her companion. Screwing up his eyes, he was looking intently at the fluffy clouds. His face looked angry, ill-humoured, and preoccupied, like that of a man in pain forced to listen to nonsense.

"I wonder you don't see it yourself," Madame Lubyantsev went on, shrugging her shoulders. "You ought to realize that it's not a very nice part you are playing. I am married; I love and respect my husband. . . . I have a daughter. . . . Can you think all that means nothing? Besides, as an old friend you know my attitude to family life and my views as to the sanctity of marriage."

Ilyin cleared his throat angrily and heaved a sigh.

"Sanctity of marriage . . ." he muttered. "Oh, Lord!"

"Yes, yes. . . . I love my husband, I respect him; and in any case I value the peace of my home. I would rather let myself be killed than be a cause of unhappiness to Andrey and his daughter. . . . And I beg you, Ivan Mihalovitch, for God's sake, leave me in peace! Let us be as good, true friends as we used to be, and give up these sighs and groans, which really don't suit you. It's settled and over! Not a word more about it. Let us talk of something else."

Sofya Petrovna again stole a glance at Ilyin's face. Ilyin was looking up; he was pale, and was angrily biting his quivering lips. She could not understand why he was angry and why he was indignant, but his pallor touched her.

"Don't be angry; let us be friends," she said affectionately. "Agreed? Here's my hand."

Ilyin took her plump little hand in both of his, squeezed it, and slowly raised it to his lips.

"I am not a schoolboy," he muttered. "I am not in the least tempted by friendship with the woman I love."

"Enough, enough! It's settled and done with. We have reached the seat; let us sit down."

Sofya Petrovna's soul was filled with a sweet sense of relief: the most difficult and delicate thing had been said, the painful question was settled and done with. Now she could breathe freely and look Ilyin straight in the face. She looked at him, and the egoistic feeling of the superiority of the woman over the man who loves her, agreeably flattered her. It pleased her to see this huge, strong man, with his manly, angry face and his big black beard—clever, cultivated, and, people said, talented—sit down obediently beside her and bow his head dejectedly. For two or three minutes they sat without speaking.

"Nothing is settled or done with," began Ilyin. "You repeat copy-book maxims to me. 'I love and respect my husband . . . the sanctity of marriage. . . .' I know all that without your help, and I could tell you more, too. I tell you truthfully and honestly that I consider the way I am behaving as criminal and immoral. What more can one say than that? But what's the good of saying what everybody knows? Instead of feeding nightingales with paltry words, you had much better tell me what I am to do."

"I've told you already—go away."

"As you know perfectly well, I have gone away five times, and every time I turned back on the way. I can show you my through tickets—I've kept them all. I have not will enough to run away from you! I am struggling. I am struggling horribly; but what the devil am I good for if I have no backbone, if I am weak, cowardly! I can't struggle with Nature! Do you understand? I cannot! I run away from here, and she holds on to me and pulls me back. Contemptible, loathsome weakness!"

Ilyin flushed crimson, got up, and walked up and down by the seat.

"I feel as cross as a dog," he muttered, clenching his fists. "I hate and despise myself! My God! like some depraved schoolboy, I am making love to another man's wife, writing idiotic letters, degrading myself . . . ugh!"

Ilyin clutched at his head, grunted, and sat down.

"And then your insincerity!" he went on bitterly. "If you do dislike my disgusting behaviour, why have you come here? What drew you here? In my letters I only ask you for a direct, definite answer—yes or no; but instead of a direct answer, you contrive every day these 'chance' meetings with me and regale me with copy-book maxims!"

Madame Lubyantsev was frightened and flushed. She suddenly felt the awkwardness which a decent woman feels when she is accidentally discovered undressed.

"You seem to suspect I am playing with you," she muttered. "I have always given you a direct answer, and . . . only today I've begged you . . ."

"Ough! as though one begged in such cases! If you were to say straight out 'Get away,' I should have been gone long ago; but you've never said that. You've never once given me a direct answer. Strange indecision! Yes, indeed; either you are playing with me, or else . . ."

Ilyin leaned his head on his fists without finishing. Sofya Petrovna began going over in her own mind the way she had behaved from beginning to end. She remembered that not only in her actions, but even in her secret thoughts, she had always been opposed to Ilyin's love-making; but yet she felt there was a grain of truth in the lawyer's words. But not knowing exactly what the truth was, she could not find answers to make to Ilyin's complaint, however hard she thought. It was awkward to be silent, and, shrugging her shoulders, she said:

"So I am to blame, it appears."

"I don't blame you for your insincerity," sighed Ilyin. "I did not mean that when I spoke of it. . . . Your insincerity is natural and in the order of things. If people agreed together and suddenly became sincere, everything would go to the devil."

Sofya Petrovna was in no mood for philosophical reflections, but she was glad of a chance to change the conversation, and asked:

"But why?"

"Because only savage women and animals are sincere. Once civilization has introduced a demand for such comforts as, for instance, feminine virtue, sincerity is out of place. . . ."

Ilyin jabbed his stick angrily into the sand. Madame Lubyantsev listened to him and liked his conversation, though a great deal of it she did not understand. What gratified her most was that she, an ordinary woman, was talked to by a talented man on "intellectual" subjects; it afforded her great pleasure, too, to watch the working of his mobile, young face, which was still pale and angry. She failed to understand a great deal that he said, but what was clear to her in his words was the attractive boldness with which the modern man without hesitation or doubt decides great questions and draws conclusive deductions.

She suddenly realized that she was admiring him, and was alarmed.

"Forgive me, but I don't understand," she said hurriedly. "What makes you talk of insincerity? I repeat my request again: be my good, true friend; let me alone! I beg you most earnestly!"

"Very good; I'll try again," sighed Ilyin. "Glad to do my best. . . . Only I doubt whether anything will come of my efforts. Either I shall put a bullet through my brains or take to drink in an idiotic way. I shall come to a bad end! There's a limit to everything — to struggles with Nature, too. Tell me, how can one struggle against madness? If you drink wine, how are you to struggle against intoxication? What am I to do if your image has grown into my soul, and day and night stands persistently before my eyes, like that pine there at this moment? Come, tell me, what hard and difficult thing can I do to get free from this abominable, miserable condition, in which all my thoughts, desires, and dreams are no longer my own, but belong to some demon who has taken possession of me? I love you, love you so much that I am completely thrown out of gear; I've given up my work and all who are dear to me; I've forgotten my God! I've never been in love like this in my life."

Sofya Petrovna, who had not expected such a turn to their conversation, drew away from Ilyin and looked into his face in dismay. Tears came into his eyes, his lips were quivering, and there was an imploring, hungry expression in his face.

"I love you!" he muttered, bringing his eyes near her big, frightened eyes. "You are so beautiful! I am in agony now, but I swear I would sit here all my life, suffering and looking in your eyes. But . . . be silent, I implore you!"

Sofya Petrovna, feeling utterly disconcerted, tried to think as quickly as possible of something to say to stop him. "I'll go away," she decided, but before she had time to make a movement to get up, Ilyin was on his knees before her. . . . He was clasping her knees, gazing into her face and speaking passionately, hotly, eloquently. In her terror and confusion she did not hear his words; for some reason now, at this dangerous moment, while her knees were being agreeably squeezed and felt as though they were in a warm bath, she was trying, with a sort of angry spite, to interpret her own sensations. She was angry that instead of brimming over with protesting virtue, she was entirely overwhelmed with weakness, apathy, and emptiness, like a drunken man utterly reckless; only at the bottom of her soul a remote bit of herself was malignantly taunting her: "Why don't you go? Is this as it should be? Yes?"

Seeking for some explanation, she could not understand how it was she did not pull away the hand to which Ilyin was clinging like a leech, and why, like Ilyin, she hastily glanced to right and to left to see whether any one was looking. The clouds and the pines stood motionless, looking at them severely, like old ushers seeing mischief, but bribed not to tell the school authorities. The sentry stood like a post on the embankment and seemed to be looking at the seat.

"Let him look," thought Sofya Petrovna.

"But . . . but listen," she said at last, with despair in her voice. "What can come of this? What will be the end of this?"

"I don't know, I don't know," he whispered, waving off the disagreeable questions.

They heard the hoarse, discordant whistle of the train. This cold, irrelevant sound from the everyday world of prose made Sofya Petrovna rouse herself.

"I can't stay . . . it's time I was at home," she said, getting up quickly. "The train is coming in. . . . Andrey is coming by it! He will want his dinner."

Sofya Petrovna turned towards the embankment with a burning face. The engine slowly crawled by, then came the carriages. It was not the local train, as she had supposed, but a goods train. The trucks filed by against the background of the white church in a long string like the days of a man's life, and it seemed as though it would never end.

But at last the train passed, and the last carriage with the guard and a light in it had disappeared behind the trees. Sofya Petrovna turned round sharply, and without looking at Ilyin, walked rapidly back along the track. She had regained her self-possession. Crimson with shame, humiliated not by Ilyin—no, but by her own cowardice, by the shamelessness with which she, a chaste and high-principled woman, had allowed a man, not her husband, to hug her knees—she had only one thought now: to get home as quickly as possible to her villa, to her family. The lawyer could hardly keep pace with her. Turning from the clearing into a narrow path, she turned round and glanced at him so quickly that she saw nothing but the sand on his knees, and waved to him to drop behind.

Reaching home, Sofya Petrovna stood in the middle of her room for five minutes without moving, and looked first at the window and then at her writing-table.

"You low creature!" she said, upbraiding herself. "You low creature!"

To spite herself, she recalled in precise detail, keeping nothing back — she recalled that though all this time she had been opposed to Ilyin's love-making, something had impelled her to seek an interview with him; and what was more, when he was at her feet she had enjoyed it enormously. She recalled it all without sparing herself, and now, breathless with shame, she would have liked to slap herself in the face.

"Poor Andrey!" she said to herself, trying as she thought of her husband to put into her face as tender an expression as she could. "Varya, my poor little girl, doesn't know what a mother she has! Forgive me, my dear ones! I love you so much . . . so much!"

And anxious to prove to herself that she was still a good wife and mother, and that corruption had not yet touched that "sanctity of marriage" of which she had spoken to Ilyin, Sofya Petrovna ran to the kitchen and abused the cook for not having yet laid the table for Andrey Ilyitch. She tried to picture her husband's hungry and exhausted appearance, commiserated him aloud, and laid the table for him with her own hands, which she had never done before. Then she found her daughter Varya, picked her up in her arms and hugged her warmly; the child seemed to her cold and heavy, but she was unwilling to acknowledge this to herself, and she began explaining to the child how good, kind, and honourable her papa was.

But when Andrey Ilyitch arrived soon afterwards she hardly greeted him. The rush of false feeling had already passed off without proving anything to her, only irritating and exasperating her by its falsity. She was sitting by the window, feeling miserable and cross. It is only by being in trouble that people can understand how far from easy it is to be the master of one's feelings and thoughts. Sofya Petrovna said afterwards that there was a tangle within her which it was as difficult to unravel as to count a flock of sparrows rapidly flying by. From the fact that she was not over-joyed to see her husband, that she did not like his manner at din-ner, she concluded all of a sudden that she was beginning to hate her husband.

Andrey Ilyitch, languid with hunger and exhaustion, fell upon the sausage while waiting for the soup to be brought in, and ate it greedily, munching noisily and moving his temples.

"My goodness!" thought Sofya Petrovna. "I love and respect him, but . . . why does he munch so repulsively?"

The disorder in her thoughts was no less than the disorder in her feelings. Like all persons inexperienced in combating unpleasant ideas, Madame Lubyantsev did her utmost not to think of her trouble, and the harder she tried the more vividly Ilyin, the sand on his knees, the fluffy clouds, the train, stood out in her imagination.

"And why did I go there this afternoon like a fool?" she thought, tormenting herself. "And am I really so weak that I cannot depend upon myself?"

Fear magnifies danger. By the time Andrey Ilyitch was finishing the last course, she had firmly made up her mind to tell her husband everything and to flee from danger!

"I've something serious to say to you, Andrey," she began after dinner while her husband was taking off his coat and boots to lie down for a nap.

"Well?"

"Let us leave this place!"

"H'm! . . . Where shall we go? It's too soon to go back to town."

"No; for a tour or something of that sort. . . ."

"For a tour . . ." repeated the notary, stretching. "I dream of that myself, but where are we to get the money, and to whom am I to leave the office?"

And thinking a little he added:

"Of course, you must be bored. Go by yourself if you like."

Sofya Petrovna agreed, but at once reflected that Ilyin would be delighted with the opportunity, and would go with her in the same train, in the same compartment. . . . She thought and looked at her husband, now satisfied but still languid. For some reason her eyes rested on his feet—miniature, almost feminine feet, clad in striped socks; there was a thread standing out at the tip of each sock.

Behind the blind a bumble-bee was beating itself against the window-pane and buzzing. Sofya Petrovna looked at the threads on the socks, listened to the bee, and pictured how she would set off. . . . *Vis-à-vis* Ilyin would sit, day and night, never taking his eyes off her, wrathful at his own weakness and pale with spiritual agony. He would call himself an immoral schoolboy, would abuse her, tear his hair, but when darkness came on and the passengers were asleep or got out at a station, he would seize the opportunity to kneel before her and embrace her knees as he had at the seat in the wood. . . .

She caught herself indulging in this day-dream.

"Listen. I won't go alone," she said. "You must come with me."

"Nonsense, Sofotchka!" sighed Lubyantsev. "One must be sensible and not want the impossible."

"You will come when you know all about it," thought Sofya Petrovna.

Making up her mind to go at all costs, she felt that she was out of danger. Little by little her ideas grew clearer; her spirits rose and she allowed herself to think about it all, feeling that however much she thought, however much she dreamed, she would go away. While her husband was asleep, the evening gradually came on. She sat in the drawing-room and played the piano. The greater liveliness out of doors, the sound of music, but above all the thought that she was a sensible person, that she had surmounted her difficulties, completely restored her spirits. Other women, her appeased conscience told her, would probably have been carried off their feet in her position, and would have lost their balance, while she had almost died of shame, had been miserable, and was now running out of the danger which perhaps did not exist! She was so touched by her own virtue and determination that she even looked at herself two or three times in the looking-glass.

When it got dark, visitors arrived. The men sat down in the dining-room to play cards; the ladies remained in the drawing-room and the verandah. The last to arrive was Ilyin. He was gloomy, morose, and looked ill. He sat down in the corner of the sofa and did not move the whole evening. Usually good-humoured and talkative, this time he remained silent, frowned, and rubbed his eyebrows. When he had to answer some question, he gave a forced smile with his upper lip only, and answered jerkily and irritably. Four or five times he made some jest, but his jests sounded harsh and cutting. It seemed to Sofya Petrovna that he was on the verge of hysterics. Only now, sitting at the piano, she recognized fully for the first time that this unhappy man was in deadly earnest, that his soul was sick, and that he could find no rest. For her sake he was wasting the best days of his youth and his career, spending the last of his money on a summer villa, abandoning his mother and sisters, and, worst of all, wearing himself out in an agonizing struggle with himself. From mere common humanity he ought to be treated seriously.

She recognized all this clearly till it made her heart ache, and if at that moment she had gone up to him and said to him, "No," there would have been a force in her voice hard to disobey. But she did not go up to him and did not speak—indeed, never thought of doing so. The pettiness and egoism of youth had never been more patent in her than that evening. She realized that Ilyin was unhappy, and that he was sitting on the sofa as though he were on hot coals; she felt sorry for him, but at the same time the presence of a man who loved her to distraction, filled her soul with triumph and a sense of her own power. She felt her youth, her beauty, and her unassailable virtue, and, since she had decided to go away, gave herself full licence for that evening. She flirted, laughed incessantly, sang with peculiar feeling and gusto. Everything delighted and amused her. She was amused at the memory of what had happened at the seat in the wood, of the sentinel who had looked on. She was amused by her guests, by Ilyin's cutting jests, by the pin in his cravat, which she had never noticed before. There was a red snake with diamond eyes on the pin; this snake struck her as so amusing that she could have kissed it on the spot.

Sofya Petrovna sang nervously, with defiant recklessness as though half intoxicated, and she chose sad, mournful songs which dealt with wasted hopes, the past, old age, as though in mockery of another's grief. "'And old age comes nearer and nearer' . . ." she sang. And what was old age to her?

"It seems as though there is something going wrong with me," she thought from time to time through her laughter and singing.

The party broke up at twelve o'clock. Ilyin was the last to leave. Sofya Petrovna was still reckless enough to accompany him to the bottom step of the verandah. She wanted to tell him that she was going away with her husband, and to watch the effect this news would produce on him.

The moon was hidden behind the clouds, but it was light enough for Sofya Petrovna to see how the wind played with the skirts of his overcoat and with the awning of the verandah. She could see, too, how white Ilyin was, and how he twisted his upper lip in the effort to smile.

"Sonia, Sonitchka . . . my darling woman!" he muttered, preventing her from speaking. "My dear! my sweet!"

In a rush of tenderness, with tears in his voice, he showered caressing words upon her, that grew tenderer and tenderer, and even called her "thou," as though she were his wife or mistress. Quite unexpectedly he put one arm round her waist and with the other hand took hold of her elbow.

"My precious! my delight!" he whispered, kissing the nape of her neck; "be sincere; come to me at once!"

She slipped out of his arms and raised her head to give vent to her indignation and anger, but the indignation did not come off, and all her vaunted virtue and chastity was only sufficient to enable her to utter the phrase used by all ordinary women on such occasions:

"You must be mad."

"Come, let us go," Ilyin continued. "I felt just now, as well as at the seat in the wood, that you are as helpless as I am, Sonia. . . . You are in the same plight! You love me and are fruitlessly trying to appease your conscience. . . ."

Seeing that she was moving away, he caught her by her lace cuff and said rapidly:

"If not today, then tomorrow you will have to give in! Why, then, this waste of time? My precious, darling Sonia, the sentence is passed; why put off the execution? Why deceive yourself?"

Sofya Petrovna tore herself from him and darted in at the door. Returning to the drawing-room, she mechanically shut the piano, looked for a long time at the music-stand, and sat down. She could not stand up nor think. All that was left of her excitement and recklessness was a fearful weakness, apathy, and dreariness. Her conscience whispered to her that she had behaved badly, foolishly, that evening, like some madcap girl—that she had just been embraced on the verandah, and still had an uneasy feeling in her waist and her elbow. There was not a soul in the drawing-room; there was only one candle burning. Madame Lubyantsev sat on the round stool before the piano, motionless, as though expecting something. And as though taking advantage of the darkness and her extreme lassitude, an oppressive, overpowering desire began to assail her. Like a boa-constrictor it gripped her limbs and her soul, and grew stronger every second, and no longer menaced her as it had done, but stood clear before her in all its nakedness.

She sat for half an hour without stirring, not restraining herself from thinking of Ilyin, then she got up languidly and dragged herself to her bedroom. Andrey Ilyitch was already in bed. She sat down by the open window and gave herself up to desire. There was no "tangle" now in her head; all her thoughts and feelings were bent with one accord upon a single aim. She tried to struggle against it, but instantly gave it up. . . . She understood now how strong and relentless was the foe. Strength and fortitude were needed to combat him, and her birth, her education, and her life had given her nothing to fall back upon.

"Immoral wretch ! Low creature!" she nagged at herself for her weakness. "So that's what you're like!"

Her outraged sense of propriety was moved to such indignation by this weakness that she lavished upon herself every term of abuse she knew, and told herself many offensive and humiliating truths. So, for instance, she told herself that she never had been moral, that she had not come to grief before simply because she had had no opportunity, that her inward conflict during that day had all been a farce. . . .

"And even if I have struggled," she thought, "what sort of struggle was it? Even the woman who sells herself struggles before she brings herself to it, and yet she sells herself. A fine struggle! Like milk, I've turned in a day! In one day!"

She convicted herself of being tempted, not by feeling, not by Ilyin personally, but by sensations which awaited her . . . an idle lady, having her fling in the summer holidays, like so many!

"'Like an unfledged bird when the mother has been slain,'" sang a husky tenor outside the window.

"If I am to go, it's time," thought Sofya Petrovna. Her heart suddenly began beating violently.

"Andrey!" she almost shrieked. "Listen! we . . . we are going? Yes?"

"Yes, I've told you already: you go alone."

"But listen," she began. "If you don't go with me, you are in danger of losing me. I believe I am . . . in love already."

"With whom?" asked Andrey Ilyitch.

"It can't make any difference to you who it is!" cried Sofya Petrovria.

Andrey Ilyitch sat up with his feet out of bed and looked wonderingly at his wife's dark figure.

"It's a fancy!" he yawned.

He did not believe her, but yet he was frightened. After thinking a little and asking his wife several unimportant questions, he delivered himself of his opinions on the family, on infidelity . . . spoke listlessly for about ten minutes and got into bed again. His moralizing produced no effect. There are a great many opinions in the world, and a good half of them are held by people who have never been in trouble!

In spite of the late hour, summer visitors were still walking outside. Sofya Petrovna put on a light cape, stood a little, thought a little. . . . She still had resolution enough to say to her sleeping husband:

"Are you asleep? I am going for a walk. . . . Will you come with me?"

That was her last hope. Receiving no answer, she went out. . . . It was fresh and windy. She was conscious neither of the wind nor the darkness, but went on and on. . . . An overmastering force drove her on, and it seemed as though, if she had stopped, it would have pushed her in the back.

"Immoral creature!" she muttered mechanically. "Low wretch!"

She was breathless, hot with shame, did not feel her legs under her, but what drove her on was stronger than shame, reason, or fear.

KATE CHOPIN

[U.S.A.]

Born in 1850, Kate Chopin (*née* O'Flaherty), married as a teenager in 1868 and became a mother of six. In 1882, after the death of her husband, she took up writing to support her family. The primary subjects in her first two books of short stories were the people of Louisiana, where she had lived for several years. The heroine of "Azélie" is a poor Cajun girl in rural Louisiana; she may seem kin to some of the Mississippi heroines William Faulkner would create in the 1930s and '40s. Chopin died in 1904.

Azélie (1894)

Azélie crossed the yard with slow, hesitating steps. She wore a pink sunbonnet and a faded calico dress that had been made the summer before, and was now too small for her in every way. She carried a large tin pail on her arm. When within a few yards of the house she stopped under a chinaberry-tree, quite still, except for the occasional slow turning of her head from side to side.

Mr. Mathurin, from his elevation upon the upper gallery, laughed when he saw her; for he knew she would stay there, motionless, till some one noticed and questioned her.

The planter was just home from the city, and was therefore in an excellent humor, as he always was, on getting back to what he called *le grand air,* the space and stillness of the country, and the scent of the fields. He was in shirt-sleeves, walking around the gallery that encircled the big square white house. Beneath was a brick-paved portico upon which the lower rooms opened. At wide intervals were large whitewashed pillars that supported the upper gallery.

In one corner of the lower house was the store, which was in no sense a store for the general public, but maintained only to supply the needs of Mr. Mathurin's "hands."

"Eh bien! what do you want, Azélie?" the planter finally called out to the girl in French. She advanced a few paces, and, pushing back her sunbonnet, looked up at him with a gentle, inoffensive face—"to which you would give the good God without confession," he once described it.

"Bon jou', M'si' Mathurin," she replied; and continued in English: "I come git a li'le piece o' meat. We plumb out o' meat home."

"Well, well, the meat is n' going to walk to you, my chile: it has n' got feet. Go fine Mr. 'Polyte. He's yonda mending his buggy unda the shed." She turned away with an alert little step, and went in search of Mr. 'Polyte.

"That's you again!" the young man exclaimed, with a pretended air of annoyance, when he saw her. He straightened himself, and looked down at her and her pail with a comprehending glance. The sweat was standing in shining beads on his brown, good-looking face. He was in his shirt-sleeves, and the legs of his trousers were thrust into the tops of his fine, high-heeled boots. He wore his straw hat very much on one side, and had an air that was altogether *fanfaron*.[1] He reached to a back pocket for the store key, which was as large as the pistol that he sometimes carried in the same place. She followed him across the thick, tufted grass of the yard with quick, short steps that strove to keep pace with his longer, swinging ones.

When he had unlocked and opened the heavy door of the store, there escaped from the close room the strong, pungent odor of the varied wares and provisions massed within. Azélie seemed to like the odor, and, lifting her head, snuffed the air as people sometimes do upon entering a conservatory filled with fragrant flowers.

A broad ray of light streamed in through the open door, illumining the dingy interior. The double wooden shutters of the windows were all closed, and secured on the inside by iron hooks.

"Well, w'at you want, Azélie?" asked 'Polyte, going behind the counter with an air of hurry and importance. "I ain't got time to fool. Make has'e; say w'at you want."

Her reply was precisely the same that she had made to Mr. Mathurin.

---

[1] *fanfaron*] like a showoff.

"I come git a li'le piece o' meat. We plumb out o' meat home."

He seemed exasperated.

"Bonté! w'at you all do with meat yonda? You don't reflec' you about to eat up yo' crop befo' it's good out o' the groun', you all. I like to know w'y yo' pa don't go he'p with the killin' once aw'ile, an' git some fresh meat fo' a change."

She answered in an unshaded, unmodulated voice that was penetrating, like a child's: "Popa he do go he'p wid the killin'; but he say he can't work 'less he got salt meat. He got plenty to feed—him. He's got to hire he'p wid his crop, an' he's boun' to feed 'em; they won't year no diffe'nt. An' he's got gra'ma to feed, an' Sauterelle, an' me—"

"An' all the lazy-bone 'Cadians in the country that know w'ere they goin' to fine the coffee-pot always in the corna of the fire," grumbled 'Polyte.

With an iron hook he lifted a small piece of salt meat from the pork barrel, weighed it, and placed it in her pail. Then she wanted a little coffee. He gave it to her reluctantly. He was still more loath to let her have sugar; and when she asked for lard, he refused flatly.

She had taken off her sunbonnet, and was fanning herself with it, as she leaned with her elbows upon the counter, and let her eyes travel lingeringly along the well-lined shelves. 'Polyte stood staring into her face with a sense of aggravation that her presence, her manner, always stirred up in him.

The face was colorless but for the red, curved line of the lips. Her eyes were dark, wide, innocent, questioning eyes, and her black hair was plastered smooth back from the forehead and temples. There was no trace of any intention of coquetry in her manner. He resented this as a token of indifference toward his sex, and thought it inexcusable.

"Well, Azélie, if it's anything you don't see, ask fo' it," he suggested, with what he flattered himself was humor. But there was no responsive humor in Azélie's composition. She seriously drew a small flask from her pocket.

"Popa say, if you want to let him have a li'le dram, 'count o' his pains that's 'bout to cripple him."

"Yo' pa knows as well as I do we don't sell w'isky. Mr. Mathurin don't carry no license."

"I know. He say if you want to give 'im a li'le dram, he's willin' to do some work fo' you."

"No! Once fo' all, no!" And 'Polyte reached for the day-book, in which to enter the articles he had given to her.

But Azélie's needs were not yet satisfied. She wanted tobacco; he would not give it to her. A spool of thread; he rolled one up, together with two sticks of peppermint candy, and placed it in her pail. When she asked for a bottle of coal-oil, he grudgingly consented, but assured her it would be useless to cudgel her brain further, for he would positively let her have nothing more. He disappeared toward the coal-oil tank, which was hidden from view behind the piled-up boxes on the counter. When she heard him searching for an empty quart bottle, and making a clatter with the tin funnels, she herself withdrew from the counter against which she had been leaning.

After they quitted the store, 'Polyte, with a perplexed expression upon his face, leaned for a moment against one of the whitewashed pillars, watching the girl cross the yard. She had folded her sunbonnet into a pad, which she placed beneath the heavy pail that she balanced upon her head. She walked upright, with a slow, careful tread. Two of the yard dogs that had stood a moment before upon the threshold of the store door, quivering and wagging their tails, were following her now, with a little businesslike trot. 'Polyte called them back.

The cabin which the girl occupied with her father, her grandmother, and her little brother Sauterelle, was removed some distance from the plantation house, and only its pointed roof could be discerned like a speck far away across the field of cotton, which was all in bloom. Her figure soon disappeared from view, and 'Polyte emerged from the shelter of the gallery, and started again toward his interrupted task. He turned to say to the planter, who was keeping up his measured tramp above:

"Mr. Mathurin, ain't it 'mos' time to stop givin' credit to Arsène Pauché. Look like that crop o' his ain't goin' to start to pay his account. I don't see, me, anyway, how you come to take that triflin' Li'le river gang on the place."

"I know it was a mistake, 'Polyte, but que voulez-vous?"[2] the planter returned, with a good-natured shrug. "Now they are yere, we can't let them starve, my frien'. Push them to work all you can. Hole back all supplies that are not necessary, an' nex' year we will

---

[2] *que voulez-vous?*] what do you want?

let some one else enjoy the privilege of feeding them," he ended, with a laugh.

"I wish they was all back on Li'le river," 'Polyte muttered under his breath as he turned and walked slowly away.

Directly back of the store was the young man's sleeping-room. He had made himself quite comfortable there in his corner. He had screened his windows and doors; planted Madeira vines, which now formed a thick green curtain between the two pillars that faced his room; and had swung a hammock out there, in which he liked well to repose himself after the fatigues of the day.

He lay long in the hammock that evening, thinking over the day's happenings and the morrow's work, half dozing, half dreaming, and wholly possessed by the charm of the night, the warm, sweeping air that blew through the long corridor, and the almost unbroken stillness that enveloped him.

At times his random thoughts formed themselves into an almost inaudible speech: "I wish she would go 'way f'om yere."

One of the dogs came and thrust his cool, moist muzzle against 'Polyte's cheek. He caressed the fellow's shaggy head. "I don't know w'at's the matta with her," he sighed; "I don' b'lieve she's got good sense."

It was a long time afterward that he murmured again: "I wish to God she'd go 'way f'om yere!"

The edge of the moon crept up—a keen, curved blade of light above the dark line of the cotton-field. 'Polyte roused himself when he saw it. "I didn' know it was so late," he said to himself—or to his dog. He entered his room at once, and was soon in bed, sleeping soundly.

It was some hours later that 'Polyte was roused from his sleep by—he did not know what; his senses were too scattered and confused to determine at once. There was at first no sound; then so faint a one that he wondered how he could have heard it. A door of his room communicated with the store, but this door was never used, and was almost completely blocked by wares piled up on the other side. The faint noise that 'Polyte heard, and which came from within the store, was followed by a flare of light that he could discern through the chinks, and that lasted as long as a match might burn.

He was now fully aware that some one was in the store. How the intruder had entered he could not guess, for the key was under his pillow with his watch and his pistol.

As cautiously as he could he donned an extra garment, thrust his bare feet into slippers, and crept out into the portico, pistol in hand.

The shutters of one of the store windows were open. He stood close to it, and waited, which he considered surer and safer than to enter the dark and crowded confines of the store to engage in what might prove a bootless struggle with the intruder.

He had not long to wait. In a few moments some one darted through the open window as nimbly as a cat. 'Polyte staggered back as if a heavy blow had stunned him. His first thought and his first exclamation were: "My God! how close I come to killin' you!"

It was Azélie. She uttered no cry, but made one quick effort to run when she saw him. He seized her arm and held her with a brutal grip. He put the pistol back into his pocket. He was shaking like a man with the palsy. One by one he took from her the parcels she was carrying, and flung them back into the store. There were not many: some packages of tobacco, a cheap pipe, some fishing-tackle, and the flask which she had brought with her in the afternoon. This he threw into the yard. It was still empty, for she had not been able to find the "key" to the whisky-barrel.

"So — so, you a thief!" he muttered savagely under his breath.

"You hurtin' me, Mr. 'Polyte," she complained, squirming. He somewhat relaxed, but did not relinquish, his hold upon her.

"I ain't no thief," she blurted.

"You was stealin'," he contradicted her sharply.

"I wasn' stealin'. I was jus' takin' a few li'le things you all too mean to gi' me. You all treat my popa like he was a dog. It's on'y las' week Mr. Mathurin sen' 'way to the city to fetch a fine buckboa'd fo' Son Ambroise, an' he's on'y a nigga, après tout. An' my popa he want a picayune tobacca? It's 'No' —" She spoke loud in her monotonous, shrill voice. 'Polyte kept saying: "Hush, I tell you! Hush! Somebody'll year you. Hush! It's enough you broke in the sto'—how you got in the sto'?" he added, looking from her to the open window.

"It was w'en you was behine the boxes to the coal-oil tank — I unhook' it," she explained sullenly.

"An' you don' know I could sen' you to Baton Rouge fo' that?" He shook her as though trying to rouse her to a comprehension of her grievous fault.

"Jus' fo' a li'le picayune o' tobacca!" she whimpered.

He suddenly abandoned his hold upon her, and left her free. She mechanically rubbed the arm that he had grasped so violently.

Between the long row of pillars the moon was sending pale beams of light. In one of these they were standing.

"Azélie," he said, "go 'way f'om yere quick; some one might fine you yere. W'en you want something in the sto', fo' yo'se'f or fo' yo' pa—I don' care—ask me fo' it. But you—but you can't neva set yo' foot inside that sto' again. Go 'way f'om yere quick as you can, I tell you!"

She tried in no way to conciliate him. She turned and walked away over the same ground she had crossed before. One of the big dogs started to follow her. 'Polyte did not call him back this time. He knew no harm could come to her, going through those lonely fields, while the animal was at her side.

He went at once to his room for the store key that was beneath his pillow. He entered the store, and refastened the window. When he had made everything once more secure, he sat dejectedly down upon a bench that was in the portico. He sat for a long time motionless. Then, overcome by some powerful feeling that was at work within him, he buried his face in his hands and wept, his whole body shaken by the violence of his sobs.

After that night 'Polyte loved Azélie desperately. The very action which should have revolted him had seemed, on the contrary, to inflame him with love. He felt that love to be a degradation—something that he was almost ashamed to acknowledge to himself; and he knew that he was hopelessly unable to stifle it.

He watched now in a tremor for her coming. She came very often, for she remembered every word he had said; and she did not hesitate to ask him for those luxuries which she considered necessities to her "popa's" existence. She never attempted to enter the store, but always waited outside, of her own accord, laughing, and playing with the dogs. She seemed to have no shame or regret for what she had done, and plainly did not realize that it was a disgraceful act. 'Polyte often shuddered with disgust to discern in her a being so wholly devoid of moral sense.

He had always been an industrious, bustling fellow, never idle. Now there were hours and hours in which he did nothing but long for the sight of Azélie. Even when at work there was that gnawing want at his heart to see her, often so urgent that he would leave everything to wander down by her cabin with the hope of seeing her. It was even something if he could catch a glimpse of Sauterelle playing in the weeds, or of Arsène lazily dragging himself about,

and smoking the pipe which rarely left his lips now that he was kept
so well supplied with tobacco.

Once, down the bank of the bayou, when 'Polyte came upon
Azélie unexpectedly, and was therefore unprepared to resist the
shock of her sudden appearance, he seized her in his arms, and
covered her face with kisses. She was not indignant; she was not
flustered or agitated, as might have been a susceptible, coquettish
girl; she was only astonished, and annoyed.

"W'at you doin', Mr. 'Polyte?" she cried, struggling. "Leave me
'lone, I say! Leave me go!"

"I love you, I love you, I love you!" he stammered helplessly
over and over in her face.

"You mus' los' yo' head," she told him, red from the effort of
the struggle, when he released her.

"You right, Azélie; I b'lieve I los' my head," and he climbed up
the bank of the bayou as fast as he could.

After that his behavior was shameful, and he knew it, and he did
not care. He invented pretexts that would enable him to touch her
hand with his. He wanted to kiss her again, and told her she might
come into the store as she used to do. There was no need for her
to unhook a window now; he gave her whatever she asked for,
charging it always to his own account on the books. She permitted
his caresses without returning them, and yet that was all he seemed
to live for now. He gave her a little gold ring.

He was looking eagerly forward to the close of the season, when
Arsène would go back to Little River. He had arranged to ask Azélie to marry him. He would keep her with him when the others
went away. He longed to rescue her from what he felt to be the
demoralizing influences of her family and her surroundings. 'Polyte
believed he would be able to awaken Azélie to finer, better
impulses when he should have her apart to himself.

But when the time came to propose it, Azélie looked at him in
amazement. "Ah, b'en, no. I ain't goin' to stay yere wid you,
Mr. 'Polyte; I'm goin' yonda on Li'le river wid my popa."

This resolve frightened him, but he pretended not to believe it.

"You jokin', Azélie; you mus' care a li'le about me. It looked to
me all along like you cared some about me."

"An' my popa, donc? Ah, b'en, no."

"You don' remamba how lonesome it is on Li'le river, Azélie,"
he pleaded. "W'enever I think 'bout Li'le river it always make me

sad—like I think about a graveyard. To me it's like a person mus' die, one way or otha, w'en they go on Li'le river. Oh, I hate it! Stay with me, Azélie; don' go 'way f'om me."

She said little, one way or the other, after that, when she had fully understood his wishes, and her reserve led him to believe, since he hoped it, that he had prevailed with her and that she had determined to stay with him and be his wife.

It was a cool, crisp morning in December that they went away. In a ramshackle wagon, drawn by an ill-mated team, Arsène Pauché and his family left Mr. Mathurin's plantation for their old familiar haunts on Little river. The grandmother, looking like a witch, with a black shawl tied over her head, sat upon a roll of bedding in the bottom of the wagon, Sauterelle's bead-like eyes glittered with mischief as he peeped over the side. Azélie, with the pink sunbonnet completely hiding her round young face, sat beside her father, who drove.

'Polyte caught one glimpse of the group as they passed in the road. Turning, he hurried into his room, and locked himself in.

It soon became evident that 'Polyte's services were going to count for little. He himself was the first to realize this. One day he approached the planter, and said: "Mr. Mathurin, befo' we start anotha year togetha, I betta tell you I'm goin' to quit." 'Polyte stood upon the steps, and leaned back against the railing. The planter was a little above on the gallery.

"W'at in the name o' sense are you talking about, 'Polyte!" he exclaimed in astonishment.

"It's jus' that; I'm boun' to quit."

"You had a better offer?"

"No; I ain't had no offa."

"Then explain yo'se'f, my frien'—explain yo'se'f," requested Mr. Mathurin, with something of offended dignity. "If you leave me, w'ere are you going?"

'Polyte was beating his leg with his limp felt hat. "I reckon I jus' as well go yonda on Li'le river—w'ere Azélie," he said.

COLETTE

[France]

COLETTE (1873–1954), *née* Sidonie-Gabrielle Colette, was born in the Burgundy region of France. Her first husband, Willy Gauthier-Villars, published her first several novels under his name. By 1905, having separated from her husband, Colette wrote under her own name many more novels and about a hundred short stories, of which "Nuit Blanche" (from *Les Vrilles de la Vigne*) is one. Colette was renowned for having female lovers, but she remarried twice. In 1912 she wed the editor-in-chief of the newspaper that she was writing for, Henry de Jouvenel, with whom she had one child before their divorce in 1925. In 1935 she married her last husband, Maurice Goudeket, who was sixteen years younger than she.

White Night (1908)

(Translated from the French by Isabella Shraiman
and Bob Blaisdell)

For Missy[1]

IN OUR HOUSE there is but one bed, too wide for you, a little narrow for us both. It is chaste, all white, all bare; not a bit of drapery veils its honest candor in plain day. Those who come to see us look

---

[1] In its first book publication, which followed its 1907 magazine publication as "Les nuits de mai sont si courtes" ("The May Nights Are So Short"), Colette dedicated the story to "M——" (a dedication later spelled out as "Missy"), for Meg Villars.

at it calmly and do not turn away their eyes with a knowing look, because it is marked, in its middle, by a single soft valley, like the bed of a young girl who sleeps alone.

They do not know, those who enter here, that every night the weight of our two bodies together hollows out a little more, beneath its voluptuous shroud, a valley no wider than a tomb.

O, our naked bed! A dazzling lamp tilted over it undresses it even more. At dusk we do not look there for the spider-gray of a knowing shadow that filters through a lace canopy, nor the pink glow of a seashell-colored nightlight . . . Star without dawn and without setting, our bed never stops blazing except to sink into deep and velvety night.

A halo of perfume suffuses it. It perfumes, rigid and white, like the body of a blessed dead. It is a complicated perfume that surprises, that one attentively breathes in, in the effort to untangle the mild spirit of your favorite tobacco from the milder aroma of your skin so clear, and this burnt sandalwood that is emanated by me; but this country scent of crushed grasses, who can say if it is mine or yours?

Receive us tonight, O bed of ours, so that your fresh valley hollows itself out a bit more beneath the fevered torpor with which a spring day in the gardens and in the woods will intoxicate us.

I lie, not moving, my head on your soft shoulder. I will surely sink, until tomorrow, into the depths of a black sleep, a sleep so stubborn, so closed off, that the wings of dreams in vain will come and beat at it. I am going to sleep . . . Only wait while I search for a very fresh place for the soles of my feet that tingle and burn. You have not moved. You breathe in long strokes, but I can sense your shoulder still alert, careful to make a hollow beneath my cheek . . . Let us sleep . . . The May nights are so short. In spite of the blue obscurity that bathes us, my eyelids are still full of sun, of pink flames, of shadows that move, swing, and, my eyes shut, I contemplate my day as one who behind the shelter of a metal shutter takes in a bedazzling summer garden . . .

How my heart beats! I also hear yours under my ear. You're not sleeping? I lift my head a bit, I imagine the paleness of your upside-down face, the tawny shadow of your short hair. Your knees are fresh as two oranges . . . Turn to my side, so that mine can steal this smooth freshness.

Ah! Let us sleep! . . . A thousand times a thousand ants race with my blood under my skin. The muscles of my calves beat, my ears quiver, and our sweet bed, tonight, is it strewn with pine needles? Let us sleep! That's what I want!

I cannot sleep. My happy insomnia twitches, cheerful, and I guess, in your stillness, the same shivering prostration . . . You do not stir. You hope I am sleeping. From time to time, your arm draws tighter around me, from tender habit, and your charming feet intertwine with mine. Sleepiness approaches, brushes me and leaves . . . I see it! It is like that heavy velvet butterfly that I chased after in the garden ignited with irises . . . Do you remember? What light, what youthful impatience exalted the whole day! A tart and hurried breeze flung a smoky streak of quick clouds across the sun, wilting in passing the too tender leaves of the lindens, and the walnut flowers fell like browned caterpillars over our hair, with the flowers of the princess tree the rainy mauve of a Parisian sky . . . The shoots of black currants that you crumpled, the wild sorrel in rosettes amid the lawn, the mint so young, still brown, the sage downy as a hare's ear—everything overflowed with a strong peppery sap that on my lips I mingled with the taste of alcohol and lemon balm.

I could only laugh and cry out, treading the long juicy grass that stained my dress . . . Your tranquil joy watched over my folly, and when I reached out my hand to pick the wild roses, you know, the pink so touching—your hand broke the branch before mine could, and you snatched off, one by one, the little curved thorns, coral-colored claws . . . You gave me the disarmed flowers . . .

You gave me the disarmed flowers . . . You gave me, so that I could lie there panting, the best place in the shade, under the Persian lilac with its ripe clusters . . . You gathered for me big cornflowers from the flowerbeds, enchanted flowers whose hairy hearts waft apricot . . . You gave me the cream from the small pot of milk, at tea time, when my ferocious hunger made you smile . . . You gave me the most golden bread, and I still see your hand transparent in the sun, lifted to ward off the wasp that buzzed, caught in the curls of my hair . . . You tossed over my shoulders a light mantle, when a long cloud towards the end of day passed slowly, and I shivered all sweaty, completely drunk with a pleasure nameless among men, the innocent pleasure of happy beasts in the springtime . . . You told me: "Turn back . . . stop . . . Let's go!" You told me . . .

Ah! if I'm thinking about you, that's the end of my rest. What hour was it that just rang? Here the windows grow blue. I hear my blood humming, or else it is the gardens' murmur, down there . . . You're asleep? No. If I brought my cheek to yours, I would feel your eyelashes flutter like the wing of a captive fly . . . You are not sleeping. You spy my fever. You protect me from bad dreams; you think of me as I think of you, and by a strange sentimental modesty we pretend a peaceful sleep. My whole body lets go, unstrung, and the nape of my neck weighs on your soft shoulder; but our thoughts love discreetly across this blue dawn, so swiftly growing.

Soon the luminous bar between the curtains is going to brighten, to blush . . . Another few minutes and I will be able to read on your beautiful brow, on your delicate chin, on your sad mouth and your closed eyelids the will of seeming asleep . . . This is the hour my weariness, my agitated insomnia, cannot be silent anymore, where I will throw my arms out of this feverish bed, and already my spiteful heels are preparing their sly kick . . .

Then you will pretend to wake up! Then I will be able to take refuge in you, with confused and unjust complaints, excessive sighs, strained nerves that curse the day that has already come, the night so swift to end, the noise of the street . . . For well I know, then you will tighten your embrace, and if the rocking of your arms is not enough to calm me, your kiss will become more tenacious, your hands more loving, and you will grant me the delight as a relief, like a sovereign exorcism that drives from me the demons of fever, anger, restlessness . . . You will give me delight, bending over me, your eyes full of maternal anxiety, you who look for, in your passionate friend, the child that you did not have.

GÉZA CSÁTH

[Hungary]

THE HUNGARIAN Géza Csáth (1887–1919) was born in the part of
Austria-Hungary now known as Serbia. He was a neurologist who
also wrote music criticism and, between 1908 and 1912, fiction. He
became addicted to morphine in 1910, and married the ill-fated
Olga Jónás in 1913, with whom he had a child. He tried to serve
in the Austro-Hungarian army during World War I but because of
his worsening addiction had to be discharged. In 1919, Csáth fled
the mental hospital where he was receiving treatment, and returned
home and killed his wife. He tried to kill himself too, but was
rescued and hospitalized; he later escaped and poisoned himself.

Erna (c. 1910)

(Translated from the Hungarian by Jascha Kessler
and Charlotte Rogers)

ERNA WAS OF course from Budapest.

A homely creature, her girlfriends remarked. And Erna was considered truly plain. The boys saw *something* in her, however, and
there were days when they said, What an oddly lovely little face!
But they said it only to themselves, and besides Erna seldom had
such good days. On the whole she wasn't pretty, she wasn't lovely,
and she wasn't charming. Erna knew it only too well, and in fact
she thought herself even homelier, more unattractive and unallur-
ing than her girlfriends did.

There was one thing though, one single thing about her that
unfailingly drew connoisseurs to her: her smell—or more literarily,

her fragrance. Her hair and her neck radiated a divine scent. Once Astalos, a sardonic fellow just admitted to the bar, getting a whiff and being thoroughly absorbed by this perfume, said to himself, I don't care if she's homely or pretty once in a blue moon or her dowry's practically nil—I'd marry her anyway . . . if her ankles were just half an inch thinner and her feet a few sizes smaller!

I might note that Astalos could have dared to disregard her ankles and feet: Erna's scent was actually marvelous enough to have compensated any man for whatever lack of feminine qualities. Astalos couldn't see it, though someone else did. Erna's piano teacher, a pleasant man with good taste and more experienced with women than Astalos, knew that having several good qualities in a woman is unimportant: face, figure, voice, manners, and style of dress are inessential. What's crucial, let it even be one of the foregoing, is that she have at least *one* good feature, and it had better be an important one.

This serious bespectacled man silently inhaled Erna for an hour a day for several weeks. At the end of the month he proposed—when the hour was over.

Erna ran through the usual program first. She played a Czerny *étude*, some of the *Études for Forty Days*, and a few exercises of Bernini that she never got right. She'd stop playing, shrug and pretend to be an untamable filly, Salome the future demon—she knew, in short, how to handle men. But let me describe how the hour went. Next came a few of Bach's *Two Part* and *Three Part Inventions*. These she managed better. Now Erna displayed her knack at counterpoint. She overemphasized the dominant voice, drowning the other out. . . . But then, one knows how women play the piano when they want to demonstrate their superior intellect.

Bach was followed by a few Chopin pieces. Now Erna pedaled, cheating, doing away with whole passages and taking off at fast tempi. Not even the devil could have handled her. The piano teacher, Stefan Balla, interrupted her, rapping, but to no avail—Erna played the "Waltz" through to the end. It never occurred to Balla that of course he should have slapped Erna's hands and it would all have been taken care of. Modern teaching methods, even in music, permit no striking—and Balla was a modern pedagogue.

At the hour's end he proposed.

Erna felt the time had come to make up for all her bitter days of lacking self-confidence, the many disappointing hours before the mirror that added up to so much suffering for this basically gentle, hence terribly vain, woman. It was clear to her from the first instant what she had to do: turn Balla down! Regardless of who he might be, even if he were the number one man in town—even then.

—No, she said, it's impossible, my dear friend, quite impossible. I'm sorry. And she shrugged as though meaning to say she wasn't to blame and had no idea how she'd placed herself in such an awkward position.

In fact, she wasn't to blame for anything. Erna had set out to achieve everything but someone's falling in love with her. What mattered to her was having her girlfriends say she was an "odd girl." What also mattered to her was that her mother, a nice, plump woman, should remark, Erna's quite the madcap! It was also her desire that her German governess declare to her gossips: *Ich kann's nicht mit Ihr aushalten*! But she never tried to please. Her odd behavior is explained by the fact that she lived in constant apprehension that someone might say, Well, well, even this homely girl wants to be loved!

She resolved that sentence in her mind, and it was unbearable. We can understand her whole character by it. It was the reason she refused to converse at length with boys who attracted her at parties; why she'd run off rudely; why she'd kiss her girlfriends so passionately, pinching them too till she drew blood. The fear of being rejected made this woman what she was. It was the reason why poor Balla, with his fine, inquisitive nose and handsome forehead— which only a man over thirty has—with his pleasant gray eyes and clean-shaven face, had to slip out of Erna's house unnoticed.

And Erna sighed in relief: she felt like jumping out of her skin. She grinned; she laughed aloud; she looked at herself in the mirror and, singing, stuck out her tongue so that the two of them, the real Erna and her reflection in the glass, touched. Who cares about Balla, wandering off on Andrássy Boulevard, his nose full of Erna, his heart full of pain! The point was that now she had realized what she'd never believed in or hoped for: there was one who loved her, who would have married her.

From then on Erna swiftly grew pretty. The desire slowly grew in her to spend more time trying on shoes and dresses. Fewer and fewer people used the word "sloppy" for her, and not often. In short, Erna saw to it that her blouse and skirt were fastened perfectly; moreover she even adjusted her skirts before the mirror according to the law of symmetry. A shoemaker of genius fashioned a pair of gorgeous shoes for her. When Astalos saw Erna's ankles in these shoes, he said, I don't know what's happened to that girl. They must have given her new legs or fixed her old ones. I don't know, but as she is now the girl's attractive and deserves the attention of the most particular of men.

Needless to add, Astalos included himself among "the most particular of men," and began courting Erna—on the banks of the Danube, at the skating rink, at the Gerbaud, etcetera, Budapest style. (Jesus Christ, but Life's shallow!) Within two weeks Astalos was wonderfully rejected. Erna needed that for her self-confidence, and so the girl sacrificed—with a sure instinct—a marriage which in other respects would have been quite adequate.

It's worth remarking that Astalos was trying to seduce Erna while proposing to her: being an adherent of the modern school, he held to the principle that one should only marry a girl one knows down to the last details. Erna didn't hold back in that game—she liked Astalos—but when it came to marrying him she said, No.

After Astalos two or three more young men suffered the same fate. Erna didn't boast of it. She didn't want to make her girlfriends envious; she wished merely to rehabilitate herself, for her own sake. And she accomplished that. What would have happened if, in addition to nature's other stinginess, Erna had lacked even that *one* compensation? The answer's easy: 1) Balla would never have proposed, so there'd have been no refusal; 2) lacking self-confidence, Erna would have neglected her looks even more and would never have sought out her master cobbler who had created the previously mentioned precious shoes for her; 3) on that premise Astalos' and the others' offers wouldn't have been forthcoming; 4) Erna would have remained forever an intolerable creature with frequent attacks of the spleen, as she had been before; 5) the whole affair would have deteriorated further when Erna passed twenty, and things would have been in even worse shape; 6) Erna would have felt herself growing burdensome to her family and begun resenting them and planning a trip abroad; 7) they wouldn't have let her go, she would have wept a lot and ceased speaking to her father and mother for weeks on end; 8) Father and Mother then secretly present her with a fiancé (30,000—not bad!)—Erna talks about her fiancé only with the most intense disgust, but the wedding comes off anyhow; 9) Erna begins talking divorce by the second month of the marriage, whereupon she is promised a slap in the face; 10) at the close of the second year, she delivers a baby girl. She's a wretched housekeeper, an incompetent mother, and an impatient, nagging shrew of a wife. She drives her husband away from home and he turns in his sorrow to cards and etcetera etcetera. In other words, Erna's life might have turned out as just described.

We know, however, that it happened differently on account of a slight but most significant accident. The moral of this story, with its ancillary combinations, is that our fate is indeed directed by small accidents. The happiness or unhappiness of our entire life may depend on accident, on small fortuitous circumstances. Erna, the intolerable nasty girl who was always like a bitter grimace or a string out of tune, disturbing and dissonant, turned out a charming, well-balanced young woman.

I think whoever marries her will do quite well.

JUNOT DÍAZ

[Dominican Republic/U.S.A.]

DROWN (1996), the first book by Junot Díaz (born 1968), was the most remarkable short-fiction debut in the American literary world since Ernest Hemingway's *In Our Time* in 1925. The novel *The Brief Wondrous Life of Oscar Wao* (2007) won Díaz a Pulitzer Prize; his second collection of stories, *This Is How You Lose Her*—just as brilliant as *Drown*—was published in 2012. "The Sun, the Moon, the Stars" is the first story from that collection. Díaz teaches writing at the Massachusetts Institute of Technology and is unmarried.

The Sun, the Moon, the Stars (2012)

I'M NOT A bad guy. I know how that sounds—defensive, unscrupulous—but it's true. I'm like everybody else: weak, full of mistakes, but basically good. Magdalena disagrees though. She considers me a typical Dominican man: a sucio, an asshole. See, many months ago, when Magda was still my girl, when I didn't have to be careful about almost anything, I cheated on her with this chick who had tons of eighties freestyle hair. Didn't tell Magda about it, either. You know how it is. A smelly bone like that, better off buried in the backyard of your life. Magda only found out because homegirl wrote her a fucking *letter*. And the letter had *details*. Shit you wouldn't even tell your boys drunk.

The thing is, that particular bit of stupidity had been over for months. Me and Magda were on an upswing. We weren't as distant as we'd been the winter I was cheating. The freeze was over. She was coming over to my place and instead of us hanging with my knucklehead boys—me smoking, her bored out of her skull—we were seeing movies. Driving out to different places to eat. Even caught a play at the Crossroads and I took her picture with some bigwig black playwrights, pictures where she's smiling so much you'd think her wide-ass mouth was going to unhinge. We were a couple again. Visiting each other's family on the weekends. Eating breakfast at diners hours before anybody else was up, rummaging through the New Brunswick library together, the one Carnegie built with his guilt money. A nice rhythm we had going. But then the Letter hits like a *Star Trek* grenade and detonates everything, past, present, future. Suddenly her folks want to kill me. It don't matter that I helped them with their taxes two years running or that I mow their lawn. Her father, who used to treat me like his hijo, calls me an asshole on the phone, sounds like he's strangling himself with the cord. You no deserve I speak to you in Spanish, he says. I see one of Magda's girlfriends at the Woodbridge mall—Claribel, the ecuatoriana with the biology degree and the chinita eyes—and she treats me like I ate somebody's favorite kid.

You don't even want to hear how it went down with Magda. Like a five-train collision. She threw Cassandra's letter at me—it missed and landed under a Volvo—and then she sat down on the curb and started hyperventilating. Oh, God, she wailed. Oh, my God.

This is when my boys claim they would have pulled a Total Fucking Denial. Cassandra *who*? I was too sick to my stomach even to try. I sat down next to her, grabbed her flailing arms, and said some dumb shit like You have to listen to me, Magda. Or you won't understand.

Let me tell you about Magda. She's a Bergenline original: short with a big mouth and big hips and dark curly hair you could lose a hand in. Her father's a baker, her mother sells kids' clothes door to door. She might be nobody's pendeja but she's also a forgiving soul. A Catholic. Dragged me into church every Sunday for Spanish Mass, and when one of her relatives is sick, especially the ones in Cuba, she writes letters to some nuns in Pennsylvania, asks the sisters to pray for her family. She's the nerd every librarian in town knows, a teacher whose students love her. Always cutting shit out for me from the newspapers, Dominican shit. I see her like, what, every week, and she still sends me corny little notes in the mail: So you won't forget me. You couldn't think of anybody worse to screw than Magda.

Anyway I won't bore you with what happens after she finds out. The begging, the crawling over glass, the crying. Let's just say that after two weeks of this, of my driving out to her house, sending her letters, and calling her at all hours of the night, we put it back together. Didn't mean I ever ate with her family again or that her girlfriends were celebrating. Those cabronas, they were like, No, jamás, never. Even Magda wasn't too hot on the rapprochement at first, but I had the momentum of the past on my side. When she asked me, Why don't you leave me alone? I told her the truth: It's because I love you, mami. I know this sounds like a load of doo-doo, but it's true: Magda's my heart. I didn't want her to leave me; I wasn't about to start looking for a girlfriend because I'd fucked up one lousy time.

Don't think it was a cakewalk, because it wasn't. Magda's stubborn; back when we first started dating, she said she wouldn't sleep with me until we'd been together at least a month, and homegirl stuck to it, no matter how hard I tried to get into her knickknacks. She's sensitive, too. Takes to hurt the way water takes to paper. You can't imagine how many times she asked (especially after we finished fucking), Were you ever going to tell me? This and Why? were her favorite questions. My favorite answers were Yes and It was a stupid mistake. I wasn't thinking.

We even had some conversation about Cassandra—usually in the dark, when we couldn't see each other. Magda asked me if I'd loved Cassandra and I told her, No, I didn't. Do you still think about her? Nope. Did you like fucking her? To be honest, baby, it was lousy. That one is never very believable but you got to say it anyway no matter how stupid and unreal it sounds: say it.

And for a while after we got back together everything was as fine as it could be.

But only for a little while. Slowly, almost imperceptibly my Magda started turning into another Magda. Who didn't want to sleep over as much or scratch my back when I asked her to. Amazing what you notice. Like how she never used to ask me to call back when she was on the line with somebody else. I always had priority. Not anymore. So of course I blamed all that shit on her girls, who I knew for a fact were still feeding her a bad line about me.

She wasn't the only one with counsel. My boys were like, Fuck her, don't sweat that bitch, but every time I tried I couldn't pull it off. I was into Magda for real. I started working overtime on her again, but nothing seemed to pan out. Every movie we went to, every night drive we took, every time she did sleep over seemed to confirm something negative about me. I felt like I was dying by degrees, but when I brought it up she told me that I was being paranoid.

About a month later, she started making the sort of changes that would have alarmed a paranoid nigger. Cuts her hair, buys better makeup, rocks new clothes, goes out dancing on Friday nights with her friends. When I ask her if we can chill, I'm no longer sure it's a done deal. A lot of the time she Bartlebys me, says, No, I'd rather not. I ask her what the hell she thinks this is and she says, That's what I'm trying to figure out.

I know what she was doing. Making me aware of my precarious position in her life. Like I was not aware.

Then it was June. Hot white clouds stranded in the sky, cars being washed down with hoses, music allowed outside. Everybody getting ready for summer, even us. We'd planned a trip to Santo Domingo early in the year, an anniversary present, and had to decide whether we were still going or not. It had been on the horizon awhile, but I figured it was something that would resolve itself. When it didn't, I brought the tickets out and asked her, How do you feel about it?

Like it's too much of a commitment.

Could be worse. It's a vacation, for Christ's sake.

I see it as pressure.

Doesn't have to be pressure.

I don't know why I get stuck on it the way I do. Bringing it up every day, trying to get her to commit. Maybe I was getting tired of the situation we were in. Wanted to flex, wanted something to change. Or maybe I'd gotten this idea in my head that if she said, Yes, we're going, then shit would be fine between us. If she said, No, it's not for me, then at least I'd know that it was over.

Her girls, the sorest losers on the planet, advised her to take the trip and then never speak to me again. She, of course, told me this shit, because she couldn't stop herself from telling me everything she's thinking. How do you feel about that suggestion? I asked her.

She shrugged. It's an idea.

Even my boys were like, Nigger, sounds like you're wasting a
whole lot of loot on some bullshit, but I really thought it would be
good for us. Deep down, where my boys don't know me, I'm an
optimist. I thought, Me and her on the Island. What couldn't this cure?

Let me confess: I love Santo Domingo. I love coming home to the
guys in blazers trying to push little cups of Brugal into my hands. Love
the plane landing, everybody clapping when the wheels kiss the run-
way. Love the fact that I'm the only nigger on board without a Cuban
link or a flapjack of makeup on my face. Love the redhead woman
on her way to meet the daughter she hasn't seen in eleven years. The
gifts she holds on her lap, like the bones of a saint. M'ija has tetas now,
the woman whispers to her neighbor. Last time I saw her, she could
barely speak in sentences. Now she's a woman. Imagínate. I love the
bags my mother packs, shit for relatives and something for Magda, a
gift. You give this to her no matter what happens.

If this was another kind of story, I'd tell you about the sea. What
it looks like after it's been forced into the sky through a blowhole.
How when I'm driving in from the airport and see it like this, like
shredded silver, I know I'm back for real. I'd tell you how many
poor motherfuckers there are. More albinos, more cross-eyed niggers, more tígueres than you'll ever see. And I'd tell you about the
traffic: the entire history of late-twentieth-century automobiles
swarming across every flat stretch of ground, a cosmology of battered cars, battered motorcycles, battered trucks, and battered
buses, and an equal number of repair shops, run by any fool with
a wrench. I'd tell you about the shanties and our no-running-water
faucets and the sambos on the billboards and the fact that my family
house comes equipped with an ever-reliable latrine. I'd tell you
about my abuelo and his campo hands, how unhappy he is that I'm
not sticking around, and I'd tell you about the street where I was
born, Calle XXI, how it hasn't decided yet if it wants to be a slum
or not and how it's been in this state of indecision for years.

But that would make it another kind of story, and I'm having
enough trouble with this one as it is. You'll have to take my word
for it. Santo Domingo is Santo Domingo. Let's pretend we all
know what goes on there.

I must have been smoking dust, because I thought we were fine
those first couple of days. Sure, staying locked up at my abuelo's

house bored Magda to tears, she even said so—I'm bored, Yunior—but I'd warned her about the obligatory Visit with Abuelo. I thought she wouldn't mind; she's normally mad cool with the viejitos. But she didn't say much to him. Just fidgeted in the heat and drank fifteen bottles of water. Point is, we were out of the capital and on a guagua to the interior before the second day had even begun. The landscapes were superfly—even though there was a drought on and the whole campo, even the houses, was covered in that red dust. There I was. Pointing out all the shit that had changed since the year before. The new Pizzarelli and the little plastic bags of water the tigueritos were selling. Even kicked the historicals. This is where Trujillo and his Marine pals slaughtered the gavilleros, here's where the Jefe used to take his girls, here's where Balaguer sold his soul to the Devil. And Magda seemed to be enjoying herself. Nodded her head. Talked back a little. What can I tell you? I thought we were on a positive vibe.

I guess when I look back there were signs. First off, Magda's not quiet. She's a talker, a fucking boca, and we used to have this thing where I would lift my hand and say, Time out, and she would have to be quiet for at least two minutes, just so I could process some of the information she'd been spouting. She'd be embarrassed and chastened, but not so embarrassed and chastened that when I said, OK, time's up, she didn't launch right into it again.

Maybe it was my good mood. It was like the first time in weeks that I felt relaxed, that I wasn't acting like something was about to give at any moment. It bothered me that she insisted on reporting to her girls every night—like they were expecting me to kill her or something—but, fuck it, I still thought we were doing better than anytime before.

We were in this crazy budget hotel near Pucamaima. I was standing on the balcony staring at the Septentrionales and the blacked-out city when I heard her crying. I thought it was something serious, found the flashlight, and fanned the light over her heat-swollen face. Are you OK?

She shook her head. I don't want to be here.

What do you mean?

What don't you understand? I. Don't. Want. To. Be. Here.

This was not the Magda I knew. The Magda I knew was super courteous. Knocked on a door before she opened it.

I almost shouted, What is your fucking problem! But I didn't. I ended up hugging and babying her and asking her what was wrong. She cried for a long time and then after a silence started talking. By then the lights had flickered back on. Turned out she didn't want to travel around like a hobo. I thought we'd be on a beach, she said.

We're going to be on a beach. The day after tomorrow.

Can't we go now?

What could I do? She was in her underwear, waiting for me to say something. So what jumped out of my mouth? Baby, we'll do whatever you want. I called the hotel in La Romana, asked if we could come early, and the next morning I put us on an express guagua to the capital and then a second one to La Romana. I didn't say a fucking word to her and she didn't say nothing to me. She seemed tired and watched the world outside like maybe she was expecting it to speak to her.

By the middle of Day 3 of our All-Quisqueya Redemption Tour we were in an air-conditioned bungalow watching HBO. Exactly where I want to be when I'm in Santo Domingo. In a fucking resort. Magda was reading a book by a Trappist, in a better mood, I guessed, and I was sitting on the edge of the bed, fingering my useless map.

I was thinking, For this I deserve something nice. Something physical. Me and Magda were pretty damn casual about sex, but since the breakup shit has gotten weird. First of all, it ain't regular like before. I'm lucky to score some once a week. I have to nudge her, start things up, or we won't fuck at all. And she plays like she doesn't want it, and sometimes she doesn't and then I have to cool it, but other times she does want it and I have to touch her pussy, which is my way of initiating things, of saying, So, how about we kick it, mami? And she'll turn her head, which is her way of saying, I'm too proud to acquiesce openly to your animal desires, but if you continue to put your finger in me I won't stop you,

Today we started no problem, but then halfway through she said, Wait, we shouldn't.

I wanted to know why.

She closed her eyes like she was embarrassed at herself. Forget about it, she said, moving her hips under me. Just forget about it.

I don't even want to tell you where we're at. We're in Casa de Campo. The Resort That Shame Forgot. The average asshole would love this place. It's the largest, wealthiest resort on the Island, which means it's a goddamn fortress, walled away from everybody else. Guachimanes and peacocks and ambitious topiaries everywhere. Advertises itself in the States as its own country, and it might as well be. Has its own airport, thirty-six holes of golf, beaches so white they ache to be trampled, and the only Island Dominicans you're guaranteed to see are either caked up or changing your sheets. Let's just say my abuelo has never been here, and neither has yours. This is where the Garcías and the Colóns come to relax after a long month of oppressing the masses, where the tutumpotes can trade tips with their colleagues from abroad. Chill here too long and you'll be sure to have your ghetto pass revoked, no questions asked.

We wake up bright and early for the buffet, get served by cheerful women in Aunt Jemima costumes. I shit you not: these sisters even have to wear hankies on their heads. Magda is scratching out a couple of cards to her family. I want to talk about the day before, but when I bring it up she puts down her pen. Jams on her shades.

I feel like you're pressuring me.

How am I pressuring you? I ask.

I just want some space to myself every now and then. Every time I'm with you I have this sense that you want something from me.

Time to yourself, I say. What does that mean?

Like maybe once a day, you do one thing, I do another.

Like when? Now?

It doesn't have to be now. She looks exasperated. Why don't we just go down to the beach?

As we walk over to the courtesy golf cart, I say, I feel like you rejected my whole country, Magda.

Don't be ridiculous. She drops one hand in my lap. I just wanted to relax. What's wrong with that?

The sun is blazing and the blue of the ocean is an overload on the brain. Casa de Campo has got beaches the way the rest of the Island has got problems. These, though, have no merengue, no little kids, nobody trying to sell you chicharrones, and there's a massive melanin deficit in evidence. Every fifty feet there's at least one Eurofuck beached out on a towel like some scary pale monster that the sea's vomited up. They look like philosophy professors, like budget Foucaults, and too many of them are in the company of a dark-assed Dominican girl. I mean it, these girls can't be no more than sixteen, look puro ingenio to me. You can tell by their inability to communicate that these two didn't meet back in their Left Bank days.

Magda's rocking a dope Ochun-colored bikini that her girls helped her pick out so she could torture me, and I'm in these old ruined trunks that say "Sandy Hook Forever!" I'll admit it, with Magda half naked in public I'm feeling vulnerable and uneasy. I put my hand on her knee. I just wish you'd say you love me.

Yunior, please.

Can you say you like me a lot?

Can you leave me alone? You're such a pestilence.

I let the sun stake me out to the sand. It's disheartening, me and Magda together. We don't look like a couple. When she smiles niggers ask her for her hand in marriage; when I smile folks check their wallets. Magda's been a star the whole time we've been here. You know how it is when you're on the Island and your girl's an octoroon. Brothers go apeshit. On buses, the machos were like, Tú sí eres bella, muchacha. Every time I dip into the water for a swim, some Mediterranean Messenger of Love starts rapping to her. Of course, I'm not polite. Why don't you beat it, pancho? We're on our honeymoon here. There's this one squid who's mad persistent, even sits down near us so he can impress her with the hair around his nipples, and instead of ignoring him she starts a conversation and it turns out he's Dominican, too, from Quisqueya Heights, an assistant DA who loves his people. Better I'm their prosecutor, he says. At least I understand them. I'm thinking he sounds like the sort of nigger who in the old days used to lead bwana to the rest of us. After three minutes of him, I can't take it no more, and say, Magda, stop talking to that asshole.

The assistant DA startles. I know you ain't talking to me, he says.

Actually, I say, I am.

This is unbelievable. Magda gets to her feet and walks stiff-legged toward the water. She's got a half-moon of sand stuck to her butt. A total fucking heartbreak.

Homeboy's saying something else to me, but I'm not listening. I already know what she'll say when she sits back down. Time for you to do your thing and me to do mine.

That night I loiter around the pool and the local bar, Club Cacique, Magda nowhere to be found. I meet a dominicana from West New

York. Fly, of course. Trigueña, with the most outrageous perm this side of Dyckman. Lucy is her name. She's hanging out with three of her teenage girl cousins. When she removes her robe to dive into the pool, I see a spiderweb of scars across her stomach.

I also meet these two rich older dudes drinking cognac at the bar. Introduce themselves as the Vice-President and Bárbaro, his bodyguard. I must have the footprint of fresh disaster on my face. They listen to my troubles like they're a couple of capos and I'm talking murder. They commiserate. It's a thousand degrees out and the mosquitoes hum like they're about to inherit the earth, but both these cats are wearing expensive suits, and Bárbaro is even sporting a purple ascot. Once a soldier tried to saw open his neck and now he covers the scar. I'm a modest man, he says.

I go off to phone the room. No Magda. I check with reception. No messages. I return to the bar and smile.

The Vice-President is a young brother, in his late thirties, and pretty cool for a chupabarrio. He advises me to find another woman. Make her bella and negra. I think, Cassandra.

The Vice-President waves his hand and shots of Barceló appear so fast you'd think it's science fiction.

Jealousy is the best way to jump-start a relationship, the Vice-President says. I learned that when I was a student at Syracuse. Dance with another woman, dance merengue with her, and see if your jeva's not roused to action.

You mean roused to violence.

She hit you?

When I first told her. She smacked me right across the chops.

Pero, hermano, why'd you tell her? Bárbaro wants to know. Why didn't you just deny it?

Compadre, she received a letter. It had evidence.

The Vice-President smiles fantastically and I can see why he's a vice-president. Later, when I get home, I'll tell my mother about this whole mess, and she'll tell me what this brother was the vice-president of.

They only hit you, he says, when they care.

Amen, Bárbaro murmurs. Amen.

All of Magda's friends say I cheated because I was Dominican, that all us Dominican men are dogs and can't be trusted. I doubt that I can speak for all Dominican men but I doubt they can either. From my perspective it wasn't genetics; there were reasons. Causalities.

The truth is there ain't no relationship in the world that doesn't hit turbulence. Mine and Magda's certainly did.

I was living in Brooklyn and she was with her folks in Jersey. We talked every day on the phone and on weekends we saw each other. Usually I went in. We were real Jersey, too: malls, the parents, movies, a lot of TV. After a year of us together, this was where we were at. Our relationship wasn't the sun, the moon, and the stars, but it wasn't bullshit, either. Especially not on Saturday mornings, over at my apartment, when she made us coffee campostyle, straining it through the sock thing. Told her parents the night before she was staying over at Claribel's; they must have known where she was, but they never said shit. I'd sleep late and she'd read, scratching my back in slow arcs, and when I was ready to get up I would start kissing her until she would say, God, Yunior, you're making me wet.

I wasn't unhappy and wasn't actively pursuing ass like some niggers. Sure, I checked out other females, even danced with them when I went out, but I wasn't keeping numbers or nothing.

Still, it's not like seeing somebody once a week doesn't cool shit out, because it does. Nothing you'd really notice until some new chick arrives at your job with a big butt and a smart mouth and she's like on you almost immediately, touching your pectorals, moaning about some moreno she's dating who's always treating her like shit, saying, Black guys don't understand Spanish girls.

Cassandra. She organized the football pool and did crossword puzzles while she talked on the phone, and had a thing for denim skirts. We got into a habit of going to lunch and having the same conversation. I advised her to drop the moreno, she advised me to find a girlfriend who could fuck. First week of knowing her, I made the mistake of telling her that sex with Magda had never been top-notch.

God, I feel sorry for you, Cassandra said. At least Rupert gives me some Grade A dick.

The first night we did it—and it was good, too, she wasn't false advertising—I felt so lousy that I couldn't sleep, even though she was one of those sisters whose body fits next to you perfect. I was like, She knows, so I called Magda right from the bed and asked her if she was OK.

You sound strange, she said.

I remember Cassandra pressing the hot cleft of her pussy against my leg and me saying, I just miss you.

Another perfect sunny Caribbean day, and the only thing Magda has said is Give me the lotion. Tonight the resort is throwing a party. All guests are invited. Attire's semiformal, but I don't have the clothes or the energy to dress up. Magda, though, has both. She pulls on these super-tight gold lamé pants and a matching halter that shows off her belly ring. Her hair is shiny and as dark as night and I can remember the first time I kissed those curls, asking her, Where are the stars? And she said, They're a little lower, papi.

We both end up in front of the mirror. I'm in slacks and a wrinkled chacabana. She's applying her lipstick; I've always believed that the universe invented the color red solely for Latinas.

We look good, she says.

It's true. My optimism is starting to come back. I'm thinking, This is the night for reconciliation. I put my arms around her, but she drops her bomb without blinking a fucking eye: tonight, she says, she needs space.

My arms drop.

I knew you'd be pissed, she says.

You're a real bitch, you know that.

I didn't want to come here. You made me.

If you didn't want to come, why didn't you have the fucking guts to say so?

And on and on and on, until finally I just say, Fuck this, and head out. I feel unmoored and don't have a clue of what comes next. This is the endgame, and instead of pulling out all the stops, instead of pongándome más chivo que un chivo, I'm feeling sorry for myself, como un parigüayo sin suerte. I'm thinking over and over, I'm not a bad guy, I'm not a bad guy.

Club Cacique is jammed. I'm looking for that girl Lucy. I find the Vice-President and Bárbaro instead. At the quiet end of the bar, they're drinking cognac and arguing about whether there are fifty-six Dominicans in the major leagues or fifty-seven. They clear out a space for me and clap me on the shoulder.

This place is killing me, I say.

How dramatic. The Vice-President reaches into his suit for his keys. He's wearing those Italian leather shoes that look like braided slippers. Are you inclined to ride with us?

Sure, I say. Why the fuck not?

I wish to show you the birthplace of our nation.

Before we leave I check out the crowd. Lucy has arrived. She's alone at the edge of the bar in a fly black dress. Smiles excitedly, lifts her arm, and I can see the dark stubbled spot in her armpit. She's got sweat patches over her outfit and mosquito bites on her beautiful arms. I think, I should stay, but my legs carry me right out of the club.

We pile in a diplomat's black BMW. I'm in the backseat with Bárbaro; the Vice-President's up front driving. We leave Casa de Campo behind and the frenzy of La Romana, and soon everything starts smelling of processed cane. The roads are dark—I'm talking no fucking lights—and in our beams the bugs swarm like a biblical plague. We're passing the cognac around. I'm with a vice-president, I figure what the fuck.

He's talking—about his time in upstate New York—but so is Bárbaro. The bodyguard's suit's rumpled and his hand shakes as he smokes his cigarettes. Some fucking bodyguard. He's telling me about his childhood in San Juan, near the border of Haiti. Liborio's country. I wanted to be an engineer, he tells me. I wanted to build schools and hospitals for the pueblo. I'm not really listening to him; I'm thinking about Magda, how I'll probably never taste her chocha again.

And then we're out of the car, stumbling up a slope, through bushes and guineo and bamboo, and the mosquitoes are chewing us up like we're the special of the day. Bárbaro's got a huge flashlight, a darkness obliterator. The Vice-President's cursing, trampling through the underbrush, saying, It's around here somewhere. This is what I get for being in office so long. It's only then I notice that Bárbaro's holding a huge fucking machine gun and his hand ain't shaking no more. He isn't watching me or the Vice-President—he's listening. I'm not scared, but this is getting a little too freaky for me.

What kind of gun is that? I ask, by way of conversation.

A P-90.

What the fuck is that?

Something old made new.

Great, I'm thinking, a philosopher.

It's here, the Vice-President calls out.

I creep over and see that he's standing over a hole in the ground. The earth is red. Bauxite. And the hole is blacker than any of us.

This is the Cave of the Jagua, the Vice-President announces in a deep, respectful voice. The birthplace of the Taínos.

I raise my eyebrow. I thought they were South American.

We're speaking mythically here.

Bárbaro points the light down the hole but that doesn't improve anything.

Would you like to see inside? the Vice-President asks me.

I must have said yes, because Bárbaro gives me the flashlight and the two of them grab me by my ankles and lower me into the hole. All my coins fly out of my pockets. Bendiciones. I don't see much, just some odd colors on the eroded walls, and the Vice-President's calling down, Isn't it beautiful?

This is the perfect place for insight, for a person to become somebody better. The Vice-President probably saw his future self hanging in this darkness, bulldozing the poor out of their shanties, and Bárbaro, too—buying a concrete house for his mother, showing her how to work the air-conditioner—but, me, all I can manage is a memory of the first time me and Magda talked. Back at Rutgers. We were waiting for an E bus together on George Street and she was wearing purple. All sorts of purple.

And that's when I know it's over. As soon as you start thinking about the beginning, it's the end.

I cry, and when they pull me up the Vice-President says, indignantly, God, you don't have to be a pussy about it.

That must have been some serious Island voodoo: the ending I saw in the cave came true. The next day we went back to the United States. Five months later I got a letter from my ex-baby. I was dating someone new, but Magda's handwriting still blasted every molecule of air out of my lungs.

It turned out she was also going out with somebody else. A very nice guy she'd met. Dominican, like me. *Except he loves me*, she wrote.

But I'm getting ahead of myself. I need to finish by showing you what kind of fool I was.

When I returned to the bungalow that night, Magda was waiting up for me. Was packed, looked like she'd been bawling.

I'm going home tomorrow, she said.

I sat down next to her. Took her hand. This can work, I said. All we have to do is try.

JAMES JOYCE

[Ireland]

IRELAND'S MOST renowned author, James Joyce (1882–1941) lived in self-imposed exile from his native country after 1912. He met the love of his life in Dublin in 1904, a chambermaid named Nora Barnacle, and lived in Italy with her and their two children until World War I, when they relocated to Switzerland. After the war, they lived in Paris for twenty years. Joyce and Nora didn't officially marry until 1931. Highly regarded for his experimental novels, particularly *Ulysses*, Joyce also wrote the more traditionally styled stories in *Dubliners* (1914), of which "Araby," a story that evokes a childhood love, was one.

Araby (1914)

NORTH RICHMOND STREET, being blind, was a quiet street except at the hour when the Christian Brothers' School set the boys free. An uninhabited house of two storeys stood at the blind end, detached from its neighbours in a square ground. The other houses of the street, conscious of decent lives within them, gazed at one another with brown imperturbable faces.

The former tenant of our house, a priest, had died in the back drawing-room. Air, musty from having been long enclosed, hung in all the rooms, and the waste room behind the kitchen was littered with old useless papers. Among these I found a few paper-covered books, the pages of which were curled and damp: *The Abbot*, by Walter Scott, *The Devout Communicant* and *The Memoirs of Vidocq*. I liked the last best because its leaves were yellow. The wild garden behind the house contained a central apple-tree and a few straggling bushes under one of which I found the late tenant's rusty bicycle-pump. He had been a very charitable priest; in his will he had left all his money to institutions and the furniture of his house to his sister.

When the short days of winter came dusk fell before we had well eaten our dinners. When we met in the street the houses had grown sombre. The space of sky above us was the colour of ever-changing violet and towards it the lamps of the street lifted their feeble lanterns. The cold air stung us and we played till our bodies glowed. Our shouts echoed in the silent street. The career of our play brought us through the dark muddy lanes behind the houses where we ran the gauntlet of the rough tribes from the cottages, to the back doors of the dark dripping gardens where odours arose from the ashpits, to the dark odorous stables where a coachman smoothed and combed the horse or shook music from the buckled harness. When we returned to the street light from the kitchen windows had filled the areas. If my uncle was seen turning the corner we hid in the shadow until we had seen him safely housed. Or if Mangan's sister came out on the doorstep to call her brother in to his tea we watched her from our shadow peer up and down the street. We waited to see whether she would remain or go in and, if she remained, we left our shadow and walked up to Mangan's steps resignedly. She was waiting for us, her figure defined by the light from the half-opened door. Her brother always teased her before he obeyed and I stood by the railings looking at her. Her dress swung as she moved her body and the soft rope of her hair tossed from side to side.

Every morning I lay on the floor in the front parlour watching her door. The blind was pulled down to within an inch of the sash so that I could not be seen. When she came out on the doorstep my heart leaped. I ran to the hall, seized my books and followed her. I kept her brown figure always in my eye and, when we came near the point at which our ways diverged, I quickened my pace and passed her. This happened morning after morning. I had never spoken to her, except for a few casual words, and yet her name was like a summons to all my foolish blood.

Her image accompanied me even in places the most hostile to romance. On Saturday evenings when my aunt went marketing I had to go to carry some of the parcels. We walked through the flaring streets, jostled by drunken men and bargaining women, amid the curses of labourers, the shrill litanies of shop-boys who stood on guard by the barrels of pigs' cheeks, the nasal chanting of street-singers, who sang a *come-all-you* about O'Donovan Rossa, or a ballad about the troubles in our native land. These noises converged in a single sensation of life for me: I imagined that I bore my chalice safely through a throng of foes. Her name sprang to my lips at moments in strange prayers and praises which I myself did not understand. My eyes were often full of tears (I could not tell why) and at times a flood from my heart seemed to pour itself out into my bosom. I thought little of the future. I did not know whether I would ever speak to her or not or, if I spoke to her, how I could tell her of my confused adoration. But my body was like a harp and her words and gestures were like fingers running upon the wires.

One evening I went into the back drawing-room in which the priest had died. It was a dark rainy evening and there was no sound in the house. Through one of the broken panes I heard the rain impinge upon the earth, the fine incessant needles of water playing in the sodden beds. Some distant lamp or lighted window gleamed below me. I was thankful that I could see so little. All my senses seemed to desire to veil themselves and, feeling that I was about to slip from them, I pressed the palms of my hands together until they trembled, murmuring: "*O love! O love!*" many times.

At last she spoke to me. When she addressed the first words to me I was so confused that I did not know what to answer. She asked me was I going to *Araby*. I forgot whether I answered yes or no. It would be a splendid bazaar, she said she would love to go.

"And why can't you?" I asked.

While she spoke she turned a silver bracelet round and round her wrist. She could not go, she said, because there would be a retreat that week in her convent. Her brother and two other boys were fighting for their caps and I was alone at the railings. She held one of the spikes, bowing her head towards me. The light from the lamp opposite our door caught the white curve of her neck, lit up her hair that rested there and, falling, lit up the hand upon the railing. It fell over one side of her dress and caught the white border of a petticoat, just visible as she stood at ease.

"It's well for you," she said.

"If I go," I said, "I will bring you something."

What innumerable follies laid waste my waking and sleeping thoughts after that evening! I wished to annihilate the tedious intervening days. I chafed against the work of school. At night in my bedroom and by day in the classroom her image came between me and the page I strove to read. The syllables of the word *Araby* were called to me through the silence in which my soul luxuriated and cast an Eastern enchantment over me. I asked for leave to go to the bazaar on Saturday night. My aunt was surprised and hoped it was not some Freemason affair. I answered few questions in class. I watched my master's face pass from amiability to sternness; he hoped I was not beginning to idle. I could not call my wandering thoughts together. I had hardly any patience with the serious work of life which, now that it stood between me and my desire, seemed to me child's play, ugly monotonous child's play.

On Saturday morning I reminded my uncle that I wished to go to the bazaar in the evening. He was fussing at the hallstand, looking for the hat-brush, and answered me curtly:

"Yes, boy, I know."

As he was in the hall I could not go into the front parlour and lie at the window. I left the house in bad humour and walked slowly towards the school. The air was pitilessly raw and already my heart misgave me.

When I came home to dinner my uncle had not yet been home. Still it was early. I sat staring at the clock for some time and, when its ticking began to irritate me, I left the room. I mounted the staircase and gained the upper part of the house. The high cold empty gloomy rooms liberated me and I went from room to room singing. From the front window I saw my companions playing below in the street. Their cries reached me weakened and indistinct and, leaning my forehead against the cool glass, I looked over at the dark house where she lived. I may have stood there for an hour, seeing nothing but the brown-clad figure cast by my imagination, touched discreetly by the lamplight at the curved neck, at the hand upon the railings and at the border below the dress.

When I came downstairs again I found Mrs. Mercer sitting at the fire. She was an old garrulous woman, a pawnbroker's widow, who collected used stamps for some pious purpose. I had to endure the gossip of the tea-table. The meal was prolonged beyond an hour and still my uncle did not come. Mrs. Mercer stood up to go: she was sorry she couldn't wait any longer, but it was after eight o'clock and she did not like to be out late, as the night air was bad for her.

When she had gone I began to walk up and down the room, clenching my fists. My aunt said:

"I'm afraid you may put off your bazaar for this night of Our Lord."

At nine o'clock I heard my uncle's latchkey in the hall-door. I heard him talking to himself and heard the hallstand rocking when it had received the weight of his overcoat. I could interpret these signs. When he was midway through his dinner I asked him to give me the money to go to the bazaar. He had forgotten.

"The people are in bed and after their first sleep now," he said.

I did not smile. My aunt said to him energetically:

"Can't you give him the money and let him go? You've kept him late enough as it is."

My uncle said he was very sorry he had forgotten. He said he believed in the old saying: "All work and no play makes Jack a dull boy." He asked me where I was going and, when I had told him a second time he asked me did I know *The Arab's Farewell to his Steed*. When I left the kitchen he was about to recite the opening lines of the piece to my aunt.

I held a florin tightly in my hand as I strode down Buckingham Street towards the station. The sight of the streets thronged with buyers and glaring with gas recalled to me the purpose of my journey. I took my seat in a third-class carriage of a deserted train. After an intolerable delay the train moved out of the station slowly. It crept onward among ruinous houses and over the twinkling river. At Westland Row Station a crowd of people pressed to the carriage doors; but the porters moved them back, saying that it was a special train for the bazaar. I remained alone in the bare carriage. In a few minutes the train drew up beside an improvised wooden platform. I passed out on to the road and saw by the lighted dial of a clock that it was ten minutes to ten. In front of me was a large building which displayed the magical name.

I could not find any sixpenny entrance and, fearing that the bazaar would be closed, I passed in quickly through a turnstile, handing a shilling to a weary-looking man. I found myself in a big hall girdled at half its height by a gallery. Nearly all the stalls were closed and the greater part of the hall was in darkness. I recognised a silence like that which pervades a church after a service. I walked into the centre of the bazaar timidly. A few people were gathered about the stalls which were still open. Before a curtain, over which the words *Café Chantant* were written in coloured lamps, two men were counting money on a salver. I listened to the fall of the coins.

Remembering with difficulty why I had come I went over to one of the stalls and examined porcelain vases and flowered tea-sets. At the door of the stall a young lady was talking and laughing with two young gentlemen. I remarked their English accents and listened vaguely to their conversation.

"O, I never said such a thing!"

"O, but you did!"

"O, but I didn't!"

"Didn't she say that?"

"Yes. I heard her."

"O, there's a . . . fib!"

Observing me the young lady came over and asked me did I wish to buy anything. The tone of her voice was not encouraging; she seemed to have spoken to me out of a sense of duty. I looked humbly at the great jars that stood like eastern guards at either side of the dark entrance to the stall and murmured:

"No, thank you."

The young lady changed the position of one of the vases and went back to the two young men. They began to talk of the same subject. Once or twice the young lady glanced at me over her shoulder.

I lingered before her stall, though I knew my stay was useless, to make my interest in her wares seem the more real. Then I turned away slowly and walked down the middle of the bazaar. I allowed the two pennies to fall against the sixpence in my pocket. I heard a voice call from one end of the gallery that the light was out. The upper part of the hall was now completely dark.

Gazing up into the darkness I saw myself as a creature driven and derided by vanity; and my eyes burned with anguish and anger.

HEINRICH VON KLEIST

[Germany]

BORN IN what is now Germany, Heinrich von Kleist (1777–1811)
had such a tumultuous life, career, and death that he might as well
have been a character in one of his own stories. For example, Kleist
and his beloved, Henriette Vogel, who was terminally ill at the time,
committed suicide together. His plays are matched in popularity by
his short fiction. "The Earthquake in Chile" (in German, "Das
Erdbeben in Chili," but in its original journal appearance called
"Jeronimo und Josefe. Eine Szene aus dem Erdbeben zu Chili, vom
Jahr 1647" ["Jeronimo and Josefa: A Scene from the Earthquake in
Chile in the Year 1647"]) is based on one or two historical facts and
a tidal wave of imagination.

The Earthquake in Chile (1807)

(Translated from the German by Stanley Appelbaum)

IN SANTIAGO, THE capital of the kingdom of Chile,[1] at the very
moment of the great earthquake of the year 1647, in which many
thousands of people perished, a young Spaniard accused of a
crime, Jerónimo Rugera by name, was standing by a pillar of the
prison in which he had been confined and was about to hang
himself. About a year previously, Don Enrique Asterón, one of the

---

[1] Chile was never a kingdom; in 1647, when an earthquake did occur, it was a
Spanish colony, part of the viceroyalty of Peru; the viceroy resided in Lima.
[Translator's note]

richest noblemen in the city, had dismissed him from his house, where he was employed as a tutor, because Jerónimo and Doña Josefa, Asterón's only daughter had fallen in love. A secret tryst, which had been revealed to the old Don—after he had expressly warned his daughter—by the malicious vigilance of his haughty son, so infuriated him that he placed her in the Carmelite convent of Our Lady of the Mountain in that city. Here, through a lucky accident, Jerónimo had been able to resume the relationship and, one night, had secretly made the convent garden the scene of his highest bliss.

It was Corpus Christi day, and the solemn procession of the nuns, whom the novices followed, was just setting out when the unfortunate Josefa sank down on the cathedral steps in labor pains as the bells began to ring. This incident created an unusual sensation; the young sinner, with no regard to her condition, was immediately thrown in prison, and scarcely had she arisen from childbed when, by order of the archbishop, she was subjected to the most harrowing trial.

This scandal was discussed in the city with so much animosity, and people's tongues dealt so harshly with the entire convent in which it had taken place, that neither the intercession of the Asterón family nor even the request of the abbess herself—who had grown fond of the young girl because of her otherwise irreproachable conduct—was able to palliate the severity with which the monastic laws threatened her. All that could be done was to have the death by fire, to which she had been condemned, commuted to beheading by decree of the viceroy, much to the indignation of the matrons and maidens of Santiago. In the streets along which the execution procession would pass, windows were rented, the roofs of the houses were leveled, and the pious daughters of the city invited their girl friends to attend the spectacle offered to divine vengeance at their sisterly side.

Jerónimo, who meanwhile had also been clapped in prison, thought he would go out of his mind when he heard about this horrible turn of events. In vain did he ponder ways of rescuing her: wherever the wings of even the most unbridled notions carried him, he came up against bolts and walls; and an attempt to file through the window grating only gained him a still more cramped dungeon when he was discovered. He flung himself down before the image of the Mother of God, and prayed to her with tremendous ardor, believing her to be the only one from whom salvation could still come.

But the dreaded day arrived, and with it, in his heart, a conviction of the total hopelessness of his situation. The bells that accompanied Josefa to her place of execution rang out, and despair took hold of his soul. Life seemed hateful to him, and he decided to kill himself with a rope that had been left to him by chance. He was just standing, as mentioned above, by a wall pillar and was securing the rope that was to snatch him from this world of sorrow to an iron clamp that was inserted into the pillar molding, when suddenly the greater part of the city sank with a roar as if the sky were falling, and buried all living things beneath its ruins.

Jerónimo Rugera was rigid with terror; and, as if all his presence of mind had been wiped out, he now held on to the pillar on which he had intended to die, in order not to fall over. The ground shook beneath his feet, all the walls of the prison were cleft, the whole structure threatened to collapse onto the street, and only the subsidence of the building opposite, occurring at the same time as the prison was slowly falling apart, prevented its complete leveling with the ground by creating an accidental supporting vault.

Trembling, his hair on end, and with knees about to buckle under him, Jerónimo slid across the now tilted floor toward the opening that the collision of the two buildings had torn in the front wall of the prison. Scarcely was he out in the open when a second earth tremor caused the entire street, already badly shaken, to cave in altogether. Unable to think how he could escape from this universal destruction, he hastened away over debris and timbers toward one of the nearest city gates, while death attacked him from all sides.

Here yet another house collapsed and, flinging its ruins far and wide, forced him into a side street; here flames were already shooting out of every gable, flashing in clouds of smoke, driving him in terror into another street; here the Mapocho River, shifting from its bed, rolled toward him, sweeping him with a roar into a third street. Here lay a heap of corpses, here a voice was still groaning beneath the debris, here people were shouting from burning rooftops, here humans and animals were struggling with the waves, here a courageous rescuer was making an effort to help; here stood another man, pale as death, speechlessly extending his trembling hands toward heaven.

When Jerónimo reached the gate and had ascended a hill outside it, he fell down there in a faint. He had probably lain there completely unconscious for a quarter of an hour when he finally awoke again and partly raised himself from the ground, his back turned toward the city. He felt his forehead and chest, not knowing what to make of his condition, and an immense feeling of bliss came over him when a westerly breeze from the sea quickened his recovering senses, and his eyes roved in all directions over the flourishing countryside of Santiago. Only the clusters of agitated people that were everywhere to be seen saddened his heart; he could not comprehend what had brought him and them to this place, and only when he turned around and saw the city in ruins behind him, did he recall the fearful moment he had lived through. He bowed his head so low that his forehead touched the ground, in order to thank God for his miraculous rescue; and, as if the one terrible impression that had been stamped on his mind had driven all earlier ones from it, he wept for happiness because he still enjoyed the charms of life with all its manifold phenomena.

Then, noticing a ring on his finger, he suddenly recalled Josefa as well; and, along with her, his prison, the bells he had heard there, and the moment preceding its collapse. Deep melancholy filled his heart again; he began to regret having prayed, and the Being that rules above the clouds seemed fearsome to him. He mingled with the people who were dashing out of the gates on all sides, busy saving their belongings, and timidly risked asking about Asterón's daughter and whether her execution had been carried out; but no one was able to give him detailed information. A woman bent over almost to the ground under an enormous load of utensils she was carrying on her shoulders and two children who were clutching her bosom, said as she passed by—speaking as if she had been an eyewitness—that Josefa had been beheaded.

Jerónimo turned aside; and, since, on calculating the time elapsed, he himself had no doubts that the execution had taken place, he sat down in a lonely wood and abandoned himself fully to his grief. He wished that the destructive power of nature would come down upon him again. He could not comprehend why he had escaped death, which his miserable soul now sought, at the time when it was offering itself to him freely on all sides. He resolved firmly not to waver even if the oaks were now uprooted and their tops were to tumble down upon him.

So, after he had wept his fill and, in the midst of his hottest tears, hope had returned to him, he arose and walked back and forth over the area in all directions. He visited every hilltop on which people had gathered; he met them on every path on which the stream of refugees still flowed; his trembling feet bore him wherever a women's garment fluttered in the breeze, but no garment clad the beloved daughter of Asterón.

The sun was again setting, and with it his hope, when he stepped to the edge of a cliff and obtained a view of a broad valley to which very few people had come. Undecided what he should do, he hurried from one to another of the individual groups, and was about to turn away again when he suddenly saw, by a brook that watered the valley, a young woman busy bathing a child in its stream. And his heart leaped at that sight: full of presentiment, he sprang down over the rocks, shouting "O Holy Mother of God!" and recognized Josefa when she timidly looked about on hearing the sound.

With what rapture they embraced, that unfortunate pair whom a miracle of heaven had saved! On her march to death, Josefa had already been quite close to the place of execution when suddenly the entire procession had been scattered by the resounding collapse of the buildings. Then her first terrified steps brought her to the nearest gate; but she soon recovered her presence of mind and turned back in haste to the convent, where her helpless little boy had been left behind.

She found the entire convent already in flames; the abbess, who in those moments which were to have been Josefa's last, had promised to care for the infant, was standing in front of the gates calling for help to save him. Josefa, undaunted by the smoke that billowed toward her, dashed into the building, which was already collapsing all around her, and, as if all the angels in heaven were protecting her, carried him out through the entrance again, unharmed. She was just about to sink into the arms of the abbess, who clasped her hands together over her head, when the abbess, together with almost all her nuns, was ignominiously killed by a falling gable of the building.

At this horrible sight Josefa stepped back, trembling; she hastily closed the abbess' eyes and, filled with terror, ran off to save from destruction her dear boy, whom heaven had restored to her. She had taken only a few more steps when she came across the crushed corpse of the archbishop as well, which had just been pulled out of the debris of the cathedral. The viceroy's palace had disappeared, the court in which her sentence had been pronounced was in flames, and on the spot where her father's house had stood there was a boiling lake emitting reddish vapors. Josefa summoned up all her strength in order to go on.

Banishing sorrow from her heart, she courageously proceeded from street to street with her prize and was already near the gate, when she also saw lying in ruins the prison in which Jerónimo had languished. At that sight she tottered and thought she would faint away at a street corner; but at the same moment the collapse of a building behind her, which the tremors had already totally shaken apart, frightened her into renewed vigor and propelled her forward; she kissed the child, squeezed the tears from her eyes and, no longer heeding the horrors that surrounded her, reached the gate.

When she found herself outside, she soon realized that not everyone who had lived in a ruined building had necessarily been crushed beneath it. At the next crossroads she stopped and waited to see whether the one who, after little Felipe, was dearest to her in the world, might still appear. She went on, since no one came and the crowd of people grew, and turned around again and waited again; and, shedding many tears, she stole into a dark, pine-shaded valley to pray for his soul, which she thought had departed; and found him here in the valley, that beloved man, and found bliss, as if it had been the valley of Eden.

She now told Jerónimo all this with great emotion, and, when she had finished, held the boy out for him to kiss. Jerónimo took him, dandled him with immense paternal joy and, when the child started to cry on seeing a strange face, stopped his mouth with endless kisses and caresses.

Meanwhile, a most beautiful night had fallen, full of wonderfully soft fragrance, as silvery-bright and calm as only poets dream of. Everywhere along the brook in the valley people had settled down in the glimmer of the moonlight and were preparing soft beds of moss and leaves to rest upon after such a painful day. And because the poor people were still lamenting—one because he had lost his house, another because he had lost wife and child, and a third because he had lost everything—Jerónimo and Josefa stole into a denser thicket so as not to sadden anyone with the secret rejoicing of their souls. They found a splendid pomegranate tree with wide-spreading branches full of aromatic fruit; and the nightingale sang its song of delight in the top of the tree.

Here Jerónimo sat down by the tree trunk and, with Josefa in his lap and Felipe in hers, they sat, covered by his cloak, and rested. The shadow of the tree, with its scattering of light, moved over them, and the moon was already growing pale again in anticipation of dawn before they fell asleep. For they had an infinite number of things to talk about, the convent garden, and the prisons, and what they had gone through for each other; and they were very moved when they thought of how much misery had to come upon the world for them to be happy!

They decided to go to Concepción, where Josefa had an intimate woman friend, as soon as the earth tremors ended; with a small loan that she hoped to receive from her they would take ship for Spain, where Jerónimo's maternal relatives lived, and remain happily there to the end of their days. Then, exchanging many kisses, they fell asleep.

When they awoke the sun was already high in the sky, and they noticed several families near them busy preparing a small breakfast by the fire. Jerónimo, too, was just thinking how he could procure food for his own family, when a well-dressed young man with a child in his arms came over to Josefa and discreetly asked her whether she would not briefly nurse the poor infant whose mother was lying injured under the trees there.

Josefa was a little confused when she recognized him as an acquaintance; but when, misinterpreting her confusion, he continued, "It would be just for a few minutes, Doña Josefa, and this child has had no nourishment since the moment that was calamitous for us all," she replied: "My silence—was for a different reason, Don Fernando; in these terrible times no one refuses to give a share of whatever he possesses." She took the little stranger, giving her own child to his father, and laid him to her breast.

Don Fernando was very grateful for this kindness and asked whether they did not wish to accompany him to that group of people who were just preparing a small breakfast by the fire. Josefa replied that she would accept that invitation with pleasure, and, since Jerónimo had no objection either, she followed Don Fernando to his family and was received most heartily and tenderly by his two sisters-in-law, whom she knew to be very respectable young ladies.

When Doña Elvira, Don Fernando's wife, who was lying on the ground with severe foot wounds, saw her hungry child at Josefa's breast, she drew her down toward herself with great friendliness. Don Pedro, too, Fernando's father-in-law, who was wounded in the shoulder, nodded to her kindly.

Thoughts of a strange kind stirred in the hearts of Jerónimo and Josefa. If they found themselves treated with so much familiarity and goodness, they did not know in what light to consider the past, the place of execution, the prison and the bell; had they merely dreamed all that? It was as if all minds were reconciled since the fearsome blow that had stunned them. They could go no farther back in their memory than to the catastrophe.

Only Doña Isabel, who had been invited to stay with a lady friend in order to see the previous morning's spectacle, but had not accepted the invitation, let her dreamy gaze occasionally rest on Josefa; but an account that was made of some ghastly new misfortune jerked her mind back into the present, from which it had barely escaped. It was reported that right after the first main tremor the city had been full of women who went into labor in the sight of all the men; that the monks had run about, crucifixes in their hands, shouting that the end of the world was at hand; that a guard who had requested the evacuation of a church by order of the viceroy received the reply that there was no longer any viceroy of Chile; that at the most fearful moments the viceroy had been compelled to have gallows erected to put a halt to looting; and that an innocent man who had entered a burning house from the back to save himself had been seized by the overhasty owner and immediately hanged.

Doña Elvira, to whose wounds Josefa was busily attending, had at one point—just when these stories were arriving most quickly, each interrupting the other—taken the opportunity to ask her how *she* had fared on that terrible day. And when, with anguished heart, Josefa recounted some of the main features of her story, she was delighted to see tears well up in that lady's eyes; Doña Elvira seized her hand and squeezed it and gestured to her to be silent.

Josefa counted herself among the blessed. With a feeling she could not suppress, she began to consider the previous day—despite all the misery it had brought to the world—a benefaction greater than any yet vouchsafed her by heaven. And, indeed, in the midst of these awful moments, in which all the earthly goods of man were destroyed and all of nature was threatened with burial, the human spirit itself seemed to open out like a beautiful flower.

In the fields, as far as the eye could reach, people of all ranks could be seen mingled together, princes and beggars, matrons and peasant women, bureaucrats and day laborers, monks and nuns. They sympathized with one another, assisted one another and cheerfully shared whatever they had been able to save to keep themselves alive, as if the universal calamity had made a single family of all who had escaped it.

Instead of the usual meaningless tea-table chitchat based on mundane events, now they narrated examples of extraordinary feats: people who had normally been of low esteem in society had shown greatness worthy of ancient Romans; there were examples in plenty of fearlessness, of cheerful disregard of danger, of self-denial and godlike self-sacrifice, of the unhesitating casting away of one's own life as if, like the most worthless possession, it might be recovered the next minute. Yes, since there was no one who had not had some emotional experience on that day, or who had not himself done something magnanimous, the sorrow in every heart was mingled with so much sweet pleasure that Josefa felt it could not be determined whether the sum of universal welfare had not increased on the one hand just as much as it had been diminished on the other.

Jerónimo took Josefa by the arm, after the two of them had silently dwelt on these thoughts for as long as they wished, and led her to and fro beneath the leafy shade of the pomegranate grove with enormous cheerfulness. He told her that, in view of this general frame of mind and this revolution in the entire social order, he was abandoning his decision to take ship for Europe; that he would risk prostrating himself before the viceroy (should he still be alive), who had always favored his cause; and that he had hopes—and here he kissed her—of remaining in Chile with her.

Josefa replied that similar thoughts had occurred to her; that, were her father only still alive, she too no longer doubted she could be reconciled with him; but that, instead of the personal petition to the viceroy, she advised going to Concepción and corresponding with the viceroy from there with the aim of reconciliation; in Concepción they would be close to the harbor in any case, and in the best case—if the affair should take the desired turn—they could easily return to Santiago. After considering the wisdom of these measures briefly, Jerónimo gave them his approval, walked around with her a little more on the forest paths, speaking about the happy times they would have in the future, and returned to their group with her.

Meanwhile it had become afternoon, and the minds of the refugees who were roving about had barely become a little calmer again—now that the tremors were abating—when the news spread that in the Dominican church, the only one spared by the earthquake, a solemn Mass would be read by the prior of the monastery himself, to beseech heaven to prevent further disaster. People were already starting out all over the countryside and hastening to the city in throngs.

In Don Fernando's party the question was raised whether or not to participate in this solemnity and join the general procession. Doña Isabel, with some anguish, reminded them what a calamity had occurred in the church the day before; she remarked that thanksgiving celebrations like this one would be repeated, and that at a later date, when the danger would be clearly past, they could give vent to their feelings all the more cheerfully and calmly.

Josefa, standing up quickly with a degree of enthusiasm, stated that she had never felt a livelier urge to lay her face in the dust before her Creator than she did right then, when He was thus manifesting His incomprehensible and lofty power. Doña Elvira declared with vivacity that she shared Josefa's opinion. She insisted upon hearing the Mass, and called upon Don Fernando to lead their group; whereupon everyone stood up, including Doña Isabel.

But when Isabel, her breast heaving violently, lagged back upon observing their little preparations for departure and, on being asked what was wrong with her, replied that she had a strange foreboding of disaster, Doña Elvira calmed her and invited her to stay behind with her and her wounded father, Josefa said: "In that case, Doña Isabel, perhaps you would take my little darling, who, as you see, is with me once again." "Very gladly," answered Doña Isabel, and made as if to take hold of him; but when he screamed lamentably over the injustice being done him and would in no way consent to it, Josefa said with a smile that she would keep him, and she kissed him until he was quiet again.

Then Don Fernando, who was very pleased with all the dignity and grace of her demeanor, offered her his arm; Jerónimo, who carried little Felipe, escorted Doña Constancia; the other people who had become members of the group followed; and in this order they proceeded to the city.

They had scarcely gone fifty paces when Doña Isabel, who had meanwhile been engaged in vehement secret conversation with Doña Elvira, was heard to call: "Don Fernando!" and was seen hastening toward the walking group with agitated steps. Don Fernando halted and turned around; he tarried for her without releasing his hold on Josefa and—when she stopped at some distance as if waiting for him to meet her partway—he asked her what she wished.

Then Doña Isabel approached him, although with reluctance as it seemed, and murmured a few words in his ear, too low for Josefa to hear. "Well," asked Don Fernando, "and what calamity can arise from that?" Doña Isabel continued to whisper in his ear with a haggard expression on her face. Don Fernando's face grew red with displeasure; he replied: "All right! Please tell Doña Elvira to calm down," and continued to escort Josefa onward.

When they arrived at the Dominican church, they could already hear the musical splendor of the organ, and a countless number of people were surging inside. Outside the doors the crowd stretched far out over the forecourt of the church, and high up on the walls, in the frames of the paintings, boys were perched, holding their caps in their hands with an expectant gaze. Light poured down from all the chandeliers; the pillars cast mysterious shadows in the twilight that was falling; the great stained-glass rose window at the far back of the church glowed like the very evening sun that illuminated it; and, now that the organ had fallen silent, silence reigned in the whole congregation as if no one had a word to say. Never did a flame of ardor leap up to heaven from a Christian church as on that day from the Dominican church in Santiago; and no human heart added a warmer glow to the whole than Jerónimo's and Josefa's!

The celebration began with a sermon spoken from the pulpit by the oldest prebendary, dressed in ceremonial robes. Raising to heaven his trembling hands, which were encircled by his surplice, he began immediately with praise, glorification and thanks that in that part of the world, which was falling into ruins, there were still people able to stammer their thanks to God. He described what had occurred at the beck of the Almighty; the Last Judgment could not be more awesome; and when, pointing to a crack that the church had sustained, he called the previous day's earthquake merely a foretaste, as it were, a shudder ran through the entire congregation.

Next, in the flow of his sacerdotal eloquence, he turned to the moral depravity of the city; he castigated the city for abominations unknown to Sodom and Gomorrah; and he ascribed it only to the infinite forbearance of God that Santiago had not yet been totally wiped out by the earthquake. But the hearts of our two unfortunates, already deeply wounded by this sermon, were stabbed as by a dagger when the prebendary took this opportunity to mention circumstantially the sin that had been committed in the Carmelites' convent garden; he termed the indulgence it had received from society "godless" and, in a parenthetical passage filled with curses, consigned the souls of the perpetrators, mentioned by name, to all the princes of hell!

Doña Constancia, tugging Jerónimo's arm, cried out: "Don Fernando!" But the latter replied, as forcefully as was consonant with his secret tones: "Doña, be silent, don't move a muscle, and pretend to faint; then we will leave the church." But before Doña Constancia had taken these ingeniously conceived measures for escape, a voice, loudly interrupting the prebendary's sermon, was already exclaiming: "Stand well back, citizens of Santiago, here are these godless people!" And when another voice fearfully asked "Where?"—while a wide circle of horror formed around them— "Here!" replied a third and, with vileness prompted by religion, dragged Josefa down by the hair so that she would have reeled to the floor with Don Fernando's son if the Don had not been holding onto her.

"Are you insane?" shouted the young man, putting his arm around Josefa: "I am Don Fernando Ormez, son of the commandant of the city, whom you all know." "Don Fernando Ormez?" shouted a cobbler, standing directly in front of him; this cobbler had done work for Josefa and knew her at least as well as he knew her dainty feet. "Who is the father of this child?" he said, turning with insolent defiance toward Asterón's daughter.

Don Fernando turned pale at that question. Now he looked timidly at Jerónimo, now he glanced quickly over the congregation to see if there was anyone who knew him. Josefa, urged on by the frightening situation, cried out: "This is not my child as you think, Master Pedrillo," and, looking at Don Fernando in extreme anguish of soul, "this young gentleman is Don Fernando Ormez, son of the commandant of the city, whom you all know." The cobbler asked: "Citizens, who among you knows this young man?"

And several of those standing near repeated: "Who can recognize Jerónimo Rugera? Let him step forth!"

Now, it happened that at the same moment little Juan, frightened by the uproar, strained to leave Josefa's breast for Don Fernando's arms. Whereupon, "He *is* the father!" a voice shouted; a second voice called, "He *is* Jerónimo Rugera!"; a third, "They *are* the blasphemous people!"; and "Stone them! Stone them!" cried all the Christians assembled in the temple of Jesus!

Then Jerónimo said, "Stop, you inhuman people! If you seek Jerónimo Rugera, he is here! Release that man, who is innocent!" The furious mob, confused by Jerónimo's statement, hesitated; several hands loosed their grip on Don Fernando; and when at the same moment a naval officer of high rank rushed over and, pushing through the press of people, asked, "Don Fernando Ormez, what has happened to you?," Don Fernando, now completely free, answered with truly heroic self-possession: "Just look at these assassins, Don Alonzo! I would have been lost if this estimable man had not pretended to be Jerónimo Rugera to pacify the raging crowd. Be so good as to take him as well as this young lady into custody for the protection of both; and," seizing Master Pedrillo: "Arrest this scoundrel, who instigated the whole uproar!"

The cobbler shouted: "Don Alonzo Onoreja, I ask you on your conscience, is this girl not Josefa Asterón?" When Don Alonzo, who knew Josefa very well, hesitated to answer, and several bystanders, in whom this kindled new rage, called: "It is she, it is she!" and "Death to her!," Josefa placed little Felipe, whom Jerónimo had been carrying up to then, in Don Fernando's arms together with little Juan, and said: "Go, Don Fernando, save your two children and leave us to our fate!"

Don Fernando took the two children and said that he would rather be killed than allow harm to befall his party. After requesting the naval officer's sword, he offered Josefa his arm and invited the couple behind him to follow him. The crowd, impressed by this procedure, made way for them with a sufficient show of respect, and they actually managed to leave the church, thinking they were safe.

But scarcely had they stepped into the forecourt, which was just as crowded with people, when a man from the frenzied throng that had dogged their steps called: "Citizens, this is Jerónimo Rugera, for I am his own father!" and knocked him to the ground at Doña

Constancia's side with a mighty cudgel blow. "Jesus and Mary!" shouted Doña Constancia, fleeing to her brother-in-law; but there were already cries of "Convent whore!" and from another side came a second cudgel blow that laid her lifeless alongside Jerónimo.

"Monsters!" shouted an unidentified man, "that was Doña Constancia Xares!" "Why did they lie to us?" replied the cobbler; "find the right woman and kill her!" When Don Fernando caught sight of Constancia's body, he burned with anger; he drew the sword, swung it and aimed a stroke at the fanatical assassin who had caused these abominations, a furious stroke that would have cut him in two had he not eluded it by a twist of his body.

But when she saw that the Don could not overpower the mob crowding in on him, Josefa cried: "Farewell, Don Fernando, you and the children!" and "Here, murder me, you bloodthirsty tigers!" and voluntarily threw herself into their midst, to put an end to the combat. Master Pedrillo felled her with his cudgel. Then, spattered all over with her blood, he cried: "Send her bastard to hell after her!" and, his blood lust still unsated, pushed forward again.

Don Fernando, that godlike hero, now stood with his back leaning on the church; with his left hand he held the children, in his right hand the sword. With every flash of his weapon an opponent fell to the ground; a lion does not defend itself better. Seven ravenous dogs lay dead before him, even the prince of the satanic horde was wounded. But Master Pedrillo could not rest until he had pulled one of the children away from his bosom by the legs and, swinging it through the air in a circle, had shattered it against the corner of a church pillar.

Then all became quiet and everyone withdrew. Don Fernando, seeing little Juan lying before him with his brains oozing out, raised his eyes to heaven in inexpressible sorrow. The naval officer rejoined him, attempted to console him and assured him that he regretted his lack of participation in those unhappy events, although it was excusable because of the circumstances; but Don Fernando said that he was not at all to blame and merely asked him to help carry away the bodies now.

In the darkness of the night that was falling they were all brought to Don Alonzo's residence; Don Fernando followed them there, shedding many tears on little Felipe's face. He spent the night at Don Alonzo's, too, and, misrepresenting the true situation to his wife, hesitated a long time before informing her of the whole extent of the tragedy—for one thing, because she was ill, and another, because he did not know how she would judge his conduct during those events. But shortly afterward, happening to be apprised by a visitor of all that had occurred, that excellent lady quietly wept her fill over her maternal sorrow and, one morning, with the last tears still glistening in her eyes, fell about his neck and kissed him. Then Don Fernando and Doña Elvira adopted the little stranger as their own son; and when Don Fernando compared Felipe to Juan and thought of how he had acquired both, he felt almost as if he should rejoice.

D. H. LAWRENCE

[England]

D. H. LAWRENCE (1885–1930), the son of a coal-miner in the East
Midlands of England, became a schoolteacher before giving up that
career, at age twenty-six, to write full-time. Despite various illnesses
and the tuberculosis that eventually killed him, he burned through
life and wrote dozens of books, among them some of the finest collections of poems, short stories, novels, travelogues, and literary
criticism in English literature. Lawrence ran off with and married
Frieda Weekley, the wife of one of his former professors, in 1912;
Lawrence often wrote fictionally and non-fictionally about the
couple's vital and volatile relationship. The critic Marvin Mudrick
considered "The White Stocking," about a newlywed couple, the
best short story ever written.

The White Stocking (1914)

I

"I'M GETTING UP, Teddilinks," said Mrs. Whiston, and she sprang
out of bed briskly.

"What the Hanover's got you?" asked Whiston.

"Nothing. Can't I get up?" she replied animatedly.

It was about seven o'clock, scarcely light yet in the cold bedroom. Whiston lay still and looked at his wife. She was a pretty
little thing, with her fleecy, short black hair all tousled. He
watched her as she dressed quickly, flicking her small, delightful
limbs, throwing her clothes about her. Her slovenliness and unti-
diness did not trouble him. When she picked up the edge of her

116

petticoat, ripped off a torn string of white lace, and flung it on the dressing-table, her careless abandon made his spirit glow. She stood before the mirror and roughly scrambled together her profuse little mane of hair. He watched the quickness and softness of her young shoulders, calmly, like a husband, and appreciatively.

"Rise up," she cried, turning to him with a quick wave of her arm— "and shine forth."

They had been married two years. But still, when she had gone out of the room, he felt as if all his light and warmth were taken away, he became aware of the raw, cold morning. So he rose himself, wondering casually what had roused her so early. Usually she lay in bed as late as she could.

Whiston fastened a belt round his loins and went downstairs in shirt and trousers. He heard her singing in her snatchy fashion. The stairs creaked under his weight. He passed down the narrow little passage, which she called a hall, of the seven and sixpenny house which was his first home.

He was a shapely young fellow of about twenty-eight, sleepy now and easy with well-being. He heard the water drumming into the kettle, and she began to whistle. He loved the quick way she dodged the supper cups under the tap to wash them for breakfast. She looked an untidy minx, but she was quick and handy enough.

"Teddilinks," she cried.

"What?"

"Light a fire, quick."

She wore an old, sack-like dressing-jacket of black silk pinned across her breast. But one of the sleeves, coming unfastened, showed some delightful pink upper-arm.

"Why don't you sew your sleeve up?" he said, suffering from the sight of the exposed soft flesh.

"Where?" she cried, peering round. "Nuisance," she said, seeing the gap, then with light fingers went on drying the cups.

The kitchen was of fair size, but gloomy. Whiston poked out the dead ashes.

Suddenly a thud was heard at the door down the passage.

"I'll go," cried Mrs. Whiston, and she was gone down the hall.

The postman was a ruddy-faced man who had been a soldier. He smiled broadly, handing her some packages.

"They've not forgot you," he said impudently.

"No—lucky for them," she said, with a toss of the head. But she was interested only in her envelopes this morning. The postman waited inquisitively, smiling in an ingratiating fashion. She slowly, abstractedly, as if she did not know anyone was there, closed the door in his face, continuing to look at the addresses on her letters.

She tore open the thin envelope. There was a long, hideous, cartoon valentine. She smiled briefly and dropped it on the floor. Struggling with the string of a packet, she opened a white cardboard box, and there lay a white silk handkerchief packed neatly under the paper lace of the box, and her initial, worked in heliotrope, fully displayed. She smiled pleasantly, and gently put the box aside. The third envelope contained another white packet— apparently a cotton handkerchief neatly folded. She shook it out. It was a long white stocking, but there was a little weight in the toe. Quickly, she thrust down her arm, wriggling her fingers into the toe of the stocking, and brought out a small box. She peeped inside the box, then hastily opened a door on her left hand, and went into the little, cold sitting-room. She had her lower lip caught earnestly between her teeth.

With a little flash of triumph, she lifted a pair of pearl ear-rings from the small box, and she went to the mirror. There, earnestly, she began to hook them through her ears, looking at herself sideways in the glass. Curiously concentrated and intent she seemed as she fingered the lobes of her ears, her head bent on one side.

Then the pearl ear-rings dangled under her rosy, small ears. She shook her head sharply, to see the swing of the drops. They went chill against her neck, in little, sharp touches. Then she stood still to look at herself, bridling her head in the dignified fashion. Then she simpered at herself. Catching her own eye, she could not help winking at herself and laughing.

She turned to look at the box. There was a scrap of paper with this posy:

> "Pearls may be fair, but thou art fairer.
> Wear these for me, and I'll love the wearer."

She made a grimace and a grin. But she was drawn to the mirror again, to look at her ear-rings.

Whiston had made the fire burn, so he came to look for her. When she heard him, she started round quickly, guiltily. She was watching him with intent blue eyes when he appeared.

He did not see much, in his morning-drowsy warmth. He gave her, as ever, a feeling of warmth and slowness. His eyes were very blue, very kind, his manner simple.

"What ha' you got?" he asked.

"Valentines," she said briskly, ostentatiously turning to show him the silk handkerchief. She thrust it under his nose. "Smell how good," she said.

"Who's that from?" he replied, without smelling.

"It's a valentine," she cried. "How do I know who it's from?"

"I'll bet you know," he said.

"Ted!—I don't!" she cried, beginning to shake her head, then stopping because of the ear-rings.

He stood still a moment, displeased.

"They've no right to send you valentines, now," he said.

"Ted!—Why not? You're not jealous, are you? I haven't the least idea who it's from. Look—there's my initial"—she pointed with an emphatic finger at the heliotrope embroidery—

"E for Elsie,
    Nice little gelsie,"

she sang.

"Get out," he said. "You know who it's from."

"Truth, I don't," she cried.

He looked round, and saw the white stocking lying on a chair.

"Is this another?" he said.

"No, that's a sample," she said. "There's only a comic." And she fetched in the long cartoon.

He stretched it out and looked at it solemnly.

"Fools!" he said, and went out of the room.

She flew upstairs and took off the ear-rings. When she returned, he was crouched before the fire blowing the coals. The skin of his face was flushed, and slightly pitted, as if he had had small-pox. But his neck was white and smooth and goodly. She hung her arms round his neck as he crouched there, and clung to him. He balanced on his toes.

"This fire's a slow-coach," he said.

"And who else is a slow-coach?" she said.

"One of us two, I know," he said, and he rose carefully. She remained clinging round his neck, so that she was lifted off her feet.

"Ha!—swing me," she cried.

He lowered his head, and she hung in the air, swinging from his neck, laughing. Then she slipped off.

"The kettle is singing," she sang, flying for the teapot. He bent down again to blow the fire. The veins in his neck stood out, his shirt collar seemed too tight.

> "Doctor Wyer,
> Blow the fire,
> Puff! puff! puff!"

she sang, laughing.

He smiled at her.

She was so glad because of her pearl ear-rings.

Over the breakfast she grew serious. He did not notice. She became portentous in her gravity. Almost it penetrated through his steady good-humour to irritate him.

"Teddy!" she said at last.

"What?" he asked.

"I told you a lie," she said, humbly tragic.

His soul stirred uneasily.

"Oh aye?" he said casually.

She was not satisfied. He ought to be more moved.

"Yes," she said.

He cut a piece of bread.

"Was it a good one?" he asked.

She was piqued. Then she considered—*was* it a good one? Then she laughed.

"No," she said, "it wasn't up to much."

"Ah!" he said easily, but with a steady strength of fondness for her in his tone. "Get it out then."

It became a little more difficult.

"You know that white stocking," she said earnestly. "I told you a lie. It wasn't a sample. It was a valentine."

A little frown came on his brow.

"Then what did you invent it as a sample for?" he said. But he knew this weakness of hers. The touch of anger in his voice frightened her.

"I was afraid you'd be cross," she said pathetically.

"I'll bet you were vastly afraid," he said.

"I *was*, Teddy."

There was a pause. He was resolving one or two things in his mind.

"And who sent it?" he asked.

"I can guess," she said, "though there wasn't a word with it—except—"

She ran to the sitting-room and returned with a slip of paper.

> "Pearls may be fair, but thou art fairer
> Wear these for me, and I'll love the wearer."

He read it twice, then a dull red flush came on his face.

"And *who* do you guess it is?" he asked, with a ringing of anger in his voice.

"I suspect it's Sam Adams," she said, with a little virtuous indignation.

Whiston was silent for a moment.

"Fool!" he said. "An' what's it got to do with pearls?—and how can he say 'wear these for me' when there's only one? He hasn't got the brain to invent a proper verse."

He screwed the slip of paper into a ball and flung it into the fire.

"I suppose he thinks it'll make a pair with the one last year," she said.

"Why, did he send one then?"

"Yes. I thought you'd be wild if you knew."

His jaw set rather sullenly.

Presently he rose, and went to wash himself, rolling back his sleeves and pulling open his shirt at the breast. It was as if his fine, clear-cut temples and steady eyes were degraded by the lower, rather brutal part of his face. But she loved it. As she whisked about, clearing the table, she loved the way in which he stood washing himself. He was such a man. She liked to see his neck glistening with water as he swilled it. It amused her and pleased her and thrilled her. He was so sure, so permanent, he had her so utterly in his power. It gave her a delightful, mischievous sense of liberty. Within his grasp, she could dart about excitingly.

He turned round to her, his face red from the cold water, his eyes fresh and very blue.

"You haven't been seeing anything of him, have you?" he asked roughly.

"Yes," she answered, after a moment, as if caught guilty. "He got into the tram with me, and he asked me to drink a coffee and a Benedictine in the Royal."

"You've got it off fine and glib," he said sullenly. "And did you?"

"Yes," she replied, with the air of a traitor before the rack.

The blood came up into his neck and face, he stood motionless, dangerous.

"It was cold, and it was such fun to go into the Royal," she said.

"You'd go off with a nigger for a packet of chocolate," he said, in anger and contempt, and some bitterness. Queer how he drew away from her, cut her off from him.

"Ted—how beastly!" she cried. "You know quite well——" She caught her lip, flushed, and the tears came to her eyes.

He turned away, to put on his necktie. She went about her work, making a queer pathetic little mouth, down which occasionally dripped a tear.

He was ready to go. With his hat jammed down on his head, and his overcoat buttoned up to his chin, he came to kiss her. He would be miserable all the day if he went without. She allowed herself to be kissed. Her cheek was wet under his lips, and his heart burned. She hurt him so deeply. And she felt aggrieved, and did not quite forgive him.

In a moment she went upstairs to her ear-rings. Sweet they looked nestling in the little drawer—sweet! She examined them with voluptuous pleasure, she threaded them in her ears, she looked at herself, she posed and postured and smiled, and looked sad and tragic and winning and appealing, all in turn before the mirror. And she was happy, and very pretty.

She wore her ear-rings all morning, in the house. She was self-conscious, and quite brilliantly winsome, when the baker came, wondering if he would notice. All the tradesmen left her door with a glow in them, feeling elated, and unconsciously favouring the delightful little creature, though there had been nothing to notice in her behaviour.

She was stimulated all the day. She did not think about her husband. He was the permanent basis from which she took these giddy little flights into nowhere. At night, like chickens and curses, she would come home to him, to roost.

Meanwhile Whiston, a traveller and confidential support of a small firm, hastened about his work, his heart all the while anxious for her, yearning for surety, and kept tense by not getting it.

II

She had been a warehouse girl in Adams's lace factory before she was married. Sam Adams was her employer. He was a bachelor of forty, growing stout, a man well dressed and florid, with a large brown moustache and thin hair. From the rest of his well-groomed, showy appearance, it was evident his baldness was a chagrin to him. He had a good presence, and some Irish blood in his veins.

His fondness for the girls, or the fondness of the girls for him, was notorious. And Elsie, quick, pretty, almost witty little thing—she *seemed* witty, although, when her sayings were repeated, they were entirely trivial—she had a great attraction for him. He would come into the warehouse dressed in a rather sporting reefer coat, of fawn colour, and trousers of fine black-and-white check, a cap with a big peak and a scarlet carnation in his button-hole, to impress her. She was only half impressed. He was too loud for her good taste. Instinctively perceiving this, he sobered down to navy blue. Then a well-built man, florid, with large brown whiskers, smart navy blue suit, fashionable boots, and manly hat, he was the irreproachable. Elsie was impressed.

But meanwhile Whiston was courting her, and she made splendid little gestures, before her bedroom mirror, of the constant-and-true sort.

"True, true till death—"

That was her song. Whiston was made that way, so there was no need to take thought for him.

Every Christmas Sam Adams gave a party at his house, to which he invited his superior work-people—not factory hands and labourers, but those above. He was a generous man in his way, with a real warm feeling for giving pleasure.

Two years ago Elsie had attended this Christmas-party for the last time. Whiston had accompanied her. At that time he worked for Sam Adams.

She had been very proud of herself, in her close-fitting, full-skirted dress of blue silk. Whiston called for her. Then she tripped beside him, holding her large cashmere shawl across her breast. He strode with long strides, his trousers handsomely strapped under his boots, and her silk shoes bulging the pockets of his full-skirted overcoat.

They passed through the park gates, and her spirits rose. Above them the Castle Rock loomed grandly in the night, the naked trees stood still and dark in the frost, along the boulevard.

They were rather late. Agitated with anticipation, in the cloak-room she gave up her shawl, donned her silk shoes, and looked at herself in the mirror. The loose bunches of curls on either side her face danced prettily, her mouth smiled.

She hung a moment in the door of the brilliantly lighted room. Many people were moving within the blaze of lamps, under the crystal chandeliers, the full skirts of the women balancing and float-ing, the side-whiskers and white cravats of the men bowing above. Then she entered the light.

In an instant Sam Adams was coming forward, lifting both his arms in boisterous welcome. There was a constant red laugh on his face.

"Come late, would you," he shouted, "like royalty."

He seized her hands and led her forward. He opened his mouth wide when he spoke, and the effect of the warm, dark opening behind the brown whiskers was disturbing. But she was floating into the throng on his arm. He was very gallant.

"Now then," he said, taking her card to write down the dances, "I've got carte blanche, haven't I?"

"Mr. Whiston doesn't dance," she said.

"I am a lucky man!" he said, scribbling his initials. "I was born with an *amourette* in my mouth."

He wrote on, quietly. She blushed and laughed, not knowing what it meant.

"Why, what is that?" she said.

"It's you, even littler than you are, dressed in little wings," he said.

"I should have to be pretty small to get in your mouth," she said.

"You think you're too big, do you!" he said easily.

He handed her her card, with a bow.

"Now I'm set up, my darling, for this evening," he said.

Then, quick, always at his ease, he looked over the room. She waited in front of him. He was ready. Catching the eye of the band, he nodded. In a moment, the music began. He seemed to relax, giving himself up.

"Now then, Elsie," he said, with a curious caress in his voice that seemed to lap the outside of her body in a warm glow, delicious. She gave herself to it. She liked it.

He was an excellent dancer. He seemed to draw her close in to him by some male warmth of attraction, so that she became all soft and pliant to him, flowing to his form, whilst he united her with him and they lapsed along in one movement. She was just carried in a kind of strong, warm flood, her feet moved of themselves, and only the music threw her away from him, threw her back to him, to his clasp, in his strong form moving against her, rhythmically, deliciously.

When it was over, he was pleased and his eyes had a curious gleam which thrilled her and yet had nothing to do with her. Yet it held her. He did not speak to her. He only looked straight into her eyes with a curious, gleaming look that disturbed her fearfully and deliciously. But also there was in his look some of the automatic irony of the *roué*. It left her partly cold. She was not carried away.

She went, driven by an opposite, heavier impulse, to Whiston. He stood looking gloomy, trying to admit that she had a perfect right to enjoy herself apart from him. He received her with rather grudging kindliness.

"Aren't you going to play whist?" she asked.

"Aye," he said. "Directly."

"I do wish you could dance."

"Well, I can't," he said. "So you enjoy yourself."

"But I should enjoy it better if I could dance with you."

"Nay, you're all right," he said. "I'm not made that way."

"Then you ought to be!" she cried.

"Well, it's my fault, not yours. You enjoy yourself," he bade her. Which she proceeded to do, a little bit irked.

She went with anticipation to the arms of Sam Adams, when the time came to dance with him. It *was* so gratifying, irrespective of the man. And she felt a little grudge against Whiston, soon forgotten when her host was holding her near to him, in a delicious embrace. And she watched his eyes, to meet the gleam in them, which gratified her.

She was getting warmed right through, the glow was penetrating into her, driving away everything else. Only in her heart was a little tightness, like conscience.

When she got a chance, she escaped from the dancing-room to the card-room. There, in a cloud of smoke, she found Whiston playing cribbage. Radiant, roused, animated, she came up to him and greeted him. She was too strong, too vibrant a note in the quiet room. He lifted his head, and a frown knitted his gloomy forehead.

"Are you playing cribbage? Is it exciting? How are you getting on?" she chattered.

He looked at her. None of these questions needed answering, and he did not feel in touch with her. She turned to the cribbage-board.

"Are you white or red?" she asked.

"He's red," replied the partner.

"Then you're losing," she said, still to Whiston. And she lifted the red peg from the board. "One—two—three—four—five—six—seven—eight—— Right up there you ought to jump—"

"Now put it back in its right place," said Whiston.

"Where was it?" she asked gaily, knowing her transgression. He took the little red peg away from her and stuck it in its hole.

The cards were shuffled.

"What a shame you're losing!" said Elsie.

"You'd better cut for him," said the partner.

She did so, hastily. The cards were dealt. She put her hand on his shoulder, looking at his cards.

"It's good," she cried, "isn't it?"

He did not answer, but threw down two cards. It moved him more strongly than was comfortable, to have her hand on his shoulder, her curls dangling and touching his ears, whilst she was roused to another man. It made the blood flame over him.

At that moment Sam Adams appeared, florid and boisterous, intoxicated more with himself, with the dancing, than with wine. In his eye the curious, impersonal light gleamed.

"I thought I should find you here, Elsie," he cried boisterously, a disturbing, high note in his voice.

"What made you think so?" she replied, the mischief rousing in her.

The florid, well-built man narrowed his eyes to a smile.

"I should never look for you among the ladies," he said, with a kind of intimate, animal call to her. He laughed, bowed, and offered her his arm.

"Madam, the music waits."

She went almost helplessly, carried along with him, unwilling, yet delighted.

That dance was an intoxication to her. After the first few steps, she felt herself slipping away from herself. She almost knew she was going, she did not even want to go. Yet she must have chosen to go. She lay in the arm of the steady, close man with whom she was dancing, and she seemed to swim away out of contact with the room, into him. She had passed into another, denser element of him, an essential privacy. The room was all vague around her, like an atmosphere, like under sea, with a flow of ghostly, dumb movements. But she herself was held real against her partner, and it seemed she was connected with him, as if the movements of his body and limbs were her own movements, yet not her own movements—and oh, delicious! He also was given up, oblivious, concentrated, into the dance. His eye was unseeing. Only his large, voluptuous body gave off a subtle activity. His fingers seemed to search into her flesh. Every moment, and every moment, she felt she would give way utterly, and sink molten: the fusion point was coming when she would fuse down into perfect unconsciousness at his feet and knees. But he bore her round the room in the dance, and he seemed to sustain all her body with his limbs, his body, and his warmth seemed to come closer into her, nearer, till it would fuse right through her, and she would be as liquid to him, as an intoxication only.

It was exquisite. When it was over, she was dazed, and was scarcely breathing. She stood with him in the middle of the room as if she were alone in a remote place. He bent over her. She expected his lips on her bare shoulder, and waited. Yet they were not alone, they were not alone. It was cruel.

"'Twas good, wasn't it, my darling?" he said to her, low and delighted. There was a strange impersonality about his low, exultant call that appealed to her irresistibly. Yet why was she aware of some part shut off in her? She pressed his arm, and he led her towards the door.

She was not aware of what she was doing, only a little grain of resistant trouble was in her. The man, possessed, yet with a superficial presence of mind, made way to the dining-room, as if to give her refreshment, cunningly working to his own escape with her. He was molten hot, filmed over with presence of mind, and bottomed with cold disbelief.

In the dining-room was Whiston, carrying coffee to the plain, neglected ladies. Elsie saw him, but felt as if he could not see her. She was beyond his reach and ken. A sort of fusion existed between her and the huge man at her side. She ate her custard, but an incomplete fusion all the while sustained and contained within the being of her employer.

But she was growing cooler. Whiston came up. She looked at him, and saw him with different eyes. She saw his slim, young man's figure real and enduring before her. That was he. But she was in the spell with the other man, fused with him, and she could not be taken away.

"Have you finished your cribbage?" she asked, with hasty evasion of him.

"Yes," he replied. "Aren't you getting tired of dancing?"

"Not a bit," she said.

"Not she," said Adams heartily. "No girl with any spirit gets tired of dancing.—Have something else, Elsie. Come—sherry. Have a glass of sherry with us, Whiston."

Whilst they sipped the wine, Adams watched Whiston almost cunningly, to find his advantage.

"We'd better be getting back—there's the music," he said. "See the women get something to eat, Whiston, will you, there's a good chap."

And he began to draw away. Elsie was drifting helplessly with him. But Whiston put himself beside them, and went along with them. In silence they passed through to the dancing-room. There Adams hesitated, and looked round the room. It was as if he could not see.

A man came hurrying forward, claiming Elsie, and Adams went to his other partner. Whiston stood watching during the dance. She was conscious of him standing there observant of her, like a ghost, or a judgment, or a guardian angel. She was also conscious, much more intimately and impersonally, of the body of the other man moving somewhere in the room. She still belonged to him, but a feeling of distraction possessed her, and helplessness. Adams danced on, adhering to Elsie, waiting his time, with the persistence of cynicism.

The dance was over. Adams was detained. Elsie found herself beside Whiston. There was something shapely about him as he sat, about his knees and his distinct figure, that she clung to. It was as if he had enduring form. She put her hand on his knee.

"Are you enjoying yourself?" he asked.

"Ever so," she replied, with a fervent, yet detached tone.

"It's going on for one o'clock," he said.

"Is it?" she answered. It meant nothing to her.

"Should we be going?" he said.

She was silent. For the first time for an hour or more an inkling of her normal consciousness returned. She resented it.

"What for?" she said.

"I thought you might have had enough," he said.

A slight soberness came over her, an irritation at being frustrated of her illusion.

"Why?" she said.

"We've been here since nine," he said.

That was no answer, no reason. It conveyed nothing to her. She sat detached from him. Across the room Sam Adams glanced at her. She sat there exposed for him.

"You don't want to be too free with Sam Adams," said Whiston cautiously, suffering. "You know what he is."

"How, free?" she asked.

"Why—you don't want to have too much to do with him."

She sat silent. He was forcing her into consciousness of her position. But he could not get hold of her feelings, to change them. She had a curious, perverse desire that he should not.

"I like him," she said.

"What do you find to like in him?" he said, with a hot heart.

"I don't know—but I like him," she said.

She was immutable. He sat feeling heavy and dulled with rage. He was not clear as to what he felt. He sat there unliving whilst she danced. And she, distracted, lost to herself between the opposing forces of the two men, drifted. Between the dances, Whiston kept near to her. She was scarcely conscious. She glanced repeatedly at her card, to see when she would dance again with Adams, half in desire, half in dread. Sometimes she met his steady, glaucous eye as she passed him in the dance. Sometimes she saw the steadiness of his flank as he danced. And it was always as if she rested on his arm, were borne along, upborne by him, away from herself. And always there was present the other's antagonism. She was divided.

The time came for her to dance with Adams. Oh, the delicious closing of contact with him, of his limbs touching her limbs, his arm supporting her. She seemed to resolve. Whiston had not made himself real to her. He was only a heavy place in her consciousness.

But she breathed heavily, beginning to suffer from the closeness of strain. She was nervous. Adams also was constrained. A tightness, a tension was coming over them all. And he was exasperated, feeling something counteracting physical magnetism, feeling a will stronger with her than his own, intervening in what was becoming a vital necessity to him.

Elsie was almost lost to her own control. As she went forward with him to take her place at the dance, she stooped for her pocket-handkerchief. The music sounded for quadrilles. Everybody was ready. Adams stood with his body near her, exerting his attraction over her. He was tense and fighting. She stooped for her pocket-handkerchief, and shook it as she rose. It shook out and fell from her hand. With agony, she saw she had taken a white stocking instead of a handkerchief. For a second it lay on the floor, a twist of white stocking. Then, in an instant, Adams picked it up, with a little, surprised laugh of triumph.

"That'll do for me," he whispered—seeming to take possession of her. And he stuffed the stocking in his trousers pocket, and quickly offered her his handkerchief.

The dance began. She felt weak and faint, as if her will were turned to water. A heavy sense of loss came over her. She could not help herself any more. But it was peace.

When the dance was over, Adams yielded her up. Whiston came to her.

"What was it as you dropped?" Whiston asked.

"I thought it was my handkerchief—I'd taken a stocking by mistake," she said, detached and muted.

"And he's got it?"

"Yes."

"What does he mean by that?"

She lifted her shoulders.

"Are you going to let him keep it?" he asked.

"I don't let him."

There was a long pause.

"Am I to go and have it out with him?" he asked, his face flushed, his blue eyes going hard with opposition.

"No," she said, pale.

"Why?"

"No—I don't want you to say anything about it."

He sat exasperated and nonplussed.

"You'll let him keep it, then?" he asked.

She sat silent and made no form of answer.

"What do you mean by it?" he said, dark with fury. And he started up.

"No!" she cried. "Ted!" And she caught hold of him, sharply detaining him.

It made him black with rage.

"Why?" he said.

Then something about her mouth was pitiful to him. He did not understand, but he felt she must have her reasons.

"Then I'm not stopping here," he said. "Are you coming with me?"

She rose mutely, and they went out of the room. Adams had not noticed.

In a few moments they were in the street.

"What the hell do you mean?" he said, in a black fury.

She went at his side, in silence, neutral.

"That great hog, an' all," he added.

Then they went a long time in silence through the frozen, deserted darkness of the town. She felt she could not go indoors. They were drawing near her house.

"I don't want to go home," she suddenly cried in distress and anguish. "I don't want to go home."

He looked at her.

"Why don't you?" he said.

"I don't want to go home," was all she could sob.

He heard somebody coming.

"Well, we can walk a bit further," he said.

She was silent again. They passed out of the town into the fields. He held her by the arm—they could not speak.

"What's a-matter?" he asked at length, puzzled.

She began to cry again.

At last he took her in his arms, to soothe her. She sobbed by herself, almost unaware of him.

"Tell me what's a-matter, Elsie," he said. "Tell me what's a-matter—my dear—tell me, then——"

He kissed her wet face, and caressed her. She made no response. He was puzzled and tender and miserable.

At length she became quiet. Then he kissed her, and she put her arms round him, and clung to him very tight, as if for fear and anguish. He held her in his arms, wondering.

"Ted!" she whispered, frantic. "Ted!"

"What, my love?" he answered, becoming also afraid.

"Be good to me," she cried. "Don't be cruel to me."

"No, my pet," he said, amazed and grieved. "Why?"

"Oh, be good to me," she sobbed.

And he held her very safe, and his heart was white-hot with love for her. His mind was amazed. He could only hold her against his chest that was white-hot with love and belief in her. So she was restored at last.

III

She refused to go to her work at Adams's any more. Her father had to submit and she sent in her notice—she was not well. Sam Adams was ironical. But he had a curious patience. He did not fight.

In a few weeks, she and Whiston were married. She loved him with passion and worship, a fierce little abandon of love that moved him to the depths of his being, and gave him a permanent surety and sense of realness in himself. He did not trouble about himself any more: he felt he was fulfilled and now he had only the many things in the world to busy himself about. Whatever troubled him, at the bottom was surety. He had found himself in this love.

They spoke once or twice of the white stocking.

"Ah!" Whiston exclaimed. "What does it matter?"

He was impatient and angry, and could not bear to consider the matter. So it was left unresolved.

She was quite happy at first, carried away by her adoration of her husband. Then gradually she got used to him. He always was the ground of her happiness, but she got used to him, as to the air she breathed. He never got used to her in the same way.

Inside of marriage she found her liberty. She was rid of the responsibility of herself. Her husband must look after that. She was free to get what she could out of her time.

So that, when, after some months, she met Sam Adams, she was not quite as unkind to him as she might have been. With a young wife's new and exciting knowledge of men, she perceived he was in love with her, she knew he had always kept an unsatisfied desire for her. And, sportive, she could not help playing a little with this, though she cared not one jot for the man himself.

When Valentine's day came, which was near the first anniversary of her wedding day, there arrived a white stocking with a little amethyst brooch. Luckily Whiston did not see it, so she said nothing of it to him. She had not the faintest intention of having anything to do with Sam Adams, but once a little brooch was in her possession, it was hers, and she did not trouble her head for a moment how she had come by it. She kept it.

Now she had the pearl ear-rings. They were a more valuable and a more conspicuous present. She would have to ask her mother to give them to her, to explain their presence. She made a little plan in her head. And she was extraordinarily pleased. As for Sam Adams, even if he saw her wearing them, he would not give her away. What fun, if he saw her wearing his ear-rings! She would pretend she had inherited them from her grandmother, her mother's mother. She laughed to herself as she went down town in the afternoon, the pretty drops dangling in front of her curls. But she saw no one of importance.

Whiston came home tired and depressed. All day the male in him had been uneasy, and this had fatigued him. She was curiously against him, inclined, as she sometimes was nowadays, to make mock of him and jeer at him and cut him off. He did not understand this, and it angered him deeply. She was uneasy before him.

She knew he was in a state of suppressed irritation. The veins stood out on the backs of his hands, his brow was drawn stiffly. Yet she could not help goading him.

"What did you do wi' that white stocking?" he asked, out of a gloomy silence, his voice strong and brutal.

"I put it in a drawer—why?" she replied flippantly.

"Why didn't you put it on the fire back?" he said harshly. "What are you hoarding it up for?"

"I'm not hoarding it up," she said. "I've got a pair."

He relapsed into gloomy silence. She, unable to move him, ran away upstairs, leaving him smoking by the fire. Again she tried on the ear-rings. Then another little inspiration came to her. She drew on the white stockings, both of them.

Presently she came down in them. Her husband still sat immovable and glowering by the fire.

"Look!" she said. "They'll do beautifully."

And she picked up her skirts to her knees, and twisted round, looking at her pretty legs in the neat stockings.

He filled with unreasonable rage, and took the pipe from his mouth.

"Don't they look nice?" she said. "One from last year and one from this, they just do. Save you buying a pair."

And she looked over her shoulders at her pretty calves, and at the dangling frills of her knickers.

"Put your skirts down and don't make a fool of yourself," he said.

"Why a fool of myself?" she asked.

And she began to dance slowly round the room, kicking up her feet half reckless, half jeering, in a ballet-dancer's fashion. Almost fearfully, yet in defiance, she kicked up her legs at him, singing as she did so. She resented him.

"You little fool, ha' done with it," he said. "And you'll backfire them stockings, I'm telling you." He was angry. His face flushed dark, he kept his head bent. She ceased to dance.

"I shan't," she said. "They'll come in very useful."

He lifted his head and watched her, with lighted, dangerous eyes.

"You'll put 'em on the fire back, I tell you," he said.

It was a war now. She bent forward, in a ballet-dancer's fashion, and put her tongue between her teeth.

"I shan't backfire them stockings," she sang, repeating his words, "I shan't, I shan't, I shan't."

And she danced round the room doing a high kick to the tune of her words. There was a real biting indifference in her behaviour.

"We'll see whether you will or not," he said, "trollops! You'd like Sam Adams to know you was wearing 'em, wouldn't you? That's what would please you."

"Yes, I'd like him to see how nicely they fit me, he might give me some more then."

And she looked down at her pretty legs.

He knew somehow that she *would* like Sam Adams to see how pretty her legs looked in the white stockings. It made his anger go deep, almost to hatred.

"Yer nasty trolley," he cried. "Put yer petticoats down, and stop being so foul-minded."

"I'm not foul-minded," she said. "My legs are my own. And why shouldn't Sam Adams think they're nice?"

There was a pause. He watched her with eyes glittering to a point.

"Have you been havin' owt to do with him?" he asked.

"I've just spoken to him when I've seen him," she said. "He's not as bad as you would make out."

"Isn't he?" he cried, a certain wakefulness in his voice. "Them who has anything to do wi' him is too bad for me, I tell you."

"Why, what are you frightened of him for?" she mocked.

She was rousing all his uncontrollable anger. He sat glowering. Every one of her sentences stirred him up like a red-hot iron. Soon it would be too much. And she was afraid herself; but she was neither conquered nor convinced.

A curious little grin of hate came on his face. He had a long score against her.

"What am I frightened of him for?" he repeated automatically. "What am I frightened of him for? Why, for you, you stray-running little bitch."

She flushed. The insult went deep into her, right home.

"Well, if you're so dull——" she said, lowering her eyelids, and speaking coldly, haughtily.

"If I'm so dull I'll break your neck the first word you speak to him," he said, tense.

"Pf!" she sneered. "Do you think I'm frightened of you?" She spoke coldly, detached.

She was frightened, for all that, white round the mouth.

His heart was getting hotter.

"You *will* be frightened of me, the next time you have anything to do with him," he said.

"Do you think *you'd* ever be told—ha!"

Her jeering scorn made him go white-hot, molten. He knew he was incoherent, scarcely responsible for what he might do. Slowly, unseeing, he rose and went out of doors, stifled, moved to kill her.

He stood leaning against the garden fence, unable either to see or hear. Below him, far off, fumed the lights of the town. He stood still, unconscious with a black storm of rage, his face lifted to the night.

Presently, still unconscious of what he was doing, he went indoors again. She stood, a small, stubborn figure with tight-pressed lips and big, sullen, childish eyes, watching him, white with fear. He went heavily across the floor and dropped into his chair.

There was a silence.

"*You're* not going to tell me everything I shall do, and everything I shan't," she broke out at last.

He lifted his head.

"I tell you *this,*" he said, low and intense. "Have anything to do with Sam Adams, and I'll break your neck."

She laughed, shrill and false.

"How I hate your word 'break your neck,'" she said, with a grimace of the mouth. "It sounds so common and beastly. Can't you say something else—"

There was a dead silence.

"And besides," she said, with a queer chirrup of mocking laughter, "what do you know about anything? He sent me an amethyst brooch and a pair of pearl ear-rings."

"He what?" said Whiston, in a suddenly normal voice. His eyes were fixed on her.

"Sent me a pair of pearl ear-rings, and an amethyst brooch," she repeated, mechanically, pale to the lips.

And her big, black, childish eyes watched him, fascinated, held in her spell.

He seemed to thrust his face and his eyes forward at her, as he rose slowly and came to her. She watched transfixed in terror. Her throat made a small sound, as she tried to scream.

Then, quick as lightning, the back of his hand struck her with a crash across the mouth, and she was flung back blinded against the wall. The shock shook a queer sound out of her. And then she saw him still coming on, his eyes holding her, his fist drawn back, advancing slowly. At any instant the blow might crash into her.

Mad with terror, she raised her hands with a queer clawing movement to cover her eyes and her temples, opening her mouth in a dumb shriek. There was no sound. But the sight of her slowly arrested him. He hung before her, looking at her fixedly, as she stood crouched against the wall with open, bleeding mouth, and wide-staring eyes, and two hands clawing over her temples. And his lust to see her bleed, to break her and destroy her, rose from an old source against her. It carried him. He wanted satisfaction.

But he had seen her standing there, a piteous, horrified thing, and he turned his face aside in shame and nausea. He went and sat heavily in his chair, and a curious ease, almost like sleep, came over his brain.

She walked away from the wall towards the fire, dizzy, white to the lips, mechanically wiping her small, bleeding mouth. He sat motionless. Then, gradually, her breath began to hiss, she shook, and was sobbing silently, in grief for herself. Without looking, he saw. It made his mad desire to destroy her come back.

At length he lifted his head. His eyes were glowing again, fixed on her.

"And what did he give them you for?" he asked, in a steady, unyielding voice.

Her crying dried up in a second. She also was tense.

"They came as valentines," she replied, still not subjugated, even if beaten.

"When, to-day?"

"The pearl ear-rings to-day—the amethyst brooch last year."

"You've had it a year?"

"Yes."

She felt that now nothing would prevent him if he rose to kill her. She could not prevent him any more. She was yielded up to him. They both trembled in the balance, unconscious.

"What have you had to do with him?" he asked, in a barren voice.

"I've not had anything to do with him," she quavered.

"You just kept 'em because they were jewellery?" he said.

A weariness came over him. What was the worth of speaking any more of it? He did not care any more. He was dreary and sick.

She began to cry again, but he took no notice. She kept wiping her mouth on her handkerchief. He could see it, the blood-mark. It made him only more sick and tired of the responsibility of it, the violence, the shame.

When she began to move about again, he raised his head once more from his dead, motionless position.

"Where are the things?" he said.

"They are upstairs," she quavered. She knew the passion had gone down in him.

"Bring them down," he said.

"I won't," she wept, with rage. "You're not going to bully me and hit me like that on the mouth."

And she sobbed again. He looked at her in contempt and compassion and in rising anger.

"Where are they?" he said.

"They're in the little drawer under the looking-glass," she sobbed.

He went slowly upstairs, struck a match, and found the trinkets. He brought them downstairs in his hand.

"These?" he said, looking at them as they lay in his palm.

She looked at them without answering. She was not interested in them any more.

He looked at the little jewels. They were pretty.

"Its none of their fault," he said to himself.

And he searched round slowly, persistently, for a box. He tied the things up and addressed them to Sam Adams. Then he went out in his slippers to post the little package.

When he came back she was still sitting crying.

"You'd better go to bed," he said.

She paid no attention. He sat by the fire. She still cried.

"I'm sleeping down here," he said. "Go you to bed."

In a few moments she lifted her tear-stained, swollen face and looked at him with eyes all forlorn and pathetic. A great flash of anguish went over his body. He went over, slowly, and very gently took her in his hands. She let herself be taken. Then as she lay against his shoulder, she sobbed aloud:

"I never meant——"

"My love—my little love——" he cried, in anguish of spirit, holding her in his arms.

GABRIEL GARCÍA MÁRQUEZ

[Colombia]

BORN IN Aracataca, Colombia, Gabriel García Márquez (1927–2014) grew up with his maternal grandparents. His grandmother told him stories with supernatural elements that she believed to be true, and which later influenced his own fantastical fiction. After going away to school, García Márquez became a journalist and remained one even after his renown as a novelist. In 1967 he published *One Hundred Years of Solitude,* one of the most popular and influential novels of the twentieth century. García Márquez won the Nobel Prize in 1982, when Colombia would have liked to persecute him for his political connections to Cuba and his literary friendship with the dictator Fidel Castro. García Márquez married Mercedes Barcha Pardo in 1958, and they were together forever after; they had two children, whom they raised in Mexico, his adopted second country. The enchanting story "The Handsomest Drowned Man in the World" (in Spanish, "El ahogado más hermoso del mundo") was first published in 1968 and was translated for English publication in 1972.

The Handsomest Drowned Man in the World (1968)

(Translated from the Spanish by Gregory Rabassa)

THE FIRST CHILDREN who saw the dark and slinky bulge approaching through the sea let themselves think it was an enemy ship. Then they saw it had no flags or masts and they thought it was a whale.

But when it washed up on the beach, they removed the clumps of seaweed, the jellyfish tentacles, and the remains of fish and flotsam, and only then did they see that it was a drowned man.

They had been playing with him all afternoon, burying him in the sand and digging him up again, when someone chanced to see them and spread the alarm in the village. The men who carried him to the nearest house noticed that he weighed more than any dead man they had ever known, almost as much as a horse, and they said to each other that maybe he'd been floating too long and the water had got into his bones. When they laid him on the floor they said he'd been taller than all other men because there was barely enough room for him in the house, but they thought that maybe the ability to keep on growing after death was part of the nature of certain drowned men. He had the smell of the sea about him and only his shape gave one to suppose that it was the corpse of a human being, because the skin was covered with a crust of mud and scales.

They did not even have to clean off his face to know that the dead man was a stranger. The village was made up of only twenty-odd wooden houses that had stone courtyards with no flowers and which were spread about on the end of a desertlike cape. There was so little land that mothers always went about with the fear that the wind would carry off their children and the few dead that the years had caused among them had to be thrown off the cliffs. But the sea was calm and bountiful and all the men fit into seven boats. So when they found the drowned man they simply had to look at one another to see that they were all there.

That night they did not go out to work at sea. While the men went to find out if anyone was missing in neighboring villages, the women stayed behind to care for the drowned man. They took the mud off with grass swabs, they removed the underwater stones entangled in his hair, and they scraped the crust off with tools used for scaling fish. As they were doing that they noticed that the vegetation on him came from faraway oceans and deep water and that his clothes were in tatters, as if he had sailed through labyrinths of coral. They noticed too that he bore his death with pride, for he did not have the lonely look of other drowned men who came out of the sea or that haggard, needy look of men who drowned in rivers. But only when they finished cleaning him off did they become aware of the kind of man he was and it left them breathless. Not only was he the tallest, strongest, most virile, and best built man they had ever seen, but even though they were looking at him there was no room for him in their imagination.

They could not find a bed in the village large enough to lay him on nor was there a table solid enough to use for his wake. The tallest men's holiday pants would not fit him, nor the fattest ones' Sunday shirts, nor the shoes of the one with the biggest feet. Fascinated by his huge size and his beauty, the women then decided to make him some pants from a large piece of sail and a shirt from some bridal brabant linen so that he could continue through his death with dignity. As they sewed, sitting in a circle and gazing at the corpse between stitches, it seemed to them that the wind had never been so steady nor the sea so restless as on that night and they supposed that the change had something to do with the dead man. They thought that if that magnificent man had lived in the village, his house would have had the widest doors, the highest ceiling, and the strongest floor, his bed-stead would have been made from a midship frame held together by iron bolts, and his wife would have been the happiest woman. They thought that he would have had so much authority that he could have drawn fish out of the sea simply by calling their names and that he would have put so much work into his land that springs would have burst forth from among the rocks so that he would have been able to plant flowers on the cliffs. They secretly compared him to their own men, thinking that for all their lives theirs were incapable of doing what he could do in one night, and they ended up dismissing them deep in their hearts as the weakest, meanest, and most useless creatures on earth. They were wandering through that maze of fantasy when the oldest woman, who as the oldest had looked upon the drowned man with more compassion than passion, sighed:

"He has the face of someone called Esteban."

It was true. Most of them had only to take another look at him to see that he could not have any other name. The more stubborn among them, who were the youngest, still lived for a few hours with the illusion that when they put his clothes on and he lay among the flowers in patent leather shoes his name might be Lautaro. But it was a vain illusion. There had not been enough canvas, the poorly cut and worse sewn pants were too tight, and the hidden strength of his heart popped the buttons on his shirt. After midnight the whistling of the wind died down and the sea fell into its Wednesday drowsiness. The silence put an end to any last doubts: he was Esteban. The women who had dressed him, who had combed his hair, had cut his nails and shaved him were unable to hold back a shudder of pity when they had to resign themselves to his being dragged along the ground. It was then that they understood how unhappy he must have been with that huge body since it bothered him even after death. They could see him in life, condemned to going through doors sideways, cracking his head on crossbeams, remaining on his feet during visits, not knowing what to do with his soft, pink, sea lion hands while the lady of the house looked for her most resistant chair and begged him, frightened to death, sit here, Esteban, please, and he, leaning against the wall, smiling, don't bother, ma'am, I'm fine where I am, his heels raw and his back roasted from having done the same thing so many times whenever he paid a visit, don't bother, ma'am, I'm fine where I am, just to avoid the embarrassment of breaking up the chair, and never knowing perhaps that the ones who said don't go, Esteban, at least wait till the coffee's ready, were the ones who later on would whisper the big boob finally left, how nice, the handsome fool has gone. That was what the women were thinking beside the body a little before dawn. Later, when they covered his face with a handkerchief so that the light would not bother him, he looked so forever dead, so defenseless, so much like their men that the first furrows of tears opened in their hearts. It was one of the younger ones who began the weeping. The others, coming to, went from sighs to wails, and the more they sobbed the more they felt like weeping, because the drowned man was becoming all the more Esteban for them, and so they wept so much, for he was the most destitute, most peaceful, and most obliging man on earth, poor Esteban. So when the men returned with the news that the drowned man was not from the neighboring villages either, the women felt an opening of jubilation in the midst of their tears.

"Praise the Lord," they sighed, "he's ours!"

The men thought the fuss was only womanish frivolity. Fatigued because of the difficult nighttime inquiries, all they wanted was to get rid of the bother of the newcomer once and for all before the sun grew strong on that arid, windless day. They improvised a litter with the remains of foremasts and gaffs, tying it together with rigging so that it would bear the weight of the body until they reached the cliffs. They wanted to tie the anchor from a cargo ship to him so that he would sink easily into the deepest waves, where fish are blind and divers die of nostalgia, and bad currents would not bring him back to shore, as had happened with other bodies. But the more they hurried, the more the women thought of ways to waste time. They walked about like startled hens, pecking with the sea charms on their breasts, some interfering on one side to put a scapular of the good wind on the drowned man, some on the other side to put a wrist compass on him, and after a great deal of *get away from there, woman, stay out of the way, look, you almost made me fall on top of the dead man,* the men began to feel mistrust in their livers and started grumbling about why so many main-altar decorations for a stranger, because no matter how many nails and holy-water jars he had on him, the sharks would chew him all the same, but the women kept piling on their junk relics, running back and forth, stumbling, while they released in sighs what they did not in tears, so that the men finally exploded with *since when has there ever been such a fuss over a drifting corpse, a drowned nobody, a piece of cold Wednesday meat.* One of the women, mortified by so much lack of care, then removed the handkerchief from the dead man's face and the men were left breathless too.

He was Esteban. It was not necessary to repeat it for them to recognize him. If they had been told Sir Walter Raleigh, even they might have been impressed with his gringo accent, the macaw on his shoulder, his cannibal-killing blunderbuss, but there could be only one Esteban in the world and there he was, stretched out like a sperm whale, shoeless, wearing the pants of an undersized child, and with those stony nails that had to be cut with a knife. They only had to take the handkerchief off his face to see that he was ashamed, that it was not his fault that he was so big or so heavy or so handsome, and if he had known that this was going to happen, he would have looked for a more discreet place to drown in, seriously, I even would have tied the anchor off a galleon around my neck and staggered off a cliff like someone who doesn't like things in order not to be upsetting people now with this Wednesday dead body, as you people say, in order not to be bothering anyone with this filthy piece of cold meat that doesn't have anything to do with me. There was so much truth in his manner that even the most mistrustful men, the ones who felt the bitterness of endless nights at sea fearing that their women would tire of dreaming about them and begin to dream of drowned men, even they and others who were harder still shuddered in the marrow of their bones at Esteban's sincerity.

That was how they came to hold the most splendid funeral they could conceive of for an abandoned drowned man. Some women who had gone to get flowers in the neighboring villages returned with other women who could not believe what they had been told, and those women went back for more flowers when they saw the dead man, and they brought more and more until there were so many flowers and so many people that it was hard to walk about. At the final moment it pained them to return him to the waters as an orphan and they chose a father and mother from among the best people, and aunts and uncles and cousins, so that through him all the inhabitants of the village became kinsmen. Some sailors who heard the weeping from a distance went off course and people heard of one who had himself tied to the mainmast, remembering ancient fables about sirens. While they fought for the privilege of carrying him on their shoulders along the steep escarpment by the cliffs, men and women became aware for the first time of the desolation of their streets, the dryness of their courtyards, the narrowness of their dreams as they faced the splendor and beauty of their drowned man. They let him go without an anchor so that he could come back if he wished and whenever he wished, and they all held their breath for the fraction of centuries the body took to fall into the abyss. They did not need to look at one another to realize that they were no longer all present, that they would never be. But they also knew that everything would be different from then on, that their houses would have wider doors, higher ceilings, and stronger floors so that Esteban's memory could go everywhere without bumping into beams and so that no one in the future would dare whisper the big boob finally died, too bad, the handsome fool has finally died, because they were going to paint their house fronts gay colors to make Esteban's memory eternal and they were going to break their backs digging for springs among the stones and planting flowers on the cliffs so that in future years at dawn the passengers on great liners would awaken, suffocated by the smell of gardens on the high seas, and the captain would have to come down from the bridge in his dress uniform, with his astrolabe, his pole star, and his row of war medals and, pointing to the promontory of roses on the horizon, he would say in fourteen languages, look there, where the wind is so peaceful now that it's gone to sleep beneath the beds, over there, where the sun's so bright that the sunflowers don't know which way to turn, yes, over there, that's Esteban's village.

GUY DE MAUPASSANT

[France]

THE RUSSIAN novelist Leo Tolstoy, in assessing Guy de Maupassant's life and work, remarked, "An artist is an artist because he sees things not as he wishes to see them but as they really are. The man, the possessor of a talent, may make mistakes, but if only his talent is allowed free play, as Maupassant gave it free play in his short stories, it discloses, undrapes the object, and compels love of it if it deserves love, and hatred of it if it deserves hatred."[1] Maupassant (1850–1893) never married and apparently never had children but continually returned to the topic of love, often through stories where first-person narrators contribute to the "free play" of conversation among friends and acquaintances, as in "A Wife's Confession" (in French "Confessions d'une femme"). Born in Normandy, France, Maupassant served in the army during the Franco-Prussian War and was a civil servant for several years in the 1870s. After the encouragement of the novelist Gustave Flaubert, Maupassant published in the 1880s more than 300 stories and several novels, which made him deservedly famous and wealthy. Maupassant died of complications from the syphilis he had contracted in his twenties.

A Wife's Confession (1882)

(Translated from the French by M. Walter Dunne)

MY FRIEND, YOU have asked me to relate to you the liveliest recollections of my life. I am very old, without relatives, without chil-

---

[1] Leo Tolstoy. "Introduction to the Works of Guy de Maupassant." In *What Is Art and Essays on Art*. Translated by Aylmer Maude. The World's Classics. London: Oxford University Press, 1950. 40.

dren; so I am free to make a confession to you. Promise me one thing—never to reveal my name.

I have been much loved, as you know; I have often myself loved. I was very beautiful; I may say this today, when my beauty is gone. Love was for me the life of the soul, just as the air is the life of the body. I would have preferred to die rather than exist without affection, without having somebody always to care for me. Women often pretend to love only once with all the strength of their hearts; it has often happened to be so violent in one of my attachments that I thought it would be impossible for my transports ever to end. However, they always died out in a natural fashion, like a fire when it has no more fuel.

I will tell you today the first of my adventures, in which I was very innocent, but which led to the others. The horrible vengeance of that dreadful chemist of Pecq recalls to me the shocking drama of which I was, in spite of myself, a spectator.

I had been a year married to a rich man, Comte Hervé de Ker—a Breton of ancient family, whom I did not love, you understand. True love needs, I believe at any rate, freedom and impediments at the same time. The love which is imposed, sanctioned by law, and blessed by the priest—can we really call that love? A legal kiss is never as good as a stolen kiss. My husband was tall in stature, elegant, and a really fine gentleman in his manners. But he lacked intelligence. He spoke in a downright fashion, and uttered opinions that cut like the blade of a knife. He created the impression that his mind was full of ready-made views instilled into him by his father and mother, who had themselves got them from their ancestors. He never hesitated, but on every subject immediately made narrow-minded suggestions, without showing any embarrassment and without realizing that there might be other ways of looking at things. One felt that his head was closed up, that no ideas circulated in it, none of those ideas which renew a man's mind and make it sound, like a breath of fresh air passing through an open window into a house.

The château in which we lived was situated in the midst of a desolate tract of country. It was a large, melancholy structure, surrounded by enormous trees, with tufts of moss on it resembling old men's white beards. The park, a real forest, was enclosed in a deep trench called the ha-ha; and at its extremity, near the moorland, we had big ponds full of reeds and floating grass. Between the two, at the edge of a stream which connected them, my husband had got a little hut built for shooting wild ducks.

We had, in addition to our ordinary servants, a keeper, a sort of brute devoted to my husband to the death, and a chambermaid, almost a friend, passionately attached to me. I had brought her back from Spain with me five years before. She was a deserted child. She might have been taken for a gipsy with her dusky skin, her dark eyes, her hair thick as a wood and always clustering around her forehead. She was at the time sixteen years old, but she looked twenty.

The autumn was beginning. We hunted much, sometimes on neighboring estates, sometimes on our own; and I noticed a young man, the Baron de C—, whose visits at the château became singularly frequent. Then, he ceased to come; I thought no more about it; but I perceived that my husband changed in his demeanor toward me.

He seemed taciturn and preoccupied; he did not kiss me; and, in spite of the fact that he did not come into my room, as I insisted on separate apartments in order to live a little alone, I often at night heard a furtive step drawing near my door, and withdrawing a few minutes after.

As my window was on the ground floor, I thought I had also often heard some one prowling in the shadow around the château. I told my husband about it, and, having looked at me intensely for some seconds, he answered:

"It is nothing—it is the keeper."

★ ★ ★

Now, one evening, just after dinner, Hervé, who appeared to be extraordinarily gay, with a sly sort of gaiety, said to me:

"Would you like to spend three hours out with the guns, in order to shoot a fox who comes every evening to eat my hens?"

I was surprised. I hesitated; but, as he kept staring at me with singular persistency, I ended by replying:

"Why, certainly, my friend." I must tell you that I hunted like a man the wolf and the wild boar. So it was quite natural that he should suggest this shooting expedition to me.

But my husband, all of a sudden, had a curiously nervous look; and all the evening he seemed agitated, rising up and sitting down feverishly.

About ten o'clock he suddenly said to me:

"Are you ready?"

I rose; and, as he was bringing me my gun himself, I asked:

"Are we to load with bullets or with deershot?"

He showed some astonishment; then he rejoined:

"Oh! only with deershot; make your mind easy! that will be enough."

Then, after some seconds, he added in a peculiar tone:

"You may boast of having splendid coolness."

I burst out laughing.

"I? Why, pray? Coolness because I go to kill a fox? What are you thinking of, my friend?"

And we quietly made our way across the park. All the household slept. The full moon seemed to give a yellow tint to the old gloomy building, whose slate roof glittered brightly. The two turrets that flanked it had two plates of light on their summits, and no noise disturbed the silence of this clear, sad night, sweet and still, which seemed in a death-trance. Not a breath of air, not a shriek from a toad, not a hoot from an owl; a melancholy numbness lay heavy on everything. When we were under the trees in the park, a sense of freshness stole over me, together with the odor of fallen leaves. My husband said nothing; but he was listening, he was watching, he seemed to be smelling about in the shadows, possessed from head to foot by the passion for the chase.

We soon reached the edges of the ponds.

Their tufts of rushes remained motionless; not a breath of air caressed them; but movements which were scarcely perceptible ran through the water. Sometimes the surface was stirred by something, and light circles gathered around, like luminous wrinkles enlarging indefinitely.

When we reached the hut, where we were to lie in wait, my husband made me go in first; then he slowly loaded his gun, and the dry cracking of the powder produced a strange effect on me. He saw that I was shuddering and asked:

"Does this trial happen to be quite enough for you? If so, go back."

I was much surprised, and I replied:

"Not at all. I did not come to go back without doing anything. You seem queer this evening." He murmured:

"As you wish." And we remained there without moving.

At the end of about half an hour, as nothing broke the oppressive stillness of this bright autumn night, I said, in a low tone:

"Are you quite sure he is passing this way?"

Hervé winced as if I had bitten him, and, with his mouth close to my ear, he said:

"Make no mistake about it! I am quite sure."

And once more there was silence.

I believe I was beginning to get drowsy when my husband pressed my arm, and his voice, changed to a hiss, said:

"Do you see him there under the trees?"

I looked in vain; I could distinguish nothing. And slowly Hervé now cocked his gun all the time fixing his eyes on my face.

I was myself making ready to fire, and suddenly thirty paces in front of us, appeared in the full light of the moon a man who was hurrying forward with rapid movements, his body bent, as if he were trying to escape.

I was so stupefied that I uttered a loud cry; but, before I could turn round, there was a flash before my eyes; I heard a deafening report; and I saw the man rolling on the ground, like a wolf hit by a bullet.

I burst into dreadful shrieks, terrified, almost going mad; then a furious hand—it was Hervé's—seized me by the throat. I was flung down on the ground, then carried off by his strong arms. He ran, holding me up, till he reached the body lying on the grass, and he threw me on top of it violently, as if he wanted to break my head.

I thought I was lost; he was going to kill me; and he had just raised his heel up to my forehead when, in his turn, he was gripped, knocked down, before I could yet realize what had happened.

I rose up abruptly, and I saw kneeling on top of him Porquita, my maid, clinging like a wild cat to him with desperate energy, tearing off his beard, his mustache, and the skin of his face.

Then, as if another idea had suddenly taken hold of her mind, she rose up, and, flinging herself on the corpse, she threw her arms around the dead man, kissing his eyes and his mouth, opening the dead lips with her own lips, trying to find in them a breath and the long, long kiss of lovers.

My husband, picking himself up, gazed at me. He understood, and, falling at my feet, said:

"Oh! forgive me, my darling, I suspected you, and I killed this girl's lover. It was my keeper that deceived me."

But I was watching the strange kisses of that dead man and that living woman, and her sobs and her writhings of sorrowing love, and at that moment I understood that I might be unfaithful to my husband.

YUKIO MISHIMA

[Japan]

THE INTERNATIONALLY CELEBRATED novelist, playwright, and poet Yukio Mishima (1925-1970) was the pen name of Tokyo-born Kimitake Hiraoka. From childhood, he was fascinated by Western writers, including Oscar Wilde, but his father disapproved of the "effeminate" writing that young Mishima produced. After being exempted from military service in World War II, Mishima became a famous author in Japan at the age of twenty-four. He was soon translated into many European languages. Meanwhile, when he wasn't writing one of his many stories and novels, he devoted himself to martial-arts and to many male lovers. He married Yoko Sugiyama in 1958 and had two children with her. His death was likely a ritual suicide after his failed attempt at inspiring a Japanese military coup d'etat.

The Priest of the Shiga Temple
and His Love (1968)

(Translated from the Japanese by Ivan Morris)

ACCORDING TO ESHIN'S "Essentials of Salvation," the Ten Pleasures are but a drop in the ocean when compared to the joys of the Pure Land. In that Land the earth is made of emerald and the roads that lead across it are lined by cordons of gold rope. The surface is endlessly level and there are no boundaries. Within each of the sacred Precincts are fifty thousand million halls and towers wrought of gold, silver, lapis lazuli, crystal, coral, agate, and pearls; and wondrous garments are spread out on all the jeweled daises. Within the halls and above the towers a multitude of angels are forever playing sacred music and singing paeans of praise to the Tathagata Buddha. In the gardens that surround the halls and the towers and the cloisters are great gold and emerald ponds where the faithful may perform their ablutions; and the gold ponds are lined with silver sand, and the emerald ponds are lined with crystal sand. The ponds are covered with lotus plants which sparkle in variegated colors and, as the breeze wafts over the surface of the water, magnificent lights crisscross in all directions. Both day and night the air is filled with the songs of cranes, geese, mandarin ducks, peacocks, parrots, and sweet-voiced Kalavinkas, who have the faces of beautiful women. All these and the myriad other hundred-jeweled birds are raising their melodious voices in praise of the Buddha. (However sweet their voices may sound, so immense a collection of birds must be extremely noisy.)

The borders of the ponds and the banks of the rivers are lined with groves of sacred treasure trees. These trees have golden stems and silver branches and coral blossoms, and their beauty is mirrored in the waters. The air is full of jeweled cords, and from these cords hang the myriad treasure bells which forever ring out the Supreme Law of Buddha; and strange musical instruments, which play by themselves without ever being touched, also stretch far into the pellucid sky.

If one feels like having something to eat, there automatically appears before one's eyes a seven-jeweled table on whose shining surface rest seven-jeweled bowls heaped high with the choicest delicacies. But there is no need to pick up these viands and put them in one's mouth. All that is necessary is to look at their inviting colors and to enjoy their aroma: thereby the stomach is filled and the body nourished, while one remains oneself spiritually and physically pure. When one has thus finished one's meal without any eating, the bowls and the table are instantly wafted off.

Likewise, one's body is automatically arrayed in clothes, without any need for sewing, laundering, dyeing, or repairing.

Lamps, too, are unnecessary, for the sky is illumined by an omnipresent light. Furthermore, the Pure Land enjoys a moderate temperature all year round, so that neither heating nor cooling is required. A hundred thousand subtle scents perfume the air and lotus petals rain down constantly.

In the chapter of the Inspection Gate we are told that, since uninitiated sightseers cannot hope to penetrate deep into the Pure Land, they must concentrate, first, on awakening their powers of "external imagination" and, thereafter, on steadily expanding these powers. Imaginative power can provide a short cut for escaping from the trammels of our mundane life and for seeing the Buddha. If we are endowed with a rich, turbulent imagination, we can focus our attention on a single lotus flower and from there can spread out to infinite horizons.

By means of microscopic observation and astronomical projection the lotus flower can become the foundation for an entire theory of the universe and an agent whereby we may perceive the Truth. And first we must know that each of the petals has eighty-four thousand veins and that each vein gives off eighty-four thousand lights. Furthermore, the smallest of these flowers has a diameter of two hundred and fifty yojana. Thus, assuming that the yojana of which we read in the Holy Writings correspond to seventy-five miles each, we may conclude that a lotus flower with a diameter of nineteen thousand miles is on the small side.

Now such a flower has eighty-four thousand petals and between each of the petals there are one million jewels, each emitting one thousand lights. Above the beautifully adorned calyx of the flower rise four bejeweled pillars and each of these pillars is one hundred billion times as great as Mount Sumeru, which towers in the center of the Buddhist universe. From the pillars hang great draperies and each drapery is adorned with fifty thousand million jewels, and each jewel emits eighty-four thousand lights, and each light is composed of eighty-four thousand different golden colors, and each of these golden colors in its turn is variously transmogrified.

To concentrate on such images is known as "thinking of the Lotus Seat on which Lord Buddha sits"; and the conceptual world that hovers in the background of our story is a world imagined on such a scale.

The Great Priest of Shiga Temple was a man of the most eminent virtue. His eyebrows were white, and it was as much as he could do to move his old bones along as he hobbled on his stick from one part of the temple to another.

In the eyes of this learned ascetic the world was a mere pile of rubbish. He had lived away from it for many a long year and the little pine sapling that he had planted with his own hands on moving into his present cell had grown into a great tree whose branches swelled in the wind. A monk who had succeeded in abandoning the Floating World for so long a time must feel secure about his future.

When the Great Priest saw the rich and the noble, he smiled with compassion and wondered how it was that these people did not recognize their pleasures for the empty dreams that they were. When he noticed beautiful women, his only reaction was to be moved with pity for men who still inhabited the world of delusion and who were tossed about on the waves of carnal pleasure.

From the moment that a man no longer responds in the slightest to the motives that regulate the material world, that world appears to be at complete repose. In the eyes of the Great Priest the world showed only repose; it had become a mere picture on a piece of paper, a map of some foreign land. When one has attained a state of mind from which the evil passions of the present world have been so utterly winnowed, fear too is forgotten. Thus it was that the priest no longer could understand why Hell should exist. He knew beyond all peradventure that the present world no longer had any power left over him; but, as he was completely devoid of conceit, it did not occur to him that this was the effect of his own eminent virtue.

So far as his body was concerned, one might say that the priest had well-nigh been deserted by his own flesh. On such occasions as he observed it—when taking a bath, for instance—he would rejoice to see how his protruding bones were precariously covered by his withered skin. Now that his body had reached this stage, he felt that he could come to terms with it, as if it belonged to someone else. Such a body, it seemed, was already more suited for the nourishment of the Pure Land than for terrestrial food and drink.

In his dreams he lived nightly in the Pure Land, and when he awoke he knew that to subsist in the present world was to be tied to a sad and evanescent dream.

In the flower-viewing season large numbers of people came from the Capital to visit the village of Shiga. This did not trouble the priest in the slightest, for he had long since transcended that state in which the clamors of the world can irritate the mind. One spring evening he left his cell, leaning on his stick, and walked down to the lake. It was the hour when dusky shadows slowly begin to thrust their way into the bright light of the afternoon. There was not the slightest ripple to disturb the surface of the water. The priest stood by himself at the edge of the lake and began to perform the holy rite of Water Contemplation.

At that moment an ox-drawn carriage, clearly belonging to a person of high rank, came around the lake and stopped close to where the priest was standing. The owner was a Court lady from the Kyōgoku district of the Capital who held the exalted title of Great Imperial Concubine. This lady had come to view the spring-time scenery in Shiga and now on her return she had stopped the carriage and raised the blind in order to have a final look at the lake.

Unwittingly the Great Priest glanced in her direction and at once he was overwhelmed by her beauty. His eyes met hers and, as he did nothing to avert his gaze, she did not take it upon herself to turn away. It was not that her liberality of spirit was such as to allow men to gaze on her with brazen looks; but the motives of this austere old ascetic could hardly, she felt, be those of ordinary men.

After a few moments the lady pulled down the blind. Her carriage started to move and, having gone through the Shiga Pass, rolled slowly down the road that led to the Capital. Night fell and the carriage made its way toward the city along the Road of the Silver Temple. Until the carriage had become a pinprick that disappeared between the distant trees, the Great Priest stood rooted to the spot.

In the twinkling of an eye the present world had wreaked its revenge on the priest with terrible force. What he had imagined to be completely safe had collapsed in ruins.

He returned to the temple, faced the Main Image of Buddha, and invoked the Sacred Name. But impure thoughts now cast their opaque shadows about him. A woman's beauty, he told himself, was but a fleeting apparition, a temporary phenomenon composed of flesh—of flesh that was soon to be destroyed. Yet, try as he might to ward it off, the ineffable beauty which had overpowered him at that instant by the lake now pressed on his heart with the force of something that has come from an infinite distance. The Great Priest was not young enough, either spiritually or physically, to believe that this new feeling was simply a trick that his flesh had played on him. A man's flesh, he knew full well, could not alter so rapidly. Rather, he seemed to have been immersed in some swift, subtle poison which had abruptly transmuted his spirit.

The Great Priest had never broken his vow of chastity. The inner fight that he had waged in his youth against the demands of the flesh had made him think of women as mere carnal beings. The only real flesh was the flesh that existed in his imagination. Since, therefore, he regarded the flesh as an ideal abstraction, rather than as a physical fact, he had relied on his spiritual strength to subjugate it. In this effort the priest had achieved success—success, indeed, that no one who knew him could possibly doubt.

Yet the face of the woman who had raised the carriage blind and gazed across the lake was too harmonious, too refulgent, to be designated as a mere object of flesh, and the priest did not know what name to give it. He could only think that, in order to bring about that wondrous moment, something which had for a long time lurked deceptively within him had finally revealed itself. That thing was nothing other than the present world, which until then had been at repose, but which had now suddenly lifted itself out of the darkness and begun to stir.

It was as if he had been standing by the highway that led to the Capital, with his hands firmly covering both ears, and had watched two great oxcarts rumble past each other. All of a sudden he had removed his hands and the noise from outside had surged all about him.

To perceive the ebb and flow of passing phenomena, to have their noise roaring in one's ears, was to enter into the circle of the present world. For a man like the Great Priest, who had severed his relations with all outside things, it was to place himself once again into a state of relationship.

Even as he read the Sutras he would time after time hear himself heaving great sighs of anguish. Perhaps nature, he thought, might serve to distract his spirits, and he gazed out of the window of his cell at the mountains that towered in the distance under the evening sky. Yet his thoughts, instead of concentrating on the beauty, broke up like tufts of cloud and drifted away. He fixed his gaze on the moon, but his thoughts continued to wander as before; and when once again he went and stood before the Main Image in a desperate effort to regain his purity of mind, the countenance of the Buddha was transformed and looked like the face of the lady in the carriage. His universe had been imprisoned within the confines of a small circle: at one point was the Great Priest and opposite was the Great Imperial Concubine.

The Great Imperial Concubine of Kyōgoku had soon forgotten about the old priest whom she had noticed gazing so intently at her by the lake at Shiga. After some time, however, a rumor came to her ears and she was reminded of the incident. One of the villagers happened to have caught sight of the Great Priest as he had stood watching the lady's carriage disappear into the distance. He had mentioned the matter to a Court gentleman who had come to Shiga for flower-viewing and had added that since that day the priest had behaved like one crazed.

The Imperial Concubine pretended to disbelieve the rumor. The virtue of this particular priest, however, was noted throughout the Capital, and the incident was bound to feed the lady's vanity.

For she was utterly weary of the love that she received from the men of this world. The Imperial Concubine was fully aware of her own beauty, and she tended to be attracted by any force, such as religion, that treated her beauty and her high rank as things of no value. Being exceedingly bored with the present world, she believed in the Pure Land. It was inevitable that Jōdo Buddhism, which rejected all the beauty and brilliance of the visual world as being mere filth and defilement, should have a particular appeal for someone like the Imperial Concubine who was thoroughly disillusioned with the superficial elegance of Court life—an elegance that seemed unmistakably to bespeak the Latter Days of the Law and their degeneracy.

Among those whose special interest was love, the Great Imperial Concubine was held in honor as the very personification of Courtly refinement. The fact that she was known never to have given her love to any man added to this reputation. Though she performed her duties toward the Emperor with the most perfect decorum, no one for a moment believed that she loved him from her heart. The Great Imperial Concubine dreamt of a passion that lay on the boundary of the impossible.

The Great Priest of Shiga Temple was famous for his virtue, and everyone in the Capital knew how this aged prelate had totally abandoned the present world. All the more startling, then, was the rumor that he had been dazzled by the charms of the Imperial Concubine and that for her sake he had sacrificed the future world. To give up the joys of the Pure Land which were so close at hand—there could be no greater sacrifice than this, no greater gift.

The Great Imperial Concubine was utterly indifferent to the charms of the young rakes who flocked about the Court and of the handsome noblemen who came her way. The physical attributes of men no longer meant anything to her. Her only concern was to find a man who could give her the strongest and deepest possible love. A woman with such aspirations is a truly terrifying creature. If she is a mere courtesan, she will no doubt be satisfied with worldly wealth. The Great Imperial Concubine, however, already enjoyed all those things that the wealth of the world can provide. The man whom she awaited must offer her the wealth of the future world.

The rumors of the Great Priest's infatuation spread throughout the Court. In the end the story was even told half jokingly to the Emperor himself. The Great Concubine took no pleasure in this bantering gossip and preserved a cool, indifferent mien. As she was well aware, there were two reasons why the people of the Court could joke freely about a matter which would normally have been forbidden: first, by referring to the Great Priest's love they were paying a compliment to the beauty of the woman who could inspire even an ecclesiastic of such great virtue to forsake his meditations; secondly, everyone fully realized that the old man's love for the noblewoman could never possibly be requited.

The Great Imperial Concubine called to mind the face of the old priest whom she had seen through her carriage window. It did not bear the remotest resemblance to the face of any of the men who had loved her until then. Strange it was that love should spring up in the heart of a man who did not have the slightest qualification for being loved. The lady recalled such phrases as "my love forlorn and without hope" that were widely used by poetasters in the Palace when they wished to awaken some sympathy in the hearts of their indifferent paramours. Compared to the hopeless situation in which the Great Priest now found himself, the state of the least fortunate of these elegant lovers was almost enviable, and their poetic tags struck her now as mere trappings of worldly alliance, inspired by vanity and utterly devoid of pathos.

At this point it will be clear to the reader that the Great Imperial Concubine was not, as was so widely believed, the personification of Courtly elegance, but, rather, a person who found the real relish of life in the knowledge of being loved. Despite her high rank, she was first of all a woman; and all the power and authority in the world seemed to her empty things if they were bereft of this knowledge. The men about her might devote themselves to struggles for political power; but she dreamt of subduing the world by different means, by purely feminine means. Many of the women whom she had known had taken the tonsure and retired from the world. Such women struck her as laughable. For, whatever a woman may say about abandoning the world, it is almost impossible for her to give up the things that she possesses. Only men are really capable of giving up what they possess.

That old priest by the lake had at a certain stage in his life given up the Floating World and all its pleasures. In the eyes of the Imperial Concubine he was far more of a man than all the nobles whom she knew at Court. And, just as he had once abandoned this present Floating World, so now on her behalf he was about to give up the future world as well.

The Imperial Concubine recalled the notion of the sacred lotus flower, which her own deep faith had vividly imprinted upon her mind. She thought of the huge lotus with its width of two hundred and fifty yojana. That preposterous plant was far more fitted to her tastes than those puny lotus flowers which floated on the ponds in the Capital. At night when she listened to the wind soughing through the trees in her garden, the sound seemed to her extremely insipid when compared to the delicate music in the Pure Land when the wind blew through the sacred treasure trees. When she thought of the strange instruments that hung in the sky and that played by themselves without ever being touched, the sound of the harp that echoed through the Palace halls seemed to her a paltry imitation.

The Great Priest of Shiga Temple was fighting. In the fight that he had waged against the flesh in his youth he had always been buoyed up by the hope of inheriting the future world. But this desperate fight of his old age was linked with a sense of irreparable loss.

The impossibility of consummating his love for the Great Imperial Concubine was as clear to him as the sun in the sky. At the same time he was fully aware of the impossibility of advancing toward the Pure Land so long as he remained in the thralls of this love. The Great Priest, who had lived in an incomparably free state of mind, had in a twinkling been enclosed in darkness and the future was totally obscure. It may have been that the

courage which had seen him through his youthful struggles had
grown out of self-confidence and pride in the fact that he was
voluntarily depriving himself of pleasure that could have been his
for the asking.

The Great Priest was again possessed by fear. Until that noble
carriage had approached the side of Lake Shiga, he had believed
that what lay in wait for him, close at hand, was nothing less than
the final release of Nirvana. But now he had awaked into the darkness of the present world, where it is impossible to see what lurks
a single step ahead.

The various forms of religious meditation were all in vain. He
tried the Contemplation of the Chrysanthemum, the Contemplation of the Total Aspect, and the Contemplation of the Parts; but
each time that he started to concentrate, the beautiful visage of the
Concubine appeared before his eyes. Water Contemplation, too,
was useless, for invariably her lovely face would float up shimmer-
ing from beneath the ripples of the lake.

This, no doubt, was a natural consequence of his infatuation.
Concentration, the priest soon realized, did more harm than good,
and next he tried to dull his spirit by dispersal. It astonished him
that spiritual concentration should have the paradoxical effect of
leading him still deeper into his delusions; but he soon realized that
to try the contrary method by dispersing his thoughts meant that he
was, in effect, admitting these very delusions. As his spirit began to
yield under the weight, the priest decided that, rather than pursue
a futile struggle, it were better to escape from the effort of escaping
by deliberately concentrating his thoughts on the figure of the
Great Imperial Concubine.

The Great Priest found a new pleasure in adorning his vision of
the lady in various ways, just as though he were adorning a Buddhist statue with diadems and baldachins. In so doing, he turned the
object of his love into an increasingly resplendent, distant, impossible being; and this afforded him particular joy. But why? Surely it
would be more natural for him to envisage the Great Imperial
Concubine as an ordinary female, close at hand and possessing normal human frailties. Thus he could better turn her to advantage, at
least in his imagination.

As he pondered this question, the truth dawned on him. What
he was depicting in the Great Imperial Concubine was not a
creature of flesh, nor was it a mere vision; rather, it was a symbol

of reality, a symbol of the essence of things. It was strange, indeed, to pursue that essence in the figure of a woman. Yet the reason was not far to seek. Even when falling in love, the Great Priest of Shiga had not discarded the habit, to which he had trained himself during his long years of contemplation, of striving to approach the essence of things by means of constant abstraction. The Great Imperial Concubine of Kyōgoku had now become uniform with his vision of the immense lotus of two hundred and fifty yojana. As she reclined on the water supported by all the lotus flowers, she had become vaster than Mount Sumeru, vaster than an entire realm.

The more the Great Priest turned his love into something impossible, the more deeply was he betraying the Buddha. For the impossibility of this love had become bound up with the impossibility of attaining enlightenment. The more he thought of his love as hopeless, the firmer grew the fantasy that supported it and the deeper-rooted became his impure thoughts. So long as he regarded his love as being even remotely feasible, it was paradoxically possible for him to resign himself; but now that the Great Concubine had grown into a fabulous and utterly unattainable creature the priest's love became motionless like a great stagnant lake which firmly, obdurately, covers the earth's surface.

He hoped that somehow he might see the lady's face once more, yet he feared that when he met her, that figure, which had now become like a giant lotus, would crumble away without a trace. If that were to happen, he would without doubt be saved. Yes, this time he was bound to attain enlightenment. And the very prospect filled the Great Priest with fear and awe.

The priest's lonely love had begun to devise strange, self-deceiving guiles, and when at length he reached the decision to go and see the lady, he was under the delusion that he had almost recovered from the illness that was searing his body. The bemused priest even mistook the joy that accompanied his decision for relief at having finally escaped from the trammels of his love.

None of the Great Concubine's people found anything especially strange in the sight of an old priest standing silently in the corner of the garden, leaning on a stick and gazing somberly at the residence. Ascetics and beggars frequently stood outside the great houses of the Capital and waited for alms. One of the ladies in attendance mentioned the matter to her mistress. The Great Imperial Concubine casually glanced through the blind that separated her from the garden. There in the shadow of the fresh green foliage stood a withered old priest with faded black robes and bowed head. For some time the lady looked at him. When she realized that this was without any question the priest whom she had seen by the lake at Shiga, her pale face turned paler still.

After a few moments of indecision, she gave orders that the priest's presence in her garden should be ignored. Her attendants bowed and withdrew.

Now for the first time the lady fell prey to uneasiness. In her lifetime she had seen many people who had abandoned the world, but never before had she laid eyes on someone who had abandoned the future world. The sight was ominous and inexpressibly fearful. All the pleasure that her imagination had conjured up from the idea of the priest's love disappeared in a flash. Much as he might have surrendered the future world on her behalf, that world, she now realized, would never pass into her own hands.

The Great Imperial Concubine looked down at her elegant clothes and at her beautiful hands, and then she looked across the garden at the uncomely features of the old priest and at his shabby robes. There was a horrible fascination in the fact that a connection should exist between them.

How different it all was from the splendid vision! The Great Priest seemed now like a person who had hobbled out of Hell itself. Nothing remained of that man of virtuous presence who had trailed the brightness of the Pure Land behind him. The brilliance which had resided within him and which had called to mind the glory of the Pure Land had vanished utterly. Though this was certainly the man who had stood by the Shiga Lake, it was at the same time a totally different person.

Like most people of the Court, the Great Imperial Concubine tended to be on her guard against her own emotions, especially when she was confronted with something that could be expected to affect her deeply. Now on seeing this evidence of the Great Priest's love, she felt disheartened at the thought that the consummate passion of which she had dreamt during all these years should assume so colorless a form.

When the priest had finally limped into the Capital leaning on his stick, he had almost forgotten his exhaustion. Secretly he made his way into the grounds of the Great Imperial Concubine's residence at Kyōgoku and looked across the garden. Behind those blinds, he thought, was sitting none other than the lady whom he loved.

Now that his adoration had assumed an immaculate form, the future world once again began to exert its charm on the Great Priest. Never before had he envisaged the Pure Land in so immaculate, so poignant, an aspect. His yearning for it became almost sensual. Nothing remained for him but the formality of meeting the Great Concubine, of declaring his love, and of thus ridding himself once and for all of the impure thoughts that tied him to this world and that still prevented him from attaining the Pure Land. That was all that remained to be done.

It was painful for him to stand there supporting his old body on his stick. The bright rays of the May sun poured through the leaves and beat down on his shaven head. Time after time he felt himself losing consciousness and without his stick he would certainly have collapsed. If only the lady would realize the situation and invite him into her presence, so that the formality might be done with! The Great Priest waited. He waited and supported his ever-growing weariness on his stick. At length the sun was covered with the evening clouds. Dusk gathered. Yet still no word came from the Great Imperial Concubine.

She, of course, had no way of knowing that the priest was looking through her, beyond her, into the Pure Land. Time after time she glanced out through the blinds. He was standing there immobile. The evening light thrust its way into the garden. Still he continued standing there.

The Great Imperial Concubine became frightened. She felt that what she saw in the garden was an incarnation of that "deep-rooted delusion" of which she had read in the Sutras. She was overcome by the fear of tumbling into Hell. Now that she had led astray a priest of such high virtue, it was not the Pure Land to which she could look forward, but Hell itself, whose terrors she and those about her knew in such detail. The supreme love of which she had dreamt had already been shattered. To be loved as she was—that in itself represented damnation. Whereas the Great Priest looked beyond her into the Pure Land, she now looked beyond the priest into the horrid realms of Hell.

Yet this haughty noblewoman of Kyōgoku was too proud to succumb to her fears without a fight, and she now summoned forth all the resources of her inbred ruthlessness. The Great Priest, she told herself, was bound to collapse sooner or later. She looked through the blind, thinking that by now he must be lying on the ground. To her annoyance, the silent figure stood there motionless.

Night fell and in the moonlight the figure of the priest looked like a pile of chalk-white bones.

The lady could not sleep for fear. She no longer looked through the blind and she turned her back to the garden. Yet all the time she seemed to feel the piercing gaze of the Great Priest on her back.

This, she knew, was no commonplace love. From fear of being loved, from fear of falling into Hell, the Great Imperial Concubine prayed more earnestly than ever for the Pure Land. It was for her own private Pure Land that she prayed—a Pure Land which she tried to preserve invulnerable within her heart. This was a different Pure Land from the priest's and it had no connection with his love. She felt sure that if she were ever to mention it to him it would instantly disintegrate.

The priest's love, she told herself, had nothing to do with her. It was a one-sided affair, in which her own feelings had no part, and there was no reason that it should disqualify her from being received into her Pure Land. Even if the Great Priest were to collapse and die, she would remain unscathed. Yet, as the night advanced and the air became colder, this confidence began to desert her.

The priest remained standing in the garden. When the moon was hidden by the clouds, he looked like a strange, gnarled old tree.

That form out there has nothing to do with me, thought the lady, almost beside herself with anguish, and the words seemed to boom within her heart. Why in Heaven's name should this have happened?

At that moment, strangely, the Great Imperial Concubine completely forgot about her own beauty. Or perhaps it would be more correct to say that she had made herself forget it.

Finally, faint traces of white began to break through the dark sky and the priest's figure emerged in the dawn twilight. He was still standing. The Great Imperial Concubine had been defeated. She summoned a maid and told her to invite the priest to come in from the garden and to kneel outside her blind.

The Great Priest was at the very boundary of oblivion when the flesh is on the verge of crumbling away. He no longer knew whether it was for the Great Imperial Concubine that he was waiting or for the future world. Though he saw the figure of the maid approaching from the residence into the dusky garden, it did not occur to him that what he had been awaiting was finally at hand.

The maid delivered her mistress's message. When she had finished, the priest uttered a dreadful, almost inhuman cry. The maid tried to lead him by the hand, but he pulled away and walked by himself toward the house with fantastically swift, firm steps.

It was dark on the other side of the blind and from outside it was impossible to see the lady's form. The priest knelt down and, covering his face with his hands, he wept. For a long time he stayed there without a word and his body shook convulsively.

Then in the dawn darkness a white hand gently emerged from behind the lowered blind. The priest of the Shiga Temple took it in his own hands and pressed it to his forehead and cheek.

The Great Imperial Concubine of Kyōgoku felt a strange cold hand touching her hand. At the same time she was aware of a warm moisture. Her hand was being bedewed by someone else's tears. Yet when the pallid shafts of morning light began to reach her through the blind, the lady's fervent faith imbued her with a wonderful inspiration: she became convinced that the unknown hand which touched hers belonged to none other than the Buddha.

Then the great vision sprang up anew in the lady's heart: the emerald earth of the Pure Land, the millions of seven-jeweled towers, the angels playing music, the golden ponds strewn with silver sand, the resplendent lotus, and the sweet voices of the Kalavinkas—all this was born afresh. If this was the Pure Land that she was to inherit—and so she now believed—why should she not accept the Great Priest's love?

She waited for the man with the hands of Buddha to ask her to raise the blind that separated her from him. Presently he would ask her; and then she would remove the barrier and her incomparably beautiful body would appear before him as it had on that day by the edge of the lake at Shiga; and she would invite him to come in.

The Great Imperial Concubine waited.

But the priest of Shiga Temple did not utter a word. He asked her for nothing. After a while his old hands relaxed their grip and the lady's snow-white hand was left alone in the dawn light. The priest departed. The heart of the Great Imperial Concubine turned cold.

A few days later a rumor reached the Court that the Great Priest's spirit had achieved its final liberation in his cell at Shiga. At this news the lady of Kyōgoku set to copying the Sutras in roll after roll of beautiful writing.

ALICE MUNRO

[Canada]

ALICE MUNRO (born Alice Laidlaw in 1931 in Wingham, Ontario), one of Canada's most renowned and beloved writers, has devoted almost her entire writing career to short stories. "How I Met My Husband" is from one of her earliest collections, *Something I've Been Meaning to Tell You*. She met and married a University of Western Ontario classmate, James Munro, in 1951, and they had three children. She divorced Munro and remarried in 1976. In 2013 she won the Nobel Prize for Literature, but has since said she will not be writing anymore.

How I Met My Husband (1974)

WE HEARD THE plane come over at noon, roaring through the radio news, and we were sure it was going to hit the house, so we all ran out into the yard. We saw it come in over the tree tops, all red and silver, the first close-up plane I ever saw. Mrs. Peebles screamed.

"Crash landing," their little boy said. Joey was his name.

"It's okay," said Dr. Peebles. "He knows what he's doing." Dr. Peebles was only an animal doctor, but had a calming way of talking, like any doctor.

This was my first job—working for Dr. and Mrs. Peebles, who had bought an old house out on the Fifth Line, about five miles out of town. It was just when the trend was starting of town people buying up old farms, not to work them but to live on them.

We watched the plane land across the road, where the fairgrounds used to be. It did make a good landing field, nice and level for the old race track, and the barns and display sheds torn down now for scrap lumber so there was nothing in the way. Even the old grandstand boys had burned.

"All right," said Mrs. Peebles, snappy as she always was when she got over her nerves. "Let's go back in the house. Let's not stand here gawking like a set of farmers."

She didn't say that to hurt my feelings. It never occurred to her.

I was just setting the dessert down when Loretta Bird arrived, out of breath, at the screen door.

"I thought it was going to crash into the house and kill youse all!"

She lived on the next place and the Peebles thought she was a countrywoman, they didn't know the difference. She and her husband didn't farm, he worked on the roads and had a bad name for drinking. They had seven children and couldn't get credit at the Hi-Way Grocery. The Peebles made her welcome, not knowing any better, as I say, and offered her dessert.

Dessert was never anything to write home about, at their place. A dish of Jello or sliced bananas or fruit out of a tin. "Have a house without a pie, be ashamed until you die," my mother used to say, but Mrs. Peebles operated differently.

Loretta Bird saw me getting the can of peaches.

"Oh, never mind," she said. "I haven't got the right kind of a stomach to trust what comes out of those tins, I can only eat home canning."

I could have slapped her. I bet she never put down fruit in her life.

"I know what he's landed here for," she said. "He's got permission to use the fairgrounds and take people up for rides. It costs a dollar. It's the same fellow who was over at Palmerston last week and was up the lakeshore before that. I wouldn't go up, if you paid me."

"I'd jump at the chance," Dr. Peebles said. "I'd like to see this neighborhood from the air."

Mrs. Peebles said she would just as soon see it from the ground. Joey said he wanted to go and Heather did, too. Joey was nine and Heather was seven.

"Would you, Edie?" Heather said.

I said I didn't know. I was scared, but I never admitted that, especially in front of children I was taking care of.

"People are going to be coming out here in their cars raising dust and trampling your property, if I was you I would complain," Loretta said. She hooked her legs around the chair rung and I knew we were in for a lengthy visit. After Dr. Peebles went back to his office or out on his next call and Mrs. Peebles went for her nap, she would hang around me while I was trying to do the dishes. She would pass remarks about the Peebles in their own house.

"She wouldn't find time to lay down in the middle of the day, if she had seven kids like I got."

She asked me did they fight and did they keep things in the dresser drawer not to have babies with. She said it was a sin if they did. I pretended I didn't know what she was talking about.

I was fifteen and away from home for the first time. My parents had made the effort and sent me to high school for a year, but I didn't like it. I was shy of strangers and the work was hard, they didn't make it nice for you or explain the way they do now. At the end of the year the averages were published in the paper, and mine came out at the very bottom, 37 per cent. My father said that's enough and I didn't blame him. The last thing I wanted, anyway, was to go on and end up teaching school. It happened the very day the paper came out with my disgrace in it, Dr. Peebles was staying at our place for dinner, having just helped one of our cows have twins, and he said I looked smart to him and his wife was looking for a girl to help. He said she felt tied down, with the two children, out in the country. I guess she would, my mother said, being polite, though I could tell from her face she was wondering what on earth it would be like to have only two children and no barn work, and then to be complaining.

When I went home I would describe to them the work I had to do, and it made everybody laugh. Mrs. Peebles had an automatic washer and dryer, the first I ever saw. I have had those in my own home for such a long time now it's hard to remember how much of a miracle it was to me, not having to struggle with the wringer and hang up and haul down. Let alone not having to heat water. Then there was practically no baking. Mrs. Peebles said she couldn't make pie crust, the most amazing thing I ever heard a woman admit. I could, of course, and I could make light biscuits and a white cake and a dark cake, but they didn't want it, she said they watched their figures. The only thing I didn't like about working there, in fact, was feeling half hungry a lot of the time.

I used to bring back a box of doughnuts made out at home, and hide them under my bed. The children found out, and I didn't mind sharing, but I thought I better bind them to secrecy.

The day after the plane landed Mrs. Peebles put both children in the car and drove over to Chesley, to get their hair cut. There was a good woman then at Chesley for doing hair. She got hers done at the same place, Mrs. Peebles did, and that meant they would be gone a good while. She had to pick a day Dr. Peebles wasn't going out into the country, she didn't have her own car. Cars were still in short supply then, after the war.

I loved being left in the house alone, to do my work at leisure. The kitchen was all white and bright yellow, with fluorescent lights. That was before they ever thought of making the appliances all different colors and doing the cupboards like dark old wood and hiding the lighting. I loved light. I loved the double sink. So would anybody new-come from washing dishes in a dishpan with a rag-plugged hole on an oilcloth-covered table by light of a coal-oil lamp. I kept everything shining.

The bathroom too. I had a bath in there once a week. They wouldn't have minded if I took one oftener, but to me it seemed like asking too much, or maybe risking making it less wonderful. The basin and the tub and the toilet were all pink, and there were glass doors with flamingoes painted on them, to shut off the tub. The light had a rosy cast and the mat sank under your feet like snow, except that it was warm. The mirror was three-way. With the mirror all steamed up and the air like a perfume cloud, from things I was allowed to use, I stood up on the side of the tub and admired myself naked, from three directions. Sometimes I thought about the way we lived out at home and the way we lived here and how one way was so hard to imagine when you were living the other way. But I thought it was still a lot easier, living the way we lived at home, to picture something like this, the painted flamingoes and the warmth and the soft mat, than it was for anybody knowing only things like this to picture how it was the other way. And why was that?

I was through my jobs in no time, and had the vegetables peeled for supper and sitting in cold water besides. Then I went into Mrs. Peebles' bedroom. I had been in there plenty of times, cleaning, and I always took a good look in her closet, at the clothes she had hanging there. I wouldn't have looked in her drawers, but a closet is open to anybody. That's a lie. I would have looked in drawers, but I would have felt worse doing it and been more scared she could tell.

Some clothes in her closet she wore all the time, I was quite familiar with them. Others she never put on, they were pushed to the back. I was disappointed to see no wedding dress. But there was one long dress I could just see the skirt of, and I was hungering to see the rest. Now I took note of where it hung and lifted it out. It was satin, a lovely weight on my arm, light bluish-green in color, almost silvery. It had a fitted, pointed waist and a full skirt and an off-the-shoulder fold hiding the little sleeves.

Next thing was easy. I got out of my own things and slipped it on. I was slimmer at fifteen than anybody would believe who knows me now and the fit was beautiful. I didn't, of course, have a strapless bra on, which was what it needed, I just had to slide my straps down my arms under the material. Then I tried pinning up my hair, to get the effect. One thing led to another. I put on rouge and lipstick and eyebrow pencil from her dresser. The heat of the day and the weight of the satin and all the excitement made me thirsty, and I went out to the kitchen, got-up as I was, to get a glass of ginger ale with ice cubes from the refrigerator. The Peebles drank ginger ale, or fruit drinks, all day, like water, and I was getting so I did too. Also there was no limit on ice cubes, which I was so fond of I would even put them in a glass of milk.

I turned from putting the ice tray back and saw a man watching me through the screen. It was the luckiest thing in the world I didn't spill the ginger ale down the front of me then and there.

"I never meant to scare you. I knocked but you were getting the ice out, you didn't hear me."

I couldn't see what he looked like, he was dark the way somebody is pressed up against a screen door with the bright daylight behind them. I only knew he wasn't from around here.

"I'm from the plane over there. My name is Chris Watters and what I was wondering was if I could use that pump."

There was a pump in the yard. That was the way the people used to get their water. Now I noticed he was carrying a pail.

"You're welcome," I said. "I can get it from the tap and save you pumping." I guess I wanted him to know we had piped water, didn't pump ourselves.

"I don't mind the exercise." He didn't move, though, and finally he said, "Were you going to a dance?"

Seeing a stranger there had made me entirely forget how I was dressed.

"Or is that the way ladies around here generally get dressed up in the afternoon?"

I didn't know how to joke back then. I was too embarrassed.

"You live here? Are you the lady of the house?"

"I'm the hired girl."

Some people change when they find that out, their whole way of looking at you and speaking to you changes, but his didn't.

"Well, I just wanted to tell you you look very nice. I was so surprised when I looked in the door and saw you. Just because you looked so nice and beautiful."

I wasn't even old enough then to realize how out of the common it is, for a man to say something like that to a woman, or somebody he is treating like a woman. For a man to say a word like *beautiful*. I wasn't old enough to realize or to say anything back, or in fact to do anything but wish he would go away. Not that I didn't like him, but just that it upset me so, having him look at me, and me trying to think of something to say.

He must have understood. He said good-bye, and thanked me, and went and started filling his pail from the pump. I stood behind the Venetian blinds in the dining room, watching him. When he had gone, I went into the bedroom and took the dress off and put it back in the same place. I dressed in my own clothes and took my hair down and washed my face, wiping it on Kleenex, which I threw in the wastebasket.

★

The Peebles asked me what kind of man he was. Young, middle-aged, short, tall? I couldn't say.

"Good-looking?" Dr. Peebles teased me.

I couldn't think a thing but that he would be coming to get his water again, he would be talking to Dr. or Mrs. Peebles, making friends with them, and he would mention seeing me that first afternoon, dressed up. Why not mention it? He would think it was funny. And no idea of the trouble it would get me into.

After supper the Peebles drove into town to go to a movie. She wanted to go somewhere with her hair fresh done. I sat in my bright kitchen wondering what to do, knowing I would never sleep. Mrs. Peebles might not fire me, when she found out, but it would give her a different feeling about me altogether. This was the first place I ever worked but I already had picked up things about the way people feel when you are working for them. They like to think you aren't curious. Not just that you aren't dishonest, that isn't enough. They like to feel you don't notice things, that you don't think or wonder about anything but what they liked to eat and how they like things ironed, and so on. I don't mean they weren't kind to me, because they were. They had me eat my meals with them (to tell the truth I expected to, I didn't know there were families who don't) and sometimes they took me along in the car. But all the same.

I went up and checked on the children being asleep and then I went out. I had to do it. I crossed the road and went in the old fairgrounds gate. The plane looked unnatural sitting there, and shining with the moon. Off at the far side of the fairgrounds, where the bush was taking over, I saw his tent.

He was sitting outside it smoking a cigarette. He saw me coming.

"Hello, were you looking for a plane ride? I don't start taking people up till tomorrow." Then he looked again and said, "Oh, it's you. I didn't know you without your long dress on."

My heart was knocking away, my tongue was dried up. I had to say something. But I couldn't. My throat was closed and I was like a deaf-and-dumb.

"Did you want a ride? Sit down. Have a cigarette."

I couldn't even shake my head to say no, so he gave me one.

"Put it in your mouth or I can't light it. It's a good thing I'm used to shy ladies."

I did. It wasn't the first time I had smoked a cigarette, actually. My girl friend out home, Muriel Lower, used to steal them from her brother.

"Look at your hand shaking. Did you just want to have a chat, or what?"

In one burst I said, "I wisht you wouldn't say anything about that dress."

"What dress? Oh, the long dress."

"It's Mrs. Peebles'."

"Whose? Oh, the lady you work for? Is that it? She wasn't home so you got dressed up in her dress, eh? You got dressed up and played queen. I don't blame you. You're not smoking that cigarette right. Don't just puff. Draw it in. Did nobody ever show you how to inhale? Are you scared I'll tell on you? Is that it?"

I was so ashamed at having to ask him to connive this way I couldn't nod. I just looked at him and he saw *yes*.

"Well I won't. I won't in the slightest way mention it or embarrass you. I give you my word of honor."

Then he changed the subject, to help me out, seeing I couldn't even thank him.

"What do you think of this sign?"

It was a board sign lying practically at my feet.

SEE THE WORLD FROM THE SKY. ADULTS $1.00, CHILDREN 50¢. QUALIFIED PILOT.

"My old sign was getting pretty beat up, I thought I'd make a new one. That's what I've been doing with my time today."

The lettering wasn't all that handsome, I thought. I could have done a better one in half an hour.

"I'm not an expert at sign making."

"It's very good," I said.

"I don't need it for publicity, word of mouth is usually enough. I turned away two carloads tonight. I felt like taking it easy. I didn't tell them ladies were dropping in to visit me."

Now I remembered the children and I was scared again, in case one of them had waked up and called me and I wasn't there.

"Do you have to go so soon?"

I remembered some manners. "Thank you for the cigarette."

"Don't forget. You have my word of honor."

I tore off across the fairgrounds, scared I'd see the car heading home from town. My sense of time was mixed up, I didn't know how long I'd been out of the house. But it was all right, it wasn't late, the children were asleep. I got in bed myself and lay thinking what a lucky end to the day, after all, and among things to be grateful for I could be grateful Loretta Bird hadn't been the one who caught me.

★

The yard and borders didn't get trampled, it wasn't as bad as that. All the same it seemed very public, around the house. The sign was on the fairgrounds gate. People came mostly after supper but a good many in the afternoon, too. The Bird children all came without fifty cents between them and hung on the gate. We got used to the excitement of the plane coming in and taking off, it wasn't excitement any more. I never went over, after that one time, but would see him when he came to get his water. I would be out on the steps doing sitting-down work, like preparing vegetables, if I could.

"Why don't you come over? I'll take you up in my plane."

"I'm saving my money," I said, because I couldn't think of anything else.

"For what? For getting married?"

I shook my head.

"I'll take you up for free if you come sometime when it's slack. I thought you would come, and have another cigarette."

I made a face to hush him, because you never could tell when the children would be sneaking around the porch, or Mrs. Peebles herself listening in the house. Sometimes she came out and had a conversation with him. He told her things he hadn't bothered to tell me. But then I hadn't thought to ask. He told her he had been in the War, that was where he learned to fly a plane, and now he couldn't settle down to ordinary life, this was what he liked. She said she couldn't imagine anybody liking such a thing. Though sometimes, she said, she was almost bored enough to try anything herself, she wasn't brought up to living in the country. It's all my husband's idea, she said. This was news to me.

"Maybe you ought to give flying lessons," she said.

"Would you take them?"

She just laughed.

*

Sunday was a busy flying day in spite of it being preached against from two pulpits. We were all sitting out watching. Joey and Heather were over on the fence with the Bird kids. Their father had said they could go, after their mother saying all week they couldn't.

A car came down the road past the parked cars and pulled up right in the drive. It was Loretta Bird who got out, all importance, and on the driver's side another woman got out, more sedately. She was wearing sunglasses.

"This is a lady looking for the man that flies the plane," Loretta Bird said. "I heard her inquire in the hotel coffee shop where I was having a Coke and I brought her out."

"I'm sorry to bother you," the lady said. "I'm Alice Kelling, Mr. Watters' fiancée."

This Alice Kelling had on a pair of brown and white checked slacks and a yellow top. Her bust looked to me rather low and bumpy. She had a worried face. Her hair had had a permanent, but had grown out, and she wore a yellow band to keep it off her face. Nothing in the least pretty or even young-looking about her. But you could tell from how she talked she was from the city, or educated, or both.

Dr. Peebles stood up and introduced himself and his wife and me and asked her to be seated.

"He's up in the air right now, but you're welcome to sit and wait. He gets his water here and he hasn't been yet. He'll probably take his break about five."

"That is him, then?" said Alice Kelling, wrinkling and straining at the sky.

"He's not in the habit of running out on you, taking a different name?" Dr. Peebles laughed. He was the one, not his wife, to offer iced tea. Then she sent me into the kitchen to fix it. She smiled. She was wearing sunglasses too.

"He never mentioned his fiancée," she said.

I loved fixing iced tea with lots of ice and slices of lemon in tall glasses. I ought to have mentioned before, Dr. Peebles was an abstainer, at least around the house, or I wouldn't have been allowed to take the place. I had to fix a glass for Loretta Bird too, though it galled me, and when I went out she had settled in my lawn chair, leaving me the steps.

"I knew you was a nurse when I first heard you in that coffee shop."

"How would you know a thing like that?"

"I get my hunches about people. Was that how you met him, nursing?"

"Chris? Well yes. Yes, it was."

"Oh, were you overseas?" said Mrs. Peebles.

"No, it was before he went overseas. I nursed him when he was stationed at Centralia and had a ruptured appendix. We got engaged and then he went overseas. My, this is refreshing, after a long drive."

"He'll be glad to see you," Dr. Peebles said. "It's a rackety kind of life, isn't it, not staying one place long enough to really make friends."

"Youse've had a long engagement," Loretta Bird said.

Alice Kelling passed that over. "I was going to get a room at the hotel, but when I was offered directions I came on out. Do you think I could phone them?"

"No need," Dr. Peebles said. "You're five miles away from him if you stay at the hotel. Here, you're right across the road. Stay with us. We've got rooms on rooms, look at this big house."

Asking people to stay, just like that, is certainly a country thing, and maybe seemed natural to him now, but not to Mrs. Peebles, from the way she said, oh yes, we have plenty of room. Or to Alice Kelling, who kept protesting, but let herself be worn down. I got the feeling it was a temptation to her, to be that close. I was trying for a look at her ring. Her nails were painted red, her fingers were freckled and wrinkled. It was a tiny stone. Muriel Lowe's cousin had one twice as big.

Chris came to get his water, late in the afternoon just as Dr. Peebles had predicted. He must have recognized the car from a way off. He came smiling.

"Here I am chasing after you to see what you're up to," called Alice Kelling. She got up and went to meet him and they kissed, just touched, in front of us.

"You're going to spend a lot on gas that way," Chris said.

Dr. Peebles invited Chris to stay for supper, since he had already put up the sign that said: NO MORE RIDES TILL 7 P.M. Mrs. Peebles wanted it served in the yard, in spite of bugs. One thing strange to anybody from the country is this eating outside. I had made a potato salad earlier and she had made a jellied salad, that was one thing she could do, so it was just a matter of getting those out, and some sliced meat and cucumbers and fresh leaf lettuce. Loretta Bird hung around for some time saying, "Oh, well, I guess I better get home to those yappers," and, "It's so nice just sitting here, I sure hate to get up," but nobody invited her, I was relieved to see, and finally she had to go.

That night after rides were finished Alice Kelling and Chris went off somewhere in her car. I lay awake till they got back. When I saw the car lights sweep my ceiling I got up to look down on them through the slats of my blind. I don't know what I thought I was going to see. Muriel Lowe and I used to sleep on her front veranda and watch her sister and her sister's boy friend saying good night.

Afterwards we couldn't get to sleep, for longing for somebody to kiss us and rub up against us and we would talk about suppose you were out in a boat with a boy and he wouldn't bring you in to shore unless you did it, or what if somebody got you trapped in a barn, you would have to, wouldn't you, it wouldn't be your fault. Muriel said her two girl cousins used to try with a toilet paper roll that one of them was the boy. We wouldn't do anything like that; just lay and wondered.

All that happened was that Chris got out of the car on one side and she got out on the other and they walked off separately—him towards the fairgrounds and her towards the house. I got back in bed and imagined about me coming home with him, not like that.

Next morning Alice Kelling got up late and I fixed a grapefruit for her the way I had learned and Mrs. Peebles sat down with her to visit and have another cup of coffee. Mrs. Peebles seemed pleased enough now, having company. Alice Kelling said she guessed she better get used to putting in a day just watching Chris take off and come down, and Mrs. Peebles said she didn't know if she should suggest it because Alice Kelling was the one with the car, but the lake was only twenty-five miles away and what a good day for a picnic.

Alice Kelling took her up on the idea and by eleven o'clock they were in the car, with Joey and Heather and a sandwich lunch I had made. The only thing was that Chris hadn't come down, and she wanted to tell him where they were going.

"Edie'll go over and tell him," Mrs. Peebles said. "There's no problem."

Alice Kelling wrinkled her face and agreed.

"Be sure and tell him we'll be back by five!"

I didn't see that he would be concerned about knowing this right away, and I thought of him eating whatever he ate over there, alone, cooking on his camp stove, so I got to work and mixed up a crumb cake and baked it, in between the other work I had to do; then, when it was a bit cooled, wrapped it in a tea towel. I didn't do anything to myself but take off my apron and comb my hair. I would like to have put some make-up on, but I was too afraid it would remind him of the way he first saw me, and that would humiliate me all over again.

He had come and put another sign on the gate: NO RIDES THIS P.M. APOLOGIES. I worried that he wasn't feeling well. No sign of him outside and the tent flap was down. I knocked on the pole.

"Come in," he said, in a voice that would just as soon have said *Stay out*.

I lifted the flap.

"Oh, it's you. I'm sorry. I didn't know it was you."

He had been just sitting on the side of the bed, smoking. Why not at least sit and smoke in the fresh air?

"I brought a cake and hope you're not sick," I said.

"Why would I be sick? Oh—that sign. That's all right. I'm just tired of talking to people. I don't mean you. Have a seat." He pinned back the tent flap. "Get some fresh air in here."

I sat on the edge of the bed, there was no place else. It was one of those fold-up cots, really: I remembered and gave him his fiancée's message.

He ate some of the cake. "Good."

"Put the rest away for when you're hungry later."

"I'll tell you a secret. I won't be around here much longer."

"Are you getting married?"

"Ha ha. What time did you say they'd be back?"

"Five o'clock."

"Well, by that time this place will have seen the last of me. A plane can get further than a car." He unwrapped the cake and ate another piece of it, absent-mindedly.

"Now you'll be thirsty."

"There's some water in the pail."

"It won't be very cold. I could bring some fresh. I could bring some ice from the refrigerator."

"No," he said. "I don't want you to go. I want a nice long time of saying good-bye to you."

He put the cake away carefully and sat beside me and started those little kisses, so soft, I can't ever let myself think about them, such kindness in his face and lovely kisses, all over my eyelids and neck and ears, all over, then me kissing back as well as I could (I had only kissed a boy on a dare before, and kissed my own arms for practice) and we lay back on the cot and pressed together, just gently, and he did some other things, not bad things or not in a bad way. It was lovely in the tent, that smell of grass and hot tent cloth with the sun beating down on it, and he said, "I wouldn't do you any harm for the world." Once, when he had rolled on top of me and we were sort of rocking together on the cot, he said softly, "Oh, no," and freed himself and jumped up and got the water pail.

He splashed some of it on his neck and face, and the little bit left, on me lying there.

"That's to cool us off, Miss."

When we said good-bye I wasn't at all sad, because he held my face and said "I'm going to write you a letter. I'll tell you where I am and maybe you can come and see me. Would you like that? Okay then. You wait." I was really glad I think to get away from him, it was like he was piling presents on me I couldn't get the pleasure of till I considered them alone.

★

No consternation at first about the plane being gone. They thought he had taken somebody up, and I didn't enlighten them. Dr. Peebles had phoned he had to go to the country, so there was just us having supper, and then Loretta Bird thrusting her head in the door and saying, "I see he's took off."

"What?" said Alice Kelling, and pushed back her chair.

"The kids come and told me this afternoon he was taking down his tent. Did he think he'd run through all the business there was around here? He didn't take off without letting you know, did he?"

"He'll send me word," Alice Kelling said. "He'll probably phone tonight. He's terribly restless, since the War."

"Edie, he didn't mention to you, did he?" Mrs. Peebles said. "When you took over the message?"

"Yes," I said. So far so true.

"Well why didn't you say?" All of them were looking at me. "Did he say where he was going?"

"He said he might try Bayfield," I said. What made me tell such a lie? I didn't intend it.

"Bayfield, how far is that?" said Alice Kelling.

Mrs. Peebles said, "Thirty, thirty-five miles."

"That's not far. Oh, well, that's really not far at all. It's on the lake, isn't it?"

You'd think I'd be ashamed of myself, setting her on the wrong track. I did it to give him more time, whatever time he needed. I lied for him, and also, I have to admit, for me. Women should stick together and not do things like that. I see that now, but didn't then. I never thought of myself as being in any way like her, or coming to the same troubles, ever.

She hadn't taken her eyes off me. I thought she suspected my lie. "When did he mention this to you?"

"Earlier."

"When you were over at the plane?"

"Yes."

"You must've stayed and had a chat." She smiled at me, not a nice smile. "You must've stayed and had a little visit with him."

"I took a cake," I said, thinking that telling some truth would spare me telling the rest.

"We didn't have a cake," said Mrs. Peebles rather sharply.

"I baked one."

Alice Kelling said, "That was very friendly of you."

"Did you get permission," said Loretta Bird. "You never know what these girls'll do next," she said. "It's not they mean harm so much, as they're ignorant."

"The cake is neither here nor there," Mrs. Peebles broke in. "Edie, I wasn't aware you knew Chris that well."

I didn't know what to say.

"I'm not surprised," Alice Kelling said in a high voice. "I knew by the look of her as soon as I saw her. We get them at the hospital all the time." She looked hard at me with her stretched smile. "Having their babies. We have to put them in a special ward because of their diseases. Little country tramps. Fourteen and fifteen years old. You should see the babies they have, too."

"There was a bad woman here in town had a baby that pus was running out of its eyes," Loretta Bird put in.

"Wait a minute," said Mrs. Peebles. "What is this talk? Edie. What about you and Mr. Watters? Were you intimate with him?"

"Yes," I said. I was thinking of us lying on the cot and kissing, wasn't that intimate? And I would never deny it.

They were all one minute quiet, even Loretta Bird.

"Well," said Mrs. Peebles. "I am surprised. I think I need a cigarette. This is the first of any such tendencies I've seen in her," she said, speaking to Alice Kelling, but Alice Kelling was looking at me.

"Loose little bitch." Tears ran down her face. "Loose little bitch, aren't you? I knew as soon as I saw you. Men despise girls like you. He just made use of you and went off, you know that, don't you? Girls like you are just nothing, they're just public conveniences, just filthy little rags!"

"Oh, now," said Mrs. Peebles.

"Filthy," Alice Kelling sobbed. "Filthy little rag!"

"Don't get yourself upset," Loretta Bird said. She was swollen up with pleasure at being in on this scene. "Men are all the same."

"Edie, I'm very surprised," Mrs. Peebles said. "I thought your parents were so strict. You don't want to have a baby, do you?"

I'm still ashamed of what happened next. I lost control, just like a six-year-old, I started howling. "You don't get a baby from just doing that!"

"You see. Some of them are that ignorant," Loretta Bird said.

But Mrs. Peebles jumped up and caught my arms and shook me. "Calm down. Don't get hysterical. Calm down. Stop crying. Listen to me. Listen. I'm wondering, if you know what being intimate means. Now tell me. What did you think it meant?"

"Kissing," I howled.

She let go. "Oh, Edie. Stop it. Don't be silly. It's all right. It's all a misunderstanding. Being intimate means a lot more than that. Oh, I *wondered*."

"She's trying to cover up, now," said Alice Kelling. "Yes. She's not so stupid. She sees she got herself in trouble."

"I believe her," Mrs. Peebles said. "This is an awful scene."

"Well there is one way to find out," said Alice Kelling, getting up. "After all, I am a nurse."

Mrs. Peebles drew a breath and said, "No. No. Go to your room, Edie. And stop that noise. That is too disgusting."

I heard the car start in a little while. I tried to stop crying, pulling back each wave as it started over me. Finally I succeeded, and lay heaving on the bed.

Mrs. Peebles came and stood in the doorway.

"She's gone," she said. "That Bird woman too. Of course, you know you should never have gone near that man and that is the cause of all this trouble. I have a headache. As soon as you can, go and wash your face in cold water and get at the dishes and we will not say any more about this."

★

Nor we didn't. I didn't figure out till years later the extent of what I had been saved from. Mrs. Peebles was not very friendly to me afterwards, but she was fair. Not very friendly is the wrong way of describing what she was. She never had been very friendly. It was just that now she had to see me all the time and it got on her nerves, a little.

As for me, I put it all out of my mind like a bad dream and concentrated on waiting for my letter. The mail came every day except Sunday, between one-thirty and two in the afternoon, a good time for me because Mrs. Peebles was always having her nap. I would get the kitchen all cleaned and then go up to the mailbox and sit in the grass, waiting. I was perfectly happy, waiting, I forgot all about Alice Kelling and her misery and awful talk and Mrs. Peebles and her chilliness and the embarrassment of whether she had told Dr. Peebles and the face of Loretta Bird, getting her fill of other people's troubles. I was always smiling when the mailman got there, and continued smiling even after he gave me the mail and I saw today wasn't the day. The mailman was a Carmichael. I knew by his face because there are a lot of Carmichaels living out by us and so many of them have a sort of sticking-out top lip. So I asked his name (he was a young man, shy, but good humored, anybody could ask him anything) and then I said, "I knew by your face!" He was pleased by that and always glad to see me and got a little less shy. "You've got the smile I've been waiting on all day!" he used to holler out the car window.

It never crossed my mind for a long time a letter might not come. I believed in it coming just like I believed the sun would rise in the morning. I just put off my hope from day to day, and there was the goldenrod out around the mailbox and the children gone back to school, and the leaves turning, and I was wearing a sweater when I went to wait. One day walking back with the hydro bill stuck in my hand, that was all, looking across at the fairgrounds with the full-blown milkweed and dark teasels, so much like fall, it just struck me: *No letter was ever going to come.* It was an impossible idea to get used to. No, not impossible. If I thought about Chris's face when he said he was going to write to me, it was impossible, but if I forgot that and thought about the actual tin mailbox, empty, it was plain and true. I kept on going to meet the mail, but my heart was heavy now like a lump of lead. I only smiled because I thought of the mailman counting on it, and he didn't have an easy life, with the winter driving ahead.

Till it came to me one day there were women doing this with their lives, all over. There were women just waiting and waiting by mailboxes for one letter or another. I imagined me making this journey day after day and year after year, and my hair starting to go gray, and I thought, I was never made to go on like that. So I stopped meeting the mail. If there were women all through life waiting, and women busy and not waiting, I knew which I had to be. Even though there might be things the second kind of women have to pass up and never know about, it still is better.

I was surprised when the mailman phoned the Peebles' place in the evening and asked for me. He said he missed me. He asked if I would like to go to Goderich where some well-known movie was on, I forget now what. So I said yes, and I went out with him for two years and he asked me to marry him, and we were engaged a year more while I got my things together, and then we did marry. He always tells the children the story of how I went after him by sitting by the mailbox every day, and naturally I laugh and let him, because I like for people to think what pleases them and makes them happy.

R. K. NARAYAN

[India]

THE FIRST language of R. K. Narayan (the pen-name of Rasipuram Krishnaswami Narayanswami), was Tamil, but he wrote all his works in English. He was born in 1906 in Madras in south India, into a family of high-caste Brahmins. Raised for the most part by his grandmother, he was well-educated but, as he told it, not successful in his first career pursuits, including teaching, and ultimately returned to what he most loved, writing. Refusing an arranged marriage, he wed his wife Rajam in 1933, when she was fifteen; she died of typhoid six years later, leaving him with a young daughter, whom he raised. Rajam's death devastated him and he left off writing for several years; when he resumed, he wrote hundreds of stories and essays, as well as thirty-four novels over the course of the rest of his life. He never remarried, and at the time of his death in 2001, at the age of ninety-four, was planning a new novel.

The Shelter (1985)

THE RAIN CAME down suddenly. The only shelter he could run to was the banyan tree on the roadside, with its huge trunk and the spreading boughs above. He watched, with detachment, the rain patter down with occasional sprays coming in his direction. He watched idly a mongrel trotting off, his coat completely wet, and a couple of buffaloes on the roadside eating cast-off banana leaves. He suddenly became aware of another person standing under the tree, beyond the curve of the tree trunk. A faint scent of flower wafted towards him, and he could not contain his curiosity; he edged along the tree trunk, and suddenly found himself face to face with her. His first reaction was to let out a loud "Oh!" and he looked miserable and confused. The lady saw him and suppressed a scream. When he had recovered his composure, he said, "Don't worry, I will go away." It seemed a silly thing to say to one's wife after a long separation. He moved back to his previous spot away from her. But presently he came back to ask, "What brought you here?"

He feared she might not reply, but she said, "Rain." "Oh!" He tried to treat it as a joke and please her by laughing. "It brought me also here," he said, feeling idiotic. She said nothing in reply. The weather being an ever-obliging topic, he tried to cling to it desperately and said, "Unexpected rain." She gave no response to his remark and looked away. He tried to drag on the subject further. "If I had had the slightest suspicion of its coming, I would have stayed indoors or brought my umbrella." She ignored his statement completely. She might be deaf for all it mattered. He wanted to ask, Are your ears affected? but feared that she might feel irritated. She was capable of doing anything when upset. He had never suspected the strength of her feelings until that night of final crisis.

They had had several crises in their years of married life. Every other hour they expressed differing views on everything under the sun: every question precipitated a crisis, none too trivial to be ignored. It might be anything—whether to listen to Radio Ceylon or All India Radio, whether one should see an English picture or a Tamil one, whether jasmine smell might be termed too strong or otherwise, a rose could be termed gaudy or not, and so forth. Anything led to an argument and created tension, and effected a breach between the partners for a number of days, to be followed by a reconciliation and an excessive friendliness. In one such mood of reconciliation they had even drawn an instrument of friendship with elaborate clauses, and signed it before the gods in the puja room with a feeling that nothing would bother them again and that all their troubles were at an end. But it was short-lived and the very first clause of the contract, "We shall never quarrel hereafter," was the first to be broken within twenty-four hours of signing the deed, and all the other clauses, which covered such possible causes of difference as household expenses, criticism of food, budget discussions, references to in-laws (on all of which elaborate understanding had been evolved), did not mean anything.

Now standing in the rain he felt happy that she was cornered. He had had no news of her after he had shut the door on her that night as it seemed so long ago. They had argued over the food as usual, she threatened to leave the home, and he said, "Go ahead," and held the door open while she had walked out into the night. He left the door unbolted for a long time in the belief that she would return, but she didn't.

"I didn't hope to see you again," he ventured to say now and she answered, "Did you think I would go and drown myself?" "Yes, that I feared," he said.

"Did you look for me in the nearby wells, or ponds?"

"Or the river?" he added. "I didn't."

"It would have surprised me if you had had so much concern."

He said, "You didn't drown yourself after all, how could you blame me for not looking for you?" He appealed to her pathetically. She nearly stamped her foot as she said, "That only shows you have no heart."

"You are very unreasonable," he said.

"Oh, God, you have started giving a reading of my character. It is my ill fate that the rain should have come down just now and driven me over here."

"On the contrary, I think it is a good rain. It has brought us together. May I now ask what you have been doing with yourself all this time?"

"Should I answer?" He detected in her voice a certain amount of concern and he felt flattered. Could he induce her to come back to him? The sentence almost formed itself on the tip of his tongue but he thrust it back. He merely asked, "Aren't you concerned with my own lot? Don't you care to know what I have been doing with myself all these months?" She didn't reply. She simply watched the rain pouring down more than ever. The wind's direction suddenly changed and a gust flung a spray of water on her face. He treated it as an excuse to dash up to her with his kerchief. She recoiled from his approach. "Don't bother about me," she cried.

"You are getting wet. . . ." A bough above shook a few drops on her hair. He pointed his finger at her anxiously and said, "You are getting drenched unnecessarily. You could move down a little this way. If you like I will stand where you are." He expected her to be touched by this solicitude. She merely replied, "You need not worry about me." She stood grimly looking at the rain as it churned up the road. "Shall I dash up and bring an umbrella or a taxi?" he asked. She merely glared at him and turned away. He said something else on the same lines and she asked, "Am I your toy?"

"Why do you say toy? I said no such thing."

"You think you can pick me up when you like and throw me out when you feel that way. Only toys are treated thus."

"I never told you to go away," he said.

"I am not listening to any of that again," she said.

"I am probably dying to say how sorry I am," he began.

"May be, but go and say that to someone else."

"I have no one else to say such things to," he said.

"That is your trouble, is it?" she asked. "That doesn't interest me."

"Have you no heart?" he pleaded. "When I say I am sorry, believe me. I am changed now."

"So am I," she said. "I am not my old self now. I expect nothing in others and I am never disappointed," she said.

"Won't you tell me what you are doing?" he pleaded. She shook her head. He said, "Someone said that you were doing harijan work or some such thing. See how I am following your activities!" She said nothing in reply. He asked, "Do you live all the time here or . . . ?" It was plain that he was trying to get her address. She threw a glance at the rain, and then looked at him sourly. He said, "Well, I didn't order the rain anyway. We have got to face it together."

"Not necessarily. Nothing can hold me thus," she said, and suddenly dashed into the rain and broke into a run. He cried after her, "Wait, wait. I promise not to talk. Come back, don't get drenched," but she was off, vanishing beyond the curtain of raindrops.

DOROTHY PARKER

[U.S.A.]

DOROTHY PARKER (1893–1967), born Dorothy Rothschild, was the fast-talking New Yorker whose voice of simultaneous toughness and vulnerability has influenced more American women humorists than anyone else. In 1919 she was a founding member of the hard-drinking, hard-joking Algonquin Round Table in Manhattan. She married Edwin P. Parker in 1917; they divorced in 1928. She was a popular writer for *Vanity Fair* and *The New Yorker,* and later a screenwriter in Hollywood. She married the actor and writer Alan Campbell in 1934, divorced him in 1947, and remarried him in 1950.

A Telephone Call (1928)

PLEASE, GOD, LET him telephone me now. Dear God, let him call me now. I won't ask anything else of You, truly I won't. It isn't very much to ask. It would be so little to You, God, such a little, little thing. Only let him telephone now. Please, God. Please, please, please.

If I didn't think about it, maybe the telephone might ring. Sometimes it does that. If I could think of something else. If I could think of something else. Maybe if I counted five hundred by fives, it might ring by that time. I'll count slowly. I won't cheat. And if it rings when I get to three hundred, I won't stop; I won't answer it until I get to five hundred. Five, ten, fifteen, twenty, twenty-five, thirty, thirty-five, forty, forty-five, fifty . . . Oh, please ring. Please.

This is the last time I'll look at the clock. I will not look at it again. It's ten minutes past seven. He said he would telephone at five o'clock. "I'll call you at five, darling." I think that's where he said "darling." I'm almost sure he said it there. I know he called me "darling" twice, and the other time was when he said good-by. "Good-by, darling." He was busy, and he can't say much in the office, but he called me "darling" twice. He couldn't have minded my calling him up. I know you shouldn't keep telephoning them— I know they don't like that. When you do that they know you are thinking about them and wanting them, and that makes them hate you. But I hadn't talked to him in three days—not in three days. And all I did was ask him how he was; it was just the way anybody might have called him up. He couldn't have minded that. He couldn't have thought I was bothering him. "No, of course you're not," he said. And he said he'd telephone me. He didn't have to say that. I didn't ask him to, truly I didn't. I'm sure I didn't. I don't think he would say he'd telephone me, and then just never do it. Please don't let him do that, God. Please don't.

"I'll call you at five, darling." "Good-by, darling." He was busy, and he was in a hurry, and there were people around him, but he called me "darling" twice. That's mine, that's mine. I have that, even if I never see him again. Oh, but that's so little. That isn't enough. Nothing's enough, if I never see him again. Please let me see him again, God. Please, I want him so much. I want him so much. I'll be good, God. I will try to be better, I will, if you will let me see him again. If You will let him telephone me. Oh, let him telephone me now.

Ah, don't let my prayer seem too little to You, God. You sit up there, so white and old, with all the angels about You and the stars slipping by. And I come to You with a prayer about a telephone call. Ah, don't laugh, God. You see, You don't know how it feels. You're so safe, there on Your throne, with the blue swirling under You. Nothing can touch You; no one can twist Your heart in his hands. This is suffering, God, this is bad, bad suffering. Won't You help me? For Your Son's sake, help me. You said You would do whatever was asked of You in His name. Oh, God, in the name of Thine only beloved Son, Jesus Christ, our Lord, let him telephone me now.

I must stop this. I mustn't be this way. Look. Suppose a young man says he'll call a girl up, and then something happens, and he doesn't. That isn't so terrible, is it? Why, it's going on all over the world, right this minute. Oh, what do I care what's going on all over the world? Why can't that telephone ring? Why can't it, why can't it? Couldn't you ring? Ah, please, couldn't you? You damned, ugly, shiny thing. It would hurt you to ring, wouldn't it? Oh, that would hurt you. Damn you, I'll pull your filthy roots out of the wall, I'll smash your smug black face in little bits. Damn you to hell.

No, no, no. I must stop. I must think about something else. This is what I'll do. I'll put the clock in the other room. Then I can't look at it. If I do have to look at it, then I'll have to walk into the bedroom, and that will be something to do. Maybe, before I look at it again, he will call me. I'll be so sweet to him, if he calls me. If he says he can't see me tonight, I'll say, "Why, that's all right, dear. Why, of course it's all right." I'll be the way I was when I first met him. Then maybe he'll like me again. I was always sweet, at first. Oh, it's so easy to be sweet to people before you love them.

I think he must still like me a little. He couldn't have called me "darling" twice today, if he didn't still like me a little. It isn't all gone, if he still likes me a little; even if it's only a little, little bit. You see, God, if You would just let him telephone me, I wouldn't have to ask You anything more. I would be sweet to him, I would be gay, I would be just the way I used to be, and then he would love me again. And then I would never have to ask You for anything more. Don't You see, God? So won't You please let him telephone me? Won't You please, please, please? Are You punishing me, God, because I've been bad? Are You angry with me because I did that? Oh, but, God, there are so many bad people— You could not be hard only to me. And it wasn't very bad; it couldn't have been bad. We didn't hurt anybody, God. Things are only bad when they hurt people. We didn't hurt one single soul; You know that. You know it wasn't bad, don't You, God? So won't You let him telephone me now?

If he doesn't telephone me, I'll know God is angry with me. I'll count five hundred by fives, and if he hasn't called me then, I will know God isn't going to help me, ever again. That will be the sign. Five, ten, fifteen, twenty, twenty-five, thirty, thirty-five, forty, forty-five, fifty, fifty-five . . . It was bad. I knew it was bad. All right, God, send me to hell. You think You're frightening me with Your hell, don't You? You think Your hell is worse than mine.

I mustn't. I mustn't do this. Suppose he's a little late calling me up—that's nothing to get hysterical about. Maybe he isn't going to call—maybe he's coming straight up here without telephoning. He'll be cross if he sees I have been crying. They don't like you to cry. He doesn't cry. I wish to God I could make him cry. I wish I could make him cry and tread the floor and feel his heart heavy and big and festering in him. I wish I could hurt him like hell.

He doesn't wish that about me. I don't think he even knows how he makes me feel. I wish he could know, without my telling him. They don't like you to tell them they've made you cry. They don't like you to tell them you're unhappy because of them. If you do, they think you're possessive and exacting. And then they hate you. They hate you whenever you say anything you really think. You always have to keep playing little games. Oh, I thought we didn't have to; I thought this was so big I could say whatever I meant. I guess you can't, ever. I guess there isn't ever anything big enough for that. Oh, if he would just telephone, I wouldn't tell him I had been sad about him. They hate sad people. I would be so sweet and so gay, he couldn't help but like me. If he would only telephone. If he would only telephone.

Maybe that's what he is doing. Maybe he is coming on here without calling me up. Maybe he's on his way now. Something might have happened to him. No, nothing could ever happen to him. I can't picture anything happening to him. I never picture him run over. I never see him lying still and long and dead. I wish he were dead. That's a terrible wish. That's a lovely wish. If he were dead, he would be mine. If he were dead, I would never think of now and the last few weeks, I would remember only the lovely times. It would be all beautiful. I wish he were dead. I wish he were dead, dead, dead. This is silly. It's silly to go wishing people were dead just because they don't call you up the very minute they said they would. Maybe the clock's fast; I don't know whether it's right. Maybe he's hardly late at all. Anything could have made him a little late. Maybe he had to stay at his office. Maybe he went home, to call me up from there, and somebody came in. He doesn't like to telephone me in front of people. Maybe he's worried, just a little, little bit, about keeping me waiting. He might even hope that I would call him up. I could do that. I could telephone him.

I mustn't. I mustn't, I mustn't. Oh, God, please don't let me telephone him. Please keep me from doing that. I know, God, just as well as You do, that if he were worried about me, he'd telephone no matter where he was or how many people there were around him. Please make me know that, God. I don't ask You to make it easy for me—You can't do that, for all that You could make a world. Only let me know it, God. Don't let me go on hoping. Don't let me say comforting things to myself. Please don't let me hope, dear God. Please don't.

I won't telephone him. I'll never telephone him again as long as I live. He'll rot in hell, before I'll call him up. You don't have to give me strength, God; I have it myself. If he wanted me, he could get me. He knows where I am. He knows I'm waiting here. He's so sure of me, so sure. I wonder why they hate you, as soon as they are sure of you. I should think it would be so sweet to be sure. It would be so easy to telephone him. Then I'd know. Maybe it wouldn't be a foolish thing to do. Maybe he wouldn't mind. Maybe he'd like it. Maybe he has been trying to get me. Sometimes people try and try to get you on the telephone, and they say the number doesn't answer. I'm not just saying that to help myself; that really happens. You know that really happens, God. Oh, God, keep me away from that telephone. Keep me away. Let me still have just a little bit of pride. I think I'm going to need it, God. I think it will be all I'll have.

Oh, what does pride matter, when I can't stand it if I don't talk to him? Pride like that is such a silly, shabby little thing. The real pride, the big pride, is in having no pride. I'm not saying that just because I want to call him. I am not. That's true, I know that's true. I will be big. I will be beyond little prides.

Please, God, keep me from telephoning him. Please, God.

I don't see what pride has to do with it. This is such a little thing, for me to be bringing in pride, for me to be making such a fuss about. I may have misunderstood him. Maybe he said for me to call him up, at five. "Call me at five, darling." He could have said that, perfectly well. It's so possible that I didn't hear him right. "Call me at five, darling." I'm almost sure that's what he said. God, don't let me talk this way to myself. Make me know, please make me know.

I'll think about something else. I'll just sit quietly. If I could sit still. If I could sit still. Maybe I could read. Oh, all the books are about people who love each other, truly and sweetly. What do they want to write about that for? Don't they know it isn't true? Don't they know it's a lie, it's a God damned lie? What do they have to tell about that for, when they know how it hurts? Damn them, damn them, damn them.

I won't. I'll be quiet. This is nothing to get excited about. Look. Suppose he were someone I didn't know very well. Suppose he were another girl. Then I'd just telephone and say, "Well, for goodness' sake, what happened to you?" That's what I'd do, and I'd never even think about it. Why can't I be casual and natural, just because I love him? I can be. Honestly, I can be. I'll call him up, and be so easy and pleasant. You see if I won't, God. Oh, don't let me call him. Don't, don't, don't.

God, aren't You really going to let him call me? Are You sure, God? Couldn't You please relent? Couldn't You? I don't even ask You to let him telephone me this minute, God; only let him do it in a little while. I'll count five hundred by fives. I'll do it so slowly and so fairly. If he hasn't telephoned then, I'll call him. I will. Oh, please, dear God, dear kind God, my blessed Father in Heaven, let him call before then. Please, God. Please.

Five, ten, fifteen, twenty, twenty-five, thirty, thirty-five. . . .

ALEXANDER PUSHKIN

[Russia]

RUSSIA'S FIRST undisputed literary genius was Alexander Pushkin (1799–1837), the great-grandson of Abram Petrovich Gannibal, who as a young boy from Africa was brought to St. Petersburg, where he was educated and became a prominent military engineer. Pushkin, on the other hand, was a dazzling poet from his teens but repeatedly got himself into hot water with the government because of his wit and careless boldness. He was a ladies' man and terribly jealous of his gorgeous wife, Nataliya Goncharova, over whom he fought the duel that ended his life. He wrote the five stories entitled *The Tales of Belkin* while waiting out a cholera quarantine in Boldino for a few months in 1830. There is no short story more charming than "An Amateur Peasant Girl," sometimes entitled, in other translations, "The Squire's Daughter" (in Russian, "Баришня Крестьянка").

An Amateur Peasant Girl (1830)

(Translated from the Russian by T. Keane)

IN ONE OF our most distant governments was situated the domain of Ivan Petrovitch Berestoff. In his youth he had served in the Guards, but having quitted the service at the beginning of the year 1797, he repaired to his estate, and since that time he had not stirred away from it. He had married a poor but noble lady, who died in child-bed at a time when he was absent from home on a visit to one of the outlying fields of his domain. He soon found consolation in domestic occupations. He built a house on a plan of his own, established a cloth manufactory, made good use of his revenues, and began to consider himself the most sensible man in the whole country roundabout, and in this he was not contradicted by those of his neighbours who came to visit him with their families and their dogs. On week-days he wore a plush jacket, but on Sundays and holidays he appeared in a surtout of cloth that had been manufactured on his own premises. He himself kept an account of all his expenses, and he never read anything except the "Senate Gazette."

In general he was liked, although he was considered proud. There was only one person who was not on good terms with him, and that was Gregory Ivanovitch Mouromsky, his nearest neighbour. This latter was a genuine Russian noble of the old stamp. After having squandered in Moscow the greater part of his fortune, and having become a widower about the same time, he retired to his last remaining estate, where he continued to indulge in habits of extravagance, but of a new kind. He laid out an English garden, on which he expended nearly the whole of his remaining revenue. His grooms were dressed like English jockeys, his daughter had an English governess, and his fields were cultivated after the English method.

"But after the foreign manner Russian corn does not bear fruit," and in spite of a considerable reduction in his expenses, the revenues of Gregory Ivanovitch did not increase. He found means, even in the country, of contracting new debts. Nevertheless he was not considered a fool, for he was the first landowner in his government who conceived the idea of placing his estate under the safeguard of a council of tutelage[1]—a proceeding which at that time was considered exceedingly complicated and venturesome. Of all those who censured him, Berestoff showed himself the most severe. Hatred of all innovation was a distinguishing trait in his character. He could not bring himself to speak calmly of the Anglomania of his neighbour, and he constantly found occasion to criticise him. If he showed his possessions to a guest, in reply to the praises bestowed upon him for his economical arrangements, he would say with a sly smile:

"Ah yes, it is not the same with me as with my neighbour Gregory Ivanovitch. What need have we to ruin ourselves in the

---

[1] [A loan institution requiring landed property as security.]

English style, when we have enough to do to keep the wolf from the door in the Russian style?"

These, and similar sarcastic remarks, thanks to the zeal of obliging neighbours, did not fail to reach the ears of Gregory Ivanovitch greatly embellished. The Anglomaniac bore criticism as impatiently as our journalists. He became furious, and called his traducer a bear and a countryman.

Such were the relations between the two proprietors, when the son of Berestoff returned home to his father's estate. He had been educated at the University of ——, and was anxious to enter the military service, but to this his father would not give his consent. For the civil service the young man had not the slightest inclination, and as neither felt inclined to yield to the other, the young Alexei lived in the meantime like a nobleman, and allowed his moustache to grow at all events.[2]

Alexei was indeed a fine young fellow, and it would really have been a pity were his slender figure never to be set off to advantage by a military uniform, and were he to be compelled to spend his youth in bending over the papers of the chancery office, instead of bestriding a gallant steed. The neighbours, observing how he was always first in the chase, and always out of the beaten tracks, unanimously agreed that he would never make a useful official. The young ladies gazed after him, and sometimes cast stolen glances at him, but Alexei troubled himself very little about them, and they attributed this insensibility to some secret love affair. Indeed, there passed from hand to hand a copy of the address of one of his letters: "To Akoulina Petrovna Kourotchkin, in Moscow, opposite the Alexeivsky Monastery, in the house of the coppersmith Saveleff, with the request that she will forward this letter to A. N. R."

Those of my readers who have never lived in the country, cannot imagine how charming these provincial young ladies are! Brought up in the pure air, under the shadow of the apple trees of their gardens, they derive their knowledge of the world and of life chiefly from books. Solitude, freedom, and reading develop very early within them sentiments and passions unknown to our town-bred beauties. For the young ladies of the country the sound of the post-bell is an event; a journey to the nearest town marks an epoch

---

[2] It was formerly the custom in Russia for military men only to wear the moustache.

in their lives, and the visit of a guest leaves behind a long, and sometimes an eternal recollection. Of course everybody is at liberty to laugh at some of their peculiarities, but the jokes of a superficial observer cannot nullify their essential merits, the chief of which is that personality of character, that *individualité,* without which, in Jean Paul's[3] opinion, there can be no human greatness. In the capitals, women receive perhaps a better instruction, but intercourse with the world soon levels the character and makes their souls as uniform as their head-dresses. This is said neither by way of praise nor yet by way of censure, but *"nota nostra manet,"*[4] as one of the old commentators writes.

It can easily be imagined what impression Alexei would produce among the circle of our young ladies. He was the first who appeared before them gloomy and disenchanted, the first who spoke to them of lost happiness and of his blighted youth; in addition to which he wore a mourning ring engraved with a death's head. All this was something quite new in that distant government. The young ladies simply went out of their minds about him.

But not one of them felt so much interest in him as the daughter of our Anglomaniac Liza, or Betsy, as Gregory Ivanovitch usually called her. As their parents did not visit each other, she had not yet seen Alexei, even when he had become the sole topic of conversation among all the young ladies of the neighbourhood. She was seventeen years of age. Dark eyes illuminated her swarthy and exceedingly pleasant countenance. She was an only child, and consequently she was perfectly spoiled. Her wantonness and continual pranks delighted her father and filled with despair the heart of Miss Jackson, her governess, an affected old maid of forty, who powdered her face and darkened her eyebrows, read through "Pamela"[5] twice a year, for which she received two thousand roubles, and felt almost bored to death in this barbarous Russia of ours.

Liza was waited upon by Nastia, who, although somewhat older, was quite as giddy as her mistress. Liza was very fond of her, revealed

---

[3] [German author (surname Richter), 1763–1825.]
[4] ["Our stamp remains."]
[5] A novel written by Samuel Richardson, and first published in 1740.

to her all her secrets, and planned pranks together with her; in a word, Nastia was a far more important person in the village of Priloutchina, than the trusted confidante in a French tragedy.

"Will you allow me to go out to-day on a visit?" said Nastia one morning, as she was dressing her mistress.

"Very well; but where are you going to?"

"To Tougilovo, to the Berestoffs. The wife of their cook is going to celebrate her name-day to-day, and she came over yesterday to invite us to dinner."

"That's curious," said Liza: "the masters are at daggers drawn, but the servants fête each other."

"What have the masters to do with us?" replied Nastia. "Besides, I belong to you, and not to your papa. You have not had any quarrel with young Berestoff; let the old ones quarrel and fight, if it gives them any pleasure."

"Try and see Alexei Berestoff, Nastia, and then tell me what he looks like and what sort of a person he is."

Nastia promised to do so, and all day long Liza waited with impatience for her return. In the evening Nastia made her appearance.

"Well, Lizaveta Gregorievna," said she, on entering the room, "I have seen young Berestoff, and I had ample opportunity for taking a good look at him, for we have been together all day."

"How did that happen? Tell me about it, tell me everything about it."

"Very well. We set out, I, Anissia Egorovna, Nenila, Dounka. . . ."

"Yes, yes, I know. And then?"

"With your leave, I will tell you everything in detail. We arrived just in time for dinner. The room was full of people. The Kolbinskys were there, as well as the Zakharevskys, the Khloupinskys, the bailiff's wife and her daughters. . . ."

"Well, and Berestoff?"

"Wait a moment. We sat down to table; the bailiff's wife had the place of honour. I sat next to her . . . the daughters pouted and didn't like it, but I didn't care about them. . . ."

"Good heavens, Nastia, how tiresome you are with your never-ending details!"

"How impatient you are! Well, we rose from the table . . . we had been sitting down for three hours, and the dinner was excellent:

pastry, blanc-manges, blue, red and striped. . . . Well, we left the table and went into the garden to have a game at catching one another, and it was then that the young lord made his appearance."

"Well, and is it true that he is so very handsome?"

"Exceedingly handsome: tall, well-built, and with red cheeks. . . ."

"Really? And I was under the impression that he was fair. Well, and how did he seem to you? Sad, thoughtful?"

"Nothing of the kind! I have never in my life seen such a frolicsome person. He wanted to join in the game with us."

"Join in the game with you? Impossible!"

"Not all impossible. And what else do you think he wanted to do? To kiss us all round!"

"With your permission, Nastia, you are talking nonsense."

"With your permission, I am not talking nonsense. I had the greatest trouble in the world to get away from him. He spent the whole day along with us."

"But they say that he is in love, and hasn't eyes for anybody."

"I don't know anything about that, but I know that he looked at me a good deal, and so he did at Tania, the bailiff's daughter, and at Pasha[6] Kolbinsky also. But it cannot be said that he offended anybody — he is so very agreeable."

"That is extraordinary! And what do they say about him in the house?"

"They say that he is an excellent master — so kind, so cheerful. They have only one fault to find with him: he is too fond of running after the young girls. But for my part, I don't think that is a very great fault: he will grow steady with age."

"How I should like to see him!" said Liza, with a sigh.

"What is there to hinder you from doing so? Tougilovo is not far from us — only about three versts. Go and take a walk in that direction, or a ride on horseback, and you will assuredly meet him. He goes out early every morning with his gun."

"No, no, that would not do. He might think that I was running after him. Besides, our fathers are not on good terms, so that I cannot make his acquaintance. . . . . Ah! Nastia, do you know what I'll do? I will dress myself up as a peasant girl!"

---

[6] Diminutive of Praskovia.

"Exactly! Put on a coarse chemise and a *sarafan*, and then go boldly to Tougilovo; I will answer for it that Berestoff will not pass by without taking notice of you."

"And I know how to imitate the style of speech of the peasants about here. Ah, Nastia! my dear Nastia! what an excellent idea!"

And Liza went to bed, firmly resolved on putting her plan into execution.

The next morning she began to prepare for the accomplishment of her scheme. She sent to the bazaar and bought some coarse linen, some blue nankeen and some copper buttons, and with the help of Nastia she cut out for herself a chemise and *sarafan*. She then set all the female servants to work to do the necessary sewing, so that by the evening everything was ready. Liza tried on the new costume, and as she stood before the mirror, she confessed to herself that she had never looked so charming. Then she practised her part. As she walked she made a low bow, and then tossed her head several times, after the manner of a china cat, spoke in the peasants' dialect, smiled behind her sleeve, and did everything to Nastia's complete satisfaction. One thing only proved irksome to her: she tried to walk barefooted across the courtyard, but the turf pricked her tender feet, and she found the stones and gravel unbearable. Nastia immediately came to her assistance. She took the measurement of Liza's foot, ran to the fields to find Trophim the shepherd, and ordered him to make a pair of bast shoes of the same measurement.

The next morning, almost before it was dawn, Liza was already awake. Everybody in the house was still asleep. Nastia went to the gate to wait for the shepherd. The sound of a horn was heard, and the village flock defiled past the manor-house. Trophim, on passing by Nastia, gave her a small pair of coloured bast shoes, and received from her a half-rouble in exchange. Liza quietly dressed herself in the peasant's costume, whispered her instructions to Nastia with reference to Miss Jackson, descended the back staircase and made her way through the garden into the field beyond.

The eastern sky was all aglow, and the golden lines of clouds seemed to be awaiting the sun, like courtiers await their monarch. The bright sky, the freshness of the morning, the dew, the light breeze, and the singing of the birds filled the heart of Liza with childish joy. The fear of meeting some acquaintance seemed to give her wings, for she flew rather than walked. But as she approached the wood which formed the boundary of her father's estate, she slackened her pace. Here she resolved to wait for Alexei. Her heart beat violently, she knew not why; but is not the fear which accompanies our youthful escapades that which constitutes their greatest charm? Liza advanced into the depth of the wood. The deep murmur of the waving branches seemed to welcome the young girl. Her gaiety vanished. Little by little she abandoned herself to sweet reveries. She thought — but who can say exactly what a young lady of seventeen thinks of, alone in a wood, at six o'clock of a spring morning? And so she walked musingly along the pathway, which was shaded on both sides by tall trees, when suddenly a magnificent hunting dog came barking and bounding towards her. Liza became alarmed and cried out. But at the same moment a voice called out: *"Tout beau, Sbogar, ici!"*[7] . . . and a young hunter emerged from behind a clump of bushes.

"Don't be afraid, my dear," said he to Liza: "my dog does not bite."

Liza had already recovered from her alarm, and she immediately took advantage of her opportunity.

"But, sir," said she, assuming a half-frightened, half-bashful expression, "I am so afraid; he looks so fierce — he might fly at me again."

Alexei — for the reader has already recognized him — gazed fixedly at the young peasant-girl.

"I will accompany you if you are afraid," said he to her: "will you allow me to walk along with you?"

"Who is to hinder you?" replied Liza. "Wills are free, and the road is open to everybody."

"Where do you come from?"

"From Priloutchina; I am the daughter of Vassili the blacksmith, and I am going to gather mushrooms." (Liza carried a basket on her arm.) "And you, sir? From Tougilovo, I have no doubt."

"Exactly so," replied Alexei: "I am the young master's valet-de-chambre."

Alexei wanted to put himself on an equality with her, but Liza looked at him and began to smile.

"That is a fib," said she: "I am not such a fool as you may think. I see very well that you are the young master himself."

---

[7] ["Good boy, Sbogar, come here!"]

"Why do you think so?"

"I think so for a great many reasons."

"But——"

"As if it were not possible to distinguish the master from the servant! You are not dressed like a servant, you do not speak like one, and you address your dog in a different way to us."

Liza began to please Alexei more and more. As he was not accustomed to standing upon ceremony with peasant girls, he wanted to embrace her; but Liza drew back from him, and suddenly assumed such a cold and severe look, that Alexei, although much amused, did not venture to renew the attempt.

"If you wish that we should remain good friends," said she with dignity, "be good enough not to forget yourself."

"Who taught you such wisdom?" asked Alexei, bursting into a laugh. "Can it be my friend Nastenka,[8] the chambermaid to your young mistress? See by what paths enlightenment becomes diffused!"

Liza felt that she had stepped out of her rôle, and she immediately recovered herself.

"Do you think," said she, "that I have never been to the manor-house? Don't alarm yourself; I have seen and heard a great many things. . . . But," continued she, "if I talk to you, I shall not gather my mushrooms. Go your way, sir, and I will go mine. Pray excuse me."

And she was about to move off, but Alexei seized hold of her hand.

"What is your name, my dear?"

"Akoulina," replied Liza, endeavouring to disengage her fingers from his grasp: "but let me go, sir; it is time for me to return home."

"Well, my friend Akoulina, I will certainly pay a visit to your father, Vassili the blacksmith."

"What do you say?" replied Liza quickly: "for Heaven's sake, don't think of doing such a thing! If it were known at home that I had been talking to a gentleman alone in the wood, I should fare very badly, — my father, Vassili the blacksmith, would beat me to death."

"But I really must see you again."

"Well, then, I will come here again some time to gather mushrooms."

---

[8] Diminutive of Nastia.

"When?"

"Well, to-morrow, if you wish it."

"My dear Akoulina, I would kiss you, but I dare not. . . . To-morrow, then, at the same time, isn't that so?"

"Yes, yes!"

"And you will not deceive me?"

"I will not deceive you."

"Swear it."

"Well, then, I swear by Holy Friday that I will come."

The young people separated. Liza emerged from the wood, crossed the field, stole into the garden and hastened to the place where Nastia awaited her. There she changed her costume, replying absently to the questions of her impatient confidante, and then she repaired to the parlour. The cloth was laid, the breakfast was ready, and Miss Jackson, already powdered and laced up, so that she looked like a wine-glass, was cutting thin slices of bread and butter.

Her father praised her for her early walk.

"There is nothing so healthy," said he, "as getting up at day-break."

Then he cited several instances of human longevity, which he had derived from the English journals, and observed that all persons who had lived to be upwards of a hundred, abstained from brandy and rose at daybreak, winter and summer.

Liza did not listen to him. In her thoughts she was going over all the circumstances of the meeting of that morning, all the conversation of Akoulina with the young hunter, and her conscience began to torment her. In vain did she try to persuade herself that their conversation had not gone beyond the bounds of propriety, and that the frolic would be followed by no serious consequences — her conscience spoke louder than her reason. The promise given for the following day troubled her more than anything else, and she almost felt resolved not to keep her solemn oath. But then, might not Alexei, after waiting for her in vain, make his way to the village and search out the daughter of Vassili the blacksmith, the veritable Akoulina — a fat, pock-marked peasant girl — and so discover the prank she had played upon him? This thought frightened Liza, and she resolved to repair again to the little wood the next morning in the same disguise as at first.

On his side, Alexei was in an ecstasy of delight. All day long he thought of his new acquaintance; and in his dreams at night the form of the dark-skinned beauty appeared before him. The morning had scarcely begun to dawn, when he was already dressed. Without giving himself time to load his gun, he set out for the fields with his faithful Sbogar, and hastened to the place of the promised rendezvous. A half hour of intolerable waiting passed by; at last he caught a glimpse of a blue *sarafan* between the bushes, and he rushed forward to meet his charming Akoulina. She smiled at the ecstatic nature of his thanks, but Alexei immediately observed upon her face traces of sadness and uneasiness. He wished to know the cause. Liza confessed to him that her act seemed to her very frivolous, that she repented of it, that this time she did not wish to break her promised word, but that this meeting would be the last, and she therefore entreated him to break off an acquaintanceship which could not lead to any good.

All this, of course, was expressed in the language of a peasant; but such thoughts and sentiments, so unusual in a simple girl of the lower class, struck Alexei with astonishment. He employed all his eloquence to divert Akoulina from her purpose; he assured her that his intentions were honourable, promised her that he would never give her cause to repent, that he would obey her in everything, and earnestly entreated her not to deprive him of the joy of seeing her alone, if only once a day, or even only twice a week. He spoke the language of true passion, and at that moment he was really in love. Liza listened to him in silence.

"Give me your word," said she at last, "that you will never come to the village in search of me, and that you will never seek a meeting with me except those that I shall appoint myself."

Alexei swore by Holy Friday, but she stopped him with a smile.

"I do not want you to swear," said she; "your mere word is sufficient."

After that they began to converse together in a friendly manner, strolling about the wood, until Liza said to him:

"It is time for me to return home."

They separated, and when Alexei was left alone, he could not understand how, in two interviews, a simple peasant girl had succeeded in acquiring such influence over him. His relations with Akoulina had for him all the charm of novelty, and although the injunctions of the strange young girl appeared to him to be very severe, the thought of breaking his word never once entered his mind. The fact was that Alexei, in spite of his fatal ring, his mysterious correspondence and his gloomy disenchantment, was a good and impulsive young fellow, with a pure heart capable of enjoying the pleasures of innocence.

Were I to listen to my own wishes only, I would here enter into a minute description of the interviews of the young people, of their growing passion for each other, their confidences, occupations and conversations; but I know that the greater part of my readers would not share my satisfaction. Such details are usually considered tedious and uninteresting, and therefore I will omit them, merely observing, that before two months had elapsed, Alexei was already hopelessly in love, and Liza equally so, though less demonstrative in revealing the fact. Both were happy in the present and troubled themselves little about the future.

The thought of indissoluble ties frequently passed through their minds, but never had they spoken to each other about the matter. The reason was plain: Alexei, however much attached he might be to his lovely Akoulina, could not forget the distance that separated him from the poor peasant girl; while Liza, knowing the hatred that existed between their parents, did not dare to hope for a mutual reconciliation. Moreover, her self-love was stimulated in secret by the obscure and romantic hope of seeing at last the proprietor of Tougilovo at the feet of the blacksmith's daughter of Priloutchina. All at once an important event occurred which threatened to interrupt their mutual relations.

One bright cold morning — such a morning as is very common during our Russian autumn — Ivan Petrovitch Berestoff went out for a ride on horseback, taking with him three pairs of hunting dogs, a gamekeeper and several stable-boys with clappers. At the same time, Gregory Ivanovitch Mouromsky, seduced by the beautiful weather, ordered his bob-tailed mare to be saddled, and started out to visit his domains cultivated in the English style. On approaching the wood, he perceived his neighbour, sitting proudly on his horse, in his cloak lined with fox-skin, waiting for a hare which his followers, with loud cries and the rattling of their clappers, had started out of a thicket. If Gregory Ivanovitch had foreseen this meeting, he would certainly have proceeded in another direction, but he came upon Berestoff so unexpectedly, that he suddenly found himself no farther than the distance of a pistol-shot away from him. There was no help for it: Mouromsky, like a civilized European, rode forward towards his adversary and politely saluted him. Berestoff returned the salute with the characteristic grace of a chained bear, who salutes the public in obedience to the order of his master.

At that moment the hare darted out of the wood and started off across the field. Berestoff and the gamekeeper raised a loud shout, let the dogs loose, and then galloped off in pursuit. Mouromsky's horse, not being accustomed to hunting, took fright and bolted. Mouromsky, who prided himself on being a good horseman, gave it full rein, and inwardly rejoiced at the incident which delivered him from a disagreeable companion. But the horse, reaching a ravine which it had not previously noticed, suddenly sprang to one side, and Mouromsky was thrown from the saddle. Striking the frozen ground with considerable force, he lay there cursing his bob-tailed mare, which, as if recovering from its fright, had suddenly come to a standstill as soon as it felt that it was without a rider.

Ivan Petrovitch hastened towards him and inquired if he had injured himself. In the meantime the gamekeeper had secured the guilty horse, which he now led forward by the bridle. He helped Mouromsky into the saddle, and Berestoff invited him to his house. Mouromsky could not refuse the invitation, for he felt indebted to him; and so Berestoff returned home, covered with glory for having hunted down a hare and for bringing with him his adversary wounded and almost a prisoner of war.

The two neighbours took breakfast together and conversed with each other in a very friendly manner. Mouromsky requested Berestoff to lend him a *droshky*, for he was obliged to confess that, owing to his bruises, he was not in a condition to return home on horseback. Berestoff conducted him to the steps, and Mouromsky did not take leave of him until he had obtained a promise from him that he would come the next day in company with Alexei Ivanovitch, and dine in a friendly way at Priloutchina. In this way was a deeply-rooted enmity of long standing apparently brought to an end by the skittishness of a bob-tailed mare.

Liza ran forward to meet Gregory Ivanovitch.

"What does this mean, papa?" said she with astonishment. "Why are you walking lame? Where is your horse? Whose is this *droshky*?"

"You will never guess, my dear," replied Gregory Ivanovitch; and then he related to her everything that had happened.

Liza could not believe her ears. Without giving her time to collect herself, Gregory Ivanovitch then went on to inform her that the two Berestoffs — father and son — would dine with them on the following day.

"What do you say?" she exclaimed, turning pale. "The Berestoffs, father and son, will dine with us to-morrow! No, papa, you can do as you please, but I shall not show myself."

"Have you taken leave of your senses?" replied her father. "Since when have you been so bashful? Or do you cherish an hereditary hatred towards him like a heroine of romance? Enough, do not act the fool."

"No, papa, not for anything in the world, not for any treasure would I appear before the Berestoffs."

Gregory Ivanovitch shrugged his shoulders, and did not dispute with her any further, for he knew that by contradiction he would obtain nothing from her. He therefore went to rest himself after his remarkable ride.

Lizaveta Gregorievna repaired to her room and summoned Nastia. They both conversed together for a long time about the impending visit. What would Alexei think if, in the well-bred young lady, he recognized his Akoulina? What opinion would he have of her conduct, of her manners, of her good sense? On the other hand, Liza wished very much to see what impression would be produced upon him by a meeting so unexpected. . . . Suddenly an idea flashed through her mind. She communicated it to Nastia; both felt delighted with it, and they resolved to carry it into effect.

The next day at breakfast, Gregory Ivanovitch asked his daughter if she still intended to avoid the Berestoffs.

"Papa," replied Liza, "I will receive them if you wish it, but on one condition, and that is, that however I may appear before them, or whatever I may do, you will not be angry with me, or show the least sign of astonishment or displeasure."

"Some new freak!" said Gregory Ivanovitch, laughing. "Very well, very well, I agree; do what you like, my dark-eyed romp."

With these words he kissed her on the forehead, and Liza ran off to put her plan into execution.

At two o'clock precisely, a Russian calèche, drawn by six horses, entered the courtyard and rounded the lawn. The elder Berestoff mounted the steps with the assistance of two lackeys in the Mouromsky livery. His son came after him on horseback, and both entered together into the dining-room, where the table was already laid. Mouromsky received his neighbours in the most gracious manner, proposed to them to inspect his garden and park before dinner, and conducted them along paths carefully kept and gravelled. The elder Berestoff inwardly deplored the time and labour wasted in such useless fancies, but he held his tongue out of politeness. His son shared neither the disapprobation of the economical landowner, nor the enthusiasm of the vain-glorious Anglomaniac, but waited with impatience for the appearance of his host's daughter, of whom he had heard a great deal; and although his heart, as we know, was already engaged, youthful beauty always had a claim upon his imagination.

Returning to the parlour, they all three sat down; and while the old men recalled their young days, and related anecdotes of their respective careers, Alexei considered in his mind what role he should play in the presence of Liza. He came to the conclusion that an air of cold indifference would be the most becoming under the circumstances, and he prepared to act accordingly. The door opened; he turned his head with such indifference, with such haughty carelessness, that the heart of the most inveterate coquette would inevitably have shuddered. Unfortunately, instead of Liza, it was old Miss Jackson, who, painted and bedecked, entered the room with downcast eyes and with a low bow, so that Alexei's dignified military salute was lost upon her. He had not succeeded in recovering from his confusion, when the door opened again, and this time it was Liza herself who entered.

All rose; her father was just beginning to introduce his guests, when suddenly he stopped short and bit his lips. . . . Liza, his dark-complexioned Liza, was painted white up to the ears, and was more bedizened than even Miss Jackson herself; false curls, much lighter than her own hair, covered her head like the perruque of Louis the Fourteenth; her sleeves à l'imbécile[9] stood out like the hooped skirts of Madame de Pompadour; her figure was pinched in like the letter X, and all her mother's jewels, which had not yet found their way to the pawnbroker's, shone upon her fingers, her neck and in her ears.

Alexei could not possibly recognize his Akoulina in the grotesque and brilliant young lady. His father kissed her hand, and he followed his example, though much against his will; when he touched her little white fingers, it seemed to him that they

---

[9] [Narrow sleeves with shoulder puffs.]

trembled. In the meantime he succeeded in catching a glimpse of her little foot, intentionally advanced and set off to advantage by the most coquettish shoe imaginable. This reconciled him somewhat to the rest of her toilette. As for the paint and powder, it must be confessed that, in the simplicity of his heart, he had not noticed them at the first glance, and afterwards had no suspicion of them. Gregory Ivanovitch remembered his promise, and endeavoured not to show any astonishment; but his daughter's freak seemed to him so amusing, that he could scarcely contain himself. But the person who felt no inclination to laugh was the affected English governess. She had a shrewd suspicion that the paint and powder had been extracted from her chest of drawers, and the deep flush of anger was distinctly visible beneath the artificial whiteness of her face. She darted angry glances at the young madcap, who, reserving her explanations for another time, pretended that she did not notice them.

They sat down to table. Alexei continued to play his role of assumed indifference and absence of mind. Liza put on an air of affectation, spoke through her teeth, and only in French. Her father kept constantly looking at her, not understanding her aim, but finding it all exceedingly amusing. The English governess fumed with rage and said not a word. Ivan Petrovitch alone seemed at home: he ate like two, drank heavily, laughed at his own jokes, and grew more talkative and hilarious at every moment.

At last they all rose up from the table; the guests took their departure, and Gregory Ivanovitch gave free vent to his laughter and to his interrogations.

"What put the idea into your head of acting the fool like that with them?" he said to Liza. "But do you know what? The paint suits you admirably. I do not wish to fathom the mysteries of a lady's toilette, but if I were in your place, I would very soon begin to paint; not too much, of course, but just a little."

Liza was enchanted with the success of her stratagem. She embraced her father, promised him that she would consider his advice, and then hastened to conciliate the indignant Miss Jackson, who, with great reluctance consented to open the door and listen to her explanations. Liza was ashamed to appear before strangers with her dark complexion; she had not dared to ask. . . . she felt sure that dear, good Miss Jackson would pardon her, etc., etc. Miss Jackson, feeling convinced that Liza had not wished to make her a laughing-stock by imitating her, calmed down, kissed her, and as a token of reconciliation, made her a present of a small pot of English paint, which Liza accepted with every appearance of sincere gratitude.

The reader will readily imagine that Liza lost no time in repairing to the rendezvous in the little wood the next morning.

"You were at our master's yesterday," she said at once to Alexei: "what do you think of our young mistress?"

Alexei replied that he had not observed her.

"That's a pity!" replied Liza.

"Why so?" asked Alexei.

"Because I wanted to ask you if it is true what they say——"

"What do they say?"

"Is it true, as they say, that I am very much like her?"

"What nonsense! She is a perfect monstrosity compared with you."

"Oh, sir, it is very wrong of you to speak like that. Our young mistress is so fair and so stylish! How could I be compared with her!"

Alexei vowed to her that she was more beautiful than all the fair young ladies in creation, and in order to pacify her completely, he began to describe her mistress in such comical terms, that Liza laughed heartily.

"But," said she with a sigh, "even though our young mistress may be ridiculous, I am but a poor ignorant thing in comparison with her."

"Oh!" said Alexei; "is that anything to break your heart about? If you wish it, I will soon teach you to read and write."

"Yes, indeed," said Liza, "why should I not try?"

"Very well, my dear; we will commence at once."

They sat down. Alexei drew from his pocket a pencil and note-book, and Akoulina learnt the alphabet with astonishing rapidity. Alexei could not sufficiently admire her intelligence. The following morning she wished to try to write. At first the pencil refused to obey her, but after a few minutes she was able to trace the letters with tolerable accuracy.

"It is really wonderful!" said Alexei. "Our method certainly produces quicker results than the Lancaster system."[10]

---

[10] An allusion to the system of education introduced into England by Joseph Lancaster at the commencement of the present [19th] century.

And indeed, at the third lesson Akoulina began to spell through "Nathalie the Boyard's Daughter,"[11] interrupting her reading by observations which really filled Alexei with astonishment, and she filled a whole sheet of paper with aphorisms drawn from the same story.

A week went by, and a correspondence was established between them. Their letter-box was the hollow of an old oak-tree, and Nastia acted as their messenger. Thither Alexei carried his letters written in a bold round hand, and there he found on plain blue paper the delicately-traced strokes of his beloved. Akoulina perceptibly began to acquire an elegant style of expression, and her mental faculties commenced to develop themselves with astonishing rapidity.

Meanwhile, the recently-formed acquaintance between Ivan Petrovitch Berestoff and Gregory Ivanovitch Mouromsky soon became transformed into a sincere friendship, under the following circumstances. Mouromsky frequently reflected that, on the death of Ivan Petrovitch, all his possessions would pass into the hands of Alexei Ivanovitch, in which case the latter would be one of the wealthiest landed proprietors in the government, and there would be nothing to hinder him from marrying Liza. The elder Berestoff, on his side, although recognizing in his neighbour a certain extravagance (or, as he termed it, English folly), was perfectly ready to admit that he possessed many excellent qualities, as for example, his rare tact. Gregory Ivanovitch was closely related to Count Pronsky, a man of distinction and of great influence. The Count could be of great service to Alexei, and Mouromsky (so thought Ivan Petrovitch) would doubtless rejoice to see his daughter marry so advantageously. By dint of constantly dwelling upon this idea, the two old men came at last to communicate their thoughts to one another. They embraced each other, both promised to do their best to arrange the matter, and they immediately set to work, each on his own side. Mouromsky foresaw that he would have some difficulty in persuading his Betsy to become more intimately acquainted with Alexei, whom she had not seen since the memorable dinner. It seemed to him that they had not been particularly well pleased with each other; at least Alexei had

---

[11] [A story by Karamzin.]

not paid any further visits to Priloutchina, and Liza had retired to her room every time that Ivan Petrovitch had honoured them with a visit.

"But," thought Gregory Ivanovitch, "if Alexei came to see us every day, Betsy could not help falling in love with him. That is the natural order of things. Time will settle everything."

Ivan Petrovitch was no less uneasy about the success of his designs. That same evening he summoned his son into his cabinet, lit his pipe, and, after a long pause, said:

"Well, Alesha,[12] what do you think about doing? You have not said anything for a long time about the military service. Or has the Hussar uniform lost its charm for you?"

"No, father," replied Alexei respectfully; "but I see that you do not like the idea of my entering the Hussars, and it is my duty to obey you."

"Good," replied Ivan Petrovitch; "I see that you are an obedient son; that is very consoling to me. . . . On my side, I do not wish to compel you; I do not want to force you to enter . . . at once . . . into the civil service, but, in the meanwhile, I intend you to get married."

"To whom, father?" asked Alexei in astonishment.

"To Lizaveta Gregorievna Mouromsky," replied Ivan Petrovitch. "She is a charming bride, is she not?"

"Father, I have not thought of marriage yet."

"You have not thought of it, and therefore I have thought of it for you."

"As you please, but I do not care for Liza Mouromsky in the least."

"You will get to like her afterwards. Love comes with time."

"I do not feel capable of making her happy."

"Do not distress yourself about making her happy. What? Is this how you respect your father's wish? Very well!"

"As you please. I do not wish to marry, and I will not marry."

"You will marry, or I will curse you; and as for my possessions, as true as God is holy, I will sell them and squander the money, and not leave you a farthing. I will give you three days to think about the matter; and in the meantime, don't show yourself in my sight."

---

[12] Diminutive of Alexei (Alexis).

Alexei knew that when his father once took an idea into his head, a nail even would not drive it out, as Taras Skotinin[13] says in the comedy. But Alexei took after his father, and was just as headstrong as he was. He went to his room and began to reflect upon the limits of paternal authority. Then his thoughts reverted to Lizaveta Gregorievna, to his father's solemn vow to make him a beggar, and last of all to Akoulina. For the first time he saw clearly that he was passionately in love with her; the romantic idea of marrying a peasant girl and of living by the labour of their hands came into his head, and the more he thought of such a decisive step, the more reasonable did it seem to him. For some time the interviews in the wood had ceased on account of the rainy weather. He wrote to Akoulina a letter in his most legible handwriting, informing her of the misfortune that threatened them, and offering her his hand. He took the letter at once to the post-office in the wood, and then went to bed, well satisfied with himself.

The next day Alexei, still firm in his resolution, rode over early in the morning to visit Mouromsky, in order to explain matters frankly to him. He hoped to excite his generosity and win him over to his side.

"Is Gregory Ivanovitch at home?" asked he, stopping his horse in front of the steps of the Priloutchina mansion.

"No," replied the servant; "Gregory Ivanovitch rode out early this morning, and has not yet returned."

"How annoying!" thought Alexei. . . . "Is Lizaveta Gregorievna at home, then?" he asked.

"Yes, sir."

Alexei sprang from his horse, gave the reins to the lackey, and entered without being announced.

"Everything is now going to be decided," thought he, directing his steps towards the parlour: "I will explain everything to Lizaveta herself."

He entered . . . and then stood still as if petrified! Liza . . . no . . . Akoulina, dear, dark-haired Akoulina, no longer in a *sarafan,* but in a white morning robe, was sitting in front of the window, reading his letter; she was so occupied that she had not heard him enter.

---

[13] A character in "Nesdorosl," a comedy by Denis Von Vizin.

Alexei could not restrain an exclamation of joy. Liza started, raised her head, uttered a cry, and wished to fly from the room. But he threw himself before her and held her back.

"Akoulina! Akoulina!"

Liza endeavoured to liberate herself from his grasp.

"Mais laissez-moi donc, Monsieur! . . . Mais êtes-vous fou?"[14] she said, twisting herself round.

"Akoulina! my dear Akoulina!" he repeated, kissing her hand.

Miss Jackson, a witness of this scene, knew not what to think of it. At that moment the door opened, and Gregory Ivanovitch entered the room.

"Ah! ah!" said Mouromsky; "but it seems that you have already arranged matters between you."

The reader will spare me the unnecessary obligation of describing the dénouement.

---

[14] ["Let me go, sir! . . . Are you mad?"]

MAX SCHOTT

[U.S.A.]

MAX SCHOTT (born 1935) has written some of the most splendid short fiction in American literature. His novels include *Murphy's Romance* (1980) and *Ben* (1990). He was a rodeo cowboy and horse trainer before he became a teacher of literature and writing at the University of California, Santa Barbara. "The Old Flame" was published first as "Murphy Jones: Pearblossom, California" (in *Ascent* magazine and then in *The Best American Short Stories, 1978*), and with its new title in his collection *Up Where I Used to Live* (1978). He has been married to his wife, Elaine Schott, since 1972.

The Old Flame (1978)

SHE'D BEEN IN low spirits and I gave her a lot of advice on how to raise them. Didn't help, but she got better. No reason why she shouldn't—nothing wrong with her but some broken ribs, and they'd healed. I remember thinking at the time that she wouldn't learn a damn thing from the accident, and that that was a pity. I couldn't decide whether I thought a harder knock would have done her any more good. The one she got seemed hard enough when it happened.

Just when she'd started feeling fairly good again, a man came along who she hadn't seen for years.

Nice-looking fellow, even yet. Lives way off in some little Nevada town she exiled him to, years back. Had to come this way on business—that's what he said in the note he wrote her.

When Margaret told me Toni'd got the letter, I said: "Did she mention the man's name?"

"Wendell," Margaret said.

"Wendell?—isn't he the one she bought that old Desert Lass mare from about a century ago?"

"Same one," Margaret said. "She had a romance with him just after her marriage broke up."

"So she tells me one thing and you another."

"Well, they're both true."

"Doesn't surprise me. Lots of buckets dipped in the well since then; wonder she even remembers him."

"It would be a wonder if she didn't. She wants us to have him over here to supper so that she won't have to spend an evening alone with him unless she decides to."

"Doesn't want to see him?"

"She wants to," Margaret said, "if she could do it without his seeing her. She's afraid he'll be struck by the change."

"He'll lie if he is," I said. "He won't turn and run."

Toni came over that night and sat down at the kitchen table with Margaret and me. More color in her cheeks than I'd seen in months and I told her so.

"Old friend of yours coming to town I hear?" She nodded. "How long's it been?"

"Eighteen years," she said, and blushed.

"That's a while. He'll be pleased to see how you've turned out."

"Thanks. He probably won't recognize me."

"I hope he's done as well. Have you heard from him over the years?"

"Not for a long time."

"You're full of curiosity then, I'll bet—only natural."

"A little," she said. She looked down and rubbed the rim of her cup with her thumb and looked up at Margaret. Seemed I was preventing a conversation, so before long I excused myself and carried my coffee into the front room and started looking over my daybook from the auction yard.

I could hear them jabbering but I couldn't make out the words. "Shut that door," I hollered. Someone shut it, and I opened the heater vent beside my chair and heard every word.

"'I don't want to see you any more,' I was going to tell him," Toni said.

"Over already," I said to myself. "Damn, they work fast!" But it turned out they were talking about a man named Ben and hadn't even arrived at Wendell yet. One thing on her mind and she'll talk about another.

"So after that I couldn't go up to Ben's stables any more and ride his horses. And after about a month of stewing I decided to buy a horse of my own. That's when I met Wendell. I bought Lass from him and took a few horse-training lessons, and I had a real wild affair with him—the first one like that I ever had where there wasn't a lot of dawdling around. A good thing there wasn't because the whole thing only lasted two weeks. He decided to go back to his wife, not because of me but because of the judge. When I met him they were separated, and he said they were going to get a divorce. But when the judge told him how much he'd have to pay, he decided to go back."

"Oh Toni, you don't believe that do you? Still?" I heard Margaret say.

"Well, not that that's why he went back, but I believe the judge had a lot to do with the timing. If the hearing hadn't been right then, he wouldn't have gone back right then. Maybe we'd have run through each other, or who knows what might have happened, I don't know. We were both only twenty-two. Anyway, the way it was it was cut off."

"What attracted you so about him?"

"Well, he was big and tall and strong and handsome—and I'd been sitting in my house for a month. It was lust at first sight."

"At first sight?" Margaret said.

"Well, if it wasn't I wanted it to be. I wanted to have an adventure."

"I don't know about that man Wendell," I said to Margaret later. "Going back to your wife just to keep out of jail—that's a new one."

"That's not all of it," Margaret said.

"I'll bet it isn't," I said, "but it's all I heard because someone closed that heater vent in the kitchen."

"I know they did," she said. "But I'll tell you some of it. His wife wouldn't let him in the house because he'd been with Toni—and he asked Toni to call her and plead his case for him—can you imagine!"

"Did she turn him down?"

"Yes, but it seems to have been just because she didn't know what to say. He took advantage of all her good feelings. He told her she was too big a temptation for him to resist. So she located him a job and loaned him the money to move. I said to Toni that he sounded a little sneaky to me. Maybe I shouldn't have."

"Did he pay back the money?"

"Yes."

"Well, maybe he's all right. He was no more than a kid himself."

When he came to town Toni called me up to say so. I stopped by her barn to meet him, and I don't know if it's to my credit, but the man did make a good first impression on me.

I found them out in the pasture looking at Desert Lass, who had her head down grazing. Wendell was curly-headed and dark-complected. "That's the kind women like all right," I said to myself.

Toni introduced us, and I stood and helped them look at the old mare.

"You know her from way back," I said.

"I'd never have recognized her," he said.

"A colt or two and they get a little dough-bellied," I said.

"Last thing a man would think of when he thought of her was belly," Wendell said. "Moved like a cat."

"A streamlined one will end up more womb-sprung than one who's on the big-bellied side to begin with," I said.

"Stands to reason," he said; "not much room in there for a colt."

"That's right," I said. "Colt has to bang out a nest for himself and the next one will stretch it on out some more."

"Must be so," he said, "from the looks of her."

"Agreeable fellow," I said to myself; "man you can talk to."

"How many's she had, Toni?" he said.

"Six," Toni said.

"My wife had seven, but one died." Toni just looked at him.

"That's too bad," I said. "Where is it you're from, exactly?"

"Gerlach," he said. "Nevada."

"I know the town but I can't place it. Where is that near?"

"Not too near anywhere," he said. "Seventy miles from Fernley."

"Fernley: I've been through there for sure. Fair-sized place, is it?"

"Fernley? About five hundred in the summer. Right on the paved road, sixty miles west of Fallon."

"Fallon: I know that place for a fact. Ate supper there and lost a game of blackjack. Hundred miles east of Reno?"

"That's right. You're up that way again, stop by. All good roads. Dirt from Fernley to Gerlach, but it's good ground and you don't even know you're in a car."

"I will," I said. "Train horses up there, do you?"

"Those boys up there don't care if their horses go crooked or in a straight line, and if they don't I don't."

"I don't blame you a bit," I said.

"I watch over some cattle for a man. Eight hundred mother cows."

"That's a lot. Have some men working under you?"

"No sir," he said. "No help but two dogs."

"Don't see how you do it," I said.

"I can press my wife into service if I have to," he said.

"Press her into service?" Toni said.

"If I have to," he said.

"Been there long?" I said.

"Gerlach? Ever since I left Los Angeles."

"You don't strike me like a Los Angeles man."

"How old's old Lass there, Toni?" he said.

"Twenty-three."

"Five when I left. Maybe I've changed some."

"Must be quite a change," I said, "to go away off to a place like Gerlach from the city."

"I don't live right in downtown Gerlach," he said. "About thirty-five miles out."

"How'd you happen to locate there?"

"This old girl right here saw an ad: 'Cowboy wanted: High desert; School bus service, house, meat and milk furnished (they meant a milk cow); Two hundred dollars a month; Northern Nevada; Apply box xxx Western Livestock Journal.' Remember that?"

"I remember," Toni said. "He wasn't a city person to start with, Murphy. He was pretty much like he is now, come to think of it."

"I believe it," I said, "but they say a person can get spoiled fast, living in town, young country boy especially. Milking that same old cow day in and day out by lantern light might look a little humdrum after your city."

"Jan milks," he said. "My wife."

"How's she getting along?" Toni said.

"Just right," he said. "Looks good, feels good—for a woman who's shelled out kids like she has and been alive as long, she gets by all right; that's what everyone says that sees her. I don't pay a whole lot of attention myself."

"That's too bad," Toni said. "I'm glad she's well."

"She does all right," Wendell said. "But you, now, you never settled. I thought you might. Once in a while I'd catch a thought floating through that you'd married and settled down—but you never." He turned to me. "Don't you think people ought to settle down, time they're our age? I understand you're a married man."

"Darned right," I said. "I've been telling her so for years. Just like talking to a log."

"It takes one to know one, Murphy—a log I mean," and Toni gave me a little push on the shoulder.

"I hadn't seen her for a long time, but she looks fine," he said. "First thing I said to myself when I saw her: 'She looks fine!' Don't you!" And he put his hand on her shoulder and shook her, and I saw her stiffen.

"Yep, I'd have known her on the street anywhere," he said, and put his hand back by his side.

Wendell went downtown to get a room for the night.

When I came home from the auction yard Toni and Margaret were busy talking in the kitchen. Usually if they're like that and I come in, they'll look at me and start to wink and whistle. But this time soon as Toni saw me she said: "I'm sorry, Murphy, if I'd known what he was like I'd never have imposed him on you and Margaret—or on myself."

"What's he like?" I said. "Seems to be a nice enough fellow from what I saw."

"Uk," she said.

"Oh, you exaggerate—unless he's done something?"

"He hasn't done anything," Toni said.

"He's a good guy," I said to Margaret. "Takes care of eight hundred cows almost by himself."

"He must be all right then," Margaret said.

"Lives up not too far from where I used to," I said.

"He's a jerk, Murphy. He has eight hundred and one cows."

"Eight hundred and a wife and two dogs," I said, "but the cows aren't his, they belong to his boss. Didn't I hear you say he's just like he always was?"

"He sort of is," she said. "It's hard to explain."

"And you used to like him. Have you changed so much?"

"I don't think so. I hope not. He used to be very good-looking, I know I'm not wrong about that."

"Good-looking man right today," I said. "You know, I believe she's still carrying a torch."

"Yeah, fat chance," Toni said. "People don't get stupider, do they? I must have had rocks in my head. Poor Jan!"

"My, my, and I have to feed him supper," Margaret said.

"Oh, he's just an ordinary fellow," I said. "Hasn't as much respect for the sex as Toni would like—but I blame his wife for that."

"What's she supposed to do—punch him in the eye?" Toni said.

He knocked on the door.

"Shall I let him in?" Margaret said.

"Do we have to?" Toni said. "Let's not!" Then darned if she didn't clap her hand over her mouth and start to have a fit of schoolgirl giggling.

"Too bad we don't have any arsenic," Margaret said.

"Phaa!" I whispered. "Now you two behave yourself! Where do you think you're going?" I said to Toni.

"The bathroom."

"Act your age, you!"

"Really, Murphy, I have to stop laughing. I'll be back."

"You're as bad as she is," I said to Margaret. "Get out of the way. I'll let him in. Go cook."

I opened the door. He'd shaved and had his hat in his hands. "Poor guy," I thought. "Come in, come in," I said. "Good to see you so soon again." I shook hands with him. "Come into the kitchen and meet my wife."

"Hello," he said to Margaret. "Smells good. Toni here yet?"

"In the bathroom doing some last-minute landscaping," I said.

"Is she?" he said. "Suits me the way she is. Older than she used to be, but looks fine."

"You bet," I said. "She'll probably ruin it."

I took him into the front room, and pretty soon she came out, which I was glad to see, and offered him and me some of my whiskey. I'm famous for not being much of a drinker, but I took a drink.

He took one too, and his flowed straight to his extremities, if I'm not mistaken. Toni was in and out of the kitchen setting the table, and he couldn't keep his eyes off her. He kept trying to get her to look at him, and she kept trying not to—and I believe she had more success.

When she was in the kitchen I said to him: "I looked at a map a while ago, Wendell, and you know, it wouldn't be a hundred miles from where you live over to where I used to live—if there was a way to get there."

"Where you from?" he said.

"Little town of Wagontire over in Oregon," I said. "Sixty miles north of Likely."

"Uh-huh," he said. "Can't place it. Good smell coming out of there."

"I'll show you on the map," I said. So I brought out a map, though I had a little trouble getting him to look at it. Toni came out of the kitchen and looked over my shoulder.

"Wendell and I were almost neighbors," I said. "Only a hundred miles from my place to his—no roads though—lava rock so thick you can't even ride a horse across. But it's the same country. My old neighbor Sterling Green, he had cattle on both sides." He sat up at the name. "Know him?"

"Know him?—damn him! I work for him."

"Hah!—you see! Margaret, come in here! You women uht—'scuse me" ("attack the man," I started to say) "—and the man works for my neighbor! Here!" And I put out my hand so he had to shake it again.

"Get Murphy another drink," Margaret said.

"Don't pay them any mind, Wendell," I said. "No wonder you take care of eight hundred cows with just a wife and a pair of dogs. He's the shortest-handedest man in the world, that Sterling, damned if he's not!"

Toni went back in the kitchen with Margaret, and I told Wendell a story or two about Sterling. No one could fault me for not being able to talk to a stranger. He didn't have to say a word or even listen.

"That's turned into quite a looking woman, that Toni," he said. "Different from what she was, but they say we most of us change a little. Took me a while to get used to it, but she looks better every time she lifts a leg. It's a wonder no one ever married her."

"She says you're just like you used to be," I said.

"I've had people tell me I haven't changed. One other old girl told me I didn't look a day older than I did twenty years ago. I told her she didn't either, but I lied to her face."

"I don't blame you," I said.

"I never pay them much mind," he said, "but if Toni says I haven't changed, that's good, the way I see it, because she liked me the way I was, and so to reason it on out, that means there's hope."

"Just between you and me, Wendell," I said, "there's no hope. If I understood you correctly, there's not a hope in the world in that direction. For many another man and boy, maybe, but not for you and me."

He'd been watching the kitchen door in case she ran by, but he turned and looked at me as if I'd said something in Greek.

We sat down to eat. Toni told us where to sit, and she put herself across at an angle from Wendell, which with only four of us was as far away as she could get. Still it was close as he'd got so far, so he proceeded to try to talk to her.

"How's business, Toni?" he said. "How're the ponies treating you?"

"Fine," she said.

"You say you had some kind of accident?"

"I'm almost all right now," she said.

"What happened?"

"A horse fell on me."

"Now what'd you go and let him do that for?" Wendell said, and laughed, big old horse laugh.

"By God she's right," I said to myself. "The man is dense, and so was I not to see it."

"I shouldn't have," she said.

"I'll say you shouldn't have. I never taught you to do like that, did I?"

"No," she said. Never cracked a smile. That chilled him a little, but he didn't give it up.

"Training those horses is no business for a woman. Don't see why you don't settle down and keep house."

"She has more than that to keep her from settling down, Wendell. She has oats to sow, so we'd better let her be. Pass Wendell those peas, speaking of oats."

Margaret and Toni both looked at me, and I was a little surprised myself, when I'd heard what I said. But it didn't phase Wendell.

"What kind of horse fell on you?—just to make conversation," he said.

"A quarter-horse stallion, four-year-old," she said.

"Conversation?" I said to myself. "If you want conversation so bad, I can give it to you." "Shouldn't have been left a stallion but he was," I said. "Man that owns him drove all the way to Texas to buy him, but he's a billy goat just the same. I wouldn't breed a mare of mine to him, I'll tell you that, Wendell!"

Wendell turned and nodded at me. Thought he could get around me with a nod. "Never crossed my mind," he said. "How'd he happen to fall over on you?" he said to Toni. "Slip?"

"No," she said, "he—"

"Slip ha!" I said (why should I let her trouble herself to talk?). "He didn't slip, Wendell. I was right there and can vouch for it, you bet he didn't slip!"

"He's really drunk!" Margaret said.

"Phaa—keep quiet," I said. "Pass that meat over to where Wendell can reach it."

"What'd he do?" Wendell said—to me this time—but I wouldn't even look at him.

"Toni," I said, "if you'd shown him that stick before you got on him that day—you know the day I mean—I believe he'd never have done it to you."

"I wish you'd said so at the time."

"I wish it too, sweetheart."

"What stick's that?" Wendell said.

"Wendell," I said, "you ask about that stick, and I'll tell you: it was a green stick, you see, cut from a bush. About yay long." I held up my hands. "At first it was green, but then the sap dried out of it and it shrank about two inches and turned kind of gray—but it was the same stick and the horse knew it.

"Well, when this horse was first brought to her he had no manners at all. Every time he saw something alive he'd try to fornicate with it: he'd get up and walk around on his hind legs and beller—you know how they do, Wendell—and his old neck would swell up like a bull-frog's." Wendell reached up and rubbed his neck, which had swollen and turned pretty red. "That's right," I said. "The horse's manners were right out of Texas. The owner calls him Golden Son of Yellow Moon or something like that, but Toni and I, we always just called him Tex. (Wendell, you just reach over and help yourself.)

"So the first day, soon as he started in to rear and squeal she stepped off and kicked him in the belly a couple of times and cut that stick from a bush. After that whenever he'd begin to titillate himself she'd pound him on top of the neck, right behind his ears: whack-whack-whack. 'Cut it out, Tex,' she'd say—way you taught her years back, no doubt."

"Darned right," Wendell said.

"Darned right," I said. "That first day it didn't keep him from carrying on, but by the next day he was sore, and by the time two weeks went by she had his attention, and if his mind happened to start to wander she'd just whisper 'Hey now, Tex' in one of his ears. Or if he was sorely tried—say if a mare walked by winking— you know how they'll do, Wendell—with her tail in the air and maybe pissing a little—why Toni'd just hold the stick up where he could see it with his big right eye."

"Murphy—eat your supper," Margaret said.

"I don't mind," Toni said.

"This will interest Wendell," I said. "She'd hold it up where he could see it and he'd subdue his old gonads.

"She rode him about six weeks—that was last winter. Then they took him home to breed a few mares with and didn't bring him back till August. And before she got on him that first time again, she found that same little old stick thrown back in a corner of the tack room. Turned gray, but that horse recognized it, you bet he did, been better if he hadn't. But at first she didn't show it to him, just clambered up in the saddle with the stick stuck in her belt, that's the pity of it. Because if he'd had a chance to carry that stick along in his mind's eye, there'd never have been any trouble, that's what I think—maybe a little pawing and squealing, but no trouble.

"He had a good picture of that stick registered in his brain and he hadn't forgotten what it was used for—but the memory had slipped way back down into his subconscious—that's the way I see it. Wasn't the smartest horse in the world anyway, and darned foolish at times—led astray by his feelings like more beasts than one since the world began—"

"Eat," Margaret said.

"But I'd hesitate to say to a man that he was outright stupid—just thickheaded. Well, we rode along—came to where there were some mares loose in a field. He looked over the fence at them and must have gone to thinking about the good old days back home, tossed his head and puffed his neck up and nickered at those mares. Rattled your jaw, didn't it Toni?"

"I don't remember."

"That's right: I forgot, she doesn't remember a thing. Anyhow, it had slipped Tex's mind that there's a time and place for everything and that there's such a thing in the world as a stick. And to jog his memory she said, 'Tex, cut it out,' took the stick out from her belt, and held it up as of old. He saw it, and it all came back to him, too much all of a sudden, and he threw himself over backwards—landed flat bang on his right side and right on top of her. Darned if I ever saw anything quite like it, Wendell. Looked like he'd been electrocuted."

"And you don't remember a thing?" Wendell said.

"No," she said. "I woke up in the hospital."

"That was unforgiving ground, too—sand, but packed down. When Tex got up and ran off she never wiggled. Scared me."

"Aw," Wendell said, "I hate to think of you lying there like that." And he laid his big right arm out on the table like a ham. I don't know if he expected her to reach across and take his hand in hers or butter it or what. "Sorry I ever got you started training those horses," he said. "A woman like you doesn't need to be in a business like that. If I didn't live so far away I'd see to it that you weren't."

"I hope *you're* drunk, too," Margaret said.

"Good thing you live so far away," Toni said. "Just how would you go about seeing to it?" And she laid down her fork and looked him right in the eye.

"Ha! Watch out, Wendell, you hound!" I said to myself. "Wendell—" I said.

"I don't know *how*," Wendell said, "but I'd stop you training those horses, because it's only right."

"Wendell, my friend," I said, "I don't know how it is in Nevada, but in Pearblossom the cats scratch. If you antagonize them, I mean. Otherwise they won't, I think. So you'll have to bark up another tree, if you can find any."

"I'll make some coffee," Margaret said.

Toni covered her mouth with her napkin.

"I didn't catch all that," Wendell said. "I haven't seen six trees since I left home, but if I said something you folks took offense at, I take it back."

"No, no—no offense, old buddy," I said. I picked his hand up and shook it. "Toni," I said, "Wendell here said he was sorry to think of you lying stretched out like that, and I really thought you were dead for a minute or two there, and it didn't make me feel so very good, I don't know if I ever told you."

She reached across and ruffled my bit of hair.

As soon after supper as she could get away with it—in fact a little sooner—she stood up, looking shamefaced: she was going to leave him with us if she could.

"You going?" Wendell said. (Dumb as he was, he was the first to see it.)

"I'm sorry to run out on you-all," she said. "I'll see you before you leave tomorrow, Wendell. Thank you," she said to us. "I'll do you a favor sometime," and she gave me and Margaret a smile, friendly but not cheerful.

"I'll give you a ride," Wendell said.

"Thanks, my car's here."

"No need at all for you to run off, Wendell," I said. "It's early. Sit right down there and I'll fix you what you've never had."

"Murphy, it's been good talking to you," he said. "You too, Mrs. Jones. Thanks for the supper."

"Goodbye," Margaret said.

"You're welcome, Wendell," I said, "but I wish you'd stay a few minutes longer."

"Can't," he said. "Where's my hat?"

"Nice to run into a fellow from up there," I said. "You take care of that good wife of yours. Tell Sterling you saw me, and if he doesn't say anything too bad about me give him my best regards. When you planning to go back?"

He winked at me. "I'm supposed to head on back tomorrow, but with luck I might stay around a day or two and see the sights."

Toni was behind him with her hand on the doorknob. She shook her head no and made a face.

"Well, then, with luck we'll see you again," I said. "But you never know about that luck stuff: sometimes a man will bow his head and pray for luck and just wind up with a stiff neck." I rubbed my neck, since he seemed to understand sign language best. Then I shook his hand, I hope for the last time.

I saw them out, and when I went into the front room again, Margaret was sitting over by the window, half in the dark, holding a magazine. "Better turn on the light if you want to read," I said.

"Shh," she said.

I walked over and looked out the window. Toni and Wendell were standing by Toni's car. Toni had her hand on the door handle, and he was standing pretty close to her. "Shouldn't eavesdrop," I said to Margaret.

"No," she said. Wendell went to put his arms around Toni, and Toni backed against her car. "Ouch," she said.

"Those ribs," I whispered.

"You may have to go out and pour water on him," Margaret said.

"Goodnight," Toni said, "I'm going home. I'll see you tomorrow before you leave."

"I feel like that horse that fell on you," he said.

"You sure do," she said. "Look: I don't want to. Can't you understand?"

"Don't want to what?" he said.

"I don't want to do anything but go home and go to bed—all by myself."

"Oh. Why don't you want to?"

"I just don't want to."

"No one will ever know, Toni," he said and pressed himself toward her.

"Will he hurt her?" Margaret said.

"No—he just hasn't got the message yet," I said.

"My God! Not yet!?" she said.

"I don't think so."

"It's just between me and you," Wendell said.

"But *I* don't want to," Toni said.

"Oh . . . you just don't want to?"

"No."

"Oh." He backed up a step and she started to open the car door.

"Toni," he said, "I just want to tell you something."

"What?"

"I'll never forget the first time I saw you."

"That's nice of you," she said. "I won't either."

"You were with Shirley."

"I remember."

"And when the two of you came walking up to the barn where I was working I said to myself: 'Now there's two plums,' and I said to you: 'Anything I can do for you girls?' and you said you were looking for a horse to buy."

"I remember," Toni said. "And I asked you if you happened to know Ben Webber. You were both in the same business, and I couldn't think of anything else to say."

"I don't remember that," he said. "I remember I said, 'Now you girls aren't really looking for a horse, are you? I'll bet you're just out joyriding around.' And you said, 'A little of both.' Or maybe Shirley said that. But I know for sure you were the one that couldn't stand still. You kept wiggling, I remember it because I remember saying to myself, 'Now this one's more of a plum than the other one.' It had to have been you because of what happened after. Because it happened with you, or I wouldn't be here now. And we had a good time, didn't we?"

"Yes," she said.

"But now you say you don't want to, without even a reason."

"No, I don't."

"Maybe it's because of that judge?"

"No, I've no hard feelings."

"That judge was enough to chill a man's ardor. I asked him, 'What if I can't pay that much?' 'Then bring your toothbrush next time,' he said. I'll never forget it. But we had a good time right up to then. When I left I at least had a reason." He put his hand on her shoulder and put his face up close to hers; he didn't seem to want to kiss her but to look in her eyes.

She didn't move a muscle, and he must have read an answer there. (I believe he was a sort of a veterinary psychologist at heart.)

"Then I won't wrestle you for it," he said.

"No, I knew you wouldn't if you ever really understood."

And she said goodnight, got in her car, and drove away.

"What an ordeal!" Margaret said. "I was wrong about his being sneaky."

ANTHONY TROLLOPE

[England]

As a young man, Anthony Trollope (1815–1882) was the unhappy and socially awkward son of the popular author Frances Trollope. Given a chance to redeem himself within the British postal service after having shown little pluck and rather poor work habits, he left London for Ireland in 1841, where he found joy in love and success not only as a postal surveyor but as a novelist. He returned to London in 1859, now a high-ranking postal official, with his wife Rose (*née* Heseltine) and their sons. He wrote forty-seven novels, all but a few of which are among the masterpieces of Victorian fiction; in English literature, Jane Austen is his only rival in the depiction of social and romantic life. As an official for the postal service, he traveled the world negotiating contracts and routes, and he wrote (often en route) dozens of short stories, many of which take place in foreign settings. "Miss Ophelia Gledd," named after the story's heroine, is an American, "the belle of Boston."

Miss Ophelia Gledd (1863)

WHO CAN SAY what is a lady? My intelligent and well bred reader of either sex will at once declare that he and she know very well who is a lady. So, I hope, do I. But the present question goes further than that. What is it, and whence does it come? Education does not give it, nor intelligence, nor birth,—not even the highest. The thing, which in its presence or absence is so well known and understood, may be wanting to the most polished manners, to the sweetest disposition, to the truest heart. There are thousands among us who know it at a glance, and can recognise its presence from the sound of a dozen words;—but there is not one among us who can tell us what it is.

Miss Ophelia Gledd was a young lady of Boston, Massachusetts, and I should be glad to know whether in the estimation of my countrymen and countrywomen she is to be esteemed a lady. An Englishman, even of the best class, is often at a loss to judge of the "ladyship" of a foreigner, unless he has really lived in foreign cities and foreign society; but I do not know that he is ever so much puzzled in this matter by any nationality as he is by the American. American women speak his own language, read his own literature, and in many respects think his own thoughts; but there has crept into American society so many little social ways at variance with our social ways,—there have been wafted thither so many social atoms which there fit into their places, but which with us would clog the wheels, that the words and habits and social carriage of an American woman of the best class too often offend the taste of an Englishman; as do, quite as strongly, those of the English-woman offend the American. There are those who declare that there are no American ladies;—but these are people who would probably declare the same of the French and the Italians if the languages of France and Italy were as familiar to their ears, as is the language of the States. They mean that American women do not grow up to be English ladies—not bethinking themselves that such a growth was hardly to be expected. Now, I will tell my story and ask my readers to answer this question: Was Miss Ophelia Gledd a lady?

When I knew her she was at any rate great in the society of Boston, Massachusetts, in which city she had been as well known for the last four or five years as the yellow dome of the State House. She was as pure and perfect a specimen of a Yankee girl as ever it was my fortune to know. Standing about five feet eight, she seemed to be very tall because she always carried herself at her full height. She was thin, too, and rather narrower at the shoulders than the strictest rules of symmetry would have made her. Her waist was very slight,—so much so that to the eye it would seem that some bond of obligation had enforced its slender compass; but I have fair ground for stating my belief that no such bond of obligation had existed. But yet, though she was slight and thin, and even narrow, there was a vivacity and quickness about all her movements, and an aptitude in her mode of moving, which made it impossible to deny to her the merit of a pleasing figure. No man would, I think, at first sight declare her to be pretty,—and certainly no woman would do so; and yet I have seldom known a face in the close presence of which it was more gratifying to sit and talk and listen. Her brown hair was always brushed close off from her forehead. Her brow was high, and her face narrow and thin; but that face was ever bright with motion, and her clear, deep, grey eyes, full of life and light, were always ready for some combat or some enterprise. Her nose and mouth were the best features in her face, and her teeth were perfect,—miracles of perfection; but her lips were too thin for feminine beauty; and indeed such personal charms as she had were not the charms which men love most, sweet changing colour, soft, full, flowing lines of grace, and womanly gentleness in every move-ment. Ophelia Gledd had none of these. She was hard and sharp in shape, of a good brown steady colour, hard and sharp also in her gait; with no full flowing lines, with no softness;—but she was bright as burnished steel.

And yet she was the belle of Boston. I do now know that any man of Boston, or stranger knowing Boston, would have ever declared that she was the prettiest girl in the city; but this was cer-tain almost to all,—that she received more of that admiration which is generally given to beauty than did any other lady there; and that the upper social world of Boston had become so used to her appearance, such as it was, that no one ever seemed to question the fact of her being a beauty. She had been passed as a beauty by examiners whose certificate in that matter was held to be good, and had received high rank as a beauty in the drawing-rooms at Boston. The fact was never questioned now, unless by some passing stranger who would be told in flat terms that he was wrong. "Yes, Sir; you'll find you're wrong. You'll find you are, if you'll bide here awhile." I did bide there awhile, and did find I was wrong. Before I left I was prepared to allow that Miss Ophelia Gledd was a beauty. And moreover, which was more singular, all the women allowed it. Ophelia Gledd, though the belle of Boston, was not hated by the other belles. The female feeling with regard to her was, I think, this;—that the time had arrived in which she should choose her husband, and settle down, so as to leave room for others less attrac-tive than herself.

When I knew her she was very fond of men's society; but I doubt if anyone could fairly say that Miss Gledd ever flirted. In the proper sense of the word she certainly never flirted. Interesting conversations with interesting young men, at which none but themselves were present, she had by the dozen. It was as common for her to walk up and down Beacon Street,—the parade of Boston,—with young Jones or Smith, or more probably with young Mr. Optimus M. Opie, or young Mr. Hannibal H. Hoskins, as it is for our young Joneses and young Smiths and young Hoskinses to saunter out together. That is the way of the country, and no one took wider advantage of the ways of her own country than did Miss Ophelia Gledd. She told young men also when to call upon her, if she liked them; and in seeking or in avoiding their society, did very much as she pleased. But these practices are right or wrong, not in accordance with a fixed rule of morality prevailing over all the earth,—such a rule, for instance, as that which orders men not to steal; but they are right or wrong according to the usages of the country in which they are practised. In Boston it is right that Miss Ophelia Gledd should walk up Beacon Street with Hannibal Hoskins the morning after she has met him at a ball, and that she should invite him to call upon her at twelve o'clock on the following day.

She had certainly a nasal twang in speaking. Before my intercourse with her was over her voice had become pleasant in my ears, and it may be that that nasal twang which had at first been so detestable to me, had recommended itself to my sense of hearing. At different periods of my life I have learned to love an Irish brogue, and a Northern burr. Be that as it may, I must acknowledge that Miss Ophelia Gledd spoke with a certain nasal twang. But then such is the manner of speech at Boston; and she only did that which the Joneses and Smiths, the Opies and Hoskinses were doing around her.

Ophelia Gledd's mother was, for a living being, the nearest thing to a nonentity that I ever met. Whether within her own house in Chestnut Street she exercised herself in her domestic duties and held authority over her maidens, I cannot say, but neither in her dining parlour nor in her drawing room did she hold any authority. Indeed, throughout the house Ophelia was paramount, and it seemed as though her mother could not venture on a hint in opposition to her daughter's behests. Mrs. Gledd never went out, but her daughter frequented all balls, dinners, and assemblies which she chose to honour. To all these she went alone, and had done ever since she was eighteen years of age. She went also to lectures, to meetings of wise men for which the western Athens is much noted, to political debates, and wherever her enterprising heart and inquiring head chose to carry her. But her mother never went anywhere, and it always seemed to me that Mrs. Gledd's intercourse with her domestics must have been nearer, closer, and almost dearer to her, than any that she could have with her daughter.

Mr. Gledd had been a merchant all his life. When Ophelia Gledd first came before the Boston world he had been a rich merchant, and as she was an only child she had opened her campaign with all the advantages which attach to an heiress. But now, in these days, Mr. Gledd was known to be a merchant without riches. He still kept the same house, and lived apparently as he had always lived; but the world knew that he had been a broken merchant and was now again struggling. That Miss Gledd felt the disadvantage of this no one can, I suppose, doubt. But she never showed that she felt it. She spoke openly of her father's poverty as of a thing that was known,—and of her own. Where she had been *exigéante* before, she was *exigéante* now. Those she disliked when rich, she disliked now that she was poor. Where she had been patronising before, she patronised now. Where she had loved, she still loved. In former days she had a carriage, and now she had none. Where she had worn silk, she now wore cotton. In her gloves, her laces, her little belongings there was all the difference which money makes or the want of money;—but in her manner there was none. Nor was there any difference in the manner of others to her. The loss of wealth seemed to entail on Miss Gledd no other discomfort than the actual want of those things which hard money buys. To go in a coach might have been a luxury to her, and that she had lost;— but she had lost none of her ascendancy, none of her position, none of her sovereignty.

I remember well where, when and how I first met Miss Gledd. At that time her father's fortune was probably already gone; but, if so, she did not then know that it was gone. It was in winter,— towards the end of winter, when the passion for sleighing becomes ecstatic. I expect all my readers to know that sleighing is the grand winter amusement of Boston. And indeed it is not bad fun. There is the fashionable course for sleighing,—the Brighton road, and along that you drive, seated among furs, with a young lady beside you if you can get one to trust you; your horse or horses carry little bells which add to the charm; the motion is rapid and pleasant; and—which is the great thing—you see and are seen by everybody. Of course it is expedient that the frost should be sound and perfect, so that the sleigh should run over a dry smooth surface. But as the season draws to an end, and when sleighing intimacies have become close and warm, the horses are made to travel through slush and wet, and the scene becomes one of peril and discomfort,—though one also of excitement and not unfrequently of love.

Sleighing was fairly over at the time of which I now speak, so that the Brighton road was deserted in its slush and sloppiness. Nevertheless there was a possibility of sleighing, and as I was a stranger newly arrived a young friend of mine took me—or rather allowed me to take him—out, so that the glory of the charioteer might be mine. "I guess we're not alone," said he, after we'd passed the bridge out of the town. "There's young Hoskins with Pheely Gledd just ahead of us." That was the first I had ever heard of Ophelia, and then as I jingled along after her, instigated by a foolish Briton's ambition to pass the Yankee whip, I did hear a good deal about her; and in addition to what has been already told I then heard that this Mr. Hannibal Hoskins, to pass whom on the road was now my only earthly desire, was Miss Gledd's professed admirer;—in point of fact, that it was known to all Boston that he had offered his hand to her more than once already. "She has accepted him now, at any rate," said I, looking at their close contiguity on the sleigh before me. But my friend explained to me that such was by no means probable;—that Miss Gledd had twenty hangers-on of the same description, with any one of whom she might be seen sleighing, walking, or dancing, but that no argument as to any further purport on her part was to be deduced from any such practice. "Our girls," said my friend, "don't go about tied to their mothers' aprons, as yours do in the old country. Our free institutions—&c. &c. &c." I confessed my blunder, and acknowledged that a wide and perhaps salutary latitude was allowed to the feminine creation on his side of the Atlantic.

But, do what I would, I could not pass Hannibal Hoskins. Whether he guessed that I was an ambitious Englishman, or whether he had a general dislike to be passed on the road, I don't know; but he raised his whip to his horses and went away from me suddenly and very quickly through the slush. The snow was half gone, and hard ridges of it remained across the road, so that his sleigh was bumped about most uncomfortably. I soon saw that his horses were running away, and that Hannibal Hoskins was in a fix. He was standing up, pulling at them with all his strength and weight, and the carriage was yawing about and across the road in a manner that made me fear it would go to pieces. Miss Ophelia Gledd, however, kept her seat, and there was no shrieking.

In about five minutes they were well planted into a ditch, and we were alongside of them. "You've fixed that pretty straight, Hoskins," said my friend. "Darn them for horses!" said Hoskins, as he wiped the perspiration from his brow and looked down upon the fiercest of his quadrupeds sprawling up to his withers in the snow. Then he turned to Miss Gledd, who was endeavouring to unroll herself from her furs. "Oh, Miss Gledd, I *am* so sorry. What *am* I to say?" "You'd better say that the horses ran away, I think," said Miss Gledd. Then she stepped carefully out on to a buffalo robe, and moved across from that, quite dry-footed, on to our sleigh.

As my friend and Hoskins were very intimate, and could as I thought get on very well by themselves with the debris in the ditch, I offered to drive Miss Gledd back to town. She looked at me with eyes which gave me, as I thought, no peculiar thanks, and then remarked that she had come out with Mr. Hoskins, and that she would go back with him. "Oh, don't mind me," said Hoskins, who was at that time up to his middle in snow. "Ah, but I do mind you," said Ophelia. "Don't you think we could go back and send some people to help these gentlemen?" It was the coolest proposition that I had ever heard, but in two minutes Miss Gledd was putting it into execution. Hannibal Hoskins was driving her back in the sleigh which I had hired, and I was left with my friend to extricate those other two brutes from the ditch. "That's so like Pheely Gledd," said my friend. "She always has her own way." Then it was that I questioned Miss Gledd's beauty, and was told that before long I should find myself to be wrong. I had almost acknowledged myself to be wrong before that night was over.

I was at a tea-party that same evening at which Miss Gledd was present; it was called a tea-party, though I saw no tea. I did, however, see a large hot supper, and a very large assortment of long-necked bottles. I was standing rather listlessly near the door, being short of acquaintance, when a young Yankee dandy with a very stiff neck informed me that Miss Gledd wanted to speak to me. Having given me the intimation, he took himself off, with an air of disgust, among the long necked bottles. "Mr. Green," she said, I had just been introduced to her as she was being whisked away by Hoskins in my sleigh, "Mr. Green, I believe I owe you an apology. When I took your sleigh from you, I didn't know you were a Britisher; I didn't indeed." I was a little nettled, and endeavoured to explain to her that an Englishman would be just as ready to give up his carriage to a lady as any American. "Oh dear, yes; of course," she said. "I didn't mean that; and now I've put my foot into it worse than ever. I thought you were at home here, and knew our ways, and if so you wouldn't mind being left with a broken sleigh." I told her that I didn't mind it. That what I had minded was the being robbed of the privilege of driving her home, which I had thought to be justly mine. "Yes," she said. "And I was to leave my friend in the ditch! That's what I never do. You didn't suffer any disgrace by remaining there till the men came."

"I didn't remain there till any men came. I got it out and drove it home."

"What a wonderful man! But then you're English. However, you can understand that if I had left my driver he would have been disgraced. If ever I go out anywhere with you, Mr. Green, I'll come home with you. At any rate, it shan't be my fault if I don't." After that I couldn't be angry with her, and so we became great friends.

Shortly afterwards the crash came, but Miss Gledd seemed to disregard the crash altogether, and held her own in Boston. As far as I could see there were just as many men desirous of marrying her as ever, and among the number Hannibal H. Hoskins was certainly no defaulter. My acquaintance with Boston had become intimate; but, after a while, I went away for twelve months, and when I returned Miss Gledd was still Miss Gledd. "And what of Hoskins?" I said to my friend,—the same friend who had been with me on the sleighing expedition. "He's just on the old tack. I believe he proposes once a year regularly. But they say now that she's going to marry an Englishman."

It was not long before I had an opportunity of renewing my friendship with Miss Gledd, for our acquaintance had latterly amounted to a friendship, and of seeing the Englishman with her. As it happened, he also was a friend of my own, an old friend, and the last man in the world whom I should have picked out as a husband for Ophelia. He was a literary man of some mark, fifteen years her senior, very sedate in his habits, nor much given to love-making, and possessed of a small fortune sufficient for his own wants, but not sufficient to enable him to marry with what he would consider comfort. Such was Mr. Pryor, and I was given to understand that Mr. Pryor was a suppliant at the feet of Ophelia. He was a suppliant, too, with so much hope that Hannibal Hoskins and the other suitors were up in arms against him.

I saw them together at some evening assembly, and on the next morning I chanced to be in Miss Gledd's drawing-room. On my entrance there were others there, but the first moment that we were alone, she turned round sharp upon me with a question. "You know your countryman, Mr. Pryor;—what sort of a man is he?"

"But you know him also," I answered. "If the rumours in Boston are true, he is already a favourite in Chestnut Street."

"Well, then; for once in a way the rumours in Boston are true, for he is a favourite. But that is no reason you shouldn't tell me what sort of a man he is. You've known him these ten years."

"Pretty nearly twenty," I said. I had known him ten or twelve.

"Ah," said she, "you want to make him out to be older than he is. I know his age to a day."

"And does he know yours?"

"He may if he wishes it. Everybody in Boston knows it,—including yourself. Now tell me what sort of man is Mr. Pryor?"

"He is a man highly esteemed in his own country."

"So much I knew before; and he is highly esteemed here also. But I hardly understand what high estimation means in your country."

"It is much the same thing in all countries, as I take it," said I.

"There you are absolutely wrong. Here, in the States, if a man be highly esteemed it amounts almost to everything. Such estimation will carry him everywhere, and will carry his wife everywhere too, so as to give her a chance of making standing ground for herself."

"But Mr. Pryor has not got a wife."

"Don't be stupid; of course he hasn't got a wife, and of course you know what I mean."

But I did not know what she meant. I knew that she was meditating whether or not it would be good for her to become Mrs. Pryor, and that she was endeavouring to get from me some information which might assist her in coming to a decision on that matter; but I did not understand the exact gist and point of her inquiry.

"You have so many prejudices of which we know nothing!" she continued. "Now don't put your back up and fight for that blessed old country of yours, as though I were attacking it."

"It is a blessed old country," said I, patriotically.

"Quite so;—very blessed and very old,—and very nice too, I'm sure. But you must admit that you have prejudices. You are very much the better, perhaps, for having them. I often wish that we had a few." Then she stopped her tongue, and asked no further questions about Mr. Pryor; but it seemed to me that she wanted me to go on with the conversation.

"I hate discussing the relative merits of the two countries," said I, "and I especially hate to discuss them with you. You always begin as though you meant to be fair, and end by an amount of unfairness— that — that—"

"Which would be insolent if I were not a woman, and which is pert as I am one. That is what you mean."

"Something like it."

"And yet I love your country so dearly, that I would sooner live there than in any other land in the world,—if I only thought that I could be accepted. You English people," she continued, "are certainly wanting in intelligence, or you would read, in the anxiety of all we say about England, how much we all think of you. What will England say of us?—what will England think of us?—what will England do in this or that matter as it concerns us?—that is our first thought as to every matter that is of importance to us. We abuse you, and admire you. You abuse us, and despise us. That is the difference. So you won't tell me anything about Mr. Pryor? Well, I shan't ask you again!—I never again ask a favour that has been refused." Then she turned away to some old gentleman that was talking to her mother, and the conversation was at an end.

I must confess that as I walked away from Chestnut Street into Beacon Street, and across the common, my anxiety was more keen with regard to Mr. Pryor than as concerned Miss Gledd. He was an Englishman and an old friend, and being also a man not much younger than myself, he was one regarding whom I might, perhaps, form some correct judgment as to what would or would not suit him. Would he do well in taking Ophelia Gledd home to England with him as his wife? Would she be accepted there, as she herself phrased it,—accepted in such fashion as to make him contented? She was intelligent,—so intelligent that few women whom she would meet in her proposed new country could beat her there;—she was pleasant, good humoured, and true, as I believed;—but would she be accepted in London? There was a freedom and easiness about her,—a readiness to say anything that came into her mind—an absence of all reticence, which would go very hard with her in London. But I had never heard her say anything that she should not have said. Perhaps, after all, we have got our prejudices in England.

When next I met Pryor I spoke to him about Miss Gledd. "The long and the short of it is," I said, "that people say that you are going to marry her."

"What sort of people?"

"They were backing you against Hannibal Hoskins the other night at the club, and it seemed clear that you were the favourite."

"The vulgarity of these people surpasses anything that I ever dreamed of," said Pryor. "That is, of some of them. It's all very well for you to talk, but would such a bet as that be proposed in the open room of any club in London?"

"The clubs in London are too big; but I daresay it might, down in the country. It would be just the thing for Little Pedlington."

"But Boston is not Little Pedlington. Boston assumes to be the Athens of the States. I shall go home by the first boat next month." He had said nothing to me about Miss Gledd; but it was clear that if he went home by the first boat next month he would go home without a wife; and as I certainly thought that the suggested marriage was undesirable, I said nothing then to persuade him to remain at Boston.

It was again sleighing, time, and some few days after my meeting with Pryor I was out upon the Brighton road in the thick of the crowd. Presently I saw the hat and back of Hannibal Hoskins, and by his side was Ophelia Gledd. Now, it must be understood that Hannibal Hoskins, though he was in many respects most unlike an English gentleman, was neither a fool nor a bad fellow. A fool he certainly was not. He had read much. He could speak glibly,—as is the case with all Americans. He was scientific, classical, and poetical,—probably not to any great depth. And he knew how to earn a large income with the full approbation of his fellow-citizens.

I had always hated him since the day on which be had driven Miss Gledd home, but I had generally attributed my hatred to the manner in which he wore his hat on one side. I confess I had often felt amazed that Miss Gledd should have so far encouraged him. I think I may at any rate declare that he would not have been accepted in London,—not accepted for much! And yet Hannibal Hoskins was not a bad fellow. His true devotion to Ophelia Gledd proved that.

"Miss Gledd," said I, speaking to her from my sleigh, "do you remember your calamity? There is the very ditch, not a hundred yards ahead of you."

"And here is the very knight that took me home in your sleigh," said she, laughing. Hoskins sat bolt upright and took off his hat. Why he took off his hat I don't know, unless that thereby he got an opportunity to putting it on again a little more on one side.

"Mr. Hoskins would not have the goodness to upset you again, I suppose?" said I.

"No, Sir," said Hoskins; and he raised the reins and squared up to elbows, meaning to look like a knowing charioteer. "I guess we'll go back;—eh, Miss Gledd?"

"I guess we will," said she. "But, Mr. Green, don't you remember that I once told you, if you'd take me out, I'd be sure to come home with you? You've never tried me, and I take it bad of you." So encouraged I made an engagement with her, and in two or three days' time from that I had her beside me in my sleigh on the same road.

By this time I had quite become a convert to the general opinion, and was ready to confess in any presence that Miss Gledd was a beauty. As I started with her out of the city warmly enveloped in buffalo furs, I could not but think how nice it would be to drive on, and on, so that nobody should ever catch us. There was a sense of companionship about her in which no woman that I have ever known excelled her. She had a way of adapting herself to the friend of the moment which was beyond anything winning. Her voice was decidedly very pleasant;—and as to that nasal twang I am not sure that I was ever right about it. I wasn't in love with her myself, and didn't want to fall in love with her. But I felt that I should have liked to cross the Rocky Mountains with her, over to the Pacific, and to have come home round by California, Peru, and the Pampas. And for such a journey I should not at all have desired to hamper the party with the society either of Hannibal Hoskins or of Mr. Pryor!

"I hope you feel that you're having your revenge," said she.

"But I don't mean to upset you."

"I almost wish you would,—so as to make it even. And my poor friend Mr. Hoskins would feel himself so satisfied. He says you Englishmen are conceited about your driving."

"No doubt he thinks we are conceited about everything."

"So you are, and so you should be. Poor Hannibal! He is wild with despair, because,—"

"Because what?"

"Oh never mind. He is an excellent fellow, but I know you hate him."

"Indeed I don't."

"Yes, you do and so does Mr. Pryor. But he is so good! You can't either understand or appreciate the kind of goodness which our young men have. Because he pulls his hat about, and can't wear his gloves without looking stiff, you won't remember that out of his hard earnings he gives his mother and sisters everything that they want."

"I didn't know anything of his mother and sisters."

"No, of course you didn't. But you knew a great deal about his hat and gloves. You are too hard and polished and well mannered in England to know anything about anybody's mother or sisters,— or indeed to know anything about anybody's anything. It is nothing to you whether a man be moral or affectionate, or industrious, or good tempered. As long as he can wear his hat properly, and speak as though nothing on the earth, or over the earth, or under the earth, could ever move him,—that is sufficient."

"And yet I thought you were so fond of England?"

"So I am. I too like,—nay love that ease of manner which you all possess and which I cannot reach."

There was a silence between us, for perhaps half a mile; and yet I was driving slow, as I did not wish to bring our journey to an end. I had fully made up my mind that it would be in every way better for my friend Pryor that he should give up all thoughts of this Western Aspasia, and yet I was anxious to talk to her about him as though such a marriage were still on the cards. It had seemed lately that she had thrown herself much into an intimacy with myself, and that she was anxious to speak openly to me if I would only allow it. But she had already declared, on a former occasion, that she would ask no further questions about Mr. Pryor. At last I plucked up courage, and put to her a direct proposition about the future tenor of her life.

"After all that you have said about Mr. Hoskins, I suppose I may expect to hear that you have at last accepted him?"

I could not have asked such a question of any English girl that I ever knew—not even of my own sister in those plain terms. And yet she took it not only without anger, but even without surprise. And she answered it as though I had asked her the most ordinary question in the world. "I wish I had," she said. "That is, I think I wish I had. It is certainly what I ought to do."

"Then why do you not do it?"

"Ah; why do I not? Why do we not all do just what we ought to do. But why am I to be cross-questioned by you? You would not answer me a question when I asked you the other day."

"You tell me that you wish you had accepted Mr. Hoskins. Why do you not do so?" said I, continuing my cross-examination.

"Because I have a vain ambition; a foolish ambition, a silly moth-like ambition, by which, if I indulge it, I shall only burn my wings. Because I am such an utter ass that I would fain make myself an Englishwoman."

"I don't see that you need burn your wings."

"Yes! Should I go there I shall find myself to be nobody, whereas here I am in good repute. Here I could make my husband a man of mark by dint of my own power. There I doubt whether even his esteem would so shield and cover me, as to make me endurable. Do you think that I do not know the difference; that I am not aware of what makes social excellence there? And yet, though I know it all, and covet it, I despise it. Social distinction with us is given on sounder terms than it is with you, and is more frequently the deserved reward of merit. Tell me; if I go to London will they ask who was my grandfather?"

"Indeed no; they will not ask even of your father, unless you speak of him."

"No; their manners are too good. But they will speak of their fathers, and how shall I talk with them? Not but what my grandfather was a good man; and you are not to suppose that I am ashamed of him because he stood in a store and sold leather with his own hand. Or rather I am ashamed of it. I should tell his old friends and my new acquaintances that it was so, because I am not a coward; and yet as I told them I should be ashamed. His brother is what you call a baronet."

"Just so."

"And what would the baronet's wife say to me with all my sharp Boston notions? Can't you see her looking at me over the length of her drawing room? And can't you fancy how pert I should be, and what snappish words I should say to the she baronet? Upon the whole, don't you think I should do better with Mr. Hoskins?"

Again I sat silent for some time. She had now asked me a question to which I was bound to give her a true answer—an answer that should be true as to herself without reference to Pryor. She was sitting back in the sleigh, tamed as it were by her own thoughts, and she had looked at me as though she really wanted council. "If I am to answer you in truth," I said.

"You are to answer me in truth."

"Then," said I, "I can only bid you take him of the two whom you love;—that is, if it be the case that you love either."

"Love!" she said.

"And if it be the case," I continued, "that you love neither,— then leave them both as they are."

"I am not then to think of the man's happiness."

"Certainly not by marrying him without affection."

"Ah;—but I may reject him,—with affection."

"And for which of them do you feel affection?" I asked;—and as I asked, we were already within the streets of Boston. She again remained silent, almost till I placed her at her own door;—then she looked at me with eyes full, not only of meaning, but of love also;—with that in her eyes for which I had not hitherto given her credit. "You know the two men," she said, "and do you ask me that?" When these words were spoken she jumped from the sleigh and hurried up the steps to her father's door. In very truth the hat and gloves of Hannibal Hoskins had influenced her as they had influenced me,—and they had done so, although she knew how devoted he was as a son and a brother.

For a full month after that I had no further conversation either with Miss Gledd or with Mr. Pryor on the subject. At this time I was living in habits of daily intimacy with Pryor, but as he did not speak to me about Ophelia, I did not often mention her name to him. I was aware that he was often with her,—or at any rate often in her company. But I did not believe that he had any daily habit of going to the house, as he would have done had he been her accepted suitor. And indeed I believed him to be a man who would be very persevering in offering his love, but who, if persistently refused, would not probably tender it again. He still talked of returning to England, though he had fixed no day. I myself proposed doing so early in May, and used such influence as I had in endeavouring to keep him at Boston till that time. Miss Gledd also I constantly saw. Indeed, one could not live in the society of Boston without seeing her almost daily, and I was aware that Mr. Hoskins was frequently with her. But as regarded her, this betokened nothing, as I have before endeavoured to explain. She never deserted a friend, and had no idea of being reserved in her manners with a man because it was reported that such man was her lover. She would be very gracious to Hannibal in Mr. Pryor's presence; and yet it was evident, at any rate to me, that in doing so she had no thought of piquing her English admirer.

I was one day seated in my room at the hotel when a servant brought me up a card. "Misther Hoskins;—he's a waiting below and wants to see yer honour very partickler," said the raw Irishman. Mr. Hoskins had never done me the honour of calling on me before, nor had I ever become intimate with him, even at the club; but, nevertheless, as he had come to me, of course I was willing to see him, and so he was shown up into my room. When he entered, his hat was, I suppose, in his hand; but it looked as though it had been on one side of his head the moment before, and as though it would be on one side again the moment he left me.

"I beg your pardon, Mr. Green," said he. "Perhaps I ought not to intrude upon you here."

"No intrusion at all. Won't you take a chair and put your hat down?" He did take a chair, but he wouldn't put his hat down. I confess that I had been actuated by a foolish desire to see it placed for a few minutes in a properly perpendicular position.

"I've just come,—I'll tell you why I've come. There are some things, Mr. Green, in which a man doesn't like to be interfered with." I could not but agree with this, but, in doing so, I expressed a hope that Mr. Hoskins had not been interfered with to any very disagreeable extent.

"Well!"—I scorn to say that the Boston dandy said "wa'all," but if this story were written by any Englishman less conscientious than myself, the latter form of letters is the one which he would adopt in his endeavour to convey the sound as uttered by Mr. Hoskins. "Well; I don't quite know about that. Now, Mr. Green, I'm not a quarrelsome man. I don't go about with six-shooters in my pockets, and I don't want to fight, no how, if I can help it." In answer to this I was obliged to tell him that I sincerely hoped that he would not have a fight; but that if fighting became necessary to him, I trusted that his fighting propensities would not be directed against any friend of mine. "We don't do much in that way on our side of the water," said I.

"I am well aware of that," said he. "I don't want any one to teach me what are usages of genteel life in England. I was there the whole fall, two years ago."

"As regards myself," said I, "I don't think much good was ever done by duelling."

"That depends, Sir, on how things eventuate. But, Mr. Green, satisfaction of that description is not what I desiderate on the present occasion. I wish to know whether Mr. Pryor is or is not engaged to marry Miss Ophelia Gledd."

"If he is, Mr. Hoskins, I don't know it."

"But, Sir, you are his friend."

This I admitted; but again assured Mr. Hoskins that I knew nothing of any such engagement. He pleaded also that I was her friend as well as his. This too I admitted, but again declared that from neither side had I been made aware of the fact of any such engagement.

"Then, Mr. Green," said he, "may I ask you for your own private opinion?" Upon the whole I was inclined to think that he might not, and so I told him in what most courteous words I could find for the occasion. His back at first grew very long and stiff, and his hat became more and still more sloped as he held it. I began to fear that, though he might not have a six-shooter in his pocket, he had nevertheless some kind of pistol in his thoughts. At last he started up on his feet and confronted me, as I thought, with a look of great anger. But his words, when they came, were no longer angry. "Mr. Green," said he, "if you knew all that I've done to get that girl!" My heart was instantly softened to him. "For aught that I know," said I, "you may have her this moment for asking." "No," said he; "no." His voice was very melancholy, and as he spoke he looked into his sloping hat. "No. I've just come from Chestnut Street, and I think she's rather more turned against me than ever."

He was a tall man, good looking after a fashion, with thick black shining hair, and a huge bold moustache. I myself do not like his

style of appearance, but he certainly had a manly bearing. And in
the society of Boston generally he was regarded as a stout fellow,
well able to hold his own,—as a man by no means soft, or green,
or feminine. And yet now, in the presence of me, a stranger to him,
he was almost crying about his lady love. In England no man tells
another that he has been rejected; but then, in England, so few men
tell to others anything of their real feeling. As Ophelia had said to
me, we are hard and polished, and nobody knows anything about
anybody's anything. What could I say to him? I did say something.
I went so far as to assure him that I had heard Miss Gledd speak of
him in the highest langauge; and at last, perhaps, I hinted,—though
I don't think I did quite hint it,—that if Pryor were out of the way,
Hoskins might find the lady more kind.

He soon became quite confidential, as though I were his bosom
friend. He perceived, I think, that I was not anxious that Pryor
should carry off the prize, and he wished me to teach Pryor that the
prize was not such a prize as would suit him. "She's the very girl
for Boston," he said in his energy; "but I put it to you, Mr. Green;
she hasn't the gait of going that would suit London." Whether her
gait of going would or would not suit our metropolis I did not
undertake to say in the presence of Mr. Hoskins, but I did at last
say that I would speak to Pryor, so that the field might be left open
for others, if he had no intention of running for the cup himself.

I could not but be taken, and indeed charmed, by the honest
strength of affection which Hannibal Hoskins felt for the object of
his adoration. He had come into my room determined to display
himself as a man of will, of courage, and of fashion. But he had
broken down in all that under his extreme desire to obtain assistance in getting the one thing which he wanted. When he parted
with me he shook hands with me almost boisterously, while he
offered me most exuberant thanks. And yet I had not suggested that
I could do anything for him. I did think that Ophelia Gledd would
accept his offer as soon as Pryor was gone; but I had not told him
that I thought so.

About two days afterwards I had a very long and a very serious
conversation with Pryor, and at that time I do not think that he
had made up his mind as to what he intended to do. He was the
very opposite of Hoskins in all his ways and all his moods. There
was not only no swagger with him, but a propriety and quiescence
of demeanour the very opposite to swagger. In conversation his

most violent opposition was conveyed by a smile. He displayed no other energy than what might be shown in the slight curl of his upper lip. If he reproved you he did it by silence. There could be no greater contrast than that between him and Hoskins, and there could be no doubt which man would recommend himself most to our English world by his gait and demeanour. But I think there may be a doubt as to which was the best man, and a doubt also as to which would make the best husband. That my friend was not then engaged to Miss Gledd I did learn; but I learned nothing further,—except this, that he would take his departure with me the first week in May, unless anything special should occur to keep him in Boston.

It was some time early in April that I got a note from Miss Gledd, asking me to call on her. "Come at once," she said, "as I want your advice above all things," and she signed herself, "in all truth, yours, O. G." I had had many notes from her, but none written in this strain; and therefore, feeling that there was some circumstance to justify such instant motion, I got up and went to her then, at ten o'clock in the morning.

She jumped up to meet me, giving me both her hands. "Oh! Mr. Green," she said, "I am so glad you have come to me. It is all over."

"What is over?" said I.

"My chance of escape from the she baronet. I gave in last night. Pray tell me that I was right. And yet I want you to tell me the truth. And yet, above all things, you must not tell me that I have been wrong."

"Then you have accepted Mr. Pryor."

"I could not help it," she said. "The temptation was too much for me. I love the very cut of his coat, the turn of his lip, the tone of his voice. The very sound which he makes as he closes the door behind him is too much for me. I believe that I ought to have let him go, but I could not do it."

"And what will Mr. Hoskins do?"

"I wrote to him immediately, and told him everything; of course I had John's leave for doing so." This calling of my sedate friend by the name of John was, to my feeling, a most wonderful breaking down of all proprieties! "I told him the exact truth. This morning I got an answer from him, saying that he should visit Russia. I am so sorry, because of his mothers and sisters."

"And when is it to be?"

"Oh! at once; immediately. So John says. When we resolve on doing these things here, on taking the plunge we never stand shilly-shallying on the brink, as your girls do in England. And that is one reason why I have sent for you. You must promise to go over with us. Do you know, I am half afraid of him,—much more afraid of him that I am of you."

They were to be married very early in May, and of course I promised to put off my return for a week or two to suit them. "And then for the she baronet," she said, "and for all the terrible grandeur of London!" When I endeavoured to explain to her that she would encounter no great grandeur, she very quickly corrected me. "It is not grandeur of that sort, but the grandeur of coldness that I mean;—I fear that I shall not do for them. But, Mr. Green, I must tell you one thing, I have not cut off from myself all means of retreat."

"Why; what do you mean? You have resolved to marry him."

"Yes, I have promised to do so; but I did not promise till he had said that if I could not be made to suit his people in Old England, he would return here with me, and teach himself to suit my people in New England. The task will be very much easier."

They were married in Boston, not without some considerable splendour of ceremony,—as far as the splendour of Boston went. She was so universal a favourite that every one wished to be at her wedding, and she had no idea of giving herself airs and denying her friends a favour. She was married with much *éclat*, and, as far as I could judge, seemed to enjoy the marriage herself.

Now comes the question: Will she, or will she not, be received in London as a lady,—as such a lady as my friend Pryor might have been expected to take for his wife?

LARA VAPNYAR

[Russia/U.S.A.]

LARA VAPNYAR was born in Moscow, U.S.S.R., in 1971, and moved with her husband to America in 1994, when she entered the graduate program at the City University of New York, and began writing in English wry short stories as well as novels. "Love Lessons—Mondays, 9 A.M.," about a young instructor teaching a subject she hasn't experienced herself, first appeared in *The New Yorker* magazine in 2003. She lives with her children in New York City, where she teaches writing at Columbia University.

Love Lessons—Mondays, 9 A.M.
(2003)

THE PRINCIPAL, MARIA Mikhailovna, was a tall, heavy woman, well over two hundred pounds, with her lower part heavier than her upper. The students nicknamed her "the Pear." When she walked, the heels of her black pumps left deep imprints in the linoleum. Without lifting my eyes, I could see that she was walking toward me. I silently prayed that at the last moment she would change direction.

From my recent experience as a student, I knew that when a principal was approaching you, it was best to keep your eyes down. I wasn't a student anymore, but I sat looking at my knees, which stuck out from under my gray pleated skirt. I hated my knees. They were bony, red, and often scratched or bruised. A little girl's knees, not a teacher's knees.

Twenty-two of us sat along the walls of the teachers' lounge. I was the youngest. In fact, I wasn't even a teacher; I was eighteen years old, only in my second year of college, but the school needed somebody to teach tenth-grade math so desperately that they hired me. The other teachers were all women between the ages of thirty and sixty, except for Sergey, the history teacher, who was twenty-five and male. All the female teachers wore dark skirts and nylon blouses. Most of them styled their hair in old, flattened perms. The young teachers used some mascara and lipstick, while the older ones wore no makeup at all and used the same cheap yellow soap that was supplied in the school bathrooms, making their faces and hands smell distinctly of school.

Maria Mikhailovna read to us from a thin brochure as she marched around the room. She had the deep, loud voice of a person who talked for a living. My mother had the same voice—she had hosted political-awareness sessions in schools and factories for years.

Although Maria Mikhailovna read very well, nobody seemed to listen. Some teachers chatted, others read *Young Muscovite,* a new daily paper that printed only shocking stories, a novelty in Russia. A few days earlier, I'd read an article about a dog that had bitten off her owner's genitals when the owner tried to rape her. And a month earlier about a gang called the Skinners, whose members kidnapped fat people, skinned them alive, and made hamburgers out of them.

Maria Mikhailovna stopped hesitantly next to me, pausing in her reading. She shifted her weight from one foot to the other, sighed, and touched the back of my chair. I stopped breathing. But then the floorboards creaked and she started walking away. I took a few quick breaths and lifted my eyes. She was definitely walking away from me, tapping the palm of her hand with her brochure.

The brochure was entitled *Sex Education: The Theses.* The Ministry of Education had sent it to every school that year to introduce sex education in the tenth grade. Now the faculty had to pick two sex education teachers. I had good reason to worry. Whenever there was an unpleasant errand or assignment that nobody wanted to do—supervising monthly school dances and weekly yard cleanings, taking students on trips to Lenin's tomb, running out to a bakery to buy a cake for the teachers' tea—Maria Mikhailovna picked me, "our young teacher." She always referred to me as "our young teacher." Her use of the word made "young" sound like a mark of inferiority and inevitable failure. Sometimes she peeped into my room during class, sticking her pink face inside the door and leaving her heavy body outside. She watched me teach for a few minutes, which made me sweat, sputter, confuse words, and drop my chalk on the floor. If one of my students so much as stirred or smiled, she said, "Shame on you! Don't you respect your young teacher?" or "We know she is young and it's very hard for her to handle you, so help her! Show some respect!" I kept my eyes down and dug my fingernails into the flesh of my palms. I wished that the most horrible things would happen to Maria Mikhailovna. I fantasized about her getting caught by the Skinners and turned into a hamburger.

Sergey wasn't very old or experienced either, but Maria Mikhailovna never referred to him as "our young teacher." She called him "our male teacher," with affection and awe, as if his gender were an admirable character trait.

Sergey had naturally just been appointed to teach sex education to the boys. He didn't mind. He seemed to know enough about sex. Every Friday, a different smug girl in nice imported clothes stood waiting for him on the school porch after classes. Every Friday, I watched from my classroom window, half-hidden behind dusty flannel curtains. At three-forty Sergey would appear on the porch, in faded jeans and a dark shirt with the top two buttons undone, carrying a wrinkled jacket and a crumpled pack of cigarettes. From my fourth-story window his back looked a little slouchy. Sergey wasn't very handsome, but it didn't matter to me. He walked up to the girl on the porch, smiled at her, gave her a peck on the cheek, and put his arm around her waist. He looked into the girl's eyes with a promising expression. I let go of the curtains and sighed.

Not that I was in love with Sergey. What I felt for him was nothing compared to what I had felt for Prince Andrey from *War and Peace,* or for the math teacher from my hometown, or for the famous actor Alexey Batalov, who played a fatally ill nuclear physicist in my favorite movie, *Nine Days of One Year.* I wasn't in love with Sergey, but I would have liked it if he looked at me with a promising expression.

Except for me, Sergey was the only one who paid attention to Maria Mikhailovna. He sat leaning forward, with his sharp elbows propped on his knees, light-brown eyes narrowed with attention, waiting for an opportunity to make a fool out of Maria Mikhailovna, which he did all the time. Back in school, he was probably one of those students who were always asking their teacher provoking questions. When Maria Mikhailovna said that our school was proud to have the lowest rate of unplanned pregnancies in Moscow, Sergey asked what the rate was for planned pregnancies. I wouldn't have wanted to have somebody like him in my class. But Maria Mikhailovna didn't mind—she responded to his quips with one of her warm, all-forgiving smiles. She smiled at him even when he didn't say anything.

Maria Mikhailovna finished reading about the disastrous effects of the lack of sex education in Soviet schools, and moved on to a chapter praising countries where sex education was highly developed. When she read, her heavily painted eyelashes blinked, and the tip of her nose moved up and down. "In the United States, *ten-year-olds* know how to use a condom!" Sergey's eyes lit up with excitement. "Ten-year-olds using condoms! I wonder what they put them on."

I dropped my gaze and tried not to giggle, biting my lower lip and digging my nails into my knees. But a little squeal of laughter sputtered out, enough to attract Maria Mikhailovna's attention. "It's easy for you young people to laugh!" When I raised my head, she was looking at me with her famous knowing smile. "You think you know everything and we older people know nothing. Well, the time has come to share your knowledge." She plopped the brochure into my lap and stopped smiling. I saw that she was serious. I also saw that the decision had been made long before this meeting and that I couldn't have done a thing about it. They all stared at me: twenty female teachers with bad perms, one unflinching principal, and one smirking Sergey.

At home, I sat on the edge of the narrow bed where I slept and stared at the brochure. My Aunt Galya had agreed to let me live in the back room of her apartment when I came to study at Moscow University. The room was so small that my feet touched the wardrobe when I sat on the bed.

I had read the brochure twice, but it wouldn't have helped if I'd read it ten times. The authors did a good job of stressing the importance of sex education and had included a detailed list of topics to cover, but there wasn't anything, not a word, not a hint, of what exactly teachers were supposed to say on those topics. On Monday,

I would have to walk into the classroom and announce to the tenth-grade girls that I was there to give sex education lessons. Would they laugh, or would there be a deadly silence? Would they ask probing questions? Would they laugh when I tried to answer them? Actually, they'd probably just exchange knowing looks, small smiles, sly winks. If I turned my back to them, I would hear stifled giggles and feel that tickling sensation in my spine that I always felt when I knew they were mimicking me.

I started crying, and a tear dropped onto the open brochure in my lap. I didn't care if it got soaked. It was useless. I wanted my mother, who was in our little hometown hundreds of miles away from Moscow. But I knew better than to call her. If I did, I would start sobbing right away, and I would drown out her voice crackling through the poor connection. During my last months at home, everything about my mother irritated me: her questions, her suggestions, her endless pestering—even the sound of her voice. I couldn't wait to hop on a Moscow train and leave for my new life. At the station, I didn't even bother to kiss her before I climbed the steps onto the train. Then I saw her standing on the platform scanning the train's dusty windows in search of me. I waved at her quickly and walked away from the window.

I wished I had somebody, anybody, to talk to. I'd been living in Moscow for a little over a year, and I'd lost touch with all of my high-school girlfriends and hadn't made any new ones. Moscow girls seemed too snobbish and too well dressed to try to approach. When I spoke to them, they furrowed their brows, as if I spoke a foreign language and they were struggling to understand me. The girls who, like me, came to the university from small towns all lived on campus. They had immediately formed a close-knit circle bound by their own specific interests. They discussed how to use forbidden electric teakettles, how to dry clothes on rusty radiators and sneak boyfriends into their rooms at night. They exchanged information about dealing with hangovers, flooded toilets, and mean Muscovites. I couldn't be a part of this set. Simply by living with my aunt, I wasn't a part of it. What is more, they considered me a Muscovite precisely because I lived with my aunt.

I saw my distorted reflection in the glossy surface of the wardrobe. I drew my knees up to my chin and moved closer to the wall. Above my head, the photographs of Aunt Galya's late husbands, Uncle Ivan and Uncle Boris, hung slightly off-center on the faded wallpaper. Ivan was in his twenties in the picture, and Boris in his fifties; both men had stubby noses and small, gloomy eyes. They could've been father and son. Every morning, Aunt Galya came into my room, climbed onto the bed, spat on the glass, and wiped the pictures with a dishrag.

I could hear Aunt Galya moving around in the living room as I wiped away my tears. The dishes tinkled as she shuffled around, humming something out of tune, clearing her throat every now and then—all sly, subtle hints that she wanted my company. The humming and throat clearing would get louder and more persistent, and soon Aunt Galya would appear at my door and ask if I wanted a cup of tea. I would have to come out and try to look enthusiastic. Aunt Galya was a distant relative of my mother. In fact, they'd only seen each other a few times. It had been very generous of her to let me live here. My mother would have gone crazy with worry if I had had to share a dorm room with three other girls—with three "drunken sluts," in her words. And it would have been base ingratitude for me to refuse to sip a cup of tea with Aunt Galya and listen to her stories.

The stories were either about Aunt Galya's dead husbands or about her countless admirers. During that year, I'd learned all their names, addictions, habits, and physical peculiarities. I'd learned, for example, that Uncle Boris had a hairy back, Uncle Ivan had small balls, and Uncle Ivan's best friend Vasiliy had even smaller ones.

Aunt Galya appeared in my doorway almost every night, holding her faded silk robe over her large breasts. Her robe used to be a kimono, but she had cut holes on one side and sewn buttons on the other. She could button it up when she wanted, but she never did. "Come, have a cup of tea with me." But Aunt Galya never served me tea. I doubted if she had tea or a teakettle, or even a pot. Aunt Galya wasn't big on cooking. She usually ate her meals at the factory where she worked. On weekends she had a bologna sandwich for breakfast, a bologna sandwich for lunch, and chocolate candies for dinner. Every time I came out of my room for "a cup of tea," Aunt Galya would put a big glossy box of candies on the table and rush to the kitchen. She came back holding a glass jar filled with a turbid greenish liquid. Moonshine. She made it herself, a fresh batch every Saturday morning, and kept it in glass jars with old faded labels: STRAWBERRY JAM, DILL PICKLES, PICKLED MUSHROOMS, EGGPLANT CAVIAR. She poured moonshine from the jar into her cut-glass tumbler, drank it slowly, ate a candy, and then poured again. She never drank more than half a liter in the course of an evening. She wasn't as strong as she used to be. Although she was fifty-seven, she looked older, and her stomach ulcer had made her complexion sallow. She spent her evenings at home, listening to the radio or simply lying on the couch.

Aunt Galya's steps stopped. She must have sat down. I heard the unsteady tinkling of the glass jar against the edge of the tumbler. Long, drunken yawns were beginning to replace her humming. That meant that she would be falling asleep soon and I wouldn't have to come out and listen to her. Yet I felt somewhat disappointed, which surprised me. Even listening to her stories would have been better than sitting here alone and mourning my ruined life. I dropped onto my hard bed with a thump and resumed crying, wetting Aunt Galya's pillow this time. I wanted my mother. If not my mother, then at least my own pillow, not this small stiff thing with its silly lace trimming.

On Monday morning, I felt better. "Maybe it won't be a disaster," I thought. I walked past the huge gray buildings of Moscow on my way to the school, and the crisp air stung my cheeks as if it were winter already. The trees were stripped of leaves but not yet covered with snow. It made the streets look wider. When I'd first moved to Moscow, the streets had seemed so strange and hostile. But after a few months I grew to like them. Moscow streets were like big rivers: wide, endless, and flowing. Everything—cars, people, autumn leaves—was constantly moving, and I felt swept up in it as I walked fast, my scarf flapping in the wind. I caught my reflection in a supermarket window. Even through its stained, poorly washed glass, I could see that I looked pretty.

The handles of my oversized canvas bag cut into my palms. The bag was weighted down by the book I had checked out from the library over the weekend. It was 980 pages, entitled *The Nature of Sexuality*. It was written by several authors, each one with a Ph.D. next to his name. The book was the only one in the library with the word "sex" in the title. I shifted the bag in my hands. Its heft was reassuring. It also contained a bright folded poster that I had copied the night before from a picture in *The Nature of Sexuality*.

I recalled that before my first math lesson I had been frightened too, but it had turned out all right. Nobody mimicked me or laughed in my face. The students sat quietly leaning over their notebooks, I didn't do anything wrong, and my voice faltered only two or three times. Maybe my sex instruction would be all right too. I had my book and my poster, and it was not as if I had no experience whatsoever. I wasn't a virgin. Or at least I hoped I wasn't. Actually, I couldn't be completely sure about it.

I arrived at school a few minutes earlier than usual, so I had time to secure my poster on the blackboard. I spread it on the table and picked out eight rusty tacks from the drawer. The poster, which I had created by gluing eight regular sheets of paper together, was large. In the center was a colorful drawing of the female reproductive organs with their Latin names shooting out from it like fireworks. Aunt Galya had peeked into my room and asked if I was drawing "chicken innards." It did not look like chicken innards at all! I had gotten the colors right, and I was especially happy with the intense purple of the uterus, a color I created by applying blue paint on top of red. I wasn't as happy with the shapes and sizes though. It proved difficult to make the poster eight times larger than the picture in the book and maintain the right proportions. I could see now that one ovary was larger than the other. But at least the poster was bright and eye-catching. Even intimidating. And that was a good thing.

I usually started my math lessons by writing some difficult equations on the blackboard and demanding that they be solved in ten minutes. I called it "warming up," but my real goal was to intimidate the students. I walked into the classroom, stumbling in my mother's pumps, with parched lips and cold trickles of sweat running down my sides. And they were sitting there, all thirty-nine of them, big, smug, scary. Everything about them was scary: their pimpled foreheads and red fingers, their blue uniforms darkened under their arms, their cracking voices, the boys' enormous feet in scuffed shoes, the girls' awkward makeup. They could eat me alive. Math was my only weapon, because I knew it and they didn't. I followed one assignment with another without a break. I gave them tests every couple of days and assigned excruciating homework. I was very strict about grading papers. They could be sure that not a single mistake would go unnoticed. Needless to say, I never smiled during my lessons. My students called me "the Math Hound" or simply "the Hound" behind my back. I didn't mind that name. They feared me. I had them under control.

The last tack bent back instead of piercing the board. I straightened its tip and punched it in, then massaged my fingers and stepped aside to admire my work. Yes, it looked scary enough. I pulled down the projector's screen to cover the poster until the appropriate time. I was ready.

The girls slowly entered the room, which looked strange with gaps where the boys usually sat. (The boys had been taken to Sergey's classroom across the hall for their class on sexuality.) It was unusually quiet. The girls moved their chairs carefully to avoid making scraping noises, talked in whispers, and exchanged shy looks. "Good morning!" I said. My voice rang out clearly in the silent classroom. Though I always said those words at the beginning of math lessons, I wasn't prepared for the girls' reaction now. Instead of groaning, then sighing, then peering at their homework, they looked up at me with strange, expectant expressions. Could it be interest? I wasn't sure, because I'd never seen my students look interested before. Then something occurred to me, something that would have made me laugh if I hadn't been so nervous. They saw me as their teacher. They thought I possessed certain knowledge of sex the way I possessed certain knowledge of math. But unlike math, sex was something they really wanted to learn. A girl in the first row was tapping her foot on the ground. Another girl by the window rubbed the pimples on her forehead with the tip of her pen. My best math student, the pretty Sveta Zotova, twisted her ash-gray curls around her finger. Suddenly, these girls didn't seem so big or tall or grown-up to me. They could have been girls like I'd once been, with their mothers telling them, "You'll figure it out when the time comes." The ground was slipping from under my feet. What if the girls were not my enemy? No, I couldn't let them fool me! I wasn't going to soften up. I would beguile them with my poster, then finish them off with Latin terminology. I unveiled my poster and spoke the sentence that I'd been working on for the last two days: "We'll begin our lessons by studying the organs responsible for sexual functions in the female body."

Aunt Galya had come home early that day and was cooking when I came in. As soon as I opened the front door, I felt waves of heat coming from the kitchen, and the sweetish smell of burnt milk crept into the hall. Apparently, something was gurgling under the lid of the big aluminum pot. I'd never seen this pot before. Aunt Galya must have borrowed it from a neighbor, along with the green apron that was tied over her "kimono." She stood beside the stove with a dishrag in one hand and a wooden spoon in the other. Every few seconds, she raised the lid, let out clouds of white steam, and stirred what was inside. Her face was flushed. "I'm making kasha! Good for your stomach," she announced. "I had another doctor's appointment today, and guess what he said? That I should eat a lot of kasha and drink less!" She poured some salt into the pot from the opening in the two-pound bag, then tossed in a handful of sugar from the sugar canister. She wiped her forehead with the dishrag and turned to me. "Want some?"

Aunt Galya served us both kasha in large golden-rimmed plates with crimson roses painted on them. We ate slowly, working from the outer edges of the plates to the center. Aunt Galya was sober and quiet. I hoped that filling myself with kasha would help me get rid of the gnawing sensation in the pit of my stomach. The kasha was hot, heavy, and gluey. I wanted each next spoonful to dissolve the memory of my sex lesson.

None of my nightmares had been realized. Nobody made fun of me, nobody laughed, nobody even smiled during my lesson. Yet somehow it seemed that what happened was even worse. I kept thinking of Vera Bunina's expression when she asked her question at the end of the hour. Vera, a quiet, overweight, somewhat slow girl, was painfully shy. For her to raise her hand and ask a question, any question, was a big deal, especially since her classmates often laughed when she spoke. She had pointed at my poster with her pale, puffy hand and asked if every woman and every girl had "that," probably wondering whether "that" was actually as huge and ugly as I had drawn it. I expected the girls to laugh. I avoided looking at Vera's homely face, thinking how it would redden and tremble at the burst of laughter. But nobody laughed. The girls sat silently staring at the poster. I wondered if some of them did the same thing that I had done back home. Shivering in our moldy bathroom, I used to put my mother's hand mirror on the floor and squat down, straining my neck to have a look at it. Afterward, I lay in bed crying, feeling frightened and appalled, because it looked so ugly. I had a startling image of myself sitting at one of the desks among the girls, looking at the poster, and feeling even more frightened and appalled.

The tears were starting to cloud and burn my eyes, and a heavy lump was rising in my throat. I tried to push it back down with spoonfuls of kasha. "It is good, isn't it?" Aunt Galya asked, blowing on hers. I nodded.

The girls had silently emptied the room as soon as the bell rang. Then, while I struggled with my rusty tacks—I wanted to take my poster off before my math lesson started—the door across the hall flung open and the boys spilled out of their classroom in groups, all blushing, excited, giggling, some even bursting out in their coarse, neighing laughs. I saw grinning Sergey in the doorway. He stood behind two of his boys, who blocked his way trying to ask him something. He scrunched his face and scratched his forehead, pretending to think hard, then he said something with a very serious expression. The boys laughed. Sergey prodded them to move them from the doorway and walked down the hall with his usual lazy gait.

I scraped kasha remains from the bottom of my plate, exposing crimson roses. I wondered what Sergey talked about in his lesson. I imagined that he shared something from his own experience. That was why the boys felt at ease with him. Then he urged them to ask questions—anything they wanted to know. I wondered if I could do the same? Just talk to the girls about my own experience, honestly, making them feel at ease with me and encouraging them to talk openly about their experiences?

No, I couldn't do that. I took another helping of kasha and began swallowing it rapidly. When I lived at home, I'd only had one unimpressive, even embarrassing, sexual encounter with a boy from my class. I couldn't possibly talk about that. Or about the fact that for the year that I had lived in Moscow nobody had asked me on a date. I tried to tell myself that it wasn't my fault, that I didn't go to parties, that I spent all my time working and studying and preparing for my lessons and my exams. But I did ride the subway and buses, and I did go to the Central Library and to art museums, and I knew that you could meet somebody at those places, but nobody had ever asked me for my phone number.

I was startled by a sudden tinkling sound. "It's time for my medicine," Aunt Galya said, pouring the green liquid from a jar labeled

EGGPLANT CAVIAR into her cup. "The doctor said that drinking is bad for me!" Aunt Galya snorted loudly. "Can you believe that? Drinking has been keeping me alive all these years! It's folk medicine. It goes way back." She drained her cup and blinked several times. She did look more alive after a drink. It brought some pink to her cheeks and made her eyes greener and brighter. Glimpses of her former attractiveness came out. I wondered if there was any truth in the stories of her glorious past love life. Often after "tea," Aunt Galya offered to share her love secrets. "Listen hard, I'm gonna teach you how to love!" she would announce while pouring out moonshine. I usually declined, making polite excuses about having to study. At other times, Aunt Galya felt like showing off her body. She would stand up, straighten her back, and say, "Just look at this! Can you see why men are so crazy about me?" I saw an aging woman in a shabby kimono, with a massive upper body, a sagging stomach, bony hips, and pale, skinny calves with twisted hairs along the bone. I saw a blotched face with small eyes the color of moonshine under heavy eyelids. Aunt Galya hardly looked like a sex goddess, especially now, when she sat staring mournfully into her empty teacup. But what if she did know something about sex? What if her love lessons were worth listening to? I had nothing to lose. I gathered up my courage and said: "Aunt Galya . . . Do you mind if I ask you a few questions?" She slowly raised her head, her expression changing from incredulous to questioning to gleeful. She moved her teacup away and ran her hand through her short, wavy hair, preparing to talk. "Aunt Galya, wait!" I rushed to my room for a notebook and pen.

In December, the schoolyard was covered with snowdrifts. The caps of soggy snow lay everywhere: on the school steps, the window ledges, the low concrete fence, and on the lilac bushes by the fence. Sharp, leafless lilac twigs broke through the snow in places, making the bushes look like gigantic porcupines. Every morning, the school janitor swept the school porch and dug a trenchlike path in the snow from the gate to the steps. There was a long patch of ice before the steps, and younger children loved to run up to the patch and glide all the way up to them, screaming with pleasure. The ice patch was also the source of another sort of students' fun, because teachers sometimes slipped and fell there. Some tenth-graders even named the ice patch "the Teachers' Spot."

I happened to witness our elderly chemistry teacher go sprawling on the spot. She spun on the ice in her bulky fur coat, struggling to get to her feet, until one of the ninth-graders came to help her. I saw how other kids stared at her from the porch and through the school windows and laughed. Even the nice ninth-grader who reached out to save her couldn't help but chuckle. In December, eight weeks into my sex education class, the Teachers' Spot had become my main concern as I walked to school. I didn't feel anxious about my lessons anymore. I thought of them as of some dull but not too unpleasant chore as I made small, cautious steps toward the school porch.

My sex instruction wasn't a success, but at least I managed to fill eight forty-five-minute lessons with information. I'd learned how to make a digestible mix from my three contradictory sources: *Sex Education: The Theses, The Nature of Sexuality,* and Aunt Galya's life stories. I usually used *The Theses* as a frame, Aunt Galya's tales for details and examples, and the mammoth *Nature of Sexuality* for emergencies. Whenever I ran out of things to say, I threw in a Latin word or two.

It was hard to steer Aunt Galya in the needed direction. When she didn't feel well, she would only talk about the deficiencies and repulsive habits of her lovers and of men in general. She slumped down on the couch with a bowl of kasha and talked about smelly breath, nasty sounds, and shriveled body parts. She could go on and on, stopping only occasionally to eat a spoonful. Finally, she would usually get up moaning, dump kasha into the garbage, and pour herself some moonshine, looking defeated and guilty. When she felt better, she would sit at the table with a box of candies and talk about her heroic qualities as a lover, laughing heartily and devouring one candy after another. "He was lying there out of breath, all drenched with sweat, and I wasn't even slightly tired! You should've seen the look on his face when I said, 'How about another go?' I thought he'd die right there." Oddly enough, those "better" sessions ended in the same way as the "worse" ones, with a portion of moonshine.

I knew that my students wouldn't be interested in any of that. Techniques and precautions were the information that they needed. And so did I, but it was awfully hard to guide Aunt Galya toward the things I wanted to know. When she yielded, I grabbed my notebook and scribbled down the precious facts to retell them to the girls later.

Yet I was afraid of students' questions. I lay in bed at night imagining what would happen if the girls asked me something. I tossed and turned, sometimes trying to figure out a way to dodge questions, sometimes simply praying that the girls would be too shy to ask me anything.

And they were shy, at first. They sat tense and silent, afraid to show any reaction to what I said. But as the lessons progressed, they relaxed more. They smiled or gasped or exchanged looks, sometimes whispering to each other. And then one day, I saw a terrifying sight—Sveta Zotova raising her hand. I had a feeling she wasn't just going to ask for permission to go to the bathroom. Her beautiful narrow hand with long fingers and manicured fingernails looked like a deadly snake. "Sometimes we want to know something in particular. Can we ask questions?" My stomach dropped. I fingered a piece of gum stuck to my desk and thought, "No! No! You can't!" But Sveta was still talking: "We could ask anonymous questions. Can we write them on pieces of paper and leave them here?" I almost let out a sigh of relief. It was the perfect solution. It would leave me enough time to consult a book or Aunt Galya.

The girls put a brown shoebox under my desk and started leaving their questions in there after Friday math lessons. There were only one or two questions each week, most of them from Sveta Zotova. I recognized her neat, firm handwriting and perfect logic: "I read that oral contraception is 97 percent safe. Does that take into account the times when a person forgets to take the pill? If not, what would be the correct percentage?" Other girls' notes weren't as good, and some were barely legible, with spelling mistakes, omitted words, and words crossed out or written over others. The questions covered everything from contraception to breast enlargement to behavior on a date. One girl (poor Vera Bunina, probably) asked, "What should I do if I am on a date and I really have to pee and I don't want the boy to know that I'm going to the bathroom?" Aunt Galya was annoyed by questions like that. "Let her pee in her pants if she is such an idiot!" I, on the contrary, loved these silly questions more than Sveta's serious ones. I could imagine my girls going out on dates and experiencing these difficulties. I liked to act out these situations in my head, with me as the main character, and think about what I would do. At times, I actually enjoyed my lessons.

About four weeks into my sex lessons, the other teachers had started treating me differently. They never asked me about my lessons, or made any remarks about them, but they actually became aware of my existence. It felt so strange, as if I'd suddenly lost a magic hat that had made me invisible all the time. They still didn't consider me a colleague—I hadn't been admitted to their gossip circle—but they nodded to me when we met in the hall and talked to me about minor events at the school: "Did you hear that a cafeteria window was broken?" They even asked me about my private life: "When are your exams?" (Younger teachers.) Or "Do you miss your mother?" (Older teachers.) I didn't feel that I was in a vacuum anymore.

Sergey started noticing me too. I caught him looking in my direction with a questioning expression, as if he didn't know what to make of me. At times, he'd stop by my room and peek in, but then leave without saying anything. Or he would stare at me and squint his eyes as he did when he wanted to make fun of somebody, but then turn away again without saying anything. I was a perfect target for him. An incompetent sex education teacher! It made me nervous but, at the same time, oddly pleased.

Maria Mikhailovna, on the other hand, began paying less attention to me. After asking me to show her my list of topics and collating it carefully with the one suggested by *Sex Education: The Theses,* she was content to let me teach. She never peeked in during my sex lessons, either because she didn't care what I was saying, or because she didn't want to be responsible if I taught the girls something wrong. I was happy that she also peeked in less frequently during my math lessons, perhaps afraid that I'd start talking about sex.

My only problem was that after a while I started doubting Aunt Galya's expertise. At bedtime, I tossed under my thin woolen blanket and wondered: "What if Aunt Galya was wrong? What if lemon juice wasn't good enough as a contraceptive? What if eating a lot of cabbage didn't make your breasts bigger? What if hair on your legs wasn't a sign of infertility? What if Aunt Galya's whole attitude toward men was wrong?" The last question bothered me the most. Aunt Galya seemed to see men as soldiers in an enemy army. Even more than that, as soldiers defeated and captured. "Don't let them sneak away!" "Make them work very hard!" "Don't let them get lazy!" "Don't reward them until they deserve it." Cold sweat broke out on my forehead when I remembered repeating Aunt Galya's words in my lessons. I looked at the portraits of Aunt Galya's late husbands, glistening softly in the moonlight above my head. They didn't look very happy. And they were both dead.

Sometimes during my math lessons I would look at the boys and wonder how much they knew about the girls' sex instruction. I wondered if Sveta shared some of Aunt Galya's wisdom with her boyfriend Sasha Smirnov? A few other girls had boyfriends from the same class too. I was sure the boys knew something now. They avoided looking at me. They sat at their desks trying to be as quiet as possible, trying not to do anything that would attract my attention. They acted as if I knew something bad about them, something that they didn't want me to know. A few times, I had the urge to go back on my words, to say that it wasn't me talking, it was Aunt Galya! And then I would think about Sergey. What if the boys talked to Sergey about my lessons? I imagined Sasha Smirnov raising his hand, lifting his big body out of the desk with a crash—he couldn't move quietly—fingering a jacket button and saying in his deep-voiced monotone, "The girls' teacher said that men . . ." I wondered what Sergey's reaction would be. Every time he looked at me with his new, questioning look, I wondered if he was thinking it was I who hated men.

Sergey finally talked to me during the lunch hour in our school cafeteria. The cafeteria served only preprepared lunches, one or two combinations each day of the week. On Fridays we could choose sardelki with beet salad or herring with mashed potatoes. I would have preferred sardelki with mashed potato, but you couldn't change a combination. The sardelki, my favorite food, had hard skins and tasted better than the usual franks. I loved how the juice burst into my mouth when I sank my teeth into them. I hated beet salad. Few things could be more appalling than chunks of overcooked beets with potatoes and carrots swimming in a pool of smelly sunflower oil, but I decided to put up with it for the sake of the sardelki.

I sat down at the teachers' table and began piercing my sardelki with a fork when Sergey tapped me on the shoulder. He stood grinning by my chair with a plate of herring and mashed potatoes. "Don't let them sneak away; make them work very hard!" He winked at me and walked to his usual place at the end of the table.

My heart jumped up and down inside my chest. I spent the rest of the lunch break waiting for Sergey to continue. I chewed hard on the sardelki and shook the excess oil off the cubes of potato and beet. I was sure that Sergey had already thought of what to say; he was only waiting for the opportunity to speak. I had the terrifying thought that he somehow, through some unimaginable source, had become aware of Aunt Galya's existence and he would ask about her. I grew tired of waiting—I almost wished that Sergey would strike sooner. I stole a quick glance in his direction. He wasn't looking at me. He was working on his lunch, pulling bones out of the herring and laying them on the edge of his plate. It was a perfect chance to escape. I left my plate and hurried out of the cafeteria. I almost made it to the exit when I heard Sergey's voice again, rustling somewhere above my ears, the words barely audible amid the cafeteria's steady rumble. I had to lift up my face to make out what he was saying. He was asking me on a date.

The following Monday, I woke up early. I had set the alarm for 8 A.M., but when I opened my eyes, the room was still dark and my fluorescent clock read only 6:30. I had come home from my date with Sergey at about 10 P.M. and had taken off my only skirt and my pantyhose before I collapsed onto my bed and fell asleep.

I stuck the tips of my toes out from under my blanket and immediately pulled them back. The room was frigid. Normally, I would have stayed in bed until the alarm clock rang, all bundled up like a cocoon, but that day I simply couldn't keep still. My limbs felt like they were filled with tight little springs, longing to be released, pushing me to move, stir, do something. I sprang off the bed and attempted to do some aerobics on the little rug by the wardrobe, but my feet kept bumping against the bed. My reflection in the mirrored wardrobe surface—barefoot, wrinkled blouse, tousled hair—seemed awfully funny for some reason. I plopped down on my bed and started laughing, pressing my hands to my mouth so that I wouldn't wake Aunt Galya. I thought of phoning home—my mother usually woke up early. I even took the receiver off the cradle, but then I put it down. I knew that I wouldn't be able to stop laughing, and my mother would think that I was crying, and it would be impossible to prove that I really wasn't. That too seemed awfully funny, and I sat and laughed until I became aware that I was famished.

In the kitchen, I sprinkled a piece of rye bread with salt and ate it standing in the doorway. Aunt Galya was stretched out on her bed in striped men's pajamas, her blanket on the floor. She slept on her back, pressing a small pillow to her chest as if it were a teddy bear. I walked over to her, covered her with the blanket, and tip-toed out of the room.

When I arrived at the school, the streetlamps were still lit, shining yellow rings of light onto the snow, making the snow seem soft and warm. The path to the porch had been freshly swept and the Teachers' Spot glistened. Aside from the school janitor with his fuzzy broom, there wasn't anybody in the schoolyard. If I slipped and fell, nobody would see me. I ran up to the Teachers' Spot, pushed with one foot, and glided to the porch without falling.

In my classroom, I opened a window, letting in an icy, swishing gust of wind. I sat down at my desk, then immediately stood up and walked to Tanya Myshkina's desk in the first row. I couldn't sit there either. I walked to the back of the room and sat in Vera Bunina's chair for a minute, then on the edge of her desk. The thought occurred to me that I was behaving just like Goldilocks, trying out my students' chairs and desks. What if I told the girls about my date with Sergey? What if I told them what a promising expression he had in his eyes? What if I told them how his hand got stuck in the knot of my scarf when he tried to unbutton my coat in a crowded movie theater? And how later he kissed me through the entire *Godfather: Part III,* pausing only when he per-ceived, with his peripheral vision, that one or another of the char-acters was about to be killed. He let me go then and watched him die, while I wished that the death would be quick. What if I told them that the best part of the date wasn't even being on a date, but walking to our meeting place at the Pushkin subway stop, because men turned to look at me when I walked. I wondered if the girls would be able to understand any of it. I imagined how I would talk to them, sitting on the edge of Vera's desk like this, swaying my legs and laughing.

Then I saw something that made the laughing springs go quiet somewhere in the pit of my stomach, replaced by the familiar sensa-tion of panic. The brown shoebox lay under my teacher's desk, looking small and deceptively harmless. I had forgotten to pick up the questions on Friday. I slowly slid off Vera's desk and walked to the box. Inside was a notebook page folded in four. My first thought was to throw it away, to get rid of it, and pretend that there wasn't anything in the box. But what if by some miracle I knew the answer? I unfolded the note. About half of the page was covered with firm, rounded letters. It looked like Sveta Zotova's handwriting, but it wasn't as neat as her usual notes—she must have been nervous when she wrote it. I smoothed the paper in my hands and read the question quickly.

I read it a second time, this time aloud, right after the bell had rung and the girls had taken their places at their desks. "I've been dating Boy X for some months now, I like him very much, we have a steady relationship. When he touches me in certain places, it feels very good. But lately I've gone out with Boy Y a few times. He doesn't read books, he has a dumb laugh and pimples."

I paused and looked out at the class. Some of the girls took quick looks around, trying to guess the author. Others seemed genuinely interested in the problem itself. With their mouths open and their brows pulled together, they strained to digest the question and possibly apply it to themselves. In the first row, Tanya Myshkina was chewing the tip of her pen so hard it seemed she might bite off a piece and swallow it. I tried not to embarrass Sveta by looking at her, but with my peripheral vision I saw that she was gazing out the window at the concrete schoolyard, twisting and twisting her curls on her finger. I cleared my throat and read the note to the end. "I don't like Boy Y at all. Why then, when he touches me in certain places, do I feel exactly the same as with Boy X?" Now they were all looking at me. They seriously thought that I could answer the question.

The ticklish springs of laughter were coming back, building up somewhere in my chest and struggling to get higher and higher. And then I said something that I'd been wanting to say for a very long time.

"I don't know!"

I enjoyed saying these words so much that it made me light-headed. I felt like hopping on one foot around the classroom singing, "I don't know! I don't know! I don't know!" The springs of laughter were growing bigger and bigger, breaking through my skin, leaving my body, filling the room. Then I heard the first sounds of giggling. I wasn't sure if it was me or one of the girls. Soon everybody was laughing, even Sveta Zotova. Soon the separate sounds became simply one loud, steady rumble in the room. I didn't hear Maria Mikhailovna open the classroom door. I couldn't hear what she was saying. I only saw the tips of her black shoes, and her pink face squeezed between the door and the door-frame, her eyelashes blinking and her lips moving. If she was saying anything about inappropriate behavior and disrespect to the young teacher, none of us could hear it.

GIOVANNI VERGA

[Sicily]

GIOVANNI VERGA (1840–1922), a playwright and novelist, often wrote of characters in his native Sicily, as in "The She-Wolf" ("La Lupa"), which (according to its translator), seems to be set in the small town of Vizzini, southwest of Catania; it was first published in a Milanese magazine and then in 1882 in *Novelle Rusticane* (*Rustic Stories*). Wealthy and educated, Verga spent much of his thirties and forties in Milan, before returning to Sicily in 1885. Never married, he had several affairs and finally a long-term relationship with a famous pianist, Dina Castellazzi di Sordevolo.

The She-Wolf (1880)

(Translated from the Italian by Stanley Appelbaum)

SHE WAS TALL and thin; her only advantageous feature was a swarthy woman's firm and vigorous bosom, though she was no longer young. She was as pale as if she were constantly suffering from malaria, and amid that pallor were two enormous eyes and bright red lips that devoured you.

In the village they called her "the She-wolf" because she never had her fill—of anything. The women used to cross themselves when they saw her go by, as all alone as a vicious bitch, with that vagrant, mistrustful gait of a starving wolf. She would bleed their sons and husbands dry in the twinkling of an eye, with her red lips, and make them follow her skirt merely by looking at them with those devil's eyes, even if they were standing in front of St.

Agrippina's altar. Fortunately, the She-wolf never came to church, neither at Easter, nor at Christmas, nor to hear Mass, nor to go to Confession.—Father Angiolino of St. Mary of Jesus, a true servant of God, had lost his soul for her.

Maricchia, poor thing, a good and proper girl, used to weep in secret because she was the She-wolf's daughter and no one would marry her, even though she had lovely belongings in her chest of drawers and a piece of landed property, like any other girl in the village.

One time, the She-wolf fell in love with a handsome youngster who had come home from the army, and was mowing hay with her in the notary's fields. This was a true case of falling in love: feeling your flesh burn beneath your fustian bodice and, as you stare at him, suffering the thirst that you feel on hot June days deep in the lowlands. But the man went on mowing calmly, with his nose to the bundles of hay, saying to her: "What's wrong, Mis' Pina?" In the vast fields, where only the crackle of the flying crickets could be heard, when the sun beat down from directly overhead, the She-wolf was tying up one bundle after another, one sheaf after another, without ever getting tired, without straightening up for a moment, without putting her lips to the flask, just so she could remain constantly at Nanni's heels, as he continued to mow, merely asking occasionally: "What is it you want, Mis' Pina?"

One evening she told him, while the men were dozing on the threshing floor, tired from their long day's work, and the dogs were howling in the vast dark countryside: "It's you I want! You're handsome as the sun and sweet as honey. I want *you*!"

"And I, on the other hand, want your daughter, who's never been married," Nanni replied with a laugh.

The She-wolf thrust her hands into her hair, scratching her temples but saying nothing; she went away and didn't show up on the threshing floor after that. But in October she saw Nanni again at oil-pressing time, because he was working next to her house, and the creaking of the press kept her awake all night.

"Take the sack of olives," she said to her daughter, "and come with me."

Nanni was shoveling the olives under the millstone, calling out "Hey!" to the she-mule to keep her from stopping, "You want my daughter Maricchia?" Mis' Pina asked him. "What do you intend to give to your daughter Maricchia?" Nanni replied. "She's got what her father left her, and on top of that I'll give her my house. It'll be enough for me if you leave me a corner in the kitchen to make a straw pallet there." "If that's the case, we can talk it over at Christmas," Nanni said. Nanni was all greasy and dirty with the oil and the olives that had been set aside to ferment, and Maricchia didn't want him on any terms; but her mother grabbed her by the hair, in front of the hearth, and said through her clenched teeth: "If you don't accept him, I'll kill you!"

The She-wolf was practically ill, and people were saying that "when the devil grows old, he becomes a hermit." She no longer roamed about; she no longer planted herself in her doorway with those lunatic's eyes. Whenever she directed those eyes at her son-in-law's face, he'd start to laugh, and he'd pull out his amulet of the *Madonna* to bless himself with. Maricchia would stay home nursing her babies, and her mother would go to the fields to work alongside the men, and just as hard as a man, weeding, hoeing, tending livestock, or pruning vines, whether the northeast and east winds were blowing in January or the scirocco in August, when the mules would let their heads hang down and the men slept on their stomachs in the shelter of a northward-facing wall. "During those hours between Vespers and Nones, in which no decent woman walks abroad," Mis' Pina was the only living soul who could be seen wandering across the countryside, over the sun-baked stones in the paths, amid the dried-up stubble in the vast fields that were lost to the view in the sultry haze, far, far off toward mist-shrouded Etna, where the sky weighed heavily on the horizon.

"Wake up!" the She-wolf said to Nanni, who was sleeping in the ditch alongside the dusty hedge, his head cradled on his arms. "Wake up, I've brought you wine to soothe your throat."

Nanni opened his bewildered eyes wide, still half-asleep, to find her standing erect in front of him, pale, with her prominent bosom and eyes black as coal, and he held out his hands waveringly.

"No! Decent women don't go around between Vespers and Nones!" Nanni sobbed, burying his face in the dry grass of the ditch, deep into it, with his nails in his hair. "Go away! Go away! Don't come back to the threshing floor!"

She did actually go away, the She-wolf did, tying up her magnificent tresses again, looking straight ahead of her, as she walked through the hot stubble, with those eyes black as coal.

But she returned to the threshing floor on other occasions, and Nanni didn't say anything. When she was late showing up, in those hours between Vespers and Nones, he'd go to wait for her at the top of the white, deserted path, his forehead all sweaty. Afterwards, he'd thrust his hands into his hair, and repeat to her on each occasion: "Go away! Go away! Don't come back to the threshing floor!" Maricchia wept day and night; she stared into her mother's face, her eyes burning with tears and jealousy, herself like a female wolf cub, whenever she saw her coming back from the fields, pale and silent each time. "Criminal!" she said to her. "Criminal mother!"

"Be quiet!"

"Thief! Thief!"

"Be quiet!"

"I'll go to the police sergeant, I will!"

"Well, go!"

And she did go, carrying her babies, afraid of nothing, not shedding a tear, like a madwoman, because by this time she, too, loved that husband who had been forced on her, greasy and dirty from the olives that had been set aside to ferment.

The sergeant summoned Nanni and threatened to put him in jail or hang him. Nanni started sobbing and pulling out his hair. He denied nothing, he made no attempt to evade his guilt. "It's temptation!" he kept saying, "it's devilish temptation!" He threw himself at the sergeant's feet, begging him to send him to jail.

"Please, sergeant, take me out of this hell! Have me killed, send me to prison, but don't let me see her again, never, never!"

"No!" the She-wolf replied to the sergeant, however. "I stipulated that I would have a corner of the kitchen to sleep in when I gave him my house as a dowry. The house is legally mine. I don't want to leave!"

Not long afterward, Nanni received a kick in the chest from a mule and was close to death, but the parish priest refused to take him the Lord's body and blood unless the She-wolf was out of the house. The She-wolf departed, and then her son-in-law was able to prepare to take his own departure as a good Christian; he made Confession and took Communion with such signs of repentance and contrition that all the neighbors and gawkers wept in front of the dying man's bed. And he would have been better off dying at that time, before the devil started tempting him again and embedding himself in his body and soul, once he had recovered. "Let me alone!" he'd say to the She-wolf. "Please leave me in peace! I've seen death with my eyes! Poor Maricchia is in total despair. Now the whole village knows! If I don't see you, it will be better for you and for me. . . ."

And he'd have liked to tear out his eyes to avoid seeing those of the She-wolf, because when they stared into his they made him lose body and soul. He no longer knew what to do to free himself from the enchantment. He paid for Masses for the souls in Purgatory, and he went to the parish priest and the police sergeant to ask for help. At Easter he went to Confession, and he performed a public penance, dragging himself along and licking the stones in the churchyard in front of the church. Then, when the She-wolf tempted him again, he said:

"Listen! Don't come back to the threshing floor, because if you come looking for me again, as there's a God in Heaven, I'll kill you!"

"Kill me," the She-wolf said, "because I don't care; but I don't want to go on living without you."

When he spotted her in the distance, amid the green fields of grain, he stopped hoeing the vineyard and went to pull his axe out of the elm-tree. The She-wolf saw him coming, looking pale and distracted, the axe gleaming in the sunlight; but she didn't retreat a single step, she didn't lower her eyes; she continued walking toward him, her hands full of bunches of red poppies and her dark eyes devouring him. "Oh, God damn your soul!" Nanni stammered.

WILLIAM CARLOS WILLIAMS

[U.S.A.]

ONE OF the most influential American poets of the twentieth century, William Carlos Williams (1883–1963) was a doctor in Rutherford, New Jersey, and published dozens of collections of poems and a few volumes of stories, several of which featured a doctor and his patients. "The Knife of the Times" was, according to Williams, about a local woman whose "experience intrigued me. She was not shocked, just amazed."[1] Williams was married for fifty-one years to Florence (or Flossie) Herman, to whom he devoted many poems and three novels.

The Knife of the Times (1932)

AS THE YEARS passed the girls who had been such intimates as children still remained true to one another.

Ethel by now had married. Maura had married; the one having removed to Harrisburg, the other to New York City. And both began to bring up families. Ethel especially went in for children. Within a very brief period, comparatively speaking, she had three of them, then four, then five and finally six. And through it all, she kept in constant touch with her girlhood friend, dark-eyed Maura, by writing long intimate letters.

At first these had been newsy chit chat, ending always however in continued protestations of that love which the women had enjoyed during their childhood. Maura showed them to her husband and

---

[1] *I Wanted to Write a Poem: The Autobiography of the Works of the Poet.* New York: New Directions, 1978. 50.

both enjoyed their full newsy quality dealing as they did with people and scenes with which both were familiar.

But after several years, as these letters continued to flow, there came a change in them. First the personal note grew more confidential. Ethel told about her children, how she had had one after the other—to divert her mind, to distract her thoughts from their constant brooding. Each child would raise her hopes of relief, each anticipated delivery brought only renewed disappointment. She confided more and more in Maura. She loved her husband; it was not that. In fact, she didn't know what it was save that she, Ethel, could never get her old friend Maura out of her mind.

Until at last the secret was out. It is you, Maura, that I want. Nothing but you. Nobody but you can appease my grief. Forgive me if I distress you with this confession. It is the last thing in this world that I desire. But I cannot contain myself longer.

Thicker and faster came the letters. Full love missives they were now without the least restraint.

Ethel wrote letters now such as Maura wished she might at some time in her life have received from a man. She was told that all these years she had been dreamed of, passionately, without rival, without relief. Now, surely, Maura did not dare show the letters to her husband. He would not understand.

They affected her strangely, they frightened her, but they caused a shrewd look to come into her dark eyes and she packed them carefully away where none should ever come upon them. She herself was occupied otherwise but she felt tenderly toward Ethel, loved her in an old remembered manner—but that was all. She was disturbed by the turn Ethel's mind had taken and thanked providence her friend and she lived far enough apart to keep them from embarrassing encounters.

But, in spite of the lack of adequate response to her advances, Ethel never wavered, never altered in her passionate appeals. She begged her friend to visit her, to come to her, to live with her. She spoke of her longings, to touch the velvet flesh of her darling's breasts, her thighs. She longed to kiss her to sleep, to hold her in her arms. Franker and franker became her outspoken lusts. For which she begged indulgence.

Once she implored Maura to wear a silk chemise which she was sending, to wear it for a week and to return it to her, to Ethel, unwashed, that she might wear it in her turn constantly upon her.

Then, after twenty years, one day Maura received a letter from Ethel asking her to meet her—and her mother, in New York. They were expecting a sister back from Europe on the *Mauretania* and they wanted Maura to be there—for old times' sake.

Maura consented. With strange feelings of curiosity and not a little fear, she stood at the gate of the Pennsylvania station waiting for her friend to come out at the wicket on the arrival of the Harrisburg express. Would she be alone? Would her mother be with her really? Was it a hoax? Was the woman crazy, after all? And, finally, would she recognize her?

There she was and her mother along with her. After the first stare, the greetings on all sides were quiet, courteous and friendly. The mother dominated the moment. Her keen eyes looked Maura up and down once, then she asked the time, when would the steamer dock, how far was the pier and had they time for lunch first?

There was plenty of time. Yes, let's lunch. But first Ethel had a small need to satisfy and asked Maura if she would show her the way. Maura led her friend to the Pay Toilets and there, after inserting the coin, Ethel opened the door and, before Maura could find the voice to protest, drew her in with herself and closed the door after her.

What a meeting! What a release! Ethel took her friend into her arms and between tears and kisses, tried in some way, as best she could, to tell her of her happiness. She fondled her old playmate, hugged her, lifted her off her feet in the eager impressment of her desire, whispering into her ear, stroking her hair, her face, touching her lips, her eyes; holding her, holding her about as if she could never again release her.

No one could remain cold to such an appeal, as pathetic to Maura as it was understandable and sincere, she tried her best to modify its fury, to abate it, to control. But, failing that, she did what she could to appease her old friend. She loved Ethel, truly, but all this show was beyond her. She did not understand it, she did not know how to return it. But she was not angry, she found herself in fact in tears, her heart touched, her lips willing.

Time was slipping by and they had to go.

At lunch Ethel kept her foot upon the toe of Maura's slipper. It was a delirious meal for Maura with thinking of old times, watching the heroic beauty of the old lady and, while keeping up a chatter of small conversation, intermixed with recollections, to respond secretly as best she could to Ethel's insistent pressures.

At the pier there was a long line waiting to be admitted to the enclosure. It was no use—Ethel from behind constantly pressed her body against her embarrassed friend, embarrassed not from lack of understanding or sympathy, but for fear lest one of the officers and Customs inspectors who were constantly watching them should detect something out of the ordinary.

But the steamer was met, the sister saluted; the day came to an end and the hour of parting found Ethel still keeping close, close to the object of her lifelong adoration.

What shall I do? thought Maura afterward on her way home, on the train alone. Ethel had begged her to visit her, to go to her, to spend a week at least with her, to sleep with her. Why not?

DOVER · THRIFT · EDITIONS

POETRY

101 GREAT AMERICAN POEMS, Edited by The American Poetry & Literacy Project. (0-486-40158-8)

100 BEST-LOVED POEMS, Edited by Philip Smith. (0-486-28553-7)

ENGLISH ROMANTIC POETRY: An Anthology, Edited by Stanley Appelbaum. (0-486-29282-7)

THE INFERNO, Dante Alighieri. Translated and with notes by Henry Wadsworth Longfellow. (0-486-44288-8)

PARADISE LOST, John Milton. Introduction and Notes by John A. Himes. (0-486-44287-X)

SPOON RIVER ANTHOLOGY, Edgar Lee Masters. (0-486-27275-3)

SELECTED CANTERBURY TALES, Geoffrey Chaucer. (0-486-28241-4)

SELECTED POEMS, Emily Dickinson. (0-486-26466-1)

LEAVES OF GRASS: The Original 1855 Edition, Walt Whitman. (0-486-45676-5)

COMPLETE SONNETS, William Shakespeare. (0-486-26686-9)

THE RAVEN AND OTHER FAVORITE POEMS, Edgar Allan Poe. (0-486-26685-0)

ENGLISH VICTORIAN POETRY: An Anthology, Edited by Paul Negri. (0-486-40425-0)

SELECTED POEMS, Walt Whitman. (0-486-26878-0)

THE ROAD NOT TAKEN AND OTHER POEMS, Robert Frost. (0-486-27550-7)

AFRICAN-AMERICAN POETRY: An Anthology, 1773-1927, Edited by Joan R. Sherman. (0-486-29604-0)

GREAT SHORT POEMS, Edited by Paul Negri. (0-486-41105-2)

THE RIME OF THE ANCIENT MARINER, Samuel Taylor Coleridge. (0-486-27266-4)

THE WASTE LAND, PRUFROCK AND OTHER POEMS, T. S. Eliot. (0-486-40061-1)

SONG OF MYSELF, Walt Whitman. (0-486-41410-8)

AENEID, Vergil. (0-486-28749-1)

SONGS FOR THE OPEN ROAD: Poems of Travel and Adventure, Edited by The American Poetry & Literacy Project. (0-486-40646-6)

SONGS OF INNOCENCE AND SONGS OF EXPERIENCE, William Blake. (0-486-27051-3)

WORLD WAR ONE BRITISH POETS: Brooke, Owen, Sassoon, Rosenberg and Others, Edited by Candace Ward. (0-486-29568-0)

GREAT SONNETS, Edited by Paul Negri. (0-486-28052-7)

CHRISTMAS CAROLS: Complete Verses, Edited by Shane Weller. (0-486-27397-0)

DOVER · THRIFT · EDITIONS

FICTION

FLATLAND: A ROMANCE OF MANY DIMENSIONS, Edwin A. Abbott.
(0-486-27263-X)

PRIDE AND PREJUDICE, Jane Austen. (0-486-28473-5)

CIVIL WAR SHORT STORIES AND POEMS, Edited by Bob Blaisdell.
(0-486-48226-X)

THE DECAMERON: Selected Tales, Giovanni Boccaccio. Edited by Bob Blaisdell. (0-486-41113-3)

JANE EYRE, Charlotte Brontë. (0-486-42449-9)

WUTHERING HEIGHTS, Emily Brontë. (0-486-29256-8)

THE THIRTY-NINE STEPS, John Buchan. (0-486-28201-5)

ALICE'S ADVENTURES IN WONDERLAND, Lewis Carroll. (0-486-27543-4)

MY ÁNTONIA, Willa Cather. (0-486-28240-6)

THE AWAKENING, Kate Chopin. (0-486-27786-0)

HEART OF DARKNESS, Joseph Conrad. (0-486-26464-5)

LORD JIM, Joseph Conrad. (0-486-40650-4)

THE RED BADGE OF COURAGE, Stephen Crane. (0-486-26465-3)

THE WORLD'S GREATEST SHORT STORIES, Edited by James Daley.
(0-486-44716-2)

A CHRISTMAS CAROL, Charles Dickens. (0-486-26865-9)

GREAT EXPECTATIONS, Charles Dickens. (0-486-41586-4)

A TALE OF TWO CITIES, Charles Dickens. (0-486-40651-2)

CRIME AND PUNISHMENT, Fyodor Dostoyevsky. Translated by Constance Garnett. (0-486-41587-2)

THE ADVENTURES OF SHERLOCK HOLMES, Sir Arthur Conan Doyle.
(0-486-47491-7)

THE HOUND OF THE BASKERVILLES, Sir Arthur Conan Doyle. (0-486-28214-7)

BLAKE: PROPHET AGAINST EMPIRE, David V. Erdman. (0-486-26719-9)

WHERE ANGELS FEAR TO TREAD, E. M. Forster. (0-486-27791-7)

BEOWULF, Translated by R. K. Gordon. (0-486-27264-8)

THE RETURN OF THE NATIVE, Thomas Hardy. (0-486-43165-7)

THE SCARLET LETTER, Nathaniel Hawthorne. (0-486-28048-9)

SIDDHARTHA, Hermann Hesse. (0-486-40653-9)

THE ODYSSEY, Homer. (0-486-40654-7)

THE TURN OF THE SCREW, Henry James. (0-486-26684-2)

DUBLINERS, James Joyce. (0-486-26870-5)

DOVER · THRIFT · EDITIONS

NONFICTION

POETICS, Aristotle. (0-486-29577-X)

MEDITATIONS, Marcus Aurelius. (0-486-29823-X)

THE WAY OF PERFECTION, St. Teresa of Avila. Edited and Translated by E. Allison Peers. (0-486-48451-3)

THE DEVIL'S DICTIONARY, Ambrose Bierce. (0-486-27542-6)

GREAT SPEECHES OF THE 20TH CENTURY, Edited by Bob Blaisdell. (0-486-47467-4)

THE COMMUNIST MANIFESTO AND OTHER REVOLUTIONARY WRITINGS: Marx, Marat, Paine, Mao Tse-Tung, Gandhi and Others, Edited by Bob Blaisdell. (0-486-42465-0)

INFAMOUS SPEECHES: From Robespierre to Osama bin Laden, Edited by Bob Blaisdell. (0-486-47849-1)

GREAT ENGLISH ESSAYS: From Bacon to Chesterton, Edited by Bob Blaisdell. (0-486-44082-6)

GREEK AND ROMAN ORATORY, Edited by Bob Blaisdell. (0-486-49622-8)

THE UNITED STATES CONSTITUTION: The Full Text with Supplementary Materials, Edited and with supplementary materials by Bob Blaisdell. (0-486-47166-7)

GREAT SPEECHES BY NATIVE AMERICANS, Edited by Bob Blaisdell. (0-486-41122-2)

GREAT SPEECHES BY AFRICAN AMERICANS: Frederick Douglass, Sojourner Truth, Dr. Martin Luther King, Jr., Barack Obama, and Others, Edited by James Daley. (0-486-44761-8)

GREAT SPEECHES BY AMERICAN WOMEN, Edited by James Daley. (0-486-46141-6)

HISTORY'S GREATEST SPEECHES, Edited by James Daley. (0-486-49739-9)

GREAT INAUGURAL ADDRESSES, Edited by James Daley. (0-486-44577-1)

GREAT SPEECHES ON GAY RIGHTS, Edited by James Daley. (0-486-47512-3)

ON THE ORIGIN OF SPECIES: By Means of Natural Selection, Charles Darwin. (0-486-45006-6)

NARRATIVE OF THE LIFE OF FREDERICK DOUGLASS, Frederick Douglass. (0-486-28499-9)

THE SOULS OF BLACK FOLK, W. E. B. Du Bois. (0-486-28041-1)

NATURE AND OTHER ESSAYS, Ralph Waldo Emerson. (0-486-46947-6)

SELF-RELIANCE AND OTHER ESSAYS, Ralph Waldo Emerson. (0-486-27790-9)

THE LIFE OF OLAUDAH EQUIANO, Olaudah Equiano. (0-486-40661-X)

WIT AND WISDOM FROM POOR RICHARD'S ALMANACK, Benjamin Franklin. (0-486-40891-4)

THE AUTOBIOGRAPHY OF BENJAMIN FRANKLIN, Benjamin Franklin. (0-486-29073-5)

DOVER · THRIFT · EDITIONS

PLAYS

THE ORESTEIA TRILOGY: Agamemnon, the Libation-Bearers and the Furies, Aeschylus. (0-486-29242-8)

EVERYMAN, Anonymous. (0-486-28726-2)

THE BIRDS, Aristophanes. (0-486-40886-8)

LYSISTRATA, Aristophanes. (0-486-28225-2)

THE CHERRY ORCHARD, Anton Chekhov. (0-486-26682-6)

THE SEA GULL, Anton Chekhov. (0-486-40656-3)

MEDEA, Euripides. (0-486-27548-5)

FAUST, PART ONE, Johann Wolfgang von Goethe. (0-486-28046-2)

THE INSPECTOR GENERAL, Nikolai Gogol. (0-486-28500-6)

SHE STOOPS TO CONQUER, Oliver Goldsmith. (0-486-26867-5)

GHOSTS, Henrik Ibsen. (0-486-29852-3)

A DOLL'S HOUSE, Henrik Ibsen. (0-486-27062-9)

HEDDA GABLER, Henrik Ibsen. (0-486-26469-6)

DR. FAUSTUS, Christopher Marlowe. (0-486-28208-2)

TARTUFFE, Molière. (0-486-41117-6)

BEYOND THE HORIZON, Eugene O'Neill. (0-486-29085-9)

THE EMPEROR JONES, Eugene O'Neill. (0-486-29268-1)

CYRANO DE BERGERAC, Edmond Rostand. (0-486-41119-2)

MEASURE FOR MEASURE: Unabridged, William Shakespeare. (0-486-40889-2)

FOUR GREAT TRAGEDIES: Hamlet, Macbeth, Othello, and Romeo and Juliet, William Shakespeare. (0-486-44083-4)

THE COMEDY OF ERRORS, William Shakespeare. (0-486-42461-8)

HENRY V, William Shakespeare. (0-486-42887-7)

MUCH ADO ABOUT NOTHING, William Shakespeare. (0-486-28272-4)

FIVE GREAT COMEDIES: Much Ado About Nothing, Twelfth Night, A Midsummer Night's Dream, As You Like It and The Merry Wives of Windsor, William Shakespeare. (0-486-44086-9)

OTHELLO, William Shakespeare. (0-486-29097-2)

AS YOU LIKE IT, William Shakespeare. (0-486-40432-3)

ROMEO AND JULIET, William Shakespeare. (0-486-27557-4)

A MIDSUMMER NIGHT'S DREAM, William Shakespeare. (0-486-27067-X)

THE MERCHANT OF VENICE, William Shakespeare. (0-486-28492-1)

HAMLET, William Shakespeare. (0-486-27278-8)

RICHARD III, William Shakespeare. (0-486-28747-5)